Smoke Dancing

10/6/64

Smoke Dancing

Eric Gansworth

To Bob,
thank you for your
enthusiasm and
articulation.

PEACE!

Eric Gansworth

Michigan State University Press · East Lansing

g green press INITIATIVE Michigan State University Press is a member of the Green Press Initiative and is committed to developing and encouraging ecologically responsible publishing practices. For more information about the Green Press Initiative and the use of recycled paper in book publishing, please visit *www.greenpressinitiative.org.*

⊛ The paper used in this publication meets the minimum requirements of ANSI/NISO Z39.48-1992 (R 1997) (Permanence of Paper).

Michigan State University Press
East Lansing, Michigan 48823-5245

Printed and bound in the United States of America.

10 09 08 07 06 05 04   1 2 3 4 5 6 7 8 9 10

LIBRARY OF CONGRESS CATALOGING-IN-PUBLICATION DATA
Gansworth, Eric L.
Smoke dancing / Eric Gansworth.
p. cm.
ISBN 0-87013-708-5 (pbk. : alk. paper)
1. Iroquois Indians—Fiction. 2. Conflict of generations—Fiction. 3. Illegitimate children—Fiction. 4. Fathers and daughters—Fiction. 5. Indian reservations—Fiction. 6. Cigarette industry—Fiction. 7. Women dancers—Fiction. 8. Indian women—Fiction. 9. Indian dance—Fiction. I. Title.
PS3557.A5196S64 2004
813.' 54—dc22
2004000268

ACKNOWLEDGMENTS
The following chapters appeared in slightly different versions in the following places: "The Last Dance," in *The Second Word Thursdays Anthology* (Bright Hills Press, 1999); "Unfinished Business," in *Nothing but the Truth: An Anthology of Native American Literature* (Prentiss Hall, 2000).

Cover design by Erin Kirk New
Book design by Sharp Des!gns, Inc.

Cover and internal paintings are all by Eric Gansworth and used with permission of the artist. Cover: "The Three Sisters (I): Embrace," oil on canvas, 24 x 36, © 1994 Eric Gansworth. Frontispiece: "Smoke Rings," oil on canvas, 36 x 48, ©Eric Gansworth 1996. Page 5: "Rabbit Dance," oil on canvas, 36 x 48, © Eric Gansworth 2003. Page 88: "Standing Quiver Dance," oil on canvas, 36 x 48, © Eric Gansworth 2003. Page 174: "Smoke Dance," oil on canvas, 36 x 48, © Eric Gansworth 2003.

Visit Michigan State University Press on the World Wide Web at: *www.msupress.msu.edu*

for the Bumblebee,

giving unconditionally

CONTENTS

ACKNOWLEDGMENTS

THIS BOOK HAS BEEN A LONG TIME IN COMING, AND THERE ARE MANY PEOPLE TO say Nyah-wheh to, in helping it along the way. As before, most significant thanks to Larry Plant, for everything, as simple as that.

Thank you to those people who have read this novel in its various drafts and who have given valuable feedback to make it a better book: Bob Baxter, Mick Cochrane, Denise David, Junot Diaz, Carole Haynes, Bob Morris, Donnie and Sherry York. Thanks also go to friends who have not read the work, but who have kept me grounded and positive, even when the drafts were not going smoothly: Bill Haynes and Mike Taylor. Thank you to Lee Francis, Bertha Rogers, John Purdy and James Ruppert, who chose to include chapters of this novel in anthologies they edited. Extra special "save my butt" thanks to Mark Turcotte, who prevented this novel from having a potentially fatal title, and to Wendy Huff, who gave me the spark for Fiction one long day driving from New York to Virginia, when I did not think I had anything more to write about. Thanks again to my second cousin Ted C. Williams, and his continually valuable book, *The Reservation.* Thank you also to my editor, Martha Bates, who delivered, concisely, the last polish needed for the final draft, in addition to having great taste in music and an astonishing array of weird stories to get me through. A thank you to Jolene Rickard, for early support of my visual work, as it would not have arrived at this point without that hand, and a thanks to

Percy and Kim Abrams, for valuable conversations concerning traditional dancing. As always, nyah-wheh to my family, still learning along with me, but more importantly, still teaching me what that word means in its many incarnations.

While actual locations, legal agreements, and historic events are part of this work's backdrop, this is a work of fiction. Names, characters, places, and incidents either are products of my imagination or have been used fictitiously. Any resemblance to actual events or locales or persons, living or dead, is entirely coincidental.

➤✦

Smoke Dancing

PROLOGUE Women's Shuffle

Fiction Tunny

Now, I was a born storyteller, but maybe you could tell that by my name. Born of lies, I guess it's not too bad a one to have. That's not my Christian name, mind you—even my mother was not that malicious—but it's the one I've been stuck with for almost my entire life. And besides, everyone knows that at the heart of fiction is where the truth sleeps, waiting to wake up and show itself, but only to those whose vision is sharp enough. You see, even in those stories that seem the most ridiculous to some—well, they keep playing themselves out to this very day. Here's one, for example. Maybe you've even heard it.

After that turtle gives up its life for Skywoman when she falls to the earth that grows on its back, and after one of the twins kills their mother, Skywoman's daughter, the three sisters spring out, never planted, from that grave—carrying on, life out of death. Those three sisters of ours, they're supposed to sustain the rest of us, but also one another: the corn, she supplies the stalks for the beans to climb; and the squash, she protects the roots, shading them with her big tough leaves; and what the beans supply, that's less obvious. She looks like she is just hanging on, something extra, but her magic seeps below the surface, flowing out through her roots, feeding the other two silently, providing for them something they can't generate themselves, making them strong, so that when the wind and the rains come, they'll dance with the fury, but in the end, they will still be standing.

Maybe some holes are punched through their leaves, some silk torn from their lovely heads, but they survive their dance, and that's the story.

That story, it's been told for hundreds of years now. Maybe you've heard a version where Skywoman fell because she was too nosy, looking through a hole in the Skyworld she wasn't supposed to; or maybe the one where she was pushed by the man in her life who didn't like her knowing more than he did. But either way, she got here and started everything. Stories are like that. Maybe you heard it where tobacco comes up with the sisters, or where it was the only thing Skywoman brought with her through that hole from her world, or where one of the sisters isn't there—but that's a pretty rare version, these days. Almost everyone accepts that there were three of them.

Now, you might think this story is out of date, that no woman was saved by the birds as she fell from the sky, that a giant turtle does not sleep under this continent, having raised itself from the ocean's bottom to give up its life for us, but you watch where Indians gather—powwows, socials— and you pay attention to the way people move. When you see three women together today, you watch—some men smile, but some slink away. Those sisters, they're not three "real" sisters, if you get my meaning. They each have to bring something different, as I said before, from different families. And what is it the beans bring? Nitrogen, one of the key elements of TNT; and if you listen, you'll hear the potential in the explosive laughter of those Indian women. And those Indian men, they want to get closer and back away at the same time—they want to know who the women are laughing at, but they are just as afraid it might be them. And some men don't want to even take the chance, don't want the women to come together; but we are survivors, and sometimes the stories unfold themselves slowly before your very eyes, so slowly you don't even know you're one of the players until you see your fingers reaching up, tender shoots wrapping around someone sturdier, steadying yourself on their strength.

Now this story starts with one sister and nearly ends with another before the third is even found. By the time I realized I was the third sister to Bertha Monterney's corn and Ruby Pem's squash, it was nearly too late to thank them. So I offer them what I can . . . which is to say everything I have. The storms around us are deadly this year, the wind and the rain tearing at us as they do, and my sisters are older than I am, much older, their dances slowing down. What they supply is obvious. My explosive nature is not quite as apparent, but the storms will know. I don't expect you to take my word for the way things might turn out, particularly with my name being what it is. The story changes with each teller, shifting like smoke in the wind, and I welcome you to listen to anyone who cares to speak up during this next year. I can only tell it in the way I know how, and that is to start at the beginning, the way Skywoman did. After she landed here, she stood on one part of that turtle's shell and started a dance, shifting her feet back and forth, blessing her new home with each shift of her feet across its back. Every time she completed the full circle, the shell expanded in size, and she continued on, gently making her way across its surface, and this eventually grew to this place we live, Great Turtle Island, or as others call it, America. This is said to be the oldest dance, the Women's Shuffle, as it's one of the first things Skywoman did.

But she did something else first, something before that, something unexpected. She survived. Sometimes things do come along in the most unexpected of ways, like Skywoman's survival from her fall, buried in the message hidden in the flight of a bird . . .

>←

PART ONE

Rabbit Dance

Okay, now, in the Rabbit Dance, the man and the woman pair up, and in the rounds of the dance, they try to keep the rhythm together as the singer takes them where he will, and if they really love each other, they should have no trouble, but if they don't, oh boy, watch out, those men will be eating their own fry bread come sundown, and we all know how nasty that is, don't we, folks? And remember, heh, heh, this here is a ladies' choice, so you men better be on your toes and ready to dance, or you're just gonna be passed right on by.

SINGER, HAUDENOSAUNEE SOCIAL

CHAPTER 1 The Last Dance

Fiction Tunny

BIRD HITS THE LIVING-ROOM WINDOW HEAD ON, TELLING ME, AS THEY DO IN suicide, that someone close to me has just passed on. Not a minute earlier, I slurped down my last cup of morning coffee and stuffed the vacuum cleaner back into its closet. The dull sound of death, glass moaning just a little, travels toward me across the carpet, freshly blank and free of prints, a blackboard in the summer. The room freezes around me for a moment in the greasy feather-oil stain—the bird's last second on earth, slapped in mid-flight across the window. I cut a path of small, quick footprints across the living room and fly out the door. The dead crow lies in the bushes surrounding the trailer, its neck flopping onto its shiny breast, when Don "Big Red" Harmony calls my name from the Big House.

Reaching the back porch, I know. Bertha Monterney is dead, and I wouldn't be surprised if Mason Rollins across the field in his shop, and all the other dancers, wherever they are, have similar stories of kamikaze birds slamming into the windows they peered through. Mason doesn't step outside the shack, though, so maybe I'm wrong. I wait a moment, but am really just putting this off.

Big Red and Bert sit at the kitchen table, as if enjoying one of those natural lulls in conversation you always see on coffee commercials, but almost never happen on the reservation. Everything looks almost normal, except for the tears dropping from the cliffs of Big Red's cheeks. Bert, she looks ready to take a break from the beadwork spread before her over the table, stopping just short of a sip from her coffee, her fingers still hooking around the nearly full cup. Her cornstalk-rigid spine still as straight as ever, not even bowing down now. She always bitches at us if we slouch, throwing whatever is close by—*TV Guide,* shoe, whatever—telling us to straighten up. So here she is—perfect posture, even in death. Man, that is just like her.

Big Red, he reaches out across the beading velvet spread on the table, and touches my hand. We sit there quiet, warmth passing between us. "Just like that," he says. "Better than being all tied up to tubes and having the numbers of your heartbeat counted down for you."

"Better than being hit walking down the road in the middle of the night," I say.

"Yeah, better than that," he says. This seems like the next natural step of our relationship, coming on down at the most curious time; but who knows, maybe that's what Bert wanted. Maybe this will be the one thing that will keep Mason Rollins away from pursuing me. Bert always was tricky like that, watching over everyone without really interfering, knowing I don't like the way Mason chases me, but never speaking to him directly about it. Big Red and I share the common routines of caring for Bert's daily needs, so this seems natural as pie. He stops by every morning to see if she needs anything. I clean her trailer and, over the last year, have begun helping her bathe, the nerve endings in her old limbs occasionally abandoning their homes, leaving the signals from her brain to knock away all they want with their ignored messages.

We stay at the table a while longer. The steam from Bert's cooling coffee breaks apart in the morning sunlight. At first, I try to call the other dancers, but at that dial tone's blank invitation, I stand frozen, not yet ready to share the truths of the suicide birds they are all expecting.

Finally, Big Red lifts the receiver away and, holding me, calls the garage where Eddie Chidkin and Chuck Trost, two of the other guys who live here, work. It's probably better this way, anyway. They won't think this is some weird joke from me. I've told some stories in my time, as I've said, but none like this would ever cross my lips. "Eddie there?" Red says into the phone, and then pauses. "Hey, get Chuck. It's Bert, come on home." He puts the receiver back down and holds me more firmly. His chest carries that familiar scent of early fall kerosene heat, pulling me closer, swallowing me as we slowly rock in the old kitchen. Even this, though, can't hold back what's rising up in me again. One mother left this earth years ago, and now the second. I haven't needed to perform a mourning dance for my father, but I might as well, as alive as our relationship is. In all real ways, I am alone. Eddie and Chuck, they burst through the door a little bit later, and together, the four of us walk out the front door to start across the field to the bright purple shack where we thought we'd find Mason "Rollin' in Dough" Rollins.

Mason's become, over the last several months, wickedly unpopular among certain segments of the reservation. In April, he opened a small business in the field next to Bert's house, selling tax-free cigarettes from the "drive-thru" living-room window of a small, sad-ass-looking shack he dragged from who knows where. It used to be back in the woods over on Moon Road. He hadn't asked the Nation's permission, and has so far just blown off their order to shut his business down until they decide if they're going to approve it.

I grab a thick plaid flannel shirt hanging on the back of a chair. The less Mason Rollins sees of my body, the better off I am. He's about ten years older than me, but he's like some horny high-school moron. I swear I can still feel his fingers on my breasts from the numerous times he's pinched me, "for a joke." Asshole. Good taste might prevent him from doing anything, but considering the color of his shack, my shirt's probably not even enough protection. I cross my arms tighter around myself the closer we get to the shack. He's not there when we walk in, letting someone else man the shop, but I bet that, wherever he is, a bird has made its way to his window.

→←

DANCERS PAST AND PRESENT MILL AROUND BEYOND THE PLATE-GLASS WINDOW OF Bert's trailer, smoking outside of the Big House, floating in and out of focus through the greasy imprint the crow left on the pane. The bird's iridescent oils fracture the late-afternoon sun even now, two days after its final flight. My fingers, unusually long, trace the bird's form in the pane. My mother always said my long fingers would either make me a piano player or a thief, and as I'd shown no musical aptitude in all my years, she had often watched me closely whenever we'd gone shopping. Of course, we haven't shopped together in a very long time. She's been dead almost four years, but even before that, we hadn't shopped in quite a while.

My fingers leave a light trace of oil around the bird's print, a small homicide-chalk outline. There should have been one of those around Bert. We never saw the autopsy report. It likely went to her family, but they probably didn't find anything really remarkable. She was, after all, an old woman—seventy-three, by last count. But if we had seen it, I bet we would have read the same words on my mother's death certificate and on the certificate belonging to Big Red's wife.

My heels clang a little too loudly on the trailer's aluminum front steps, as the large beaded barrette, one of Bert's last pieces, shifts in my hair. My mother, she would have hated this dress—"too slutty." She would have had problems with this whole affair, when you come right down to it.

"Bert was not a witch," I mumble aloud, answering my mother's pushy voice in my head. "She was just traditional, is all. And what's wrong with that? What did Jesus Christ ever do for you? Did he put running water in your house?" My mother, Deanna Johns, faithful member of the Tuscarora Nation Protestant Church, died young of intestinal problems, developed over years of her raw sewage seeping into her drinking-water well. She was the first. From their houses with all the modern conveniences, even garbage disposals, some of the Chiefs dismissed the coroner's speculation with the ridiculous evidence that no one else had died of such a thing. Can you believe that?

Most of us have gotten off lucky with the Chiefs' refusal to let town water into the reservation—just a *skaht-yeh* full of cavities. We got fluoride treatments once a year when we were in elementary school, washing over a year's worth of neglect every spring, but that's about it. Rotting teeth must be one of the traditions they want to preserve with their "pure" well water.

Funny, though—my mother still had most of her teeth when she died. She always was a stubborn one. She begrudged every last one she lost to rot. Even in the hospital, near the end, her stubbornness made her nearly refuse visits from me, her own daughter. The issue between us? I had legally changed my last name to my father's a few months before, on my eighteenth birthday, an act of which, you can imagine, my mother had most sincerely not approved. On my admittedly occasional visits, her prime motivation for even speaking to me had clearly been religious conversion. Things would be better if I would just do that one thing. She constantly yakked away that Bertha Monterney had stolen me with a spell—one so powerful, it was even able to grab a good Christian girl like Patricia, as she still called me, and lead me down the witch's path. Since she died, Big Red's boy, Two-Step, is the only one who doesn't call me Fiction.

In the past, I usually reminded her that if it hadn't been for Christians, Indians might still be thriving groups instead of statistical anomalies. She and I were the last two of a line of Onondagas living among Tuscaroras, a line extending as far as the reservation itself did, way back to the 1700s. And then, somewhere around the time Haudenosaunee people were given the new name Iroquois, we stuck together for our own survival; regardless of which of the Six Nations you came from—Onondaga, Tuscarora, Mohawk, Seneca, Oneida, Cayuga—it didn't matter. This last generation, though, they flourished among the rows of pews within the well-established Protestant Church, their ears long empty of the Longhouse songs. Those ears, nearly filled with the contents of missionary hymnals, found room for one more phrase, "racial purity," whispered over the airwaves of World War II in the translated speeches of a psycho, somehow just missing the insanity altogether, maybe losing it in the translation.

First my mother, and then I, myself, experienced the trick of lowered status in a community that generally claimed to accent the "unity" end of the word. Our family had always enjoyed the same treaty rights all members of Haudenosaunee Nations have. Those rights, they'd been negotiated with New York State, allowing us to maintain the small parcels of land, reservations, as supposedly sovereign land. We paid no property or school taxes, and had access to the state-funded health clinic, but the two of us specifically had slowly been given the message. The sighs and the rolling of the receptionist's eyes, showing off her whites, any time either of us stepped into the clinic, so consistent that I wanted to slap those rolled whites right out of her head; the mailbox flyers announcing Council meetings for Nation members only; "Nation-members-only" dances at the socials—these things told us in pretty damned loud voices that we were different.

My mother, she always pretended she never got those messages. Right up to the end, she didn't recognize it had been her own blindness that had driven me like a fast car from there and into Bert's traditional dance group in the first place. Bert welcomed everyone in, and her house was probably the only one on the Nation that welcomed complete Haudenosaunee representation. Even some Algonquins belonged to the group, relocated from Maniwakee and welcomed in as any other. Bert's father had been Mohawk,

I think, and never felt totally at home out here. My mother never understood the desire to be accepted without the strings, without needing a new personality for your new friends.

"D'you say something?" Eddie Chidkin asks, as I step up and bum a smoke.

"Not to anyone who could hear. Let's go." We all squeeze into Chuck Trost's car. In the rearview mirror, square in front of me, the features of my mother and father swim across my skull, shifting and working their way out, my mother's perfect front teeth generally masking the rotten molars of my father. The traits Bert passed on to me—they've burrowed way deeper, almost hibernating now.

>‹

THE NONDENOMINATIONAL MISSION—THE ONLY CHURCH THAT WOULD ALLOW A Longhouse service within its walls—holds a deep gap between the crowd at the front and the few folks stuffed into the last pew's far corner. Those in the back are the only people I don't recognize in the whole place. Mason, finally home from who knows where, slides over in his pew, puts his arm on the pew's back, and motions with his head for me to join him, to sidle up next to him. Big Red and his boy Two-Step entice me with bug eyes from the first row, and I slide easily into the custom-sized space between the two.

Big Red continues to give me that large-eyed look, so I glance down to see if I am sitting on his hand or something, which I'm not. He finally points to his wrist, where no watch lies.

As the speaker begins, recounting a brief history of Bert's dancers— her proudest achievement—I whisper, "Christian trouble," leaning over and pressing into Big Red's bulky frame in order to reach his ear with my secret. He frowns and passes me a stick of his namesake gum. Now, Big Red, he'll do just about anything for anybody on this whole reservation, except give up even a single stick of gum, even if he has a Plen-T-Pak. I must have had pretty bad breath. This doesn't come as a total surprise, as I was out late last night. Sometimes even toothpaste is no match for a fermented tongue.

We're all taking Bert's death a bit differently. Bartending down at The Den, I've gotten into the habit of just staying beyond my shift. You know, I'm not bad looking, maybe even better than average, no fry-bread queen is what I'm saying, and these ludicrous spandex outfits I have to wear at work—bear claws on black leather thongs hanging off at strategic points and all that nonsense—make my coping choice pretty cost-effective. I never, ever, pay for a drink, and refuse most offers of drinks while I'm on duty. Even on a bad night, there's always Mason Rollins to count on.

Of all of us, though, Red is taking this the hardest. Only four or five sentences have left him since he shouted that morning. It seems like Bert doesn't want him singing for any other group of dancers than hers, and somehow silenced him when she left this world. He's been the group's primary singer for as long as I can remember, and that's at least the last twelve of my twenty-two years. The group is over thirty years old, long-standing enough for Big Red to have been one of the early dancers and to have graduated to singer, as his body rhythms slowed and his poor posture could no longer be corrected with a shout and a well-thrown *TV Guide.*

He holds the title of most consistent member, welcoming new dancers and using their idiosyncrasies for the group. Eddie is Bert's other primary singer, and Red had pegged him for that role from the day he had moved into the Big House. Eddie never settles in anywhere completely, and Bert's place is no exception, though he takes an active role in keeping the house up, performing whatever minor repairs are needed at the moment. Whenever there's time, he works on his room with precision, arranging and rearranging the room into neat stacks of items: true-crime magazines, rolled-up posters that never seem to make it to the walls, boxes filled with who knows what, all organized from smallest to largest. His room is a miniature city, its pathways allowing him access to all of his piles, his closet, and his bed. He proudly revealed it to me shortly after I moved in, and I recognized, as Big Red had years before, that this man would always keep the beat.

Bert welcomed me, as she had every person willing to be one of us: the only rules are that you have to dance and have to perform some chores around the house. I take . . . took . . . care of Bert's needs, mostly. The other women dancers have moved on to families of their own, breeding the next generation in drafty trailer back-bedrooms in the rhythms they keep with their husbands or boyfriends. Right now, I'm the only woman living in the Big House. Even Bert, she hadn't actually lived in it for several years.

Behind the Big House stands a single-wide trailer, just the right size for her. She liked the privacy when she wanted it, making trips up to the house every day, if for nothing more than to eat. She had fallen into the habit of eating with her dancers from the very beginning. Otherwise, things would have fallen apart a long time ago, torn up in the lonely storms we all battle. The feeling she made in that space was really what her children—as she'd always called us—had come to her for in the first place.

We had all fallen out with our own families and eventually wound up on her doorstep. But she made us more than a family—she made us proud. We're competition-caliber dancers: Smoke, War, even Rabbit. How do you think most of our women have snagged some good men for themselves? If it's East Coast—you name it, we do it. We all have our own specialties— mine is Smoke, where you have to anticipate where the singer and drummer are going to take you—but our pride and drive rests with the group. Across the whole Northeast powwow circuit, we are feared and respected— the only worthy combination, she often said as we set out for the floor.

We bury Bert over in Calvary Cemetery (which most folks mispronounce "cavalry"), over on Torn Rock Road on the upper mountain, where the graves overlook the escarpment and the town of Lewiston, below. The ground is still pliable enough for digging. The members of the small last-pew group keep their distance again, afraid they might hear Bert calling from inside of her casket. Her likeness runs around inside of their features, emerging suddenly and then disappearing again as they move cheeks, eyes, lips. They keep their distance, while the casket is lowered into the earth and late September leaves dance gently on the grounds, politely hiding earlier passings.

After we plant her, all of us—Bert's dancers that is—regroup back at her house, coming together as we never have before. The relatives decide to skip this part. Some dancers haven't been inside in years, and they eye the place, playing back their own times, changing the furniture, peeling the paint and wallpaper to their layers, forcing the television to vanish. They don't see the holes in the plaster, the places where hardwood floors have transformed into plywood, the occasional cardboard wall, bulging out and frowning with the effort of keeping the fiberglass insulation in.

No one has brought us the condolence casseroles that usually accompany a funeral, not even a goddamned ham-and-cheese-sandwich tray. Mason puts on some coffee, but he hasn't taken the idea far enough to use the huge party urn. "Remember this?" I ask, opening the tall cupboard.

"What about it?" he asks. The Mr. Coffee holds enough for about six, yet those who have filled their cups wait. I set the coffee to brew, and even Mason waits, after he takes a sip and realizes no one has joined him.

Bert's cupboards are a guidebook to the cycles she had us all live by. She believed we were hers for good. Her fridge and cupboards always hold enough to make supper for as many people as might show up on any given day. She refused to be caught unprepared. Just like she always made us, we all take part in this preparation, pulling down home-canned peaches we put up mid-season, an industrial-size jar of sweet pickles Eddie bought from the warehouse club, a leftover turkey breast I smoked earlier this week for sandwich makings, blackcap jam Big Red's mother-in-law Ruby Pem always gave Bert during Midwinter Ceremony, bricks of commodity cheese, and the loaves of bread Bert baked every Sunday.

All this and more sit in the fridge, unaware Bert has died. There, on the center shelf, is a large ceramic-sealed kettle that can house only one thing—corn soup. It must be the final kettle from last year's braids of Indian corn that Bert kept hanging in the attic, cooking us up a batch only when we needed to renew. There were a few more braids than usual this last year, Mason having donated some he had gotten in trade for some smokes. She hadn't mentioned this kettle. I pull it from the cold shelf and dipper out amounts in smaller pots to heat on the stove. The blind, eyeless, lyed corn, puffed and swollen from its hours of hardwood-ash cooking, moves silently in its broth as it heats above the low flame.

Two-Step digs a big Valu-Pak of miniature candy bars from the ancient flour-milling cupboard. "Hey!" Eddie says, "I thought I was the only one she shared her secret hiding place with!"

"Guess not, Candy-Boy," Two-Step says, and everyone laughs, though I had also thought I was the only one, and probably others had felt that way too.

"You okay?" Mason asks, wrapping his arms around my shoulders from behind, pressing himself into me.

"Fine." I pull away fast and pour a bowl of the hot soup. When we each have a full plate, bowl, and cup, and his hands are fully occupied, we all move into the living room, locked into the confines of a certain, unseen perimeter we can't and won't break free from. Bert's sagging furniture welcomes us, tries to comfort us in tattered and worn padded arms as we mumble out that quiet after-funeral conversation.

"It's kind of weird, but I think she knew. You know, they say some people do," I say, turning to Chuck, sitting next to me on the couch. I don't really know him that well, but Eddie's talked about him for years, and all the stupid shit they do at the garage, like taking the tanks off their motor-cycles so they can fill them with county gas. Would seem just as easy to pay for a tank of gas. How much can it be? Chuck looks at me, but doesn't seem to be listening. As far as I know, my breasts have not at any time in the recent past acquired the gift of speech, and I am no ventriloquist, yet all his attention seems focused there. It's like some damned syndrome! For the moment, though, this keeps at least one person between Mason and me, and that's the way I like things. Chuck is only using his eyes.

"She always took her bath at night, just before bed, but that day, she wanted to take it in the morning, you know, almost like she didn't want to die dirty or something. Right after her bath, she went up to the house and, as I was straightening up, this huge bird—I don't even know what the hell kind it was—crashed into the door glass and opened the door wide, just flying around the room like crazy before plowing into the living-room win-dow and killing itself." The first part is true, but the rest is to see how closely Chuck has actually been listening. This has become a trademark of mine. I don't know where the stories come from. They just leap out of the holes in my teeth and are out my mouth, flying around the room by them-selves before I can stop them. I guess I deserve my name.

Someone knocks on the front door. Big Red gets up and returns a moment later with my father, Chief Jacob "Bud" Tunny. My father, he nods to most people in the room, but looks over me as if I am nothing more than another piece of Bert's resigned furniture, in the same manner he has since I legally adopted his last name, revealing the horns he wore before he put on the Chief's official ones—the horns he wore with Protestant women other than his wife, from other than his tribe.

"I have Bertha Monterney's will here," he says, raising a slim blue plas-tic folder. He sets it on the large floor-model television set in the corner. "Everything seems to be in order except—and I hate to bring this up so soon, but you're all going to have to leave here—her life insurance only covered the funeral. There's still the digging and clean-up fee . . ."

"What about her relatives?" Chuck asks, leaning in the living room's archway.

"Well, they don't have the money, so they said the Nation could have the house as payment. So, you're going to have to leave."

"How much was it?" Mason crawls out of the couch and pulls his wallet from his back pocket. He thumbs several crisp Benjamin Franklins from it.

"That's the Nation's concern. Besides, your money's no good to us. In the same way you don't recognize our wisdom, we don't recognize the dirty money you bring in," my father says simply. All of his replies have the sound of an Emergency Broadcast System test, dull and emotionless, yet full of the potential for disaster, able to say the words "nuclear attack" as blandly as "this is only a test."

"Three hundred. Least it was when we buried Bev a few years ago," Big Red says, moving his bulk into the room, speaking some of his first words since Bert's death. I nod in agreement, though my father keeps his back to me.

"You took this place for three hundred dollars?" Mason's face begins to grow flat with anger—his features ironed rigid from the inside out.

"It's more than that, now," my father says, attempting to wave Mason away as he would one of those carcass-eating bluebottle flies.

"How much more?" Mason ignores my father's flicking fingers.

"The Nation must be compensated. It's the way things have always been in our community, and though you might be able to change some things with those hundred-dollar bills of yours, this won't be among them," my father rattles out in his Emergency Broadcast System voice.

Mason rushes to the telephone and dials a number with some serious attitude. He lifts the receiver to his ear and frowns, clicking away at the hang-up buttons on the phone's base.

"It's too late. The Nation has already had the phone lines cut. Bertha won't be needing one anymore. It's all part of my duties. Electric will be stopped in one week's time, no more. That ought to give you all more than enough time to remove your belongings." My father leaves the living room and rushes out through the entry without even bothering to look back. Mason starts to follow him, but Big Red reaches for his shoulder.

"It ain't right, man. Bert wouldn't like you starting shit in her house. She always went by tradition, even down to respecting Chiefs who might not be deserving it at the moment. You know that," Big Red says. He's a little over ten years older than Mason, and he still speaks in a voice Mason can hear. Though he works midnights for Mason at the purple shack, taking the job after growing gray and tired from a lack of work, he still holds an easy authority.

"Well, I ain't Bert."

"But you're here. C'mon." Red nudges him back into the living room, where we all ignore the folder. None of us are anxious to see what Bert's death holds for us on paper. Silence surrounds us, and we sit for what seems like hours in the fading light, growing into gray shadows of ourselves. The folder on the television glows with the news hidden inside it, the only light in the living room.

A sound grows from the darkness, low at first, and I initially mistake it for a faraway engine, driving closer and closer. The far corner fills with movement, and only when his bulk blocks out the window's faint light do I recognize the shape as Eddie leaving the room.

The sound sharpens, clarifies, as Big Red opens his mouth wide, seeming about to yawn, and the high, soaring note arches out from his diaphragm, reverberating off his esophagus, never even grazing his teeth as it spreads throughout the room. It lasts hours, vibrating the room—a giant tuning fork, filling us with all the sounds and feelings he's been holding prisoner in the base of his lungs since he found Bert at the kitchen table. Eddie runs back in carrying bone and dried-corn rattles, one snapping-turtle rattle, two drums and sticks. The bone rattles glide into the right hands and wait, silent. Eddie hands the snapping-turtle rattle to Red, passes the first drum to Chuck, and then waits—the stick vibrating for a moment before he brings it down to meet the drum, as Red raises the snapping turtle, and the corn's first collision sends its waves out into the room. Chuck joins Eddie on the cue, and the two begin a mourning song in earnest. The other rattlers follow suit, the hard dried corn knocking against the bony bull-horn shells, whispering for us to rise.

We, the group of twenty or so of Bert's "children" who have not succumbed to late-night car wrecks, overdoses, cirrhosis, or any other twentieth-century saviors, bloom out of her listless, patient furniture—germinated Indian seed-corn leaving the dead husk and cavity-filled cob her body has become—and we grow out into the world, our feet moving softly on the warped wooden floor, shining with the brilliance of thirty years of children dancing away from their pasts. Our own glow, sunlight on silk, drowns out the meager, cold light my father has tried to bathe us in with his documents, as we fall into our own rhythms, our potential futures, for our first, and last, dance together.

><

CHAPTER 2 Redman's Drop

Mason Rollins

AT THE BOTTOM OF REDMAN'S DROP, THE DRIVER'S SEAT OF MY PALE SILVER Chevette embraces me in a way the woman in my passenger's seat won't. No matter what I offer her, no matter what we have shared, no matter how many times I've gently reached over and touched her thigh, obeying when she removes my hand, she won't hold me like a lover in the late hours would. The heater hums the blues in the September air. These deep green shadows will soon be turning, showing off their skeletal innards. The fall apples' scent drifts down from Bud's orchards and into the Chevette's heating-vent ducts. Not really—that's more like one of her bullshit stories—but it would be cool. My next car will be able to do that. Unlike hers, the stories I tell are going to come true.

This is all part of the future that grows around me like a demanding weed, creeping and taking hold wherever it can. In my future, we look out over the escarpment from my beautiful new mansion, sipping a glass of Dom Perignon, my hand on her tight little ass, firm like one of her father's apples, and this time she doesn't move away, or slap me, or anything like that. When we drain our glasses, we toss the crystal out over the cliff and watch as it blends into the atmosphere. We listen for its last bit of existence, the quiet musical jingling of it smashing on the rocky hill bottom, and maybe then we laugh a little. She doesn't know why we're laughing, because all she can see are the glasses we've just wasted. She can't see the freedom in knowing you can always buy more, if you've got it. She can't see how I've sat here a half-dozen times over the past several months, deep in my bucket seat, when she has refused to come home with me—playing out that scene and wondering who owns this fragment of the reservation, listening as the sound of shattering glass grows more and more clear each time—crystal clear.

"Look, Mason. I gotta get to work. If you're not gonna give me a ride the rest of the way, let me know now, and I'll walk. But you can be sure as shit I won't be riding with you again—making me walk up this damn hill, getting all sweaty for work." Fiction Tunny has her own way of shattering things like fine crystal—this moment, for example. If she didn't know I wanted to be with her, why'd she accept the ride in the first place? Particularly wearing this outfit. I can picture it sweaty, glistening damp in all the right places. I might just like to see her climb this hill, and then I could pick her up again at the top and re-offer her the ride, filling my lungs with the scent of her sweet juices.

"So, how'd you like to live in one of these, someday?" Through the tree tops, we can catch glimpses of the houses and property at the ridge's top. These big old houses, not actually "game-show luxurious," but pretty fine all the same, belong to folks who were smart enough to stake them out when this reservation was divided up, and it probably also helped that their voices were heard crystal clear by those doing the dividing. They'll never sell. They overlook the edge of the reservation, where its border drops off into nothingness. The steep wall was ripped from the earth thousands, maybe hundreds of thousands of years ago, by the Niagara Falls—the escarpment a part of the scar left by the water's erosion line, impressive and bold, like me. But at the bottom, down here in the earth's rich embrace, where these trees quietly enjoy the sun, ignoring the development all around them . . . now, this is a possibility.

After some weeks of asking around, calling in every information favor owed me, my far cousin and former dancing colleague Eddie Chidkin drops that the piece belongs to a relative of one of my very own employees—Big Red Harmony's mother-in-law, Ruby Pem. This old woman is from Eddie's clan—Deer—is, in fact, its Clan Mother, trusted with keeping the clan alive and thriving. She's about eighty, that shaky age where she can no longer be counted on to appear at the Feast on New Year's Day. When I heard that, man, you can bet I got to work on trying to up my financial base. I would definitely have enough to offer her for certain by next summer, but I've never been the waiting kind. When Ruby eventually lets go, that asshole Bud—excuse me, Chief Jacob Tunny—might just somehow figure a way to claim it for the Nation. I need to make sure he never even gets a shot.

"Oh, yeah, Mason, maybe my dad'll leave me enough to buy some of that land when he dies, and I'll go into the family business. What do you think? Fiction Tunny Apples, homegrown in your own backyard, falling not very far from the family tree. Come on, I gotta go, really, or I'll be selling no wine before its time," she says, getting all agitated, looking at her watch, like she hadn't just looked at it a minute ago.

"How about if I pay you? Just to sit here and talk with me. You could call in sick. What d'you make there in a night, anyway? Thirty, forty bucks? I can handle that."

"You gonna keep paying me, day after day, to listen to your nonsense? 'Cause they're gonna fire my sorry ass if I miss another day. They barely let me get the time for the funeral, and then when I told them I need the tenth day after she died off for her death feast—man, they just hit the freakin' roof. They thought ten days was too soon to take off another day. You know, they've never heard of that. White folks don't hold Ten-Day Feasts. When I tried to explain, my old boss poured a draft and threw a bag of pretzels on the bar and told me to have my own feast, instead of missing another day. Can you believe that shit?"

I'm not sure I can believe it. Her stories are pretty close to the way things might be, so sometimes I just can't tell. This is one of those times. Either way, I won't be having her tonight, that's for certain. Just like every other night.

I slam my old Indian car into first gear, after a few tries, and start up the hill. The transmission is going. Bud's gleaming Lincoln rounds the sharp bend near the top of Redman's Drop, making the wide Y-swoop at the hill's sloping peak, heading toward the dike. What the hell, I figure, and lean on the gas trying to catch up with him. My car doesn't want to take the hill at the same speed I do, and by the time I catch sight of the Lincoln again, Bud is easing that bad boy into his hidden driveway, sliding into his orchards. Those Tunnys make a bundle on their orchards, but I wonder how much Nation money goes into buying those Lincolns. It'd be easy for him to snatch up, since Bud doesn't allow anyone else to see the Nation books.

"Mason, what are you doing slowing down? We are not going there! I'm serious, damn it!"

"Hold your horses, I just wanted to make sure Bud was going home." I never know if she wants me to call him her dad or not, so I stay on the safe side with her, at least on that topic. She doesn't have a lot of credibility out here. I could probably take her and bang her right here in the car, and no one would ever believe her; but that's not the way I like to do things. She should be riding on my lap because she wants to be there. "I'll have you there in time. How much you got left?"

"Five minutes."

"No problem." In five minutes, I expect to sit in Bud Tunny's living room. So I wind us down Pem Brook at seventy miles an hour, the fastest this bitch will go, and dump Fiction off at The Den, and by the time I follow Bud's path to his house, my hard-on is gone down enough so nothing shows when I get out. No car is in sight. Garage-door opener, I guess, hopping up to the porch and flicking both knockers on the double doors. Behind me grows the expanse of the Tunny family orchards, following the north wall of the dike like foot soldiers. His tall hedgerow stands guard, hiding this big-ass estate from the road, and through it all, the long road making up Bud's driveway. Of course, most of us have seen the layout anyway from the top of the dike—probably the reason he doesn't like us swimming up there, but I guess he feels if we don't have to see it every day, we won't mind so much.

During Christmas vacations when I was a kid, my first fortunes were grown among these rows. Pruning back to get the right kinds of growth for these apple trees, bullying them to produce while we froze our asses off, was one of the few jobs a ten-year-old reservation kid could get. I'd already been living off and on at Bert's by that age, my folks both having jobs. Every Christmas vacation morning, Bert hauled anyone who wanted to work down here at seven o'clock and picked us back up, seven at night. Bud had a little heater on in the shed out back where we could warm up, but he docked you the whole hour if you stayed more than five minutes in the shed, so most of us just bundled up and stuck it out.

Every kid who went had to give Bert a dollar a day for gas and lunch money, but no one minded. Bud paid a dollar an hour, so if we weren't too lazy, we could come away with eleven dollars free and clear at day's end, way better than the piecework most other apple growers in the area offered, and you didn't have to wait until you were fourteen to work at Bud's. I was ten, but some of the other kids were easily around eight years old, maybe seven. He had ladders set up wherever he wanted us to work in the orchards on any given day.

We never worked picking in the fall. I always wanted to do that, to taste those apples I had forced into good posture, like Bert had me, but it was back to school in the fall, with no break until after harvest time was over. One night, when I was about fourteen, I snuck back into Bud's orchards to finally have that taste . . . to discover labels attached to the heads of various rows. Bud's apples were raised for industry, and here I thought he had cut some deals with local fruit stands all that time. One of the companies dealt in a commercial hard-cider drink. And every year, we watched Protestant-proud Bud making all kinds of noises on the Temperance League, always presenting the polyester ribbon awards for the best anti-drinking posters in the elementary school's annual Temperance Poster Contest.

I only received one of those strips of ribbon once. I'd saved some of my pruning earnings and paid Chuck Trost a dollar to make my poster. Even then, at seven years old, Chuck had been a crackerjack artist, building a polyester rainbow for his grade's category; but his rainbow was dominated by white, the First-Place ribbon. The poster I won with featured a Chevy careening off the side of Redman's Drop. Its driver, an electrified skeleton, floated in midair, somehow having hit live wires after jumping from the tragically moving vehicle. A twelve-pack of Genesee fell big as life over the escarpment's ledge in the poster's right-hand corner. Neither Chuck nor I had known how to spell Genesee, so the twelve-pack boldly sported the name all the old hard-core rez boys had given the beer: "Genny." Though I was three years older than Chuck, that boy could still draw better than anyone in any of the grades. The prize of two dollars is years long gone, but I still have the First-Place ribbon I snagged, dingy yellow with age, some of the gold-leaf letters crumbling off, so the ribbon is now for "Fist-Place." I like that just as well—probably better.

"Yes? What is it? Jacob isn't home," Bud's wife says. A skinny old woman, wrapped in gray polyester, Twila's rose-shaded face offers the only color she holds. She's turning into old, dried fruitwood herself.

"Yes, he is. I saw him pull in here not three minutes ago." I'm not buying into that bullshit game, and I prop myself against one of the awning pillars, one knee lifted, boot heel hooked into the lowest groove, just to let her know.

"Well, he's gone back among the rows, and I don't know when he's coming back. Maybe if you make an appointment, I'll have him get back to you," Twila continues, closing the door.

"That's okay, I'll wait. I got time," I say back, just before the door clicks shut. All I can think of, though, is that I don't have time, that I am not at The Den, watching Fiction slinking around in that shiny outfit of hers, wanting to peel it back, like a ripe, slick skin, kneeling in front of her as I grip her ankles and snap that outfit free. A sliding-glass patio door opens at the back of the house, and Twila's wispy nasal voice carries her husband's name down through the woods, being absorbed by the solid wall of the dike. Counting silently to myself, I reach only nine before Bud appears at the porch's edge from around the side of the house in a pair of house slippers, making my new hard-on disappear awful fast.

"Hi, Bud."

"What do you want?" He steps up on the porch and doesn't even offer me a hand as I rise.

"One of them dollar-an-hour jobs pruning your apples for you." Always a gentleman, I brush dust from the seat of my jeans and then hold out my dusty hand for Bud to shake. "How 'bout it?"

"My workers get three dollars an hour, and they get their lunch hour, too." He looks at my open hand, but passes on gripping it.

"Minimum wage is four and a quarter."

"What do you want?" Bud repeats.

"Let's you and me talk."

He remains still at first, but when I reach for the door handle, he moves quickly, drawn like I'm siphoning him with threats of violation.

Inside, he directs me into his study at the back of the house. He closes the door and sits behind a broad desk backed up to a set of plate-glass doors resting in carved oak frames, the pattern matching the desk. Those frames are solid—not veneer. I might not yet be able to afford quality, but I've got an eye for it. If nothing else, this man has style. His study overlooks the woods and the dike, its rising expanse behind him, a wall of earth forced to stand up straight. Bud sits and, in the afternoon sun, becomes a faceless silhouette against the edge of the reservation. As I make myself comfortable, Bud clears papers from his desk and shoves them into file folders randomly.

"Bertha Monterney's will is not up for discussion. The place belongs to the Nation now, period. These decisions might seem very unfair to someone who . . . someone like you, but it was all for the best. These are complex matters. In fact, there's one other issue with that will, but it's one that doesn't concern you. It concerns that young woman who's planning to live in Bertha's trailer, that Johns girl." Even after all this time, he won't admit that Fiction's his daughter, and though I don't have any idea where he's going with that, I can't afford to get sidetracked here. I am at an advantage. He has no idea where I'm going with this, either, and his sensitivity to Bert's house is pretty clear. He knows he fucked us over. That piece of information is worth storing for later. Could be useful.

I start.

"Now, cigarettes ain't in such high demand you could make a big living on just selling them, but hey, let's face it—with smokes, there's the advantage of the built-in customer. The customer with needs. And if you can give 'em what they want cheaper'n they can get it anywhere else . . . well, you know the way I'm makin' money." Of course, Bud knows.

>‹

THE TREATY RIGHTS I SCORED BIG TIME WITH IN MY BUSINESS ARE THE SAME rights Bud and his family have been using for—oh, easily the last several generations. Those same treaty rights Bert ranted on and on about all through our dance practices finally came in handy for me. The Canandaigua treaty suggests anything bought or sold within the reservation's boundaries can't be taxed by the state, and this is solidified by no less than the United States Constitution. I had this all checked out. Bert wasn't shitting us after all. Bud Tunny's family, discovering they had an entire income base on which they could not be taxed, offered their produce at a price so far below their competitors that businesses were just lining right up to take those apples off their hands. Bud's family became the most popular suppliers in the area. The state ignored this situation. The Tunnys claimed they were only doing what the treaty allowed for, but everyone knew about the politician dinners the family's men had always attended, dinners with state officials. A half dozen other businesses thrived too, from time to time, on the reservation—a general store, several roofing companies, a couple of junkyards—but only with the Chiefs' Council's permission.

I didn't go that route. As I planned it, Mason Rollins's Smoke Shop just appeared one day on the opposite side of the dike, near the reservation's south border. I painted the little shack I bought for fifty bucks and dragged from the swamps of Moon Road a bright purple, with bold white letters on the trailer's side, just like the colors of the treaty wampum belts, directly shouting SMOKES ALMOST ¹/₂ OFF, and I painted this half-assed-looking cigarette next to the words, just in case.

I didn't want anyone to recognize that old shack. If they knew some old jock had died drunk sitting on the pot in there, his drawers down around his ankles, his kids just wanting to make back some of the burial money, I'd never get anyone to work for me. Too many active ghosts out here already. You hear them sometimes, mostly when you don't want to, telling you what to do; but no ghosts have been paying my bills as far as I can tell, so they can just keep their damned mouths shut.

I cut the grass down into a circular-shaped driveway, saturated it with vegetation killer, and had a few loads of crushed stone dumped there to prevent the grass from growing back. That was all I needed for customers to keep on coming.

I took my initial inspiration from Bud himself, even down to location, and it worked like a charm. The land I got is on the opposite side of the dike from Bud's place—it's like a giant wall between us—except I am right on the border, perfect for my purposes. So, any time he looked at my place, he had to see how close the dike had come to taking the whole southwest corner, had to see what his father had done to us. 'Course, it also helped that this was Bert's land.

My customers find the fifty-cents-a-pack savings worth the trip out to the reservation, none caring they're evading New York State tax laws, some maybe even liking that aspect of their habits. The business is popular enough that any time of day or night, at least a few cars are lined up, the owners patiently waiting to satisfy the needs of their nagging bodies. All this on a borrowed five thousand dollars.

"So ANYWAY, THIS IS GONNA BE BIG. I'M WORKING OUT THE DETAILS RIGHT NOW so I can carry more brands, maybe even some Canadian brands eventually, and you know how that's gonna hit. They're already shopping for everything over here, their inflation's so high. Offer 'em smokes, they'll be lining up."

The elements of Bud's face that I can see remain still. "I can't give you your electric back. You should have come to the Nation with your idea in the first place." He opens the middle drawer of his desk and begins sorting paper clips, putting them all in one small compartment. When he finishes, he moves on to rubber bands.

"Well, that's fine. I'll keep my electric the way it is. It's fine. That's not why I came." I had hoped Bud might consent to rerouting the shop's electricity back where it should be. Sometimes, my stubbornness doesn't pay off as well as I would like. I've been ignoring the Nation's crabbiness with my business and their demand that I shut down, but Bud's a little more clever than I've given him credit for. He's found ways of making me notice. A few days after their demand, the Nation sent down an order that I was not to receive electricity at the reservation site. The power company, as always, obeyed the Nation's orders and discontinued service. Within two days, though, bam! I was back in business. I just had my lines rerouted and buried. They now emerge over the border onto a white farmer's property. I leased the small patch of land where the lines surface and connect with outside lines, circumventing the Chiefs, all perfectly legally. Now, I would have preferred not to go through this hassle, particularly with my new plans, but that's the way it goes.

I rehearsed this discussion all last night, after Fiction turned me down at The Den for the five-hundredth time, as I lay on the slim cot in the smoke shack's bedroom. Besides the small pockets where a few ratty chairs sit, the shack's filled with cases of cigarettes stacked more or less alphabetically by brand. The tobacco odor stuck to my clothes at first, and finally I moved all of my stuff back to my old room at Bert's house, where I showered. I can't yet afford to have a well dug, so the shack has no running water. With the earliest profits, I picked up a microwave, and went down to a boating-supply shop and bought one of those portable sanitary toilets, the sort that are basic equipment on the yachts moored in the Lower Niagara River in Youngstown, that part of the river that continues below the Niagara Falls, eventually washing into Lake Ontario.

➤❮

YOU SEE, I HAVE SPENT YEARS RIDING A BICYCLE THROUGHOUT NIAGARA COUNTY, searching out the steepest hills possible, aside from the impossibly straight wall of the dike—its surface almost perpendicular to the earth—for which we have Bud's father to thank. Ezekiel Tunny messed things up for us—giving the state, in an undisclosed deal, the invitation to eat up a third of the reservation. Redman's Drop is probably the most challenging hill in my immediate riding area. It begins gradually in Lewiston, but grows wickedly difficult, twisting up at a forty-five-degree angle for the rest of its quarter-mile stretch.

I first tried riding my bicycle up it when I was fifteen, but I failed, dropping out after the lowest bend, exhausted, even with my ten-speed in first gear. After that initial defeat, I tried smaller hills, gradually working my way up. The trick is to only work as well as you can manage for the long haul. One of my early challenges had been the ramp road leading to the Youngstown Yacht Association—or YYA, as the members called it among themselves—in the lower Niagara gorge. While preparing to ride the hill, I often eavesdropped on club members, learning the language of wealth. No big surprise there; their discussions concerned work, or stocks, or other money issues.

Even after I had "graduated" from the yacht-club hill, I returned frequently and sat at one of the benches overlooking the river, listening and learning about the things rich men said and did. I was in training. I learned of the ways they kept themselves dignified, even out in the natural and unpredictable element of the river. I learned along the way of the portable sanitary toilet, where they simply carried out their waste in a handy little chemical-filled suitcase from below the commode. They dumped it, never having to see or smell the end products of their own bodily functions. Now that I have the shitter, the yacht can't be too far behind.

Redman's Drop took me the entire summer to conquer, but the week before the school year was to begin, I wheezed my way on up to a stop at the road's left branch, facing toward the center of the reservation, having kept a slow, relentless stride in first gear. I celebrated simply, with the school year rapidly approaching in the setting August sun.

The hill had taken cars in ice storms and drunk drivers on clear moon-lit nights, indiscriminately, but it was not going to take me. It had been nicknamed Redman's Drop several generations ago because it was a wicked hill to navigate, its turns awkward and random, and many rez boys lost their lives dropping their cars over its steep edge. Some time over the years, no one's really sure when, a state road sign was erected, officially naming the road as Redman's Drop Road. The hill road had been carved into the escarpment ridge at the reservation's northwest border, a few miles down the road from where we now sit and look at the future.

✌

"Anyway, I came to offer the Nation a business proposition. Like I was saying, with Canadian smokes, this can only get bigger. I want the Nation to succeed as much as anyone, so now's your chance to get in on the ground floor." I don't want to sound like some swampland salesman, but for all of my hanging around at the yacht club, I still have not mastered the language of big business. But it doesn't matter too much. Bud wouldn't recognize the dialect if he heard it.

Though the Tunnys have always been invited to political dinners, they're probably treated like strange and potentially dangerous dogs: patted and complimented, only taken as seriously as the deadliness of the bite they could deliver. When I make it to those dinners—and I will—I'll eat with them, not at the side of the table. I'll be wearing the same kinds of clothes they wear, not those damned beaded bolo ties Bud has made his trademark.

"In order to get all the brands in I want, I need a bigger building than my little house there. Now, I'll be able to do it on my own, but it's going to take me a bit longer than I want. So, if the Nation wants, we can half and half the start-up costs and the profits. And I'm telling you, it's gonna be big. The Picnic Grove—this time next year, you'll have all the improvements you been talking about, and then some. And the Council House—that too. New siding and new roof. Maybe even running water. The way I figure—"

Bud slowly shakes his head, back and forth. He stops shuffling around in his desk and stares directly at me.

"The Nation's money is a serious matter. I don't think they would approve of the idea. It's too much money for money's sake. Pretty soon your skin will start fading. You'll look like the *cree-rhooh-rhit* you invite out here with your bargains. I am going to have to say no. Now if you'll excuse me, I have to get things ready to complete Bertha's burial, and—"

"Wait a minute. You're supposed to be representing the Nation. How do you know what they want? You haven't even brought this up in open Council. You haven't even given me the chance to tell them what it's all about. What the fuck kind of 'people's voice' is that?"

"I was raised to be in this position," Bud begins, "because the Clan Mothers knew I would have the vision to represent the people—even if, especially if, they weren't around to be their own voices. You came from nowhere. You were raised to wind up on Moon Road, drinking away like all those other do-nothings out here. You should be silent, now, and consider yourself fortunate. You're lucky we haven't stopped your business, yet. We can, you know. You didn't bring it to—"

"I don't think you can," I say, simply. "You've already tried, and if you could actually stop my business, I'm sure you wouldn't have waited 'til now, so don't give me your bullshit, Bud." I pause and then, smiling, continue. "You'd like me to be down on Moon Road, wouldn't you? Just drunk and passed out, shit and piss in my drawers and puke in my hair, as long as I was quiet. You could just keep running your little traditional Protestant Church government, filling your own pockets and worrying about the seventh generation of the Tunny family. Well, there are other families out here. And they remember what your father's vision brought to this reservation—that dike right outside your window here, and who knows what's leaking out of those barrels he let be buried everywhere. Everywhere but around your house, anyway. How much was he paid for that? Did it go into the Nation's books?"

"Those books are none of your concern."

"You're the voice of fewer people than you think, Bud. This reservation knows how you work. Your daughter inherited her first name from you, too, and everyone knows it. You've been trying to walk away from her since the day she was born. People have eyes, Bud." Cutting him off with my purposeful exit, I leave the house and head down the driveway. "And you ain't the only Chief! You might think you are, but you ain't." From behind me, Bud yells something about denying Fiction is his daughter, and some other shit about Johnnyboy Martin's lack of power; but I climb into my car as if I hear nothing more than the river water lapping against the rocks inside the dike. Bud shouts from his porch in my rearview mirror as I head past the orchard and out onto the road.

I drive around the reservation—the gold fillings in my teeth, like radio antennae, bringing voices, conversations from behind those closed doors. Some houses and trailers offer really strong reception. Ten guys—former dancers all—had, with Bert's vote of confidence, loaned me five hundred dollars apiece as start-up money. Of those ten, three chose shares in the company, and the other seven took their loan money back when I offered, a month into the venture. Another twenty-five houses belong to relatives, either of those few people I employ, or of those who loaned me the money, or my own. About forty houses deliver static—distorted stories, pieces missing—this from the Chiefs and their immediate relatives. Even though Johnnyboy ain't always in agreement with Bud, he usually goes along, so they look like they're still a working Council. From around sixty houses, though, I receive nothing but dead air, radio-silence-obscured opinions on my recent adjustments.

Sixty is a dark number, a little heavy for an unknown, but I believe they'll end up on my side of the tally in the end. I can see the future. How can they not want city running water and sewer lines, a community center, maybe even an apartment complex? These things will come. They will come ripping up fully formed through the earth, giant glaciers of modern life, the water lines massive snakes burrowing beneath the reservation, pulling it moaning into the twentieth century as the rest of the country welcomes the twenty-first. And I will offer all of this to the Nation, when I hit the big time, and then we'll see who's listening to Bud.

I hoped it would be sooner, but I can wait. What Bud said was true, I have to give him that. Not about Fiction, of course. Anyone can just look at the two of them and see it. But Johnnyboy's voice is a whisper next to Bud's, and pursuing that quiet Chief, or any of the others, would be a pointless activity. I need a voice with the power to produce echoes, shock waves—a voice like my own. Bud will regret not bending to my will, and not handing over the ten thousand as the Nation's half of the investment. What's wrong with him, anyways? He likes what money can buy. I have enough to make the improvements, but not on as big a scale as I could have with the Nation backing me. I'll have to lose the interest my cash is making, and in reality, I'm also going to have to risk losing everything if the business fails. But it won't. I will make it happen—with or without them. It just means more for me.

These thoughts vanish as I leave the reservation and close my bank accounts without a second thought. At "Lumber" Jack's, I place an order for one of those prefabricated barns, paying in cash, in one hundred and three sturdy bills, casually snapping each hundred-dollar bill on the counter, finally showing my tax-exempt Nation ID card and requesting delivery to my old purple shack, smiling, knowing the sales-tax treaty rights extend to anything purchased off the reservation that's delivered by the seller to a reservation address. The clerk gives me that annoyed "tax-card look," but I continue to smile nonetheless, and even tell the sour gentleman who takes my cash and address to have a nice day, tell him it's been an incredible pleasure doing business with him, nearly as good as sex. "Actually, maybe only as good as a handjob with baby oil," I finally offer—I don't know why—as I leave and the clerk reddens, either in rage or embarrassment. I don't care one way or the other.

At the county garage, Eddie Chidkin and his fellow clock-watchers punch out for the day, as he confirms that the land below the hill belongs to Ruby Pem. I definitely don't want to start making risky overtures to Big Red over nothing. I've worked long and hard on Red to gain his trust, and really, it came only at Bert's hands, and now she's gone.

Red's trailer sits back in a nice little crowd of trees on Snakeline Road, his majorly rusted truck resting comfortably in the rutted driveway. Music comes from the trailer's far end, and some wicked banging from its back side. In a makeshift lean-to in the back, Red looks up from some project, startled at my knock.

"We don't get too many guests." He pulls the vent mask away from his face and checks his palms for varnish drips, before grasping my extended hand and accepting my dinner invitation.

We putt off the reservation, my old Chevette almost going in slow motion with three people in the car, even though the kid in the back seat is no more than a weed. I am going to take them to a nice steak place in the city, but I never make it past The Den, the roofers' bar where Fiction is at this very moment tending bar, pulling me in. I can feel her in there still, can almost smell the sweat and Lycra glistening on her as she flirts for quarters. It probably helps that I dropped her off there myself a couple of hours ago, but it's more than that. My hands—feeling her hard nipples, small nuggets of gold, from here—turn the wheel sharp just before we are beyond the driveway. The Chevette rocks as we bump over the curb and come to a stop in the parking lot.

"Listen, man," I say, after we have knocked back a few, and I have gotten an eyeful of that nice ass. Empty plates, recently holding thick, greasy burgers and fries, litter the table. Two-Step doesn't finish his, but he's working on his third Pepsi. "I got big plans, you know. Big plans for the whole reservation. What do you think, kiddo? What would be the best thing to come to the reservation?" Fiction gleams under the fluorescents in her black spandex catsuit, tucked into black cowboy boots—and, wrapped around her boots, braided leather bands, a few bear claws hanging from them. The bands match the leather necklace she wears. This outfit is designed to go with the den theme of the bar, with its looming stuffed bear's head mounted over the bar—not nearly as interesting to look at as Fiction is. I have admired this incredible woman for years, and usually have to invent reasons for coming here to ogle her in the daytime. She knows I've brought the two Harmonys here to keep an eye on her, and she's kind of kept as much distance as she can from us and still be a decent bartender, but her eyes never stray too far. She can't fool me.

". . . ash parks," the kid says. "That would be great."

"What?"

"You know, one of those splash parks. With the wave pool, and all those water slides." The kid seems to be getting geared up for the park already, and it really ain't a bad idea. To give people running water is one thing, but to give them a constant reminder, a shrine to running water, that is something else entirely. I file this idea. It's way down the line, but I have plenty of time.

"Fiction!"

She's putting clean glasses away and pretends to just now look in our direction as she rubs some spots from one. She bends over to reach two Labatts from the cooler.

"Have a seat for a few minutes." She makes a small face—just for a second, but it's there—and looks around the room. The only other three customers are at the pool table, and their bottles are full, so she sits down. I take one of the bottles from her tray and hand it to Red, and slide the other one in front of her. "For you." I stuff a ten-dollar bill in her tip glass.

"Thanks." She lifts the bottle and drains a third of it on her first drink. "Hey, you coming over tomorrow to help me with Bert's stuff?" she asks Two-Step. He nods, as she sets the bottle on the table and, seeing how much she's downed, shrugs her shoulders and drinks some more. There's something weird between those two. Maybe it's just the shit with losing Bert's house and all. Bud's going to be a much smarter opponent than I ever thought.

"So, me, Big Red, and Two-Step were just talking about the future. What do you think of a splash park on the reservation?"

"You mean one of those big places, with the pools and the slides and the—"

"Yeah, one of those places. What do you think?"

"Well, you know, they had one of those things down in Texas some-where, I think it was down outside Lubbock—you know, Buddy Holly's home town? And one day their wave pool was just full of this nasty, slimy see-through stuff. It was flaking up everywhere, so they thought the filter system must have been messed up or something. And when they went into the system, you know what they found?" The kid stares intently, but I've already dismissed her story and am instead watching her breasts, as she sways with emphasis in her conclusion. Harmony begins laughing even before she can finish.

"A big, giant water snake had been holed up in there, and it was shed-ding its skin into the system. They had to call in some guys from one of those big zoos in California to handle it—San Diego, San Francisco, one of those. And when they finally got it out into the pool where they could cap-ture it, it was over thirty-five feet long. Its head was big as a TV screen, and I'm talking floor model," she says, holding her arms out about a yard.

"Fiction, when you get a chance," someone calls from the pool table.

"Other than that . . ." She grabs her tray and makes a "who knows" face.

"You're full of shit. That story's ridiculous."

"No more ridiculous than a splash park at home. Christ, my mom didn't even have fuckin'—excuse me, freakin'—running water, and you're talking about a splash park? Keep dreaming. Thanks for the beer." She returns to the bar, laughing, and though it's me she's laughing at, I can't shut my eyes of her. That laugh won't stop me.

"So anyway, that's a pretty good idea, kiddo. But, you know, things like that, they cost an awful lot of money . . ."

"No shit, Mason. Why do you think we don't have any of that stuff? No money," Harmony says, finishing his beer. "Thanks for the supper, by the way. We don't get out too often, either."

"But I could do it with a little help."

"Well, I don't know anyone with a couple million worth of help. Christ, I barely have enough to keep my truck from dying. I gotta rely on you and your business to keep me in Bondo." Red keeps an extra twenty in his boot pocket to lend if someone might really need it, and he thinks I'm setting him up for the touch. I haven't won his trust.

"C'mon. Let's take another ride." The Harmonys walk out the door ahead of me, and I flip Fiction a fifty and one more tip. "Expect a visit from your father some time real soon. I don't know what it's about, but I'm guessing it ain't good." Her face reveals nothing, but this information has upset her. Her tight little biceps flex, and the bear claws around them clink together. I want to stay, offer some comfort and get a little closer, but my plans with Harmony for the night are not yet over.

We hit a number of other places around the reservation, and after dropping the kid off to go to bed, finish with a twelve-pack at the bottom of Redman's Drop, in my favorite spot. I give Red the night off, with pay. The twelve-pack is Heineken, not the Genesee my old tragic poster boy downed years ago—I have no intentions of slipping off the hillside, and a classier brand of beer is the start. I know the difference, even if Red doesn't. Those yacht-club guys would never drink Genesee. We sit on the Chevette's hood, soaking the ticking engine's warmth up through our jeans, faint hints of the travels we've made, the twelve-pack perched coolly between us.

Just before arriving at this border, we were at the opposite end of the reservation, parked behind the shop and Bert's old house at sunset—a kind of home for both of us. I linked our lives as her dancers and how we have lost so much—all the truth, certainly, but a truth that will definitely appeal to him—and when I had this idea firmly wedged into his consciousness, I brought him here, to this edge, to the future. I need Red to talk with his mother-in-law, Ruby, about the piece of land—and now, after I tell him the first stages of my plans, they grow even more solid in my own head. He agrees to consider going with me, to help represent my idea—even seems a little excited about the prospect.

The water-park idea has grown in my head, flooding everything else out. Now, on the car's cooling hood, I look into the deep green of growing twilight and can clearly see one of the strongest attractions: an enormous water slide—the biggest ever—with steps built into the escarpment cliff, leading to the top, maybe even an escalator of some sort. I'll call the slide the Maid of the Mist. Even as this thought clears, I revise it. Surely, the white-run Niagara Falls Chamber of Commerce can't own the copyright on our legend of the maid's selfless acts to save her community. Riders will have two options: they can ride down the slide, or rent canoe-shaped inner tubes, to sacrifice themselves to Hinu, the thunder god.

In the swelling darkness, I can see more of the future: the artificial-wave pool growing out of the underbrush, its waves rising and crashing; a lazy-river inner-tube ride called Hinu's Cave that will take riders behind the water slide, into manmade caves blasted from the escarpment's stone cliff wall, much like that old legendary Maid's final resting place, where she met the thunder god; a steam room/hot-tub area called The Mists; a "tunnel-of-love" ride for young couples, and old ones for that matter—a place where I will make love to Fiction Tunny after hours, where she will sacrifice herself to me, consummating my dreams with her in the wet darkness. It grows.

I will turn back time. I will bring Niagara Falls back where it belongs: with the Indians. I will conquer Redman's Drop, make it completely my own, force it to take back the waterfall it passed on. I will wash away the Chiefs' government, will wash all other forces away, and I will elude them in the mists. Red says something, but in the darkness, I can't hear above the pounding cascade in my ears.

><

CHAPTER 3 Harvest Moon Eclipse

Bud Tunny

BLOOD WELLS UP, PUSHING THROUGH THE DAMAGED SKIN OF MY FINGER, pinched in the toolshed's padlock. My skin, not as tough as it used to be, reminds me I'm getting to be an old man. "Son of a bitch" slips out of me, though it is not my custom to curse in the graveyard. The younger generation has little regard for their elders, these days. They want to forget us and the sacrifices we've made on their behalf. To some of them, I am ancient, past my prime—muscles shrinking and the hair on my scalp thinning rapidly. They have all noticed. My body mocks me as they do. Their eyes were on me only as I delivered the old woman's will, not after I left that decrepit house. I am not what I once was to them. As they grew up, I was their Chief, making important decisions, guiding them into the future. Back then, they would hope I would wave to them, take notice, smile. Now, even when I do wave, some of them pretend they don't see me. Regardless, I make it a point to display my respect, most times.

On occasion though—today, for example—the curses and kicks force themselves from within. And today, this causes me much grief and a cracked window pane. My angry face splits in two on the tiny pane, reminding me my wrath only causes me trouble. There was really no point in kicking the door, but it gave me some satisfaction. Even a Chief can lose control—a real Chief, mind you. One who has to make hard decisions.

Nobody shall make comparisons between me and the fools I must share the Council with, particularly the lowly sheep Chief Johnnyboy Martin, who now glances up from the grave at the slight snapping sound. He is a Turtle Clan man, but if there were a sheep clan, he would surely belong to it instead, he's such a follower. Return to your digging, old man—all you are good for. To speak these words out loud would be unacceptable, so they are buried as surely as the old woman. Johnnyboy walks over now, across the dusky resting place, and gently presses his withered hand on my shoulder.

"Would you like me to take care of it, Jacob?" he asks, using my Christian name. His yellowed eyes gaze. Cowardice seeps to the surface of those eyes like the blood in my hand. Johnnyboy would never, if he lived another seven generations, be able to carry out the necessary actions this day requires. To tell the truth, I almost look forward to my duties tonight, as uncharitable as that might sound. Someone must perform them. Johnnyboy has not done anything requiring balls in many a year, probably not even siring his own children; but fatherhood is a subject I do not much care to speak of.

"No, it won't take but a minute." One more thing, always one more thing. The crack is clean and could have gone maybe two weeks before replacement, if this had been the past. My face merges and splits across the shifting pane. It would have been simple to pass the keys to those gravediggers, but the young people these days cannot be trusted, even with their palms flat against the leaves of a Bible. Before you know it, they would be getting duplicate keys made and having strong drink out here in the resting place. So these days, they perform their duties and leave the tools for me to deal with as soon as I am able.

In the old days, Dreamer dug all of our graves. Certainly, he indulged in the liquors himself, many a time, but he was a part of the community; he took his duties with great seriousness. The Nation grew so used to Dreamer as our escort to Heaven that when he passed on, there was no one to cut through the earth for his plot. Who trims the barber's hair?

The Chief, that's who. So I assumed the digging early on the morning of Dreamer's funeral. That hole, my first, occurred over ten years ago, and the young men I finally found, Harold and Danforth Mounter—two of Harris and Shirley's boys from, curiously, over on Dead Man's Road—are drunken brothers. Young and fairly reliable, they're still not completely trustworthy—completely, the way Dreamer was—but they do perform the job. They are young, and the young are a sad sight these days.

"Those boys do a nice job. Those flowers should last a few days. Those boys clean 'em up, then?" Johnnyboy rattles. They did a fairly decent bit of honest work filling in, but the floral arrangements look, from this distance, like rubbish heaped up on the mound. Most are small, tasteless bunches.

The fake-satin ribbon on one reads "Happy Dancing" and "Love, Fiction" in embossed cardboard letters, swooping out in opposite directions from beneath a mix of bright red carnations and some gaudy purple flower. As often happens, I am reminded at every turn of some ugly task I have been sternly avoiding. Yesterday, the Sunday-paper headline shouted NEW FICTION. It happened to be the book-review section, but that accursed name keeps leaping out at me, pushing against my insides, like an unexpected bout of gas in church.

Though it is only five o'clock, the fat September moon already lurks in the gray late-afternoon sky, waiting for the light to leave that plane, conspiring to remind me of where I must go. It is getting late. Twila will be expecting me home in about an hour for supper. I say my goodbye to Johnnyboy, slowly climb into my Lincoln. Even the new-car scent filling the interior doesn't change my mood.

My Lincoln is the only one within the bounds of the Nation. Given hard work, any member of my Nation could drive one, but they seem content to wander the roads and the back paths in cars held together with duct tape and putty, taking full advantage of the fact that New York State inspection, like all other United States laws, means nearly nothing out here. Some drive cars that are merely skeletons of cars—a chassis, an engine, and a driver's seat. Few appreciate the finer elements of trusting a known name. But some do.

If only she would stop using my last name, I would not mind her so much. In fact, up until four years ago, I had been able to almost forget the year and a half I'd made my monthly full-moon sojourns with the girl's mother to one of my smaller, satellite orchards on Dog Street, near the woman's house. We'd almost never spoken, the woman and I, but whenever the moon reached its fully bloated stage, there we would be, both appearing along the attentive rows. My Lincoln would pull down the rutted pathway, lights off, and after the car went to idling, she would emerge from the leaves, only her beautiful teeth glinting in the moonlight through lips parted to meet mine. Each month, those perfect teeth, so rare among our women, invited me to lick them, over and over.

Winter nights, we found each other on the broad back seat of my Lincoln, exploring the complicated choir of our secret lovemaking. The harmonies, blending our moans and the leather upholstery's creaking with the Lincoln's own rhythm, rocked in the white-shrouded pathway and the humming December east winds. Summers, though, we embraced among the high, wild weeds, blossoming like the trees all around us.

In the second spring, she took longer rising from the damp, new-grown weeds, and in May, her midsection was beginning to obscure the moon as she stood to her full height. By fall, her belly would totally eclipse the pale moon, harvesting the evidence of my weakness. The last time she vanished among the creeping buds in my rearview mirror, my only satisfaction was knowing it was not my problem that Twila and I had such difficulty multiplying.

The woman might have stood in the rows waiting for me the next month. She might have waited a long while before realizing I would not be returning. Across the sanctuary of the church the next Sunday, she offered not even one glance in my direction. Never again did she. It was almost as if we no longer existed in the same universe. She continued to attend church, even as she grew larger, and her church clothing made way for the loud colors of maternity clothing, particularly second-hand maternity clothing. The speculation grew as steadily as she did during the unofficial Protestant Church social hour—which followed the official, in the parking lot—as to who the father was. Toward the ninth month, half the men on the reservation, married and unmarried, and several from the Onondaga reservation, nearly three hours away in Syracuse, were mentioned. As far as I knew—although they would never say anything in earshot, anyway—my name was never included among the list of candidates.

When the little girl was born, the woman gave the child her last name, which was as things should be. She brought the child to church right from the beginning. The baby's long tendril-like fingers were immediately noticeable. From that point on, my own gnarled extremities stayed deep in my pockets whenever possible, though the woman said nothing. As of four years ago, though, my buried fingers no longer mattered. My wife and I had two girls of our own. Fiction, as the girl's now known, did what she had strictly out of spite.

Today's activities, though, have nothing to do with that. It's in the Nation's best interest, I repeat to myself, even out loud, all the way to the corner of Pem Brook and Clarksville Pass, the border road near where Bertha Monterney's house stands. The road itself is not Nation land, but all the land on its north side is—including Bertha's house and, at its edge, Mason Rollins's place, the current thorn in my backside. This is what being a Chief has come down to—having your *hetch-eh* serve as a pincushion for your community's troubles.

The Lincoln meanders the long way around to the Monterney woman's place, where Rollins's activities are easily viewed. One of my daily rituals includes a trip around the Nation, concluding with a slow drive down Clarksville and then Pem Brook toward my home, to glimpse the ramshackle place where Rollins sells cigarettes. Against my opinion, the Nation has decided Rollins is merely growing into the role of "undesirable." We've never encountered a young one like Mason Rollins before, or an Elder, for that matter. He was raised like any other child within the Nation, under the guidance of our leadership, and should have obeyed us when we ordered him to close his shop. But he did not. He seemed to have not even heard us.

The Haudenosaunee Confederacy system has worked for hundreds of years; some members claim the United States of America's Articles of Confederation are based on the teachings of the Peacemaker, but given the state the outside country is in, this seems not a desirable boast. The Confederacy's existence, though, has allowed the six tribes of Cayuga, Oneida, Onondaga, Mohawk, Seneca, and Tuscarora to stay fairly intact as Nations. Even the overbearing outside culture, pushing at us constantly— taking, at first, small pieces, and then larger and larger—has little effect. Within the Confederacy, however, some have faltered. Some Nations have given in to electoral systems of government. If the people don't like what their leaders are doing, they simply vote those leaders out. The trust element is gone. How can a leader feel responsible for the next seven generations if the present one is willing to vote him out after two years? The changes in those governments started with someone like Mason Rollins, someone grown deaf to the wisdom of the Chiefs. If he is allowed to thrive, dark times will be on the horizon for the Tuscarora Nation. The whole younger generation needs a good shaking to get their hearing back.

The deaf business, with its patient line of customers, crowds the first driveway, but the Continental bounces easily up the rutted path to Bertha Monterney's trailer. Outside the large, decrepit house next door, groups of people, like ants, complete the day's removal of huge items and strap them to equally decrepit-looking pickup trucks. They won't be working for much longer. The dark is growing the way it does in the fall, as if someone suddenly throws a huge black blanket over the sky at dusk. The trucks pull out of the driveway, and the Lincoln's brilliant headlights die as it glides to a stop at the trailer, near the back of the property. Even in this scarred driveway, its suspension allows me the smooth entrance suited to a Chief. Trading for new every two years is worth every cent.

The gravel yard crunches beneath my feet, sliding toward the deepest of the ruts, which are slowly transforming themselves into puddles in the frequent September rain. Foggy rock-and-roll music from Rollins's place fills the thick air, fairly warm for this time of year. Humid almost, it clings to my lungs like gauze as I clomp onto the rickety aluminum front step and knock, leaning my head into the living room. The girl wanders in from the hallway, carrying a cardboard box loaded down with wide ribbons of brightly colored polyester clothes I would never allow my wife to buy, though we have arrived at that era in our lives when all women seem to wear them.

"Hi. C'mon in. Just cleaning out Bert's things. Figure I'd take 'em down below the school, where they got that clothes-giveaway box by the clinic. Well, I guess you know. You probably started that program, huh?" The girl drops the enormous, bright box on the couch and tucks her Marlboro T-shirt back into her dungarees. Strong drink weighs heavy on her breath, but this is not at all a surprise. "Have a seat."

"No, no. That was the nurses down to the clinic. Chiefs' Council just signed the papers approving it."

"Coffee? Tea?"

"Coffee." Why does she have to be so ungodly pleasant? Deep in my head, there must be things for which she may be disliked. The same big one keeps unearthing itself, glistening with truth beneath the dirt, and eventually, with effort, submerges again. Using that would require acknowledging the evidence her long fingers speak.

"Here you go. Cream and sugar's on the table. There's artificial sweetener in the cupboard above the stove. That's what I use," she says, smoothing her T-shirt evenly against her trim torso.

"*Nyah-wheh.*" The milk on the kitchen counter smells all right, and a few drops fall into my coffee, turning the rich, clear liquid slightly murky. Some things should stay dark, the way they were meant. "You know, there was a mistake in Bertha Monterney's will. I thought I should mention it. She had not checked with us, you know." The coffee, against my lips, is louder than my words.

"Why'd she have to check with the Nation about her will? I never heard of that. It was all her stuff. What could be wrong with it?" The house across the way is dark. The others called it a night shortly after the Lincoln pulled in. This is too bad. She would be less likely to wade into histrionics if others were around.

"Well, you don't know everything about the Nation. There are closed Council sessions, for Nation members only. Matters of Nation integrity. Matter of fact, that is precisely what is wrong with her will. You see, you are Onondaga."

My statement floats between us. Finally, the girl raises her eyebrows. "I know that. I know the rules of matrilineal society," she starts in the bored voice of a tour guide reciting lines grown virtually nonsensical through repetition and lack of real meaning. "Your tribal identity is based on who your mother is—if she is Tuscarora, you will be Tuscarora, if she is Onondaga, you will be Onondaga . . ." She pauses, and when she begins again, her voice gains the sharpness of a favorite paring knife. "Regardless of who your father is."

"That is right." How can she be so stupid? "So, Bertha Monterney could not give you this piece of land. Now, you can have the trailer. She passed that on to you fairly and squarely, right in the will, but the land . . . the land belongs to the Nation, now."

"What!" She flies from the couch, hovers in front of me like a hummingbird but does nothing, jerking her head slightly as if listening to some inner voice. My loudest Chief voice recites Nation rules in response.

"No Tuscarora can give land away, unless it is to another Tuscarora." My right hand pounds every word into the palm of my left. "It's always been this way. Now, you can leave the trailer here for the winter and move it to one of the trailer courts in the spring, but you can't live here. The power will be cut the same time as the house. You have a week to close it up, or do whatever you plan to do, but that's it."

"Well, I'll just move it to that land my ma had at the cross of Snakeline and Torn Rock."

"You can't have that, either. You're Onondaga. You can't own land out here! Have you no ears? You have to move to a trailer court that belongs to a Tuscarora, or move off Nation land. Those are your choices." The voice has moved beyond loud, though this young woman is not two feet from me.

"My ma owned land, and she was Onondaga! She owned the land her house is on and that stretch down at the end of Snakeline!"

"Well, now calm down. There's no need for shouting. Your mother could have either sold that to a Tuscarora or given it to one. Since she still had it when she passed on . . . it also . . . went to the Nation. Your mother was an unusual case. Your mother was a . . . she received that in special consideration." My voice lowers, unable to conjure any other phrase to describe this situation from my past.

"Consideration for what? Letting you fuck her among the apple trees?" she offers, her sharp knife-tongue slicing again.

My left hand suddenly leaves graceful, long streaks across her right cheek. She looks almost like a John Wayne–style Sioux warrior. "Wipe that shitty little grin off your face, or I will. You have no idea what you're talking about." Only she can do this to me, lead me down this path.

"You slap your other daughters when they tell you the truth?" She sips from her coffee cup and sets it down on the table, stretching, distorting the harsh impact lines across her cheek with a loud, wide-mouthed yawn, as if she's preparing for hibernation. "Aww, fuck it. I'm not leaving . . . Dad. I'll just stay right here."

"Who do you think you are?" She smirks her answer in her Marlboro shirt. She probably got that from Rollins, along with that attitude. We'll see what happens to those who defy the Tuscarora Nation. She's not even one of our own. Maybe that's why she has no respect for my role.

"I know who I am. Don't you?" she continues, spreading her own lengthy fingers in the air between us, not knowing what she is touching with her long, thin accusations.

"Who the fuck do you think you are!" The end table extends an invitation, and an object with the satisfying weight of ceramic is delivered into my hand. The small table lamp shatters with sweet release, the bulb moaning a low popping sound, slamming into the wall next to her. We are in the dark, and there are freedoms there, where one doesn't have to see one's actions. Why didn't she know? The sharp sound of a fist on skin, like a drum being beaten, calling, begging—some invitations one cannot resist. Nothing dirty, I can assure you that. That is not who I am! But some songs nearly as strongly can cause a man to lose his way along the path.

That she escapes, and I hobble to the door—lean on the jamb, cupping my swelling balls with my right hand—has nothing to do with that, and everything to do with the way she runs her life. She is a ball-grabber to the very end. Their rubbing against my leg as I walk makes them throb like rotting teeth, small explosions telling me she needs lessons in respect. Mason Rollins's shack lurks across the field, amply lighted by several blue-eyed street lamps burning cold, turning all his customers' cars a sickly liver color.

"See what you started?" The voice leaving me is shattered and thin, a voice not my own, almost womanish. "This young bitch thinks she can just stay here." The words wander out across the weeds, though the only answer back is more rock-and-roll music. "Soon, no one will be listening to the Chiefs. Be just like the white world." The moon highlights field and trees, moon shadows playing in the chill breeze, it is so bright. The leaves dance, but there are no signs of the girl.

"I know you're out there!" The bush line does not answer back. "You think you can just go on staying here?"

Back in the living room, the matching lamp from the other side of the couch comes on bright in my hand. Throughout the trailer, the lights come on with easy turns. When every light is burning, I go outside and stand in the driveway, admiring the glow from the windows. "You'll know how it's going to be. I'll show you!"

Back inside, I take up a spear—an old dancing prop, I imagine—leaning in the corner. The living room lamp explodes a moment later, beginning the darkening of the girl's home with a resounding shatter.

The broken pieces crunch beneath my feet, following me to the back bedrooms where other lamps shatter. In the bathroom, with one even sweep, I decapitate the entire line of five large globe vanity lights mounted over the mirror, all condemned conspirators in electricity. I finish in the kitchen, over the stove where I had, a while earlier, poured a vague spot of cream into my black coffee. She needs to find out the hard way what life without electricity is going to be like, and it is a Chief's responsibility, above all, to teach respect. Some lessons are harder than others to receive and to give.

"There." The Lincoln awaits me. Tonight, I shall sleep soundly with the satisfaction of fulfilling my duties, but I will have to change my undershirt before crawling beneath the blankets with my wife. The perfect crescent tracing the girl's teeth throbs an arc across my collar bone, and the top seam of my undershirt rests damp and sticky against it. She has broken my skin. She has her mother's teeth, I will grant her that. Only at the drive-way's edge do my headlights engage, lighting the way ahead of me and leaving the woman who calls herself my daughter—no, she is my daughter—alone in the darkness, filling my rearview mirror. I cannot see myself in it at the moment, and this is the only way this story can be told—in the dark, where blood wells up.

>‹

CHAPTER 4 Unfinished Business

Fiction Tunny

I COULDN'T IMAGINE THE FURY OF MY FATHER'S MOVES, THE WAY HE DROPS ME to this couch with one kick to the belly, slapping over and over. I manage to block some hits and dodge others, slapping back when I can get a hand up. At one point I get close enough and I bite, sinking into the soft flesh above his collar bone—my canines ivory thorns, driving deep, nearly meeting below the surface in the muscle—but he pulls up, and I release him. For the brief second he stands off balance in front of me, I get my foot up and shove him further out.

"Oh, you want to kick? I'll show you kicking. You'll never dance again, you bitch," he shouts, his fingers closing tight around his palms, and he starts in again, punching my thighs down like he is kneading fry-bread dough, and then stepping on my feet with one heavy work boot, shifting his weight to keep me pinned, kicking my shins with his other foot. Though his face is full of shadows, he's smiling. He's not going to stop until I'm dead.

Blocking his vicious hands with my left arm, driving it up—he keeps going for my face, maybe hoping to slap his features clear off its surface—I simply reach out my other hand and encircle his nuts with my fingers. He doesn't even realize my goal until I have his entire small bundle gathered up tightly in my fingers, just before I squeeze. Passing his crumpling form, I run for the bushes and hide. Though my eyes gleam with the full-moon light in the rearview mirror of his Lincoln, he doesn't seem to see me, shouting in all directions before finally leaving.

I get ahold of Minnie Crews—one of my old friends who will probably retire from dancing now that Bert's gone—from a pay phone across the road, and she rushes right over and takes me to the emergency room. She doesn't ask any questions as we ride to the hospital, and in her rearview mirror, new bruises arise like shadows on my skin.

Behind the curtain, and wearing only this nasty paper gown—after they take pictures and x-rays—I slide the nickel from the pocket of my jeans, crumpled on the floor, and flip it. The coin lands heads—Indian side up—so I tell the emergency-room doctor I fell down a flight of stairs. Not one of my more original stories, but it will have to do; I'm in no shape to be creating convincing epics on the spot.

Bert, she gave me this—my first slice of personal medicine, an Indian-head nickel—when I first moved into her house four years ago. The old Indians used to keep four items of personal medicine with them at all times. I saw that in a movie once. At eighteen, I didn't know too many old Indians on the reservation—mostly those at the Indian table on bingo night down at the Lewiston Number Two Fire Hall, and Bert too, of course.

That day four years ago, she reached into her apron pocket and handed me the nickel—her dark and stiff fingers enclosing mine—and told me to keep it at all times, that I'd know who I was with that. "You listen," she said, "when white people mention that kind of nickel, they always call it a buffalo nickel. But you won't call it that."

The coin Indian looked amazingly like Lee Howard from down on Dog Street. Lee Howard . . . I had always assumed everyone called him "Nickel Man" because he smoked a lot of weed. At one of the bigger powwows in Ottawa my first summer dancing, one of the vendors sold T-shirts with the nickel's image on it; in addition to the nickel itself, blurry faded images of its path followed its arc across the shirt. The caption read: IT'S ABOUT TIME FOR THE INDIAN TO COME UP HEADS AGAIN.

From the moment she passed it on, the coin helped me make decisions. Once, I read a friend's college book for a course in casino gambling, only to discover it was really a math course on statistics and probabilities; but I continued anyway. Once I start something, I can't stop.

The probabilities are fifty-fifty on the coin, and having just moved from my mother's smothering Christian household to Bert's communal traditional one, I was comfortable with those odds. If my coin came up heads, I went the traditional way, and if it landed buffalo side up—the bullshit side—I went the white way. So, four years and hundreds of flips later, amidst the whirring and whining of emergency-room technology and misery, the coin winks in the air with its potential to go either way. The buffalo nearly invites me to tell them one of the reservation's Chiefs beat me because I'm his illegitimate daughter, but it comes up with Lee Howard's stoic face looking sternly into the past. So, these next few months will be dedicated to healing.

Even three days later, as October begins, I ache pretty bad. Normalcy has been pretty easy to fake for the most part, with my long-sleeve spandex at work and only Two-Step knowing what happened, and to be honest, I wouldn't have even told him, but we spend so much time together, there was no avoiding it. My movements are stiff like a robot's as I jam storm-window plastic into the couch's cracks, sliding the translucent material across the cushioned surfaces. This sealing things in their own little protective sacs is one way to safeguard furniture that's going to sit unused for long months, furniture that will not know the intimacies of life, of lost dimes and quarters—lost heads and tails—the potential of what those coins could do, the knowledge of what they'd done in the past.

It's taken me these three days just to recover from my father's rage. My flipping nickel was right; I have to respect the traditions, even if those in the power positions are not doing right by the people. Sure as hell not doing right by me, anyway. My body is the map of my father's insanity. Dark purple traces him here, paintings of his steel-toed boot prints and his wicked fingers.

I bury Bert's furniture in the milky sheets—her belongings, her whole lifestyle—as well as burying the lovely old woman herself. The plastic sobs as I rock and shake on the couch for a time, overcome. Cleaning up the light-bulb massacre took up my whole morning, every shard of glass and ceramic a reminder of what I am up against, just waiting for me to slip so they can work their way in again. Valium would have been nice to find under the cushions, or something else to get through this week—anything to soften the glaring wound of my present life—but no such luck.

"Here, Trish. I found some more in the back-bedroom closet," Two-Step says. Two-Step Harmony, Big Red's twelve-year-old son, he's a born dancer, even in walking, showing the potential his name suggests. He comes floating into the room on some breeze I can't feel, carrying a few more rolls of the window-cocooning material. "Still hurting, huh? I'm telling you, Trish. I was down at the shop visiting Eddie that night. You remember, my dad and Mason dumped me off at home—but I knew Eddie was covering for my dad at the shop, and he came and picked me up to keep him company. I could prove Bud was the one that did it. I heard his voice. Why won't you?"

"Who's gonna believe someone named Fiction?" My father was likely responsible for my name early on, planting the seeds of doubt in the Nation's mind, preparing for the time he would be exposed. After a while, I just accepted it, cultivating a talent for the tightest, most believable stories, living up to the name with honor. Nearly everyone here still stays away from Christian names, and once you get a community nickname, it has a tendency to stick.

The photos on the wall watch us—individual shots of Bert's dancers, each captured in mid-performance—thirty years' worth. The earliest are black-and-whites, which have become brown-and-yellows, growing as fragile and brittle as the dance-prop feathers Bert kept in her storeroom for new dancers, those who come without tradition of their own. Bert, she always said you only need to come with a hunger for tradition, and not just for corn soup and fry bread. This is a future Two-Step has before him, taking on the traditions, and he can't risk his future on me. If we lost the case, who knows what might happen to this boy and his father.

"Your picture was supposed to complete this wall. I guess it's still down at Prints Charming. I'll have to go through Bert's things and find the slip. They need the slip at that place."

"Yeah, that would be nice. A shot of my last competition."

"I thought I was the one named Fiction."

"You are. I'm done. It's just not the same. First my ma, now Bert. There's no reason to dance if they're not in the crowd."

"Well, what about your dad?"

"Yeah, I don't know. Maybe I'll change my mind, but I don't think so." He sits down and looks at the last empty spot on the living-room wall. Bert just last week rearranged all of the pictures. At Grand River in August, Two-Step had taken First in Young Men's Traditional Dance. Though his regalia wasn't the greatest, made up of some mismatched pieces and some bead-work apparently created by a colorblind beader, he had shone through any-way. The old woman, she had a sense for these things: "This time," she told me idly that day, hobbling closer to the main grounds. Bert, she just snapped that image of Two-Step—a resigned tourist preferring the lenses of her own eyes to the distance sights of her Minolta—but an instant smile appeared through Two-Step's feathers and movements. Bert knew. Two-Step walked away with the prize, and she slid the little film canister into her oversize powwow bag.

One night last week, after Bert's bath, we watched the *Wheel of Fortune*, dancing with the rabbit ears for better reception as we did almost every night, each trying to shout out the solution before the other and scolding the clueless contestants for wasting their hard-earned money on vowels— or worse yet, ceramic Dalmatians. Bert, she promptly stood up and pushed the couch away from the wall, not even bothering to let me get off of it. A sudden bout of cleaning mania seemed unlikely, but this seemed potentially more interesting than the fabulous Dining Room Showcase. We'd lost the game to static and snow when Bert leapt up, anyway.

She carefully stacked the photos, leaning them against one another in the proper order on the couch, a cast of forty-nine frozen Indian dominoes lying spent on her cushions. They had rested on that wall for the five years I'd known Bert, in their seven neat rows of seven photos each. Each time Bert received one of her camera messages and added another First-Place winner, she had just tacked another nail up, dropping to a new row after seven, guided by some sort of photographic typewriter rules.

She coaxed all the nails out gently, harvesting them perfectly straight from the wall, and then renailed them in at random places. Her hand and mouth finally barren of nails, she picked up the top photo, the most recent, and hung it on the last nail pounded. A pattern of concentric circles emerged as she followed through. The last photo she hung—the first taken—was one of Big Red Harmony, who in addition to working the late shift at Mason Rollins's Smoke Shop, set up a vendor's table on the powwow circuit when he could swing it. She had placed his fragile picture in the center of the photo rings.

She stepped back, ignoring the staticky ghosts of Pat and Vanna entirely. The outermost circle was empty at the top—a photographic horseshoe, keeping all the others within its circle of luck. She sat back down and waited for *Jeopardy* to start.

The day before she died—in the middle of her bath, where she usually made bold statements, fending off the humiliation of needing someone to help her bathe—she dropped a casual explanation of her new design, without all that mysticism bullshit so many believe should accompany all Indian acts. Two-Step's picture would complete the circle started by his father. She would officially have taught two generations of dancers.

"Maybe I'll get up to seven—I got a few more walls," she later said, watching TV after her bath, sweeping her arm broadly to encompass her entire living room.

What sorts of things are in store for Two-Step? Though Bert joked about it, every generation of Indians was supposed to look out for the next seven generations; but I have trouble enough worrying about the *next* generation. Who's going to teach them to dance?

Two-Step drops rolls of plastic into a chair that vaguely matches the couch, from some time when avocado green was a popular color. We could almost be siblings, though we're not even related by blood. He's a feminine-looking sort, sweet almost, and since this often needs disproving, his wiry limbs are tight, flexible small muscles.

He turns and smiles gently in an apparent effort to comfort me from across the room, and when I smile back, he leaves the room, continuing to explore the other areas of Bert's trailer. As happens, my grief eventually passes in wispy clouds.

In the cracks of the padded piece, pressing against the hard coiled springs hidden below its surface, my fingers brush against something metal, flat and circular, a disc. The video-game token gleams dull in the fall light, a small disappointment. It's worn down to its original copper color, the fake-gold, brassy finish long rubbed off by countless HIGH SCORES and GAME OVERS.

On one side, the twin fish of Pisces chase one another and stare blandly at me—their cold, common metal eyes unblinking—not unusual iconography for video tokens; but the flipside holds the image of two women, swimming in air, imitating the positions of the Pisceans. The women are naked. I would guess they don't distribute this sort of token at the mall, where the average age of the average customer is fifteen.

I almost throw it out, but my clan is Eel, and I can't discard a token meant for me to find. Fish, eel—they're members of the same family, right? It'll keep company with my nickel. These barenaked ladies should stay with me, at least for a little while. Somehow, Bert meant for me to find it. Otherwise, why would she have willed me the trailer and put me through the horror of what my father did in the name of "The Nation"? I flip the token a few times. I'm good at this. I can flip a coin with my right hand and guide it to land on a finger tip on my left. Women swimming, fish swimming gracefully over and over through the air. I snap the token down on the kitchen table and finish covering the couch in its filmy shroud.

In the steaming whistle of my tea water, Two-Step reappears from the back hallway, his arms filled with three large economy-size coffee cans and several Land O' Lakes margarine tubs he found on the floor of Bert's closet. His eyes peek out over the top.

We shuffle the stuff to the kitchen table, the stove clicking a backbeat for us as the surface coils cool. The trailer has electricity for four more days, the stove sings to me. Then it's exit, stage left. Four more days—can they spare it? My father, though he still fails to acknowledge his seminal role even after his unique christening, passed on the word during our pleasant visit that the Chiefs' Council is allowing me a week to get my things in order.

From the first tin, I pull one item, then rummage around inside the can. Two-Step looks in his tin and arches his neck to see what mine holds. I wrap a towel around the table's edge as an embankment and spill the contents of my can onto the table. He follows immediately with his and the other. The last can empty, the table is covered with over a hundred pill canisters from the reservation clinic.

"So . . . holy shit! I didn't know Bert was that sick." Mason Rollins leans in the trailer door, the sun cutting him a long and dark shadow across the living-room carpet. As he came up the driveway a few minutes before, I slid that tarnished token into my palm and flipped: Women—exposure; I would tell him the truth, straight out. Fish—I'd be slippery, elusive, fish; I'd tell a story.

"Oh, yes, barely navigating. We were all amazed she lived this long— not that you'd know." Fish. Two-Step gives a slight nod to my wink, almost as if a breeze has somehow caught just his head. "Big Red found her at the table, you know. Her eyes were all bugged right out of her head from years of all that"—I glance down at the table—"digi . . . digitalis." Two-Step shakes his head slowly, with the tragedy my story calls for.

"Jeez. Red told me she looked like she had just fallen asleep."

"Didn't want to make you feel guilty."

"About what?"

"Don't know. You got something to feel guilty about?" Everyone's got something they're carrying around that they don't want, as simple as that.

"No . . . So, uh . . . you're really gonna do it? You're gonna let the Chiefs pull that shit on you?"

"No choice."

He clears another place at the table and then reaches for another mug from the cupboard.

"Have a seat." He's going to be here a while, so I might as well invite him to sit down. That's what Bert would have done. He was one of her dancers years ago, even before the powwow circuit took off, when competitions occurred at the National Picnic, county and state fairs, regional field days, and the annual border-crossing celebration.

Mason is startled at the framed photo of himself in full regalia on the wall, maybe not knowing a part of him still lived with Bert. He asks if he can take it. It leaves a void on the wall, a missing tooth in a perfect smile, but I have no right to keep it from him. The picture is at least eight years old—from before he made the leap from the dancing circles to the ghost circles under barroom beer glasses.

"Thanks." He sets the photo down on the table. "What do you mean, 'no choice'? I found choices." He points his chin out the south kitchen window toward the small, purple, oversized-outhouse he has turned, like lightning, into a successful small business.

"Well, maybe you're a little skinny bit smarter than me." The smokeshack lights are shining brightly, even in daylight, despite the Chiefs' order to cut the electricity.

"I don't even have any land, legally, and even if I had what's supposed to be mine, it isn't anywheres near white land, anyway. So I couldn't do what you're doing. Besides, it's what the Nation wants."

"Well, I think you've got options."

"This didn't change your life, any. You're not 'exploring options,' are you?"

He nods and says he has to go. But before he leaves, he puts the picture back on the wall, though not from the place he had taken it. He nods and heads to the door. "By the way, it's kind of dark in here. Don't you have any lamps?" he asks, leaning in the door again.

"The magnetic forces in electricity are slowly pushing people to insanity and causing cancers worldwide. It was in the Sunday supplement."

"Oh."

"It's no wonder no one believes anything you say, making up shit like that. Why do you do that?" Two-Step says, after Mason is out of hearing range.

"Look. It's right here," I counter, reaching for a magazine featuring power lines and the letters EMF written in a scary design across the top. He flips through the magazine to find the article as I put the picture back where it belongs. Mason walks up the driveway to the Big House, probably going to see his cousin Eddie. He still seems so positive he's going to score with me. He's cute, and certainly has a steady income, but those creeping hands of his say just way too much about where he believes his place in the world is. It is the one thing really right with Big Red. When he puts his hands on me, it's for me, not him.

Maybe Red needs a live-in baby-sitter. The thought of living with him makes me smile at my cleverness for having found a way to keep thinking about him for just a few more minutes, though it would be weird trying to treat Two-Step as some kind of son. Shit, I've barely been able to take care of myself. If I moved in, it would only be to allow Red to hit the Southwestern powwow circuit in the winter months, anyway, bring in more cash for Two-Step and him; and besides, Two-Step spends most of his time with me as it is. Red just might go for it. And maybe he'd want to take me with him; but then what would be the reason? Shit, my storytelling skills are slipping. This one is bad all around. All kinds of gaping holes. Red's struggling like the rest of us. If he's working midnights at Mason's shop, things must be pretty bad. That grief and panic seep into me again, a dark mold growing around my insides, weighing me down.

One of the pill bottles from the table idly fills my hand. The neat label reads: "Wampum Shell Purple." Other medicine bottles in this group have the odd prescriptions of "Squash Blossom," "Cornsilk," "Ivory Bone," "Crow Feather," and "Sky Blue Glass."

The childproof cap easily lifts off the "Sky Blue Glass" with one twist. I am an adult now. A few hollow glass pills spill out into my hand from the tipped bottle. My palm disappears into the pure, blue, wide-open atmosphere filling in its furrows—my life line, my love line, my death line. My funneled hand pours the sky back into its stale medicinal bottle.

"Your gram still beading?"

Two-Step scrunches up his face in trying to conjure an answer, but this clearly doesn't help, and he smiles, shrugging his shoulders. Ruby Pem, the late Bev Harmony's mother, is one of the better-known beaders from the reservation and was an early proponent of the treaty allowing us to sell beaded souvenirs to tourists at the parks, including Prospect Park, the biggest tourist attraction in the area—the falls itself. No one else can now do any vending at the park, unless contractually connected with the state parks department.

Now, I have neither intention nor skill to become a beadwork maker or vendor. I don't know a thing about beadwork. While Bert worked on her beading, the TV was a more interesting draw. She offered to show me time and time again over the years, but my bored eyes always wandered away after a few minutes. Her hands moved too quickly for me to follow anyway. But none of this means the beads will be entirely useless to me now.

The two options of my nickel call to me from my pocket. I could sell the beads to Ruby, or to any number of people if Ruby doesn't want them. There are plenty enough bottles here to give me a little survival cash. The beads belonged to a dead woman; they hold strong power—the power of the past. They'll be valued by any good beader from the reservation. In my pocket, my fingers hit both coins—more than two options.

The coins slide easily onto my thumbs to flip. I've never tried a double flip before. My future spins out of control in the afternoon sun. Traditional ways. Fabrication. Outside ways. Truth. Lee Howard, fish, buffalo, and naked women blur, become one, flying and falling as gravity pulls them in. My probabilities are shot.

My hands come up and clap the two coins passing one another before me, closing the arcs of their paths shut prematurely. The coins, sliding back into my pocket, will mingle forever. The surest bet is one in which you have a stake in all aspects. Like that, I am suddenly complete. It's not a matter of probabilities; it's a matter of balance. In the four coin sides, I have my four medicines. Learning to balance their influences will be the trick.

"I knew you couldn't do a double flip," Two-Step says. "Hey, are we gonna do any more tonight?" My future has just been decided, and all of the enshrouding we spent the afternoon involved in doesn't matter anymore. "I'm gonna go see if I can catch a ride at least to Snakeline and Dog Street from someone at the shop. You want I should ask my dad if Gram still beads? He might know." Big Red should know. He still takes his mother-in-law's work, and other pieces from almost anyone else who has goods to sell, on consignment to powwows.

"No, that's all right." If I need Ruby, I'll have to go see her in person, anyway.

"If you wanna take it to court, I'm here."

Two-Step heads up to the Big House as I flick the fluorescent ring on over the table—the only light that survived my father's tirade—and open a large margarine tub marked UNFINISHED BUSINESS in Bert's hand. The tub contains a partially completed piece of beadwork. It is a gauntlet.

Its black velvet background holds the traces of my touches, afterimages of the place where I try to connect with Bert. My fingertips ride rough over the raised, three-dimensional leaves and roses making up the design. Strangely, no thorns exist here. Maybe that was what hadn't been completed. A needle and thread protrude from the beaded stem.

Bert, she would have wanted all of her business affairs completed. Slipping the needle back through the work, I begin a slow healing dance with the gauntlet, unraveling and reconstructing, watching and feeling the beads and the weave. As the night grows long, the war-glove's designs vanish and reappear, revealing in confidence the glove's secrets, its web of supports, its strengths, its weaknesses. I follow its ghosts, becoming more fluid with every row. The repetitive movements of Bert's dance instruction permeate this group of hollow glass globes. I absorb the gauntlet, row by row, into my fingers, warmly replacing the aches and bruises.

Even when I break for some food, the patterns in the work weave themselves deep into my brain. Outside, the moon blooms and withers while Mason's lights remain, beacons of things to come. I do not sleep—there will be time for that later—but I do pause briefly to rip the shrouds of plastic from the furniture.

At one point—it occurs to me that it must be past midnight—Big Red's truck sits out behind the smoke shack. In the living room, here, a teenage Red balances perfectly still, his left leg arched high in the air while his right arm arches fiercely from behind: Thunder Dance, in the center of a small Indian universe. He's still carrying on that warrior tradition, providing for the future, working the midnight shift at the smoke shop for his boy, and still as good-looking as when he was eighteen—better-looking, actually. Life has worn him like the comfort of clothes you've worn into perfection.

In the back bedroom, I find what I'm looking for in one of Bert's various purses. The Prints Charming receipt is in her powwow bag, where it has been this whole time. I slide the tag onto the nail at the photo horseshoe's top, where tomorrow, Two-Step's picture will complete the circle. The gauntlet calls me back to the table.

Bert tried to ensure I would carry on, passing on the trailer, the beads, the pictures, and everything else. She wouldn't have wanted her things to be wrapped in cold storage. The two coins sit comfortably in my jeans pocket, polishing one another—Lee Howard caressed by the naked women, and maybe even smiling for the first time ever, warming his cold metal cheeks and showing his silvery teeth. Tradition can't work without truth. Before the four days are up, my father will know this. The courts aren't my only option for truth.

I take up a needle as my own for the first time and look at the beads. Bert's gauntlet forms in my mind, complete, with new touches that can come from nowhere but inside me. Adding myself, I select two of the amber bottles and set them close beside me. "Ivory Bone" will come a little later— for my thorns—and bring serious weight; but the beginning must have something to carry me through. The gauntlet rose sits dark and obscure, nestled in its black velvet garden. It needs some sunlight, needs to be exposed in the open air, to dance in the freedom of breezes. I crack the lid of the sky and jab my needle in. Piercing myself a line of it, I begin to rise.

><

CHAPTER 5 A Six-Chair Night

Fiction Tunny

WHEN THAT KNOCK COMES, THOUGH I LIFT THAT OLD LAPBOARD GENTLY AND smoothly, it startles me enough to almost dump the whole damned thing. As it is, a bead container spills, and the miniature shiny globes bounce across the room's hardwood floor, dashing away under the legs of the chairs filling the room. Ruby, across the way, she waves her weathered hands in that sign language toothless people use—unknown yet precise; her hands tell me she'll get the door herself. It is her job as Clan Mother to maintain, to protect the old ways, and even here, as decrepit as she is, she must welcome any who come to her door. "If you don't protect the roots of your ways," she told me over beads last week, "the surface may look fine, but all the connections have rotted, and it is just a matter of time before the whole thing falls in on itself."

My delinquent beads continue to scatter, and I set my board on my chair, to remember which one I've been sitting in. This is an old Hansel-and-Gretel trick I learned my first time in this house of chairs—which, like me, have a tendency to lie. You learn one you can trust and you stick with it. No man has learned that lesson about me yet, but maybe I haven't given the one I want enough of a chance to see the truth in me, waiting to emerge.

Well, anyone coming to the door still gives me the jitters, and apparently it doesn't even need to be my own door. The shaking isn't as noticeable now as it was right after the beating. Some part of me believes he might come back for a second go-round, and you know, Ruby is his Clan Mother—it's possible he could come here, though they've drifted. Trying as she has, even the heavy, blanketing leaves of a Clan Mother can't stop corruption that forms on the inside—the kind that spreads silently. Ruby, her influence spreads across the reservation like aggressive squash vines; but some kinds of rot are just unstoppable.

A few sawed-off ends of lacrosse sticks rest at strategic places around the trailer in case my father decides to spread the rot my way again. For the winter, a new deep and narrow pocket in my coat keeps them in easy grabbing reach, so one of the sticks can be at hand whenever I walk the roads, which—not owning a car, you know—is a frequent circumstance. Next summer, I'll have to devise some way to tuck one of these mini-clubs into shorts or a halter, but for now the grip and weight of that handle, as my feet clock along the cold asphalt, is comfort enough.

Maybe by summer he'll have forgotten how I outsmarted him, though the truth-telling part of me still jumps and jabs me in the ribs, assuring me he'll never forget. He has copies of the pictures, after all. I wonder where he keeps them, and how he explained the certified package to Twila. His wife had most definitely wondered after the contents of the package he had to lay his name on the line for, personally.

Of course, the original Polaroids they took at the hospital and passed on to me are tucked safely away. They would be a necessity, if I ever decide to take it to trial. Well, really, I can't do that. That would betray our way of life. Working within it, getting below the surface nonsense, is my only real option. So the originals are put away, but copies were easy to do, really, and they only cost me six bucks. I just took the originals down to a printer's shop where they advertised color photocopies, made copies, and neatly prepared the package for my father.

The small pile of things he got included the copies of the photos, and copies of medical reports one of the nurses had slipped to me. "Just in case you change your mind about pressing charges against that staircase you fell down," said this woman, whose face held the sympathetic look of someone familiar with the taste of a man's fists, as she pressed the sealed envelope into my hand in the emergency room. A typed note in the package also informed him a Tuscarora would come forward shortly with a request for electrical and telephone service, and a notice that Deanna Johns had willed him a piece of land, upon which he was now laying claim, and also which he was going to rent out. I worked really hard on getting the words just right, just official-sounding enough.

At the end of the note sat a small postscript, simply stating that sound traveled very well on crisp fall evenings, that identifiable shouts could probably be heard clearly for quite a remarkable distance. This is a sort of blackmail, but that doesn't matter anymore. I will reside in my rightful place.

Big Red, he said everything went very smoothly when he delivered the copy of the deed to my father at his home. Red, he never asked me why I wanted my land in Two-Step's name, likely figuring it had something to do with the fact that I'm Onondaga, but he could see no harm in taking over "official" ownership. We've known each other a long time. I've been watching Two-Step since he was in diapers, and Red was the one who introduced me to Bert when I first got interested in dancing. Growing older and more involved in Bert's dancing group, I had also kept an eye on Two-Step at all the competitions Red couldn't make, which were getting more frequent, with the demands of the smoke shop. He said he'd be happy to put the papers in his name.

We moved the trailer with not one single problem. Mason Rollins had already been making some improvements in his business and rented some heavy machinery to smooth out the land. They still had the drive-thru window when they'd moved the business to the new building, but the customers could park and enter the building now, too. Big Red, he asked if he could borrow the payloader and some other pieces over the weekend, when they weren't being used, and Mason, he agreed without a question. We cleared the land enough for the trailer and arranged to have it moved in two days, with an assurance from the electric, gas, and phone companies that they'd be out to hook up service the following Monday.

To try and push down this shaking tic, and to further my skills, I continue with Bert's beadwork. There are limitations in my work, mind you, and I've come to a roadblock in a particularly unique Iroquois design—the three-dimensional floral pattern—having used up all of the knowledge Bert's silent boxes, bottles, and cans offered. No matter how hard I try to re-create thorns on the beadwork, they don't stand up in the same raised pattern the leaves and petals fall into. The silence of Bert's work sent my voice over the lines to Ruby Pem's telephone in a plea for some lessons.

Ruby, at first she informed me that her beading days had been over for a while. But when she finally recognized me as her grandson's baby-sitter all his growing-up years, she promised to teach me more about beading than would stick in my young brain; she promised to give me a better beading foundation than anyone since a woman of her generation has received. The lessons began, but she immediately explained there was no technique for beading thorns. They were to be assumed hidden among the petals and leaves. Even with this setback, every afternoon I hitch or walk to Ruby's right after my shift. Something will eventually show itself that can be adapted to create my thorns. I'm not giving up that easily.

It's been a few weeks now, as the sunlight fights its losing battle and the year creeps on down to its own end, and the knock on Ruby's door sends my beads running for cover, quietly letting me know the beads are not completely healing. But I've got time.

Ruby, she's also tried to teach me in her own roundabout, maddening way why my father and I will never walk along the same path. She says we're caught in some damn Haudenosaunee pecking order. The Haudenosaunee, the Six Nations, used to be the Five Nations; and even though the Tuscaroras joined way back in the 1700s, the other Five Nations take every opportunity to remind them they were not original members of the Confederacy. Even now, in Grand Council, where the Chiefs from all the Nations meet to deal with issues of Confederacy importance, the Tuscaroras may sit at the Council, but they don't have the same voice all the others do. Some Senecas, I have heard, refer to the Confederacy as "The Five Nations and the Tuscaroras." As you can imagine, this kind of pisses them off, after two hundred years of this shit, but what can they do—leave? Jump off the Confederacy and out into the white world?

Of course they're not going to leave; but they can make things as miserable as they want to for anyone living in Tuscarora territory. Ruby, she's quick to tell me not all Tuscaroras feel this way; but enough do. So what it boils down to is a lot of my grief comes from a two-hundred-year-old, short-sighted decision. In the same way they'll be forever reminded that they have been merely allowed in, they'll continue to remind me and any other non-Tuscaroras out here that we've also merely been allowed in. If I could, I'd just give them the equal chair.

But we are fond of tradition, and this circle of bad treatment seems to be as sturdy as the beads that now roll away from me in all directions as Ruby leaps to the door. The woman's fingers might have long given out, forcing her to quit beading, but other than that, her eighty-year-old body flies about the house as if on wheels. By the time most of my beads are scooped up and corralled, Ruby has snapped the door open and welcomed the new visitors, brushing her withered vines of fingers against the late November snow on their shoulders.

"*Chewaent,* Roo," Red says, passing a twenty-dollar bill directly into her apron. She jabs her clumsy hand to deflect it, but can't grasp it well enough, so she shakes one of her bent fingers at him. Mason Rollins, he nods, as Ruby shakes his collar of cold. While the three greet one another in the fading snow dust, I close my containers. Today's lesson is over, and it's getting late, anyway. I gather my things up into the same old woven powwow bag Bert always used.

"Roo, this is Mason Rollins. You know him, don't you?" Ruby, she looks him over carefully as he unbuttons his old wool coat.

"Your ma Bonnie Wilkes's girl, married Herb Rollins's boy?" With the older set, people are never identified for who they are on the reservation— except for maybe people like Brian Waterson, who took over the old medicines when Hillman died—but for who their folks are, what roots they're protecting with their lives. As you get older, and the folks you grew up with age at the same rate, it seems the younger folks are only varied extensions of the real folks.

"Yup. That's my gram and grampa you just named." Ruby nods, mulling over his answer, while Mason folds his coat over his arm and stays in the entryway with his boots dripping, staring longingly at the active fireplace turning one whole corner of the room orange with its glow. She finally tells them to come in and sit by the fire, gathering their coats from them as they make their way through her crowded living room to its radiant end.

"Come on, sit down. I have enough stew on for ten more if they wanted to show up," she says, hanging their coats up and tugging at my coat, which I just finished buttoning. "But take care to sit in a chair with all its legs, or you'll be warming yourself from the outside in with that stew," she says— seemingly to the room itself, rather than to anyone in it.

"I gotta get going," I say, already unbuttoning my coat, regardless. The stew has been simmering in Ruby's tiny kitchen the entire afternoon. I had gotten so used to the aroma, I'd almost forgotten its presence, only noticing it again when the door opened, inviting all sorts of frozen smells in as contrast. The cutting blast from the men's entry also served as a reminder of the several-mile walk in the early dark ahead of me.

The dead season often comes quickly and unexpectedly to this area, whenever it has a mind to, sometimes so quick, the kids need to wear winter coats while trick-or-treating, disguising their clever costumes in the dull shrouds of winter. This year isn't that bad, but almost. By the second week of November, the small cricks have developed frozen glazes over their surfaces every morning, so thick they only melt to free-floating chunks by the time sundown occurs and the freezing starts all over again. In Big Crick, patterns emerge in the water's freezing and thawing, gigantic squash blossoms of ice—even here, flowers—suspended in fluid pathways. New patterns bloom in this frozen garden every evening. At first I only glimpsed them in the moonlight, but later my handy flashlight would refract light twisting on the lower levels, where inches below the frozen designs, the water still danced to its final, unknown destination. The designs are somehow familiar, but the memory floats away before it firms up.

Looking forward to this beautiful display is my way of keeping the cold and fear away. The black roads go on forever, some evenings, their dull, frigid surfaces absorbing whatever faint life comes from distant porch lights and offering nothing more. Every snap among the frosted woods flanking the roads between the sporadic houses is my father, coming for me from the wild. He's waited me out, knowing what time I leave Ruby's.

This belief is most strong by the orchard where I was conceived, the frosted and weathered branches drooping amidst the dead weeds, the entire area barren and desolate. How many people had walked this road and seen my father's car, rocking with his delinquency? How many people heard my mother moaning in her stupid bliss? These are questions the frozen waterways and their beautiful designs block, even able to vanquish thoughts of the bacteria lurking just below the water's surface. This day has been so cold, I bet the cricks didn't even thaw, and no new patterns will greet me on my long walk. Nothing will offer to keep my mind from exacting my father's revenge in every brittle winter twig snapping under hungry animal feet. So when Ruby asks me to stay, it doesn't take much coaxing. Just one bowl, I promise myself, hanging my coat back up on the old rack.

"Mmm. Where'd you get moose, Roo? I haven't had any since that last Maniwakee competition. Moose stew and Filix's french fries! Can't beat it for nothin,'" Red says through mouthfuls.

"Oh, you know, one of them Mounter boys, Royal. He drinks too much, but he's generally a good boy. That's right where he was, up Quebec way. You know that's where their dad, Harris, is from, and sometimes he takes those boys with him up on his trips. He brought me some pieces, and I keep 'em all frozen up for special occasions."

"What's so special about today?" The others sit in the now-crowded corner, where they slurp from mismatched bowls. Mason has taken the chair I used earlier. Before I can look for another negotiable seat, Ruby stops me.

"Sometimes, it's special enough to be safe in a house when the wind is bitin' mean outside. Now you go get yourself a bowl. You been here long enough, you ain't company no more. You know where they are," she says, huddling closer to the fading fire. "And drag over one of them lame chairs, too, will you? This feels like it's gonna be a four-chair night," she adds, rubbing her hands and returning to her interrogation of Mason, as I make my way back through Ruby's obstacle course of disabled furniture. When I first came here with Two-Step, I couldn't imagine why the woman kept her house so crowded.

That first time, man, I thought we must have mistakenly come on a day when Ruby was throwing a party, but that turned out not to be the case. The living room looked more or less the same each time I came, and tonight is the most company I've seen the old woman have, aside from Two-Step and me. Her living room seems to be perpetually set up for a spontaneous game of musical chairs, minus the music—Ruby listens strictly to an AM talk-radio station, where a rez boy deejays. I became even more perplexed that first day when I picked one of the twenty or so chairs in the room to sit in, and as I was crouched near the chair's seat, Ruby, she screeched a warning that one was off-limits.

The old woman offered me a different chair and tried comforting me by saying that particular chair fooled a lot of people. That one would be next, she assured me, though what the chair would be next for was unclear.

Now, balancing my bowl in one hand, I examine the herd of chairs and select an especially dense one—splay-legged with some missing or splintered rungs—lugging it behind me through the ranks of decommissioned seats; it's a cold night already.

"Nyah-wheh," Ruby says. "Oof! Too heavy for my old, thick, dull hands. Here." She pushes it Mason's way; he gets up from the seat he's been occupying and, eyeing the unstable legs, attempts to sit in the new chair. He looks as if some initiation prank is being played on him—one which he has no recourse but to play into. "No, no. Put it in there. Can't you see the legs are no good?"

Mason, he lodges the chair in the middle of the huge fireplace as instructed, and then offers me the nearby chair, brushing against my ass when I pass too close by him. He ventures out into the chairs to find a stable one among the herd. Finally locating one, he returns to the fireside with it, and Ruby, she continues as if there has been no pause, offering no explanation for having chosen dining-room chairs as her preferred type of fuel. Man, I could come up with a good one, but this is her place.

"You the one that has that little shack down by the Pass, or is that your brother?"

"That would be me. I don't have a brother."

"Why'd you paint it the color of the treaty belts?"

"Uh, well, I didn't really pick the color with that in mind," Mason says, and I can't tell if he is lying or not. It would be like him to do something like that, but he's not likely that witty. Pausing a little and then smiling, he says, "Got your attention, though, didn't it?"

"So does the smell of dog *oo(t)-gweh-rheh,* but that don't mean I'm gonna chase it down. Matter fact, I usually go the other way. Things all have their time and place, and maybe mine is passing, but at my age, I can't trust m'eyes and might could step right into the middle of things."

"Well, it's not there anymore, anyhow. I got some new buildings up— bigger. Brand spanking new, just built. That old shack is part of history, now," Mason says, sounding like a used-car salesman, but with an unidentified product. I'm already buying my Marlboros from his shop and have seen the expanse of the new store with its wider selection. Though the other, identical building next to it is intriguing, it's not my place to ask.

"Well, I better get going. If it gets too dark, I'll be falling into Big Crick or something. Ruby, you want some help with these dishes before I go? I almost hate to leave, that stew was so good."

"I'll give you a ride home. No one should be walking in this kind of weather," Mason says, rising from his chair.

"Uh, Red, would you mind giving me a ride? I got some questions I wanted to ask you anyway, about next week's schedule." I do not want to be out on the road alone with Mason Rollins. Could be almost as deadly as meeting my father.

"I guess I'll just stay and keep your mother-in-law here company. Maybe help her with the dishes," Mason chirps, speaking to Red but staring at me, tossing a noisy bundle of keys to Red and bringing his own bowl, and Ruby's, into the kitchen.

"Here, take some home with you," Ruby calls. "It'll build up your legs for those long walks. We got to protect you, make you strong; wouldn't want you withering on us, now—be heavy on our minds and on our hearts," she continues, following Red in and rooting around inside of what appears to be an old wardrobe. The wardrobe is filled with night stands of varying shapes and sizes that have been haphazardly nail-mounted to its inside surfaces. The drawer she peruses is dedicated entirely to old margarine containers. She eventually finds one she thinks is the exact size I should take and fills it from her kettle.

➤◄

"I BET THE ONLY TALKING GOING ON IN THAT HOUSE IS THE DISHES TALKING TO the cups in the hot water."

Red laughs at my comment as we pull onto the road in Mason's new Thunderbird. It's actually a "new to Mason" Thunderbird, a few years old. "They got lots of stuff to talk about," Red mumbles. "Mason wants—"

"What? What could he possibly want from her, beading lessons?" I laugh at the idea of Mason Rollins hunched over some kitchen table, looping beads to get some extra survival money, and maybe opening up a beadwork shop. It's the first time in weeks, and man, does it feel good. A beading shop actually isn't a bad idea. There's always people coming out here to look at the "Real Indians," even more since Mason opened his smoke shop. It's a natural.

"I don't know if I should tell you."

"Don Harmony! For Christ sakes! I just about raised your boy for the last four years. Why shouldn't you tell me?" Red's secrecy is nearly as insane as the image of Mason with a beading needle. I touch his hand.

"Well, you are Bud's daughter . . . and, you know . . . Hey! What's so funny?"

"Sorry, Red. That was just so . . . Never mind. Keep your secret, if it's that important."

"Hey, wait . . . what did you want to know about the schedule? Nothing's changed."

"I was just kidding. I really don't want to know anything about it. I just wanted to spend some time with you." We sit in the awkward silence as I mutely curse my name and reputation. As intimately as I know Bert's . . . no, *my* trailer, it still doesn't feel like home. It would be really nice to spend some time with someone in it, even just talking, sharing someone's company. No, not just someone. If I'm going to start telling the truth, I better tell it to myself, first. I want to spend time with him there, no one else. I'd just put on some music and we could relax. Maybe I would even take the phone off the hook. No, not that far—particularly with the price getting my utilities installed has been, I couldn't go that far.

"Jeez, Fiction, you should keep a light on if you're gonna be coming home this late."

"I don't usually get home this late. But I do keep one on. I got one of my living-room lights on a timer. Wait here for a minute, will ya?" Something else is not right about my trailer, aside from the fact that the timer light isn't on. That could be anything. It's a cheap timer. Maybe the clicker just loosened. But the trailer still looks a bit funny. The large pane of broken glass lying against the trailer's side clarifies. It was the lack of reflection from Big Red's headlights that I noticed as we pulled up.

"Somebody's shot my windows out," I yell. He runs up and joins me immediately, wrapping an arm over my shoulder, trying to coax me away as he looks around for any tracks. I shrug him off and run to the door, needing something before we can leave. Inside, the trailer looks curiously like one of those scenes in the snow globes that seem to appear everywhere at Christmas time, the snow drifting and sparkling, caught in Red's headlights through the broad pane.

The living-room table lamps, of course, are no longer there. The kitchen overhead fluorescent ring still sparks on, though—once again, unnoticed. Some things are missing. The box in the closet where my original documents rest is there, and I clench it hard enough to bow the cardboard ends. Red stands to the side of the broken picture window, staring out it, an oblivious actor in this winter-wonderland scene.

I close the trailer's curtains—can't do much else with the place, and I certainly can't stay there. The temperature is dropping even further. Red convinces me Ruby wouldn't mind some temporary company until he can get the panes replaced. We've left the car doors open, and even with the heat on, the rearview mirror has frosted over in the few moments we've been inside the trailer. I verbally guide him out the darkened driveway, never letting go of the box.

We arrive a short while later. At our entrance, the other two look up from Ruby's fireplace, where they've been discussing the loss of land to the

New York State Power Authority. The room is more crowded than when we left. That Ruby, she must have snagged Mason to go out back and bring in more of her broken chairs, maybe explaining that Red collects the chairs for her when he goes into the city on Big Trash Nights, hunting for the treasures white folks often unwittingly throw out. Once, he picked up an old sewing table and, after stripping it down, sold it to some antique dealer in the city for five hundred bucks.

Any wooden chairs he finds, he brings here, dumping them behind her house. Ruby, she has an idea this method is cheaper than buying cordwood, and the old woman secretly likes the company of her ailing furniture, keeping it useful until the very last moment of its life.

The door slams itself shut in the wind, and Ruby's chairs are vacant again a while later. It has taken an agreement from me to do some work for Mason in return for his financing of my replacement windows before the men will leave, though. I'll be tending bar for a New Year's Eve party he's throwing. He promises he'll get his money's worth when I mention that it doesn't seem like a fair trade for him. You know, how many people can he invite?

The next bowl of stew Ruby has just served warms me from the inside out, but it's going to take more than that to stop the shaking. In front of the fire, she offers a sturdy-looking chair with thick legs, but she pushes one cross-support with her foot, thick varicose veins winding their way down, mapping her path as a Clan Mother. First that support falls from the chair, then the others, all dropping from the shifted legs, and the soft corruption within is revealed. Though the men seem to have bought my story—that I thought kids had done my windows in—she doesn't believe it in the slightest. She knows, as well as I, who acted out a bad vision on my place.

"Sometimes," she says, "a chair seems strong on the outside, sturdy—when in reality, it lacks support, rotting from the inside. And when that chair begins to show some signs of rot on the outside, maybe they'll even cover it, protect it for a little while longer. Now, it's true that with this kind of help, this chair might trick some others for a while, and when they take what it has to offer, they fall with it—maybe get splinters, maybe even a broken leg. But they'll remember those injuries, and eventually they will learn. When they choose their next chair, they'll be more cautious. They'll test it, maybe. And maybe they'll ask others for advice. That's where I can help; but maybe it's time for me to speak up even before they sit down. Before they ask."

The chair burns easily, its supports stacked like bones beneath it in the fireplace. Before long, the chair is engulfed, and Ruby asks me to grab another. The ones she calls her own and those that have been designated for the fire, they all seem equal. I have no idea how she was able to chose a Chief from among all the men of her clan—a leader from a group of supposed equals. I can't even distinguish a good chair from a bad one. Then again, the man she chose was my father.

I touch one. It looks like the others, but there is something slightly off in its posture, and it wobbles beneath my fingers. I drag the chair next to the fireplace, and Ruby nods in satisfaction. This room is full of choices, and I refuse to let myself shake, even in the cold. It's going to be at least a six-chair night.

><

CHAPTER 6 Curbside Phoenix

Big Red Harmony

IT'S GOING TO TAKE ANOTHER SWEEP. THE SWIRLING FORMATIONS, SOMETIMES almost perfect spirals in the night sky, keep on coming as my boy and I climb from my truck at the end of Fiction's driveway. I've known Fiction for years now, but since Bert's death, we've been spending a lot more time together. Funny, I still can't bring myself to call her Patricia. Her real name is, I don't know, somehow too intimate. Maybe soon, though, maybe soon. She's begun to see me with new eyes, too. Before, maybe to her I was who I am to everyone else: a man who used to be all muscle—tight, firm, solid with work—but who took off years ago, leaving a puffier guy who has trouble buttoning his jeans after a big meal. One who burps too much at bad times; one who cuts his own hair to save money. But she can still see that man who left; maybe she knows where to find him, how to bring him back.

Since Two-Step turned nine three years ago, old enough to help, I always bring him plowing. It wasn't just when he turned nine. More like when the contaminated well water we'd been drinking finally caught up with my wife, the same way it had caught Deanna Johns the year before, and washed her on down to Calvary Cemetery. The boy is all I got left in the world. My folks are still alive, but Bert's flock, now there's my real family. Even their big place in my life, though, doesn't in any way touch my loss.

My boy is the only other person who feels it almost the way I do. Like me, he drank the same water she had, but somehow we came away untouched. No explaining this magic connection, but respecting it, that's another matter. So we do, oh, just about everything together we can, even down to spending long nights plowing the reservation together. I usually make a driveway's first sweep and drop my boy off up to the house front, so he can shovel the porch and make a walkway clearing where the plow might cause a buildup. He's a good boy like that.

This new truck's got so much more juice than my old baby that I probably get the first part done in easily a third of the time, but on bad nights, I take another sweep through the reservation. I wasn't the old truck's first owner, and drove it for over ten years myself—and toward the end, it mostly just wheezed when I stepped on the gas. Still, I long for the hulk resting behind my trailer, losing itself to the seasons—an ailing monument to a time when I had a full family and a full plowing docket.

When the snow began spitting early this November, I didn't even bother mounting the plow on my old baby. The reservation climate has grown a little more hostile since Mason Rollins expanded his smoke-shop complex with the two new buildings, and besides, the old mounts might not even hold the plow. My plowing days, like my loving days, were over. I couldn't afford it, anyway—hadn't been able to for years, really. But every year, when the snow lays itself down thick as a commodity-cheese sandwich, that need to head out and slice through it takes me all the way.

When I was a boy, living at Bert's house as part of the first wave of unofficial foster children, she would make us stay indoors while she went out and shoveled that endless driveway herself. We all stood by the front window, the heating radiator hissing warmth out at us so we hardly felt the draft creeping in from the towels stuffed and taped around the panes. Only after she completed the work did she come back in and bundle up those of us who wanted to play in the snow.

In the fall of the year I got the old truck—in my Carborundum days, before all the plant shutdowns and layoffs—I also invested in a used plow from the swap sheet. Bev, that's my wife, argued that we really couldn't afford it. She wanted me to wait until the next year for the plow; but I got it anyway, pigheaded, arguing my own side—that we'd make the cost of it back easy in the first bad storm that blew through. That hadn't been so. The storm came, as always, in November, and I jumped on out in the dusting and locked that plow in place even as the first patches spotted our lawn.

I was dead wrong about the amount of money I'd make plowing. More often than not, I refused the crumpled-up bills that bundled folks held out to me from their porches. They blocked off most of their rooms with blankets—living in one room in an effort to keep the kerosene bills down low—and I'd just wave and smile, pulling out of the cleared driveway. After a while, they just watched out their windows, smiling and waving back as I rumbled by, finishing up in five minutes what would have taken them probably three hours.

Bev and I had ourselves a lean Christmas that year. We only bought gifts for Roger—as my boy Two-Step was known until he reached the age of eight. The boy opened his gifts that year like he thought someone might just take them away if he didn't get them open fast enough. We sat on the couch, knowing we had done right. But throughout the day, folks stopped by, carrying packages, gifts for the family. Some I knew only from the waves that passed between us on cold, stormy nights. Many of those boxes held food—cakes, cookies, a huge Mason jar filled with corn soup, even an already cooked turkey on a platter, stuffed with corn bread and still warm from the oven.

One package, a box wrapped in the Sunday funnies, contained this huge, bulky Navy pea coat that looked big enough to wrap Bev and Roger in, as well as my big old self. A note pinned to it confirmed that Bert sent the coat. It had been in the wrapping paper she favored, but several others had also discovered this extra use of the *Niagara Cascade* Sunday comics. The note said she had discovered this like-new coat down at the North End City Mission and, with a few of her own special treatments, it might be handy for plowing in. She always told me to dress warm for playing in the snow.

I hadn't lived at Bert's house for over nine years, and here she was, still trying to look out for me; but she'd been so wrong-headed about the size. I opened the coat to discover finally that she'd ripped out whatever lining had been in it, and had sewn in a new flannel lining, with goose-down padding filling in the spaces my body would not. It was a perfect fit. Bert had guessed the right amount of down to give the old coat a snug, well-insulated fit.

⇥⇤

NOW, TEN YEARS LATER IN FICTION'S DRIVEWAY, THAT SAME OLD COAT RESTS ON my back. It's a little more snug around the gut, as most of my clothes are, but it's kind of a comfort, like someone tugging me back to some unknown place, pulling gently on the sides of my shirt.

That coat might still be here, but the old truck is gone for good. And Bev is gone. I've tried to forget this. Sometimes I walk in the trailer thinking she must be in the bathroom, or the bedroom, or shopping, or something—anything but where she really is, over in Calvary, where she's recently gotten new company in Bert. The going to the cemetery was the hardest part of Bert's funeral, seeing my wife two rows away, turning back to her elements in the September ground.

Her death was senseless, but everyone who's lost someone thinks that. We suspected our water was bad, our well contaminated by our own sewer, particularly with what everyone believed about Deanna Johns's death; and yet we kept drinking it anyway, avoiding the price of bottled spring water. She just got sick one day and never got better. She died of a combination of an acute bacterial infection and dehydration, they said, her body finally refusing water altogether. Even now, after three years, she still appears every time I buy bottled water. She lurks somewhere just outside of actual vision, mingling in the refraction of light in the pure water. It'll be years before I can drink a glass of water in peace. Beer took water's place for a while there; but when Mason Rollins offered a job, I straightened right up, taking the midnight shift—working while my boy slept, hiring Fiction to come to the house in the early morning to get him up for school.

Through those long nights, over the years, I grew on very intimate terms with that old truck, coaxing it when necessary, swearing and punching it other times. It was my snowplow in the long winters, and my junking truck the rest of the year. Me and the truck would scour others' throwaways past midnight on Big Trash Night for salvageable items. It even gained a name a number of years later, when I'd been laid off.

Junking became a means of survival. Unemployment just wasn't enough. Discoveries like that treasure of a sewing table I often brag about finding and selling are rare, but enough scroungeable scrap metal I could sell to junkyards eased our financial troubles a bit. And sometimes couches, chairs, and other furniture found their way into my truck. Though not in the best of shape, they were always welcomed on the reservation by someone needing them. And there's never a shortage of those folks. Someone's always got a son or daughter moving home from the city, needing a couch to sit or sleep on, or another table to feed everyone who has a chair and a mouth. It's hard work, but it maintains an excitement about the possibilities.

Some specific areas of the city produced the best trash, usually in the areas that have an *x* somewhere in their names, particularly a snotty French silent one. One night, during a summer junking expedition in the ritzy DeVeaux area—which I always pronounce "Devo," like the punk band—I came across a particularly large mound in front of a really nice house on that street.

Where I was digging, some guy pulled up the driveway in a deep green Jag. He wandered over, glowing and weaving in his tennis whites like some tasteful, sporty ghost. He leaned his hand on a wardrobe—half of which sat perfectly intact while the rest of it, shattered planks, lay casually inside, the secret formal clothing of trees. His arm rested on the wardrobe for a few seconds, and then he thought better of this situation, standing in his driveway with a stranger in the middle of the night, and retreated a few feet. "You aren't going to find any curbside phoenix there, my friend," he said, smirking—sharp and articulate—his polished teeth cutting straight through the *x*, even filtered by the alcohol mushiness of a few after-match drinks. He wandered away, gliding through the night to his Jag. The garage door magically opened and closed. Security lights glared on a minute later, likely not to benefit my search.

I threw the wardrobe into the truck's bed, trying to prove the DeVeauxian wrong. Behind the wardrobe on the curb lay the shattered remnants of what appeared to be a beautiful oak coat rack that had, as its main focus, a nearly life-sized relief carving of the FTD guy. I couldn't tell much about it as I grabbed up the pieces—an uncracked beveled mirror, a bunch of shaped spindles, and the broken and naked florist—and threw them in, too. If nothing else, Ruby would have some pretty fancy kindling, come winter.

Whenever daywork on some local farms or anywhere else grew scarce, I took to trying to rebuild the Mercury coat rack. My boy told me the god's proper name, and that he was the messenger of the gods, a good speaker, clever—kind of like a Haudenosaunee runner, carrying important messages among the Nations, tribe to tribe, chief to chief. Bev died that same summer, and one of the ways I tried driving her absence from the house was to fill it with the sounds of creation—or in this case, re-creation. The broken god lay in a heap in the corner of my built-on shack out the trailer's back door. I named the pile "Pinocchio" after a while, making friends with the carving that winter in the cold shed, my breath pluming out, delicate vanishing feathers, as I worked on the rack's bottom.

The bottom consisted of an umbrella rack, the spindles creating a steady base shaped like an inverted Victrola horn. Some of the spindles were broken so badly, there was no way to fit them back on, and others were just plain missing. It seemed hopeless at first, but the piece nagged at me unexpectedly. I eventually returned to it and carved my own, using an intact spindle as a guide.

Mounting new coat pegs in Mercury's widespread arms and filling in gouges and chips, stripping and refinishing the god took me nearly all winter. Even with all the fragments gathered and accounted for, Mercury had no midsection—no belly, no chest, and no heart. As it turned out, the various pieces of his anatomy all came together in the back of the mirror, so that, when assembled, he appeared to race away behind the mirror as you checked your coat and scarf.

The piece, finally completed in the spring, stood over six feet tall and took up an entire corner of our small trailer. I had indulged in fantasies of selling him for thousands of dollars the entire time I'd worked on him, but I couldn't. An appraisal did confirm it could have sold for four thousand dollars in Buffalo. I did, however, act out my other fantasy.

A few Polaroids of the rack later found their way back to the right house in DeVeaux. They set easily into the front-door frame, along with a note that said: "You were wrong about the curbside phoenix." I started walking away, but turned around and pulled out another sheet from my pocket notebook, where I keep track of the furniture items people need most desperately. I replaced the first note with a new one. "You were wrong," it said, and then I signed it "Curbside Phoenix," placed it with the photos, and never looked back.

Ever since the tennis ghost had first slurred that phrase, it played in my head like some beautiful song. The sharp, hard, noisy *x* sounded like it could cut your tongue out if you weren't careful speaking it. I had found this dictionary while junking the year before. It was missing a few pages, but other than that, it was okay. I probably wouldn't ever need those words that had flown away on the missing pages anyway. "Phoenix" was there where it should have been.

Secretly, I hoped this might replace the name I've been stuck with since I was a young guy. That's the thing about the reservation. You never get the name you want. Everyone in the dance group knew I always carried a pack of Big Red gum, and used to hit me up for it on competition mornings. I was agreeable at first; you know, I'll share anything I have. But most of these guys were bumming gum from me to hide their hangover breath from Bert, and that wasn't right. So I started telling them I didn't have any, though they could see me chewing a stick anyway, and some of them were ballsy enough to point this out. They mocked me out for what they felt was my stinginess. That's when my name became Big Red.

You can probably understand why I like Curbside Phoenix better. The image that came to my mind was of a beautiful, spread-winged bird, rising out of a pile of trash. When it got warm enough outside that year, I traded Chuck Trost some ugly chair he'd always liked in return for him painting a version of my fantasy image on the truck's doors, with the legend CURB-SIDE PHOENIX below the image. He only had standard paints then, so the painting was clumpy and streaky with brush marks, not at all like the new one.

The paintings on the new truck consist of essentially the same images, but these were painted with an airbrush, so my truck looks just like those fancy ones down at the Monster Truck shows at the Convention Center. I was working late one night last month at the new, bigger smoke shop, which still has a drive-thru window, when this gleaming black truck pulled up to the window with the perfect image of my eternal bird gracing its sides. The plate numbers were already in my little notebook when Mason Rollins's face was revealed from behind the tinted window, laughing in the driver's seat.

><

"SO, HE JUST GAVE THIS TO YOU?" FICTION ASKS, UNSCREWING THE PLYWOOD WE mounted over her window frames while we'd been getting the panes replaced. Someone had shot out the young woman's windows a couple of weeks ago, but she refuses to discuss the matter, at least with me.

"Just like that."

"What strings?"

"No strings."

"No strings, my ass. I can tell when you're lying."

"How?"

"They don't call me Fiction for nothing."

"Funny. You got that off, yet?"

"One more second. Okay. Two-Step, grab that end when it drops, okay?" she says, not waiting for a response as the large sheet of plywood slides noisily from her window, revealing the gaping opening of her glassless picture window.

"No strings, really?" she asks as we coax the frame gently into the wall. We work one window at a time around the trailer, stopping after every couple of windows to come in for a cup of tea and a thawing out. There are strings, but strings I can live with—have, in fact, for the past ten years. Mason bought the new truck for three thousand dollars at a police auction. It was seized material, some drug smuggler. Mason said it was pretty stupid to be smuggling in such a flashy vehicle—that such activity required a certain amount of discretion—but he wasn't about to pass up a great deal because of someone else's lack of subtlety. I was a little concerned about what he wasn't saying; but for now, he's the boss. Handing over the keys, he told me that in the winters, instead of working at the shop, my job was to plow out any driveways on the reservation that needed it.

"So, I'm just doing what I always done, and now I'm getting paid for it." I drain my teacup and head toward the bathroom. We have just finished installing her last window. The entire job took over three hours, and a new, dense layer of snow now clogs the driveway. "Matter of fact, he even gave me a Sunoco card to use for when I'm plowing, but he said I wouldn't be needing that for long. He's paying for it all. Insurance, registration, everything. He said it's like a company car, but one that's strictly mine. Papers're all in my name. You coming with us?"

"Nah, I wanna straighten up around here, now that we got the windows in. Besides, I gotta admire my beautiful view. You don't know what it's like having to look at plywood scenery all the time. I was beginning to think I worked down at 'Lumber' Jack's. Started carrying a tape measure around with me everywhere, but I had to stop that pretty quick," she says, holding the measure out in front of her. We'd been using it to figure which windows were supposed to go where. Today, it's too damned cold for trial and error. "No one wanted to ask me out. Guess they thought I was gonna measure it before I said yes or no." We both laugh, and my boy turns red. "Don't worry, I won't ask you for a few more years, when you're done growing."

"I'll be out in the truck," my boy mumbles, blooming even redder and heading for the door.

"Here. Start her up." He catches the keys expertly and hurries out the door. After he closes it, we laugh some more. "You shouldn't tease him like that. Now he'll be worried about the size of his dick the rest of his life."

"Why should he be different from any other man?" She pulls the tape measure's tab out a few inches and flicks it back in, a metallic snake's tongue. "Let's see if you measure up to your name?" I step over and unzip my fly, blushing a little myself for the moment, glad of the nickname. Something keeps me from zipping back up. "Get outa here." She pushes my shoulder as we laugh more, but I think her laughter covers up a desire to see this through to the end. Mine does.

"So, I could stop by after we finish our rounds and I drop him off," I say in the roomful of silence, still standing close. Fiction looks out the window, seeming not to notice. "Uh, you know, check your windows for drafts, make sure we got 'em all caulked up right." The caulking gun in my hand is proof of my full intention for the rest of the evening. My truck rumbles in the snow, my boy revving the engine periodically as a reminder of his presence. "Or maybe I could just stop by tomorrow. That might be—"

"No. Tonight would be . . . nice. I could have some more tea steeped when you come in," she says, though I haven't given a time. "We could sit in front of the fireplace and watch the flames pop and dance long into the night."

"You don't have a fireplace."

"Oh, yeah. We could sit on the couch without the TV or lights on, and look out at the winter and be glad we're not in it."

"Deal." Outside, sharp daggers of cold dig into my throat. It took all I had to not bend forward those few inches and kiss her as she stood looking out through her new windows. What other elements of her life have been shattered that are closed to me? Those bruises didn't get there by any accident, no matter what she says. But she won't share it. Her life dances that cloudy line her name suggests.

"Move over."

"Can I drive?"

"Sure, head down near your gram's. We'll start there, give you some practice driving before we get down to business." The boy is stunned at my answer, and I walk around to the other side. We seize along Fiction's driveway as my boy tries to get the hang of standard shift, while I tilt my head to watch her diminish; but instead she grows, somehow filling the entire rearview mirror, pressing against its fragile prison, separated from me only by the melted grains of sand. I've broken some glass in my time.

We head on into the storm, and as we glide on down Torn Rock, Fiction waits in front of her window for my headlights to appear. A guilty hard-on makes itself known, and I try to concentrate on caulking her windows, the reason I am supposed to go back there. We pass by the cemetery, and this distraction is no longer a concern.

"Here, drop me off here, and then go down and do that patch at the bottom of Redman's Drop, you know the one—give you some practice before we get to the first real driveway—and then come back up for me. And be careful, the Drop can be a little tricky in this weather. Keep it in first or second."

The boy pulls out, and then I wander over to the vague snow-hump I believe to be Bev's grave. Of course it's Bev's grave; how do you forget something like that? I brush the snow from the stone, revealing her carved name and date of passing, stuffed with snow as the rest of the stone blows clean.

"Hey, Babe. It's me. 'Course it's me, like you don't already know that. You know, I feel kind of stupid talking to this piece of rock. Feel like there should be some violins playing in the background, or maybe some dead leaves blowing around or something. But the leaves are all buried. Anyway, you already know why I'm here. And it ain't to get your permission or anything. Christ, if you gave it, I'd probably jump sky high with a heart attack. So, don't say anything, okay?

"Anyway, she's great with Two-Step . . . Roger . . . I know you used to hate that name, but Christ, you should see him on the circuit. He took First this past summer. Better than I ever was, and I was a pretty good traditional dancer in my time. She watches over him when he's out on the pow-wow circuit. She seems to know how to be a mother, even though she doesn't have any kids. And no, we haven't been trying to make any, I swear. Anyway, Roger's getting up there to where he probably don't want all that much mothering anyway, but what I mean is . . . is, she's responsible. So, I'm just telling you, Babe, and this don't mean I love you any less. It's just that, well, I still need some goodness in my life, and I know you'd want that, and . . . I don't know, mind you, but I think she could use some, too. Some that I could give her. I'm still watching over your ma. Christ, she's gonna be burning probably that whole forest of junked chairs I brought her this winter. Hey, listen, Two . . . Roger's gonna be coming up soon. I better get out to the road. He's driving. At twelve, can you beat that! I gotta go. Love you."

My boy grinds gears up the hill, finally. The truck stops, and the stone gradually grows faint and pale in the swirling winter behind us as we pull out.

"So, why'd you have to go see Ma?"

"I didn't. I had to take a leak."

"Right at the graveyard?" He exaggerates every syllable. "I don't think so, Dad."

"Here, here. What the hell are you doing?!" I grab the wheel and we swerve across the road. "Hit the brakes!" The boy does as he's told, but leaves the truck in gear, and it lurches to a stop, stalling on the dotted passing lines.

"What? I was just pulling into that driveway is all." My boy's wide eyes shine in the dash lights.

"We don't go to that driveway. That's Bud's."

"Yeah, I know it's his. Why don't we? Just because he's a Chief don't mean he can make the snow stop falling in his driveway."

"Yeah. I know. It's just . . . never mind. I'll tell you which driveways to go down. Go on down there, to Justin Time's place."

"Justin hates when people call him that, Dad."

I point to an entrance swarming with cheerful reflectors, shimmering in the headlights over the snowbanks. It is four driveways away.

"Yeah, but we always used to—"

"Things are different this year. Just drive."

"But, Dad—"

"Hey! You wanna drive, or not?" We look at one another for what seems like hours. In that time, there are still no real answers for him. Finally, the horizon glows with a pair of distant headlights, and it is an excuse to end the silence. "Sorry. Just . . . just drive, okay? Hurry up. There's a car coming. You'll be smashing up my new truck."

Two-Step starts the truck, and we heave out into our proper lane as the approaching car passes by us. It's Bud Tunny's Lincoln, and it pulls into the driveway behind us, promptly getting stuck as soon as all four wheels are in the plugged drive.

"Go on. Get going." He moves, creeping along the road, keeping an eye locked to the mirror.

"Oh, shit. All right, turn her around." We reach Bud a few minutes later. He stands outside his driver's-side door, trying to push the car, step on the gas, and steer at the same time. We step up behind the Lincoln and start pushing. Bud hops in, steers it off the road entirely, and throwing it into park, gets back out.

"*Nyah-wheh.*" He shakes our hands.

"Jacob." I use his real name, attempting respect. "You want I should plow this out and you can pull right up? Only take about five minutes." The air between us whips around my offer, and Bud's gaze remains focused on the growling truck.

"*Gwah(t)-ess!* Never with his money! I'd sooner walk a hundred miles in five-foot drifts than benefit from any of that dirty cigarette money. It goes against our ways, and you know it." To prove his point, it seems, Bud grabs a bunch of shopping bags from his trunk and labors up his heavily drifted drive. Not quite a hundred, but enough to prove his point. I had similar encounters a few weeks ago, when the first heavy snow hit. I'd gone out, as instructed, and began slicing through the driveways.

This was fine for the first few, but then on the fourth driveway, some-one came from the house and said pretty much the same statement Bud just recited, and then told me to get the hell off of their land. Sporadically through the night, my new truck received similar responses—even from some of the elders I'd plowed out for years, and who couldn't possibly shovel out their own driveways.

"Trust me?" I ask my boy, watching Bud disappear into the night. Two-Step nods, and I put my arm around his bony shoulders. "Let's go. Even without those folks, we still got a shitload of driveways to take care of."

"Can I still drive?"

"I wouldn't even call what you did 'driving.' But yeah, you can still do whatever it is you wanna call it."

"So, what's up? Is it this split on the reservation over the shop? The way all the traditionals feel? You know, some people think we should stay with the old ways, respect our ancestors. That why you were talking to Ma?" he asks, downshifting and lowering the plow as we hit the first drive-way. He's a natural. Must have been watching, all these years.

"Your mother did that. The filthy water that killed her had nothing to do with tradition. Mason Rollins is offering us survival."

The boy doesn't reply.

"Sorry. No, it's none of that." He remains quiet. "Now, leave me alone or I'll take you back to Fiction's and she'll get out her measuring tape," I try to joke with my son.

"Right. We almost done? I'm tired."

"We just started, but you got years ahead of you. I'll drop you off at Gram's when we finish her driveway, and you can stay there tonight while I finish the rest myself." When my boy finishes shoveling her path, I tell him I'll pick him up in the morning, that the storm is getting worse and that I'll probably be out most of the night.

"Okay. But Ma would probably want you to do those other driveways too, you know," he says, shutting the truck door and running up to his grandmother, standing in the door with a steaming coffee for me. He runs it back out to me, and I nod, watching him go in and then leaving to give the rest of my scheduled driveways a once-over.

I get to Fiction's about an hour later. She has placed two tumblers on the coffee table, and alongside them a bottle of wine sits in a bucket filled with snow. Her hair is damp and smells of shampoo.

"I needed to warm up, and the hot water seemed like the best method at the time," she says, twisting her long ponytail in a towel. "You want some wine? That might thaw you out some." She pours the glasses without waiting for a response.

"Boy, you sure have changed from the time I first introduced you to Bert." I drain half of the large glass with one gulp.

"Times change. People grow up." She refills my glass and helps me off with my bulky coat. "This thing don't fit too well." She tugs at the sleeves as I yank myself free from the other end.

"Times change. People grow fat." I pat my slightly rounded belly.

"Not so fat," she replies, rubbing it too. Her hand follows the line of my belly around to the side and I melt into a full, long embrace, feeling the slickness of her ponytail on my cold cheek. We pull back and she sits down on the couch, near the window.

"No draft."

"No shit. I caulked them while you were plowing. What do you think I am, the helpless female?"

"Well, I don't know. You sure get into some funny situations. You ever gonna tell me the story of your windows getting shot out?"

"It's like this. When a bullet traveling out of the barrel of a gun hits glass, it shatters the—"

"And you have no idea who did it."

"I didn't say that, did I? Anyway, I don't want to talk about it. Here, have some more wine. I got this whole bottle and it just doesn't keep, so we gotta finish it."

"Well, if we're gonna, you know, uh, be together, we should at least be honest."

"Who said we were gonna be together? You're almost twenty years older than me, dirty old man." She raises her eyebrows. "I thought you were coming to check my windows."

"Well, I thought, you know, the tape measure . . . you said sit in the dark . . . I just thought . . . Sorry, I better get going." I reach for my old pea coat.

"You thought right. C'mere." She pulls the tape measure from under her couch cushions and gets up to meet me in the middle of the room. She reaches her arms around me in another hug and then brings them slowly around to my belt buckle. I kiss her neck, smelling deeply the wild and sweet scent lingering there. She crouches a little, fumbling around my belt buckle. "Forty-two," she exclaims in an exaggerated voice, pulling back with her long fingers across a point on the tape measure, presumably at forty-two inches. "Man, I guess you are fat, after all."

We laugh and continue to embrace. She reaches over and clicks the light off. I mumble that she won't be able to read her measuring tape that way, and she replies that she doesn't care. In the dark, slowly, we learn each other's body, entirely, in soft caresses. I rub my face into the front of her flannel shirt, unbuttoning it slowly, kissing every inch of newly exposed flesh. I stop at her bra, leaving it on—I can't go that far, yet. Her thin collarbone rests between my lips. She unbuttons my shirt, tracing her fingers along the faint line of soft baby hair that leads from my belly to my navel and then down, disappearing in the waistband of my jeans. Her fingers slide deeper, softly tugging at the hair there and pulling gently back. We writhe in unison, almost avoiding what we know will end the evening for us. Finally, I smooth my hand away from the small of her back to her wonderfully soft bottom, lifting her toward me. She reaches below the arc of my belly, unbuckles my belt, and undoes my jeans, letting them drop gracelessly to the floor.

I step out of them, slipping her bra from around her shoulders as she thumbs my shorts down, tugging them away from my stiffness. I crouch, shrugging them the rest of the way off and stepping out of them, as I unbutton her jeans and slide them and her panties from her simultaneously, releasing her from the denim. The soft dark hair of her mound carries the same shampoo scent. I leave a trail of kisses up her torso to help find my way back, finally arriving at her neck. The ridge of her right ear softly leans against my lips, and pressing the small of her back with one hand, I guide myself in gently with the other. It has been too long. We slowly descend on her living-room carpet below her new, draftless picture window, leaving the storm to its own devices.

LATER, AS WE LIE IN HER BED, THE BREATHING OF HER DREAM JOURNEY IS SLOW, rhythmic, a song in the darkness. The deejay talking on her digital clock radio lets me know it's after three. Out in the living room, her picture window fills with this stubborn bitch of a storm. My vague reflection mimics me in the clean glass. I do have a bit of a paunch, but other than that, I'm in pretty good shape. My back muscles, my lats, spread behind me in the reflection. They'll be sore tomorrow. I flex them, and they flare. Wings— those guys at the health club I used to belong to in the Carborundum days called them wings, a century ago.

I gather up my clothes and sit on the couch to get dressed. With this storm, another sweep is almost mandatory, and whether they want it or not, every single driveway on this entire reservation is going to be clear in the morning. We all need to rise from our own shit. I wrestle the old pea coat on, but it tugs, constricting my back. I leave the coat on her couch and head out into the storm. My truck has excellent heat and warms up fast, and besides, I have simply just outgrown that coat.

PART TWO

Standing Quiver Dance

Okay, now, Standing Quiver Dance. This used to be an old-time traveling song, when we had much journeying to do, into paths we didn't know so well. Used to be, we'd sing and dance this around a quiver just full of arrows in the center, and always did it first, even though lots of you ladies out there like the Rabbit Dance first. Now, with our permanent homes and Nation lands, we still do this, asking for the good fortune, in hunting and in warfare. We can't get too lazy now, 'cause you never know with borders like ours when you're gonna need some luck with your arrows.

SINGER, TUSCARORA SOCIAL, TUSCARORA NATION

CHAPTER 7 The Sharpest Vision

Bud Tunny

A SINGLE SHOT AT THIS END OF THE NATION'S BOUNDARIES RIPS THROUGH THE morning air, and then another; it has begun. Atop the reservoir, the sun rises over the community it is my life's duty to shepherd. My hands are a bit stiff, but my vision remains as sharp as ever. Five stories below, at least seven hunters from my Nation wander through my vision in the immediate area, though whether they are from the Young Men's team or the Old Men's team is unclear. The area is certainly as full of as many hunters as the Lord has provided game for. There are no fishes and loaves within the borders of my Nation. We must provide as much for ourselves as we can, and learn to live with this.

The wind at my back tries to bite at me around my collar and scarf, slicing—this very morning dropping in temperature easily ten degrees colder than the three-degree mark we've been stuck at for the past week. The weatherman on the radio this morning says the new year'll be ushered in two days from now at temperatures well below zero, as if he can truly predict the movements of the Lord, the Creator, across the face of this world.

In the fading shot echo, the Hunt has commenced, one team gaining in game over the other. The final count, later, will determine which team has provided the most game for the Feast, which team has the sharpest eyes and the sharpest skills. My fingers, thick and stiff with the arthritis slowly creeping into my joints these last few years, play over the safety switch on my loaded rifle. The heavy padded gloves don't help, with their restrictive movement. The late December wind chews at my achy joints, making them throb even worse. Though I've been on the Old Men's team for nearly twenty years, this is the first year I actually feel like I belong there. There is no shame in being old within our community. To acknowledge age is to grant respect to the wisdom that comes with it. It was a different matter when my people let me remain on the Young Men's team longer than I should have. They waited until the woman I am married to had a child by me. They ignored my first child—the one born to a woman who was not my wife, a woman who was nobody's wife. But all of that is in my past.

To the south and west of me, the water—its top layer a shifting, frozen mass—blossoms fresh, small sunlight jewels on its surface, almost five square miles of river water, baptizing the reservoir's inside walls. Most times, though my house sits at the edge of its northern border, I keep away from the top of the reservoir—or "the dike," as it has come to be known over the past thirty years. I make this journey once yearly, from the north border to the south, at the beginning of the Hunt, to remind myself of my father's history, to keep it clearly in my mind when considering the future.

In the east, the rest of the Nation folds out before me, behind me: my father's legacy. The Continental parked in my garage at the reservoir's northern edge will be warm when I eventually descend, thanks to my remote starter, but that is a while in coming. At the south wall, terrible things have grown this year, and the perimeter road leads me there.

This tremendous containment system was built in the time my father was Chief. There are other landmarks here of my father's vision as well— the chemical barrels buried deep in certain places within the Nation, for instance—but none of his other sins so visible and undeniable as this.

I was not a part of the chemical companies' contracts, but those have been mostly forgotten anyway. But neither did I have anything to do with the contract no one will let me forget: how my father was fooled, and we as a Nation were eventually beaten by the U.S. Supreme Court, losing a fifth of the Nation's land for the Niagara Power Project, to store the Niagara River's potential power. Though we fought with nearly everything we had, when the Supreme Court overturned a ruling we had truly won, we had no choice but to accept our defeat. Some of us accepted other things, as well.

A vast new house appeared here in the reservoir's shadow for me, and other settlements were also offered to my father and his family. We were recently married, and my new bride and I, just starting out, were living with my parents in their home. The state offered, in relocating my family, to build me a house as well as building my father's.

Anyone else from the Nation would have taken the deal, most definitely, had it been offered. But it hadn't been. Any others who had to be relocated had received a small cash compensation for their troubles. This was not my fault. Nor was it my father's, I say to myself, trying to sound emphatic in my head, as I always attempt when it comes to this day. Giving up my house would not change the lives of the others. All I can do is try to ensure those things will not happen while I am Chief, until the day I die.

My Clan Mother Ruby Pem's house sits here at the place where Dog Street ends, a reminder that in the past it had continued on, into what is now deep beneath the freezing water. It's likely she knows I am up here, as she seems to know my every move before I do—almost every move, anyway. There is no light or movement, but her eyes are on me—as they were on my father when her view of the western end of the Nation's expanse was replaced by the neat and orderly walls of this reservoir. She knew she was the only reason it stopped where it did, that my father did not dare displace a Clan Mother in his last negotiation concerning the Nation's land.

At the corner, Rollins's buildings stand, and the new violations he's planned are revealed even from this distant vantage point. This scene is a grim one. At the barbed-wire barrier on the perimeter, normally a turning point, I descend instead, immersing myself in the woods growing behind the grounds. The trees have grown up dense in the thirty years since the reservoir arrived, strong and forgiving of those violations of their roots, and I am at ease in their company.

Nearby, a small, uneven gravel area that had once been a driveway leads to a house long keeled over and rotted back into the earth, returning itself slowly to the Lord's earth, leaving now only a fragile skeleton of soft wood supports jutting from the snow here and there—as things should be. The residents had left when they thought they were going to be displaced, and they never came home. I have no idea where they are now.

Snow crunches under my feet in my arc toward the edge of the woods, the crumbing traces of house, a safe distance. It looks like the New Year's

Day Feast might be a bit sparse this year. Six days ago, the brief warm spell we enjoyed ended abruptly with a shift in pressure, and in the winds came the drop: layers of melting snow flash-froze, its usual camouflaging insulation removed.

After a few cold trails, I come out near the bush line, but stay in the brush, where the full back of Mason Rollins's tobacconist store sprawls before me. In the two months since Bertha Monterney's death, much has happened on the land next to her house. The girl's trailer is gone, as ordered, though the deep ruts dug in its removal are still visible, leaving deep shadows in the snow. She will not cast significant shadows in my life for much longer, that is certain.

Rollins's decrepit, ramshackle place is gone, and a monstrous two-story preconstructed building stands in its place. A similar, larger building sits next to it, sidled up nearly to the old woman's house. The dead woman's land was a concern from the beginning, and when the Nation lost a good portion of it, my concern grew. We had no plans for it, except to let the old house join the other houses of past generations, returning to the ground, so the seventh generation would have something to work with—and this is important enough.

Rollins's ascent to prosperity doesn't really concern me too much. Why shouldn't our people prosper? Sometimes, though, the power that comes with the money doesn't create a smooth environment. When you can grant your own wishes in a matter of minutes, you have no time to consider the implications for your later life, or for those who come after you. These rapid changes tell me Rollins is rising to that level of opportunity. They tell me a king's ransom is being generated at the store. Behind the buildings lie something new to worry about. They've been here for nearly a month, and while I had a sense of them from above, I couldn't judge the intimidating size of the two underground gasoline-storage tanks until now, here, on the same level—a pair of giant suppositories, bloated white slugs waiting to be slipped into the Nation's bowels.

The ground's frozen too hard to be dug now, but Rollins and his crew will start tearing into the tender spring earth as soon as they can—certainly no later than the end of March. As I raise the gun, somehow the safety flips off, probably just caught on my finger. The sight through the jeweled telescopic lenses is the closest I've been. The hunting is lousy, anyway.

I'm not a smoker and don't believe in Rollins's business. I guide those I can to not get involved, tell them that it can only bring grief. Rollins is playing with the state, and he is young—an upstart who knows nothing about the dance he's beginning. My father thought he knew what he was doing, too. The reservoir stands as a monument to the last dance Tuscaroras had with the state of New York.

The people followed my father blindly, trusting him as they should trust a Chief; but they really trusted those words my father kept repeating: "I am doing what is in our best interest." Their blindness hadn't been unwarranted; he'd even gone to jail for their benefit in his attempts to halt the reservoir's construction. By the time people began truly protesting the events out here, the United States stepped in and reminded us just how shaky our sovereignty can be. These people are now the community Elders, older and considerably wiser. Tradition dictates that the Elders are the wisest, but tradition has gone the way of the language—taught in elementary-school classrooms and lost by graduation from high school.

Many young people have followed Rollins, as if he were wise, his insights banded together in neat stacks of fifties and hundreds. The Elders, silenced into Senior Citizens, are now supported as infants, fed bitter fare by the state's Meals on Wheels platter. They call, between bites, to ears deafened by the flicking of disposable lighters and the ringing of cash registers.

We did the only thing we could. When Rollins offered us a building for Senior Activities like the two he just raised, we refused. The state has taken away our Elder status, but we will not let one of our own reduce us to board games, card games, and road trips we could not have made when we were responsible for the community; we will not let him confirm our loss. We sent back the money he had donated, with a note informing him that tobacco was created as a way for people to thank the Lord, the Creator; tobacco was a gift, not a commodity with which to gain profit. How do you put a price on the Lord's gifts? we asked.

Rollins put the returned money in a bank with the Tuscarora Senior Citizens as the account's holder, mailing back the statement book and another note to the Elders, asking us why we hadn't felt that way when we'd allowed one of our Chiefs to sell out a fifth of the reservation for a chance at prosperity. He seems to think the comparison is flattering.

The note and the bank book are now secreted away in a safe-deposit box, where all significant reservation information is kept: birth records, death records, the roll books identifying legal members of the tribe, legal agreements between the Nation and the state and country, historical photographs, and now its first documented encounter with Mason Rollins. It will not be the last. My scope roams over the gasoline tanks and the anonymous second building. People come and go from this building, carrying boxes in and leaving empty-handed, their long early-morning shadows mimicking them. This could all be stopped, right now.

A cold draft slips into my collar, gnawing at my neck, and then a frozen metal point presses against the back of my head. Stepping forward, away from the point, I turn around.

"I wouldn't do that if I were you, Bud," Mason Rollins says and stands before me, dressed in a white camouflage snowsuit. The suit is made of some lightweight material that doesn't rustle in the winter wind, the way most nylon does. "Could get messy." He clicks the safety off his weapon. I am in the cross hairs.

"It's not surprising that you would use an illegal weapon." I shift my safety back on and lean my rifle on one of my boot toes. Rollins keeps his safety in the off position.

"This is the Hunt. Anything goes, remember? There's no such thing as illegal today. D'you forget the traditional rules?" The rules were designed when there was no convenience of running to the grocery store if the Hunt had been bad. They had been designed for survival, the lack of which was something this upstart young snot has never even had to consider.

Rollins holds the sleek crossbow casually, clearly still aimed at me. Its shiny, polished black helve rests easily along his muscled arm—obviously custom-designed. He slides a cigar from a zippered pocket in his suit.

"Cuban?"

I shake my head, and Rollins sticks the cigar into his own mouth.

"You're killing our Nation."

"With one cigar? I don't think second-hand smoke is *that* serious. Maybe you're right, though. The smoke might scare away the animals." He slides the cigar back inside his suit and zips the pocket shut.

"You know what I mean. I've seen other Nations. One of that kind of shop leads to another and then to another. Pretty soon, all you have is one big tobacconist store. Nothing left for the seventh generation."

"*Oo(t)-gweh-rheh!* I'm ensuring there'll *be* a seventh generation. Change, man—that's what we're all about. If you're so traditional, why don't you follow the Peacemaker's example. The reason we survived is 'cause that guy dealt with his situations head on—he adapted. That's all I'm doing. That guy had vision, like me. I got vision," Rollins says quietly, never changing his quiet hunting tones.

"The only vision you have is bad vision." Imagine Rollins aligning himself with the greatest hero of the Haudenosaunee. There's no point in explaining the blasphemy of such a statement. The Peacemaker gave us unity, formed the Confederacy, showing us a single arrow can be broken easily, but that a group of arrows bound together is nearly unbreakable. First, other tribes met with our formidable front and were conquered or absorbed, and by the time the settlers brought their way to us, we'd already been organized enough to stand our ground, maintain our territory. If it hadn't been for the Peacemaker, we'd be wandering around in the pathetic lands of what's now the Midwest, the most useless land in this country. We have the Peacemaker to thank for everything, and this fool compares himself to that man. He's not even wise enough to know he shouldn't stand alone. Clearly, he hasn't seen the evidence the Peacemaker provided in the bundle of arrows.

"Why do you believe the state is just going to sit by and let all that tax money walk away while you get rich?" I know something of the Peacemaker's ways, including the move of making sure the most formidable enemy is convinced to join you. This stupid, arrogant boy, though, if he heard that part of the story, would believe he was being talked about. This boy has no idea that the state is a far more dangerous enemy than he could ever be. The boy doesn't know the state only lets an Indian rise if there is something to be gained—the way my father rose.

➤◄

THE STATUS OF MY FATHER, EZEKIEL TUNNY, HAD GROWN IN DIRECT RELATION TO the number of feet New York State took for the reservoir. As soon as negotiations began, he was invited to all of the most prestigious parties and benefits, where it was not uncommon for one to pay over one hundred dollars a plate, and where they argued with him and seduced him simultaneously. The first time he attended such an event, he thought he could take the plate with him—at that price, he felt he should get something. "And you will," he was informed by one of his politician friends. He was told these dinners were acts of solidarity, and that when he needed the state at some point, he could rely upon it. These dinners were insurance, he was finally told.

My father had his picture taken at these dinners with just about every politician in New York. He squinted in each of them, smiling a wide grin, displaying his own plate—a clean, straight line of porcelain teeth. When my mother asked why he had smiled so wide, he told her he was supposed to—that and to say "cheese" at the same time. She wondered what smiling had to do with cheese, and he told her he guessed he was supposed to be thinking of all the commodity cheese the government distributed to the Nation every six months, one brick per household, five bricks per Chief's household. She often commented that he was squinting so hard, she could not even see his lovely eyes in the pictures. He always said "nonsense," but knew she was right.

As my father lay dying a few years later, his false teeth abandoned in a bedside drinking glass, he told me to come into his room alone. Though Johnnyboy Martin would take my father's place, being a member of his clan, it was understood that I would one day inherit a position as Chief. Whenever the Deer Clan Chief passed, I would step immediately into his place, taking the horns before a week was up. I'd been bred for it. My Clan Mother had designated me years before because my father was a Chief, and having lived that life, I knew the inner workings of what it took. She also chose me because I inherited my father's acute vision.

"Now you listen," my father said in the sick room. "Don't let your vision get all blurry when there's money involved. If your time in this duty is anything like mine, you'll be seeing lots of funny things. And there'll be times you'll be asked to see things through a gentle fog, a mist—and times when you're asked to not see things at all.

"And throughout these, usually, you'll be asked to smile for a picture. The picture is taken to remind you who you have made promises to. When you smile for the camera, you must close your eyes down as tight as you can, but they remain open, too. This is a hard feat, but you will have your sharpest vision then, and you will need it. Let your squinty-sharp eyes guide you. See what you see, and not what you are told to see.

"When the state came in, I saw different from everyone out here. They saw what they were told to see by their friends and relations—that they would get more if they held out for more. I saw, eventually, when we began to lose, that the state was going to take the land whether we sold it or not;

so I figured we should at least get something for it. The cash settlements, the relocations, and the reduction of the reservoir's size so it would take less of our land, those were all things I had succeeded at." He told me more things about politics, but most wasn't news. I am observant, and in my father's declining years, in addition to serving as a runner in Chiefs' Council—a silent observer of all proceedings—I had made acquaintance with many of the important people I'd be needing to deal with from the state. Most came to the funeral, their own recognition gesture of the power change. Though there were no photographs taken, the politicians who attended had made sure they sent along a condolence note which made mention of their attendance. It began then, as I took note of those names and offices.

The photographs of my father are put away in the safe-deposit box with all of the other important documents of Nation history. Helping my mother sort through all of my father's belongings, taking what I would eventually need for my new position, I collected those photos from her wall shortly after the funeral and took possession of them.

We had gone through most of the house when my mother brought me to the root cellar, just off the family room that took up most of the main basement. She handed me the key and stepped back. A thick, dark stench blew out of the room as if forced from within when I opened the tightly sealed door. Waving my hand in the air did not help. My mother handed me a large blue flashlight.

The root cellar was stacked floor to ceiling with drab rectangular card-board boxes, all claiming the same legend on the sides: GOVERNMENT SUR-PLUS—NOT FOR RESALE. The commodity-cheese packages rotted and oozed black stench in the root cellar of my father's house—my mother's house.

Back in the kitchen, my mother explained over tea what those boxes meant, and that they would shortly be my responsibility. The doctors having given my Chief probably less than a year to live, my training period was rapidly coming to a close. The cellar full of years' worth of the Chief's five-brick allotment spoke volumes in its hellish stench. The Chief's family was supposed to get the same allotment everyone else did, and the four extras were to be distributed—at the Chief's discretion—to those families which were more needy than others.

"But how do you decide between needy and needier" my father had always told my mother, locking the extra bricks in the cellar, slowly build-ing a moldy shrine to his indecisiveness. He believed if he gave a brick to some families and not to others, greed and jealousy would bloom in his clan. So he kept them all hungry. The hunger would motivate them. Taking the cheese in the first place was probably not one of the Nation's smartest moves, but the other Chiefs had all wanted it, and it was not too much of a price to pay. The others could deal with their clans as they saw fit, but he kept his prepared for independence. "Relying on the state to feed you is like relying on a strange dog not to bite you," he often said. He allowed his clan's people the minimum set up in the agreement, but his discretion called for none of the surplus.

In taking on his responsibilities, I continued attending the same sorts of dinners my father had gone to, but refused to have my picture taken, claiming it was against Indian beliefs, and the fools believed. My alliances would not be known quite as easily as my father's had. The cheese I stored and saved for the Feast—it allowed me indulgences, and my clan couldn't possibly argue with such a huge donation coming from them. I'm smart—smart enough to know that Rollins sees things unlike anyone else from this Nation—and if the old ways are going to survive, I'll have to see the future Rollins sees, whatever twisted vision he has, and stop it in its infancy. Rollins doesn't know the outside government, doesn't know the things it can do and has grown fond of doing over the long years.

"I KNOW MORE ABOUT THE GOVERNMENT AND THE TREATIES THAN YOU THINK, Bud," Rollins says. He slides his wallet from another pocket, flipping the transparent sleeves until he arrives at his red Nation identification card, and—otherwise never changing his position—begins. "This reads 'Exemption from all taxes unless imposed by his or her own nation, band, or tribe. U.S. Constitution, Article Six, Section Two and Amendment X-I-V'—What is that? Fifteen?—'Section Two.' I know the government can't do anything to me and the tax laws, unless you allow them to. They can't shut me down or collect taxes on my products sold on sovereign land. Our future is in this strip of property," Rollins continues softly, sweeping his arm wide and then sliding the wallet away. Something moves just beyond Rollins's shoulder, nearly hidden by the ridiculous rearview mirror he has mounted on his sunglasses. I click the safety off my rifle and lift the sights to my eyes, pointing it in Rollins's direction. Rollins quickly brings his arm around and turns, raising the crossbow.

Lunging forward, I fire. For just a second, the deer stands indecisive and confused, and then its right eye is gone in a bloody mess as it is knocked to the earth. The buck, down for a few seconds, stands, its antlers sagging with my shot—clean through the ridge at the center of its head. It looks to the woods, and in that second, Rollins, glancing into his scope, releases his arrow. It opens a neat slice between ribs and continues on into the field. The buck folds forward, its heart pierced.

"It's all in your hands," he says, loading another arrow onto the crossbow and returning to the conversation as if it had not stopped. "And Bud, if you sign us over, we'll come for you. You won't have to worry about the seventh generation anymore; you'll have your hands plenty full with the next generation . . . us.

"Bud . . . one more thing. You can have the buck. It wouldn't be right for me to bring in one of your clan members."

"Of course, I'll take it. My shot brought it down in the first place. You're merely trying to claim my kill as your own."

"Yeah, okay, if you say so. Besides, my guess is that the Young Men are gonna win the Count, even without it. You can take it out through the woods to the white side, where you need a license I'm betting you don't have, or you can pull it through my parking lot. Or maybe you want to drag it up the dike the way you came. Your choice, Bud," he laughs, patting a sack at his side, apparently full of game.

Rollins turns and disappears into the woods. He walks on some kind of snowshoe of a type I have never seen before. They're traditional in shape, but seem to be made of some synthetic material, rendering them nearly silent, even in the frozen snow.

The deer lies exposed in the field. Its left eye holds the same stunned look it had when I fired. It should have been a perfect shot, no visual obstructions except Rollins—and he was a minor one—but the sight was cloudy, smudged by my thumb or something. I'd fired anyway. I'd been too confident—too sure that the deer was exposed, that it had offered itself to a human of its clan—but I won't make that mistake again.

I gut the deer and drag it across the field to Clarksville Pass, hiding it in the bushes near the road's edge. Somewhere along the trail, the antlers rip free, and the tattered head now lies exposed to the winter sun, clotted and mangled. Retrieving them would require a farther walk if I trace my trail than if I just cut the clearest path to the reservoir and my waiting car, beyond. The longer I stand here deciding, the more likely it is that I'll lose this deer. The law won't be on my side once I step beyond the Nation border, and I'll have to stuff the deer into my trunk as quickly as possible, breaking their laws.

I cannot, will not, walk across his parking lot. The antlers will have to stay in the field's furrows, sinking under the increasing snow cover, driven even deeper by heavy feet—or maybe at some point found along the way, in the spring's thaw. The morning sun, winking brilliantly on the cold white metal of the gasoline-storage tanks, leaves hot ghosts burnt onto my eyes, like those other chemical tanks, years and years ago. I squint in defense. The sharpest vision is necessary at a time like this, but even losing my footing in the frozen ruts of this field, I am unable to take my eyes off the gleaming tanks.

><

CHAPTER 8 Frostbite

Big Red Harmony

THE NEW SNOWSUITS AND THE CROSSBOWS MASON BOUGHT HIS CREW WORK like magic, keeping us far from frostbite and granting a snagger's eye, allowing us to deliver bulging and straining sackfuls of small game to the Old Gym before heading up to the shop for final party preparations. Most of Mason's guys are on the Young Men's team, but since I have my boy, I'm wedged square in the Old Men's. The kitchen here seems like the soundproof booth on one of those old quiz shows, and none of these contestants seems to be in the lead.

Almost every year I can remember, this place is like an anthill—women running like crazy back and forth, laughing, lying, or sometimes just needing to exaggerate about their men's hunting skills. It was easy back then to snatch bits of food with the other kids when the women were busy. And when I hit six and got my first Christmas shotgun, the single piece of game I dragged in—a scrawny squirrel—delivered all kinds of words from the women at the tables. In all this time, no Feast kitchen has soaked up sound the way this one does; man, it's like the Bounty paper towels of sound in here. These women cluster in two distinct groups, and they aren't the women for Old and Young Men's teams, I can tell you that; and I can also tell you the members of only one of them look at me and my sack.

"Hi, Don. What'd you bring in?" Nancy Harmony, my mom, asks, taking my burlap bag. This is one of the few occasions during the year when our paths cannot help but cross.

"Oh, you know, an assortment." She takes my bag and empties it on one of the long tables filling the room which are designated as "Old Men's tables."

"Probably bought it all," floats up from a voice somewhere in this crowd of women. You could almost see it, like those cartoon word balloons, the letters all with a layer of ice on them. These women busy themselves sorting the other kills lying on the table—and this is not a large number—moving my pieces awkwardly like they were poisoned or something, and finally, though officially a sorter at the Young Men's tables, my mom yanks the pieces, snapping rabbit necks and making pheasant wings almost spread, and flings them to their proper piles. I don't let the door hit me in the ass when I clomp down the slushy, well-salted back steps.

I didn't truly expect my mom to come to my rescue in this group of women with very sharp knives. Really, I have a hard time even thinking of her as my mother. She farmed me out to Bert's all those early years so she and my dad could work two jobs each, racking up the first reservation color TV, and then the first reservation microwave, stereo, hot tub . . . and that list goes on and on. Their house is busting full of luxuries I was never home long enough to use. They're not mine in any sense.

Instead, fighting for a turn at the heating register in Bert's living room, eating commodity peanut butter on toasted week-old bread, that was home. My folks' house was like a major department store, and I didn't have the cash. So even when they came to get me for a weekend here and there, I asked to go back to Bert's before Saturday night was up. Didn't want to miss popcorn and movie night—staying up late, sometimes until one-thirty, watching the scary late-night movies. Dancing practice still supposedly came at eight-thirty the next morning, but she let us sleep until almost ten—unless there was a big competition written on the gigantic gas-station calendar tacked to the living-room wall.

Here, at the Gym, my mom nods goodbye through the door pane. My idling truck floods the air with a cloud of exhaust smoke, filling my lungs with its sweet, dark fragrance. That building, once so spectacular, gigantic, now sits decrepit and fragile in the smoky haze of my rearview mirror. If I were to break the mirror—a quick flick of the wrist, like the one you use to take a bleeding rabbit out—the whole building would rain down in old shards and slivers of its former life; but there's been no scarcity of bad luck out here.

The Phoenix bounces west, and the new shop eventually looms gleaming in the windshield. The jammed parking lot says it's going to be a great end to a shaky year. Even Mason's reserved spot at the back of the building is taken. I pull up onto a plowed mound and, climbing from the cab, throw the emergency brake on. An Acura, huddling guilty in Mason's parking space, sports Canadian plates. His gamble pays off.

Inside, six girls work the registers like crazy typists, and the stock guys just about run to keep product on the shelves. Arms strain as everyone in the crowd is bundled high with cartons of cigarettes like gift packages. The storeroom grows rapidly empty these days. Mason'll have to place another order—maybe even double it—for most of the Canadian brands on the second day of the new year, when outside business resumes.

November sure was a tight one, I tell you. Mason had ordered all the popular brands from over the border and offered cutthroat low prices, but it sure wouldn't do any good if they didn't know we were here. He sunk his last profits into two billboards over the thruway, selecting that same pink you usually see advertising massage parlors (who knows why) to announce that "Smoke Rings" was now open and carrying a full complement of Canadian brands at up to thirty percent off. Every day since those signs appeared, the checkout lines in the shop have been more or less the same as they are today—folks waiting loaded down for twenty minutes, even with all six registers going.

"Hey!" I call out. The four guys playing poker in the second-floor break room turn quick, giving the look that says they've been stretching their coffee break for at least an hour too long. "Ain't a one of you got a chance at winning. Y'all got poker faces worth shit. You ready for tonight?"

They nod slowly, grinning that free-beer-and-food grin.

"All right, six o'clock. See you there." Their voices, swearing at—or to—one another about having been caught, follow me down the hall.

"Those guys working out?" Mason asks, shuffling papers at his desk and handing me, in one hand, order forms to fill out based on the information from the stack of old forms he holds in his other—the carbon marks that keep this business going.

"Oh, yeah. You know, it's just that it's New Year's Eve. They're just all jazzed up about the party, is all. They work hard."

"How's it coming, anyway? We gonna start on time?"

"Jeez, I don't know. I imagine. Fiction's been over there a couple hours, easy. Those guys were already setting up when I let her in. Wanna go see?" Mason locks all of the financial papers in his desk before pushing the chair in. He claims he chose me as manager because he thinks I know what's going on, that I seem to know the reservation—not who's taking land from whom, but the serious, real issues: who's working, who isn't; who needs a job, and who needs, maybe, just a loan to get out from under the bills; a bunch of other things he couldn't, and really didn't want to, keep track of. That skill doesn't take anything but a good pair of eyes. He doesn't trust me with all his secrets, though, and that's okay too, I suppose.

The parking-lot salt usually does the trick, but this New Year's cold freezes it—uncut diamonds littering the lot, mixed with crushed cigarette butts, which usually don't look like anything except cigarette butts. Lately, though, Mason says they've been looking an awful lot like receipts. "Dirty receipts" is what Bud would likely say, but as far as I know, he hasn't crossed onto this property in a long time. We probably look goofy in the matching polymer jumpsuits and insulated boots Mason bought, but that freeze doesn't touch us.

He's proud of these suits, though we look like we're ready to be cleaning up hazardous waste. I shouldn't complain; the suits were my idea. Along with inventory, I sometimes suggest things that might do the community some good, and Mason usually listens. My workers don't mind coming in during this stubborn cold stretch, all moving pretty freely in their suits. The suits were pretty stiff on the wallet. Even with the quantity discount, they came in over two-fifty apiece; but my workers' attendance proved the decision had been a good one. And there was the benefit that hadn't occurred to any of us. Mason gave time off to anyone who wanted to participate in the Hunt.

Today, at the Old Gym, it was plain to see that the Young Men's game table was piled way higher than the Old Men's. Most everyone at the party tonight will be younger, too. They're the ones who can really see that the old ways are just that, meant for people unwilling to grow. I may be getting up there, but I've still got room. I'm not that attached to the Old Gym.

Tonight will be the first time most folks will see this place, and though the construction scents of drywall dust, adhesive compounds, and paint still linger, Mason's new recreation building welcomes you in like an old friend waiting for you to come home. He's been keeping the reason for this place a big secret until just the right moment, spilling it only on the invitations we sent out for tonight's big bash. The only people allowed in have been construction and Chuck Trost, who did some special work for Mason on one of the walls—and now, with only a few hours to go, Fiction. With the way *ee-awk* spreads around here, though, just about anyone with an ear could have gotten a description—something Mason's been counting on.

The main floor is decked out with fifty tables, all in swooped crepe-paper tablecloths and streamers. A few people dot the room, running like chickens in these last couple of hours beforehand, setting up centerpieces on the tables. Pink Floyd plays low over the sound system, those bluesy moans of "The Great Gig in the Sky" soaking into my skin, making me almost tired.

Fiction arranges and rearranges the bar, shuffling bottles and swaying with the music. Our boots echo through the nearly empty building. Above us, my boy pores over the electronics, adjusting headphones around his ears, in the glassed-in area that will be this evening's deejay booth.

"What's he doin' up there?" Mason asks.

"Two-Step? He's deejaying tonight. I figured he could use the cash as much as anyone else. Besides, it'll keep him out of trouble. He usually stays with Fiction when I'm working, but, you know, she's gonna be here."

"I love that song," Mason says at the sounds of shuffling currency opening the next song on the album, "Money," waving his hand at me. He shakes his arm wildly at my boy, who finally spots him and quickly turns the volume down. Mason raises his thumbs and waves his arms harder until my boy cranks it up, vibrating champagne glasses.

I saw the group on that tour. Behind them, above the colored lights and dry ice hiding the band, a giant circular movie screen projected hypnotic images throughout the show; but as the coin and cash-register rhythm vibrated the auditorium through the opening bars, the screen turned into a giant coin, flipping and falling into a huge room full of coins. Dollar bills floated by as well, as the band started to jam the song proper. A factory assembly line came into view on the screen: an endless row of albums rolled off the presses ready for shipping to adoring fans everywhere.

I heard somewhere that the physical vinyl discs that records were pressed on cost somewhere under twenty-five cents to manufacture. The rest of the price tag was straight-out profit for distribution among all the names on the contract. And as the years had gone on, and compact discs replaced vinyl, I heard something else: that compact discs cost even less than vinyl to produce; but since they have a longer life span, and people won't be buying third and fourth copies to replace scratched copies—as I had done with my favorite albums, this one included—the higher price was for the estimated loss of duplicate sales.

I used to think for the longest time that this was just a bunch of bull-shit, that records couldn't possibly cost that little; but now the story seems closer to a generous lie. Watching Mason's first major shipment of American and Canadian cigarettes come in was like watching that movie all over again, knowing the gap between what he paid and what he charged was nearly as much as what the record-industry pirates had made, and he could still offer a deep enough discount to drive out any competition. And the plans he's going to reveal tonight are big—so big he can hardly wait for the great thaw. If he could have paid someone to rush the winter, he'd do just that.

Fiction nods at us with the beat. The music throbbing as loudly as it does, none of us even attempt conversation, and instead share the synco-pated rhythms briefly, and then we wave and head for the back stairway.

At this end of the gallery sit Mason's two offices. The first, his public office, is filled with all promotional junk from tobacco companies. He reaches two Marlboro mugs from the wall above the coffee machine and fills them. Handing one to me, he eases himself into the leather chair behind the desk. I gently sit on the matching couch, not wanting to crease it. The entire time, I swear the coffee will leap from my mug and force itself into the fibers of his creamy, pale-purple carpeting. This kind of thing happens any time I am around swank—not that I'm around it much.

"The caterers here yet?"

"Yup, went over the checklist myself. Enough for five hundred, just like you ordered. Don't you think that's a little high, Mason? Who do you expect to show?"

"Five hundred. Half the reservation. Shit, I'm hoping we run out. You know what that'll mean." We both oversaw the invitations personally, dis-tributing one to every household on the reservation, even one to Bud Tunny. As Mason became more successful, he gained a selective invisibility. Over the last month, whenever he's gone grocery shopping, some people we've known our whole lives began looking right through him, even if they were reaching for the loaf of bread right next to the one he just grabbed, or scop-ing out the same cuts of meat for supper. Some were obvious, and he didn't bother waving to those, but others he spoke to—and it was as if the store had somehow absorbed whatever sound he made, swallowing his hellos and his comments on the high price of beef. This hasn't happened to me, yet, but given some of the responses to my plow, I may be disappearing shortly.

When the doors open tonight, we'll watch closely to see who crosses the threshold. This cold might keep some away, though. The invitation made special note that Mason rented several vans to shuttle people in, so they wouldn't have to risk DWIs. This was another of my suggestions. The cops'll surely be keeping a special eye on the reservation borders this evening. Of course, folks still have the option to drive if they so desire—there's parking aplenty. All anyone has to do who doesn't want to drive, though, is step to the end of their driveway at around ten to six, and one of the vans will be by shortly. Or they can call ahead and request a pickup, something a number of people have done. So a little more than two hundred folks are already guaranteed to show, but they're the obvious ones: employees and relatives.

><

TWO HOURS LATER, THE LINES ARE DRAWN. FOLKS COME ROLLING IN, STOMPING the winter from the bottom of their boots and rushing to reserve places. Some lay coats on the backs of chairs at tables near the buffet—others, nearer the bar. Priorities, I guess. They all gawk, wandering through the room, admiring the centerpieces, the decorations, and the high-mount speakers for the sound system, playing low in the background again.

The big white curtain against the far wall catches some notice, but only momentarily. The room's filled with way more interesting things than a plain old curtain. Lines form almost immediately at the bar and buffet, where tables are filled with rolls and roast beef for Beef on Weck, chicken wings, pizza, shrimp cocktail, cheese platters—anything we could think of that they would not be put off by. Mason made sure the thinly sliced roast beef, horseradish, and salt-encrusted rolls are here, as well as the hot wings. He wants them knowing this event is a homegrown affair, so he included these foods invented here at home. I'm not so fancy an eater, and if he mentioned something on the caterer's list and I responded with a "what the hell is that?" the item in question was immediately crossed out.

The thing he wanted the most had, of course, been the hardest to obtain. We had a bitch of a time getting anyone to supply corn soup, as it was all tagged for the Feast, but I was able to squeeze one kettle from the mother of one of my workers, and at two hundred dollars, it was about five times more than I've ever paid for a kettle in my life. We probably could have hired someone to cook up "lazy-man's corn soup," with store-bought hominy and Liquid Smoke seasoning to add with the kidney beans and pig hocks, but folks would have known the difference. I always do. The taste of real wood-lyed corn can't be stuffed into a bottle.

"Hey! Wondering what happened to you guys. You threw this party, go on and join it," Fiction shouts from behind the bar as the stairwell door locks behind us.

"You go join it," I say, changing my direction, approaching her.

"Can't. Gotta job to do," she says, opening us a couple of Heinekens and pouring them headless and smooth into tall glasses, handing them over in her silky movements.

"*Nyah-wheh.*" I take a long pull from it. "Go on, get something to eat. You got a long night ahead of you. I'll watch this place for a few." Kissing her, I gently push her out. Mason joins me behind the bar.

"Okay. Be right back."

"Take your time." My hands tingle, still feeling the warmth of her body beneath them, still cupped to her shape, and hopping onto her bar stool, I don't let them break form. The bottom of her tip jar on the bar is lined with a couple of dollar bills and some change. Mason removes two hundred-dollar bills from his wallet, gives me a wink, and deposits them in her jar. She rushes back, carrying a plate piled with a mountain from the buffet.

"Okay, thanks, hon. It all looks so delicious. I don't know why you didn't charge for this, Mason. All the bars in the city are gettin' seventy-five, eighty bucks a couple for a spread like this."

"Go on, eat, and then come back when you're done. Take your time," he says. "Go on. Go with her."

"No, I'll stay here," I say.

"Well, listen, while you guys fight it out—here, take this. I don't think I missed anything." She hands the plate our way and examines it.

"*Nyah-wheh,* again," I say, dipping a chicken wing into the blue-cheese dressing and taking a bite, enjoying the homegrown mixture of burning spice and sharp, cold dressing.

While Fiction eats and talks with some of the other dancers, a few people come up to the bar. Most snag their free drinks, pay a quick thank-you, and rush back to their tables. A big burly guy, Gary Lou Howkowski—who, although he's half white, has the same sharp hawk nose and high cheekbones his mother and dead actor brother had—comes up and shakes Mason's hand, asks for a gin and tonic, and stays awhile, until I have finished with the others standing in line.

"You know, this is a good thing. You'd a had more folks here, too, if they wasn't afraid."

"I got about three hundred."

"Even still."

"Well, afraid of what? That I wouldn't let 'em in?"

"No, man. Afraid of the Chiefs. That's why I couldn't get my old man to come here. He still thinks I shouldn't be here. Like, I'm waiting at the road like the invitation says, and he come out to try and talk me out of it again, and we see these headlights slowing down, and the old man grabs me like this here," he says, lifting his shoulders like a marionette, "and pushes me into the bushes. It was Bud Tunny's Lincoln rolling on by. My old man recognized the Lincoln headlights." He finishes the drink and Mason makes him another.

"So, what's your point, man?"

"Bud was looking to see who was coming to this here party, that's what. My old man thinks I got something to lose if I show support for you, something he don't. My ma was Tuscarora, but my old man's white as a sheet. After she passed on a couple years ago, he's just a white man living in an Indian house. My dead movie-star brother might be the most famous man from this reservation, but none of that matters where my dad's status is concerned. Why do you think I moved back in?" I shake my head, and Gary Lou continues. "I got a voice in Council. He don't. If they try to throw him out, I can still speak in Council.

"You look around you, here. Most of these folks ain't got much to lose. A good half of 'em's not on the roll books. Those folks over there is Mohawk. Those ones is Seneca. Shit, your bartender's Onondaga. You see, they been living with the idea for years that the Chiefs could cut their electric and phones, and they can't even speak against it. You and me, though . . . if they did that to us, we could go to Council."

"I don't believe in that shit. Council don't work," Mason says, taking a long pull from his brew.

"You might not think so, but it's still pretty strong with lots of people out here. They respect the decisions. You'd do well to pay attention to Council."

"You seem to know quite a bit about it."

"Sure, my ma was always involved in Council."

"You want a job? I could use someone who knows so much."

"Nope."

"Why not? I could pay pretty good." Gary Lou shakes his head again and takes his drink from the bar.

"They already messed around with your life."

"So, I got around it. Without going to Council."

"We don't all have that kind of money. And we don't all live right next to the border. You got lucky."

"Luck don't have anything to do with my life."

"Look, I don't wanna argue with you. I just wanted to thank you for throwing such a nice party. You wanna ask someone how to beat the Chiefs, you ask your bartender."

"Huh? Fiction?"

"She's Onondaga, she's broke, and Bud hates her; but she's still got more than you."

"She's a bartender. How do you figure she's got more than me?"

"She's still got electric. I'd ask her." Fiction comes back to the bar, tipping a cardboard soup bowl to her mouth, draining the last of the corn-soup broth from it. "See ya later," Gary Lou says, walking away as Fiction gets situated between us.

"Hey, how'd you like our deal to be erased and I pay you for your bartending here tonight?"

"Nah. Look, I said I didn't want any charity. You had my windows replaced, and I bartended for free tonight—that was the deal." She's already taught him that valuable lesson. Folks don't like to be given things. Their loyalty is better gained by some kind of cooperation. With her, it was an even trade. He offered right away to replace her windows, that night at Ruby's when we'd shown back up with her news that her windows had been shot out. But she refused, until he offered her the opportunity to work it off.

The same sort of deal was worked with Chuck Trost. He couldn't offer either Chuck or Fiction jobs—they're already employed—but the exchange system worked. Now Chuck's got a top-of-the-line airbrush paint setup, if he wants to go into that as a sideline. Mason bought all the equipment and paid Chuck very well for some work he did—my truck, and some more work that'll be revealed later this evening. Fiction busies herself refilling the garnish trays, cutting slices of various fruits and plopping them into the appropriate compartment.

"You didn't even listen to my offer."

"I don't care. I said I would bartend."

"Okay, then. How about selling me some information?" I shrug my shoulders, not wanting to get involved, but I'm not about to leave, either. I know some of how she got her power back on—I helped with that one— but there's still all kinds of mysteries about her. It's like she's frozen me out of certain areas in her life. And Mason thinks I don't know any better, but I can tell he still hasn't given up on her entirely, and I don't want him finding and thawing out any of those secret places.

"What?"

"How did you get electric and phone hookups?"

"Long story. Don't you have to get back to hosting this party? You keep hanging around here and all those rumors about your drinking are gonna get way out of hand. Hey, Floyd, what can I get ya?" She turns to Floyd Page, one of the roofers who hangs out at The Den, as he comes up.

"What rumors?" Mason asks, after Floyd leaves.

"Gotcha." She smiles and pulls herself slowly away.

"Come on, we gotta go," I say to Mason before he can get any further into this. Across the room in the entryway, several members of the Niagara Falls Small Business Association and their spouses stand. They actually came.

"Ladies, gentlemen, come with me." Mason regally leads the small group up the front stairs to a suite next to the deejay booth, also overlooking the main floor. However, that suite and the double offices at the building's opposite end have one-way privacy glass installed. A similar spread covers a serving table in that room, but we had rock-lobster tails, steamed crab legs, and stuffed mushrooms added to this arrangement—all kinds of nasty shit, but I guess it's supposed to be impressive. "Please, help yourselves. I'll be back up later to join you," he informs them as I go about maintaining the main-floor party.

Throughout the evening, he spends his time going back and forth, back and forth, between the two parties—speaking with as many people as possible and dancing with a few young ladies later in the evening, when folks have generally finished eating and my boy has cranked the sound system. Toward midnight, he excuses himself for the last time from the smaller party and walks to the main floor, grabbing a microphone we've had installed there for this evening.

"Okay, okay. I've got just a couple of announcements to make, and then you can go back to dancing or eating or drinking, or however you're celebrating the coming of the new year with us. But here's how I'm celebrating. First of all, I'd like to thank you all for coming to this, the first of many events to take place at the Tuscarora Recreation Building, the T.R.B.—easy to remember—'the Tribe,' we like to call it. From next Monday on, we'll be open from noon until midnight, twelve to twelve. There's gonna be pool tables, video games, and all that kind of stuff. And we're gonna have a small grill, do things like wings and pizza, burgers and all that, so bring your appetites. And if you need a place for a big family gathering, you can reserve this one—no hassle about if you're on the roll books or not—first come, first serve, so keep that in mind.

"Starting tomorrow, though, the first of the new year, I have bigger news. I am offering health insurance to anyone from the reservation who wants it, for only five dollars a month per household. No more Nation Members Only health clinic. Applications will be handed out tomorrow at the Feast, and also during New Yah. If for some reason you don't get one, just come here to the T.R.B. and you can pick one up." Members of the crowd clap, cheer—and some deliver echoing war whoops, songs of triumph.

"Okay, okay. Just one more announcement, I promise," he continues, edgy to wrap this up, walking over to the white curtain when they've quieted a bit. "This is a little early, but I see an exciting future for our people and I want to share it with you here, tonight," he says, gripping the rip cord. "This spring, as soon as the thaw comes, we start construction on . . ." He pauses dramatically, watching the neon clock on the back wall climb to twelve, and then snaps the cord. The sheet flutters to the floor in the new year's first few seconds. ". . . Smoke Rings Smoke Shop and Fuel Island."

Exposed from behind the sheet, amid some flashy, controlled indoor fireworks, is an enormous reproduction, nearly twenty-feet high, of a painting he hired Chuck Trost to design and paint, featuring Great Turtle Island—the giant turtle Haudenosaunee legend says this continent is created on the back of. But on this turtle's back, instead of the Great Tree of Peace—a white pine with its roots growing in the four directions—oil derricks and gas pumps erupt from the shell. Directly above the turtle, concentric smoke rings float in an orderly fashion, growing smaller the higher they reach. They surround a giant, white, burning cigarette—together roughly the shape of the white pine. The eagle still floats close to the uppermost, smallest ring—as it traditionally has—looking to the horizon, watching for enemies; but this eagle is made up of the crossed gasoline-nozzle shapes. This scene all sits against a backdrop of a repeated pattern consisting entirely of the purple and white of the George Washington Covenant Wampum Belt—the treaty belt that defines the relationship between the tribal government and the outside government, the treaty that defines our sovereignty.

Two miniature spotlights illuminate the piece from below, and Mason's silhouetted and back-lighted figure is dramatic, standing out sharply against the image of the large beaded figures holding hands in solidarity that make up the wampum belt. We tested endless positions with him and the lights the day before and, finding this one the most effective, laid masking tape X's on the places his feet should stand.

His audience gets their initial peek at the logo for approximately five seconds before the power goes out in the entire building. The turtle and the smoke tree are the last things most see for a few minutes in the orange afterglow of the spots, as we hear gunshots from various places—reservation fireworks. Mason shouts for people to hang on while he finds out what happened, but I'm already on it. This might be the last event the Recreation Building ever puts on. Has it really come to this? Probably less than a minute passes in the dark before I reach the auxiliary generator and fire her up. The lights are back on before Mason can reach the restricted stairwell. Off the rez, these would have just gone on automatically when the lights went out, but we didn't have to build to code, so this was one of Mason's shortcuts.

He scratches at the lock and I release it from my position on the other side. I ask him to come outside.

"Okay, sorry about that. The spots just blew a fuse; I think we got it. C'mon! It's New Yah! New Yah!" he yells to the crowd before we walk out. Some people shout "New Yah!" back, and the party picks up a bit again. I motion for Two-Step to get things moving, and my boy responds with an appropriately lively tune.

"C'mere. I got the generator going, so the building should be all right for the rest of the night. Put this on and come and have a look." Mason takes the snowsuit and slips it on as we step outside.

"Wow. How'd you get this down from the office so fast?"

"I didn't. I don't have a key to your office. That's my suit." We cross the parking lot to the far side of the shop, the beaded black leather jacket Fiction made for me keeping me only marginally warm. A small, isolated lightning storm takes place on the far side of the shop, throwing off blue highlights from behind its dark silhouette. "Here, look. The old trick— someone shot out the transformer." The blasted metal construction still sputters arcs of blue in the dark. The smoke shop sits in darkness, occasionally visible in a particularly bright spark blast. "We're gonna be out of outside power for at least a couple days, but I think the generator should hold until then. You know, you might want to see if someone wants to work. I know you were gonna shut down so everyone could go to the Feast, but I think you might ask. You shouldn't leave this place unguarded."

"Here, man, take this. You're gonna freeze." He climbs out of the suit and hands it over.

"Oh, jeez. What are you, fuckin' crazy?"

"Take it."

"Well here, take this, then." The leather jacket isn't much, but it's better than nothing. "You know, if you woulda just kept the damn thing on, we'd be in the building by now." We run back to the building, nearly falling with every step.

"How many of your guys sober enough to be safely armed tonight?" he asks, slapping at his arms and legs in the back hallway, trying to jump-start his oil-thick blood flow.

"Jeez . . . three, tops. Don't forget, they been at it since six. That's a while."

"Well, get 'em, and meet me upstairs in ten minutes." He tries to fix his hair to look presentable, heads up to the suite, and excuses himself from the businessmen's party, telling them he hopes they've enjoyed themselves, and that he'll be in contact, soon . . . blah, blah, blah. He runs the length of the gallery and grabs his snowsuit from his office, fumbling it on as he clomps down the stairs. He enters the main room and finds the microphone.

"Okay. Now, listen up. Everything's fine. Party as long as you want. But

I thought you should know that, ah . . . that someone shot out the transformer for this whole place. Seems like that other side, and you know who I mean by that . . . well, it seems that they don't want you to have a recreation building. That's all I can think. I guess we got to get ourselves a real eagle to watch for our enemies. But they ain't gonna stop us. All it means is more jobs. Since we don't have that eagle yet, I'm gonna need to hire some with eagle eyes. I'm gonna need some security folks, plain and simple, because you deserve to have a place you can celebrate in and have a good time in without worrying. So, in a couple days, come on down if you want a job. I'd ask you right now, but I don't have enough of these here snowsuits, and it's too damn cold to ask people to go out there without the right kind of protection. So, uh, thanks again for making tonight a success." He sets the microphone down, and Two-Step turns the music back up. During his speech, I've been making stops in the crowd. When he's done, we run back to the staircase.

Four of my men wait at the top of the stairs. They've all gone to their lockers and retrieved their suits. "Remind me to get you a key to this," Mason says, unlocking the office. He won't remember that tomorrow, but he'd better remember to hand my jacket back before the night is over. He seems to have forgotten he's wearing it, but Fiction glared at me when he wore it to make his announcement. He hands us each a rifle from a rack he released from its secret panel, I assume, when he got his suit. I had no idea he even had secret panels built into the offices. The idea is just so secret agent–like, so childish.

"Okay, there's six of us. What's the best way to cover this whole place with just us?"

"Probably four on this building: two on the roof, one at each door. That leaves two of us for the shop. Those two will just have to move around more. But first, we should get the shop generator going, or your pipes are gonna freeze," I offer.

"Okay, but no light over there. You guys stay here. Me and Red'll go over to the other place. If they're gonna go after anything, it's gonna be the smokes. I can't imagine they'd do anything to the people. Roof access is over there." He points to metal rungs mounted on the wall as we run down the stairs.

"Hey, wait. Here." I hand the spotlights to one of the guys. "Run an extension cord to the roof and shine these out into the fields, just in case."

Some men from the party approach me near the door. They want to help tonight, claiming they're sober enough and want to see "the tribe" survive. I must give them a weird look, because they clarify they're talking about the T.R.B. Man, he is persuasive. They've already adopted this nickname he gave the place just a few minutes ago. They step outside with me and walk to the shop. Shivering while Mason unlocks the door, they are easily convinced that waiting is a smart idea. The dedication it took for them to even come forward is good enough for right now, but frostbit loyalists aren't worth shit.

The spots, so brilliant in the room, look like flashlights suffering from dying batteries in the night sky. The men on the ground point to them and then change their direction, heading toward the parking lot. A few minutes later, three 4-wheel-drive trucks leap out of the back lot and tear through the frozen field, shining their own hunting spotlights across the frigid ground. Their lights reveal two snowmobiles sitting together near the field's far end.

One peels off through the woods, the trucks digging down in pursuit. The other one seems to have some trouble, its driver shaking the machine in some ridiculous attempt to get it started. At the trucks' approach, the snowmobile's driver and rider jump off and run deep into the woods, the trucks still in pursuit.

"Come on, let's go. Where's the Phoenix parked?" Mason says, lifting the roof hatch and crawling in.

"What? Where? Come on, Mason," I try, staying firm on the roof, trying to hang on to him with reason. "What about up here? Those guys can handle things just fine."

"I'm not missing out on all the fun." He pauses. "Red, I'm going—with or without you. Now which is it?" He reaches inside his snowsuit and pulls my truck's key from the leather jacket he hasn't yet returned, as he disappears down the hatch. What can I do?

By the time I reach the ground and have the door locked behind me, Mason has pulled up in the Phoenix. Minutes later, we're off cutting through the field, shattering the ice in frozen ruts.

Approaching the abandoned vehicle, Mason slows the truck to a halt and hops out, grabbing his rifle. He pulls the trigger, shooting the snowmobile's gas tank. The explosion lights the entire field, now empty of any vehicles except those on our side. Our side—jeez, listen to me. The other trucks move deeper into the wild. Mason's face is a hideous red in the light, bunched in a mean-spirited laughter—a face I don't know and really don't want to—and for a few seconds I am away from this all, back junking, having only to trust my own abilities and actions. I open my mouth to speak, but have nothing to say. The early January wind jumps in and sends sharp needles from my sensitive teeth straight up into my brain, so intense I have to screw my eyes shut for a few seconds until the feeling passes. When I open my eyes, the fire is dying down, and Mason is walking back to the truck, his usual face returned. "Let's go," he says, climbing into the passenger's side as if we were doing nothing more than running an errand. "I got a party to finish hosting."

>‹

LATER, IN THE DARK ON THE SMOKE SHOP'S ROOF, AND BACK IN MY OWN JACKET, I watch those loyal headlights bounce around in the fields—eagles flying in the fiercest of weather—and I wonder exactly what they are loyal to. Mason walks back this way across the almost empty lot. It's after two, and the party is breaking up. He joins me, and we watch the last few cars leave. Fiction has gotten a ride home from someone else. I don't even know who. I'm probably going to be here all night.

"I bet there won't be any talk at the Feast tomorrow of snowmobiles or wandering in the woods. And I wonder who might be showing up claiming some minor frostbite from the Hunt," Mason laughs, and he lights a Havana, the smoke mixing with his steaming breath in the subzero night. Though no one from the Young Men's team will make that claim, or have a need to, there is nothing to laugh at in the possibility of someone freezing to death over electricity.

>‹

CHAPTER 9 Winter Garden

Fiction Tunny

THE NEWS THESE KIDS BRING IS INADVERTENT, UNINTENDED, AND IT'S IN THEIR cold faces and hands, not their voices—the expected eruptions through snow crust, tender new shoots of life—that I discover part of what this new year is bringing me. I haven't heard of any collisions happening last night, but that event would not have been an incredible surprise, particularly on New Year's Eve. This roadside Russian roulette is a newer tradition, tacked on to a more long-standing reservation dance.

In the old days, kids pounded their way through the deep New Year's snow, making sure even those old timers, the ones refusing to mark their days by the outside world's calendar, would know the new year had arrived. Normally, those elders wouldn't care for such things, you know—like George Washington's birthday, or Columbus Day—but this was just a little bit different. Somewhere along the way, the Midwinter Feast got moved around a little—shifted, even as some of us might not have wanted, to line up closer to schedules that were already beginning to reshape us. All those big holidays that ended up affecting so many people's work schedules was part of it: that week at the end of December when a lot of factories just shut right on down until the first of the year—stuff like that likely caused the shift. Who knows?

Anyway, so the kids' shouting also announced that the Feast would be starting in just a bit, though really, they'd have known all along, what with the Hunt and everything else going on for the Feast, especially all that cooking. The exchange—the cookie for the news—must have grown right out of Feast preparations. After folks out here discovered New Year's Eve parties, sometimes the kids carried news of ends, telephone-pole deaths, as well as their news of beginnings. Who could deny these kids, withstanding the cold to ensure their message got through, something from the kitchen? Not me, anyway.

This first bunch of voices arrives long before the actual kids they belong to, loud and happy, hit the steps. The clock on my night table can't be right. The sky outside my window is shrouded in darkness, so it can't be noon, and no kids come for New Yah at midnight. Me, I was glad for the dark, anyway—my eyes were probably going to be a little sensitive today.

Well, if those kids want to go out in the dark, they'll get served in the dark, too. It just can't be midnight. That New Year's Eve party went at least until three or four, and I stayed to the very end, way after the transformer was shot out.

My shabby quilts would not do any Indian proud, so they're left in the discretion of my bedroom, and outside of them, my sweats don't seem to insulate in the least. With no Indian blankets for me, the thermostat gets my attention before the kids draw me back with their greeting. "New Yah! New Yah!" I shout, opening the door to a chorus of the same. These kids clustered on my steps are anonymous bundles of layered winter clothing, secret agents, only their eyes exposed through slits in their warmth. The car in my driveway, though, clearly belongs to Minnie Crews, one of the neutrals—those people who could still New-Yah at any house on the reservation. Anyone who cared to show up at my house would be served, mind you, but the numbers'll be low this year, for certain.

When I was a little girl, my mother and I had two New Year's rituals we never missed. She was never a drinker of any sort, so on New Year's Eve, we used to drive into Niagara Falls and visit the Festival of Lights, a Chamber of Commerce gimmick to sucker tourists into our shitty winters. I mean, really, who on earth would want to come and see the falls in December, its mist pluming up and coating your body and car with spray that, if you stayed still long enough, might freeze you solid, right to the spot? So the city, every winter, came up with this idea to string up thousands of colored lights all over the south end of the city, surrounding the park with a warm glow in the middle of our snowstorms. You have to admit, it's gorgeous, but mostly it's too damned cold to walk around in it much—better if you drive around seeing the lights changing the nighttime snow to all the colors of the rainbow. The whole section of the city is transformed into a giant piece of beadwork—lighted beads resting on a soft, white blanket of velvet.

We would drive the broad circuit of the few blocks where everything was concentrated, catching glimpses, driving as slowly as we dared, trying to avoid getting rear-ended, and then we'd walk the few blocks in the snow after parking in one of the free lots that were not so close to the attractions, watching the lights grow from a few lonely strands to the wild figures of deer and angels, soldiers and sleighs, all made of light, brilliant ghosts of our dying city.

Eventually, we would arrive at the Winter Garden, for hot chocolate and whatever other treats we might be able to afford that year, waiting for midnight. I have no idea who came up with this idea, and now it just has "stupid" written all over it, but no one could see it then. The Winter Garden is this huge four-story building made of glass and I-beams—a giant, stylish greenhouse in the middle of downtown, where, as the name suggests, plants flourish all winter long, even all kinds of bizarre ferns that don't live around here naturally, relocated and left to thrive or die in this glass tower. Steps and elevators are built into it, so you can walk around inside and admire this odd jungle, feel like you're out in the natural world; but if you look—and really not even all that carefully—you can see the landscaping, the manipulation, the pruning, cutting things back so they do not grow wild and unsightly. It is indeed a garden, and not a jungle at all. Birds get fooled all the time and somehow find their way in there. I wonder if any ever find their way back out, or just bang their bodies against the glass until they give up or die.

As midnight approached on New Year's Eve, we would ride the elevator up to the third or fourth floor, along with a million other people it seemed, to watch the fireworks being shot off over the falls to welcome in the year. After that, the place cleared out pretty quickly, and if you stayed a little later, which we did one year because my mother wasn't feeling so hot, spending her first hour of the new year in the ladies' room, you got to see the ghosts leave. At exactly one in the morning, as we made our way through the streets back to our old car, all those thousands of lights suddenly switched off, leaving us in the dark, our feet crunching the snow—the only sound except for the music from bars where people were still celebrating late into the night.

I liked the fireworks and all, but the whole time we were there, every year, I was on the lookout for Big Red Harmony. He was a married man back then, and certainly off-limits and way older than me, but he was always a fiercely handsome man. Bert's group used to do a special New Year's Eve dance performance every New Year's Eve at The Turtle, the local Indian museum—this really cool building shaped like a turtle, right across the street from the Winter Garden. Sometimes, when the dancers were on break, they would run over to the Garden to get something to eat from one of the vendors, or a smoke, or who knows what else; but sometimes they just wanted to get out of The Turtle for a little while. I believed then they were probably sneaking a drink, too, but that was before I knew much about Bert and her group, and that no one could ever drink on the day of a dance or they would be asked to leave the group, and before I knew this New Year's Eve performance was her idea, her way of keeping her dancers safe and alive to see another year.

I started admiring Red at about the age of ten or eleven, and though I never thought we would wind up together, it was great to see him in the Winter Garden. We never spoke, back then. My mother, she had convinced me that all of Bert's dancers were living in a pagan house, which she said was the house next door to the devil's own home; but I wanted to get close, just the same.

Only a glass partition separated Red and me, and on that other side my reflection stood next to him, almost as if that other me, the real one, who was clever and smart and maybe just a little bit older, could strike up a conversation with him and maybe be his Rabbit Dance partner; but then he would move and pass right through my reflection, yet another ghost, and I'd be alone again, waiting for my mother to feel better. Stupid, I know, but what do you want from a twelve-year-old girl who went to church on Sunday and Youth Group on Wednesday nights?

He must have noticed me even then, though. I about died the first time he called our house, a couple of years later. I don't know what I was thinking—probably something dumb like he was divorcing and was interested in a date, or something like that—but of course it was that I had reached baby-sitting age, and he and Bev were in a need. My mother was very iffy about it at first, making me take my Bible with me in my bag and forcing me to promise I'd read some of the more exciting stories from my old Children's Bible Stories Picture Book to Red's boy, reminding him the stories were true, first.

We traded stories, Roger and me. I told him about the Ark, and the Garden of Eden, and even a toned-down version of the Tower of Babel, and Lot's wife—these were the kinds of Bible stories I liked best—and some weren't in the picture book, so I told these to him in my own best way of making them exciting. In turn, Roger introduced me to the dancing life he'd grown up in, and since that first year, I had always looked forward to New Year's Eve in the Winter Garden, where my mute reflection no longer had to do the talking for me.

And during those years, the morning after our trips to the Festival of Lights and the Winter Garden, my mother still got me up early on the first morning of the year and took me out all alone to go New-Yahing, though plenty of neighbors every year offered to pile me in with their crew of shouters. Every January first, she idled in our old car while I stomped my way through dense, unplowed paths to doorways opened way before I could shout my announcement that the new year had come; but I was rewarded for my news all the same—some cookie, cupcake, or piece of fruit neatly dropped in the sack I carried. The early January winds were always so sharp and cutting, though, I doubt very much my small-child voice was actually heard by anyone, except through those already-opened doors. My mother's reason for insisting I went solo eventually became more clear when we drove past my father's driveway each year—the only door I never faced, open or shut—as if my mother somehow felt he needn't be aware of the passage of years.

"C'mon in. Here, stand over here by the heat and I'll get you guys something." The kids yank their layers of gloves off and hold them over the floor registers while I reach for the batch of Forgotten Cookies, touching the fragile meringue sweets, nearly glowing in the early light, to make sure they've come out all right. Bert's specialty—this year was the first time I've tried them alone. She always liked their simplicity, the fact that she could fire up her old oven, throw those cookies in, shut the oven off and not have to worry over them until the next morning's first New-Yahers showed up on the doorstep. "What time is it, anyway? Aren't you guys a little early?"

"Nope. Quarter to seven. We been up since six, but our ma wouldn't let us go out 'til six-thirty. Uh, Fiction, when is this heat supposed to come on?"

one of the kids asks, standing away from the register, delivering that unexpected news.

I drop tinfoil-wrapped cookies in their sacks and lower my hand to the register. I ask one of the taller boys to turn on a light and check the thermostat, but even as the boy reaches for the switch, it clicks—my electricity is off. Of course the thermostat won't work without electricity. All that gas and no way to utilize it. "You guys see any downed lines on the way over here?" The kids shake their heads simultaneously as silence is all that comes from my telephone receiver. "So much for calling the electric company."

These particular kids, carrying only the news of the new year, stand around uncomfortably, having no idea how to abandon me with grace, but anxious to do so. The oven requires no thermostat, and even the grumbling of gas igniting warms me—I am that cold. "Yes!" I shout. "Hey, would one of you guys have your ma call the electric company for me and tell them they need to send a crew out?" My hands float inside the open oven.

"Sure," they say in unison and pile out the door. I have a candle mounted and in a hurricane globe in less than a minute. The thermometer reads a little over forty degrees and now slowly climbs in the oven heat. The lights must have gone off sometime in the middle of the night for the temperature to have gotten in the thirties. The living-room clock confirms that the electricity went off at exactly twelve o'clock—midnight.

A knock at my door accompanies my boiling tea water a few minutes later. No shouts, can't be kids. Minnie's car sits in the driveway.

"Hi. Thanks for calling, but you didn't have to come back. You got kids to cart around the rez." Her car is empty, though. "Where are your kids? I'm okay; go on with them. I got the oven on. What? You want 'one for the driver'?" I laugh—that old lie isn't one of mine. Just about every kid scams more cookies, claiming that.

"You mind if I come in? Got something to tell you, and you probably ain't gonna like it."

"Sure. C'mon in. Don't worry about the snow. It'll melt. Well, maybe not today. You want some tea? I can't make coffee. All's I got is a Mr. Coffee and, you know, it needs electric." Minnie, she stands near the oven, rubbing her hands in front of it. "So, what'd they say? They won't be able to get anyone out here for the downed line 'cause of the holiday? I'll tell you right away, that's bullshit. It's mandatory that they keep repair crews on." I don't actually know if this is true, but it sounds as if it should be. "At least on call."

"There ain't any downed line, Fiction," Minnie says. "And it ain't a shot-out transformer, either. When I called, Niagara Mohawk told me that the Nation demanded two months ago, in writing, that your electricity be turned off. Effective January first. They said their hands were tied. That they had to go by whatever decisions get made out here, and that you had to take it up with the Nation if you want your electric back on." Minnie, she pours boiling water into the two cups and fixes the tea as I stare at her. "I don't know anything about it. I haven't gone to a Council meeting in a long time. But I know they been having a lot of them the last few months. I just figured they had to do with Rollin' in Dough Rollins. Coulda been at one of them meetings. Here," she says, handing me the cup. "Is there anything I can do?"

"Thanks. Yeah. Actually there is. Go on and finish taking your kids New-Yahing—you know, that's a mother's job—but then come back and pick me up at noon for the Feast. If you could do that, I would really appreciate it."

"Well, yeah, of course I can do that; but Fiction, why would you want to go to the Feast? Some of those people just cut off your power." Minnie halts for a minute. "They got your phone, too, didn't they? Even more so, why do you want to go?"

"Just . . . If you can just do that, if you can just be here at noon, I would totally appreciate it. Oh, one more thing. Can I borrow your watch 'til you get here? I don't have one, and all my clocks are—"

"Sure, sure. See you then." The watch says I have a few hours, as Minnie's car drifts off into the morning, and that sound is eventually lost in the voices of new kids at my door.

Red, he drives on over here around eight-thirty, after calling my number only to be informed it had been disconnected. He offers to stay, but there's too much to do in the minutes ticking by. His expression strikes me like a gut punch, but I help him on with the jacket I recently finished making for him and gave him for Christmas. It's a motorcycle leather jacket that came into my hands from the Salvation Army—the "Dig-digs"—for twenty bucks.

The intricate beadwork patterns on it are all mine. Once I learned how to use the leather needle, I finished it off with a large version, nearly covering the entire back, of his Curbside Phoenix sign—with one major alteration. Here, the phoenix is clearly a Snipe—Red's clan. He should have that connection with his real family, though he seems to feel like flying from them most of the time. At first, the jacket was a practice piece, for learning under Ruby, but my constant working and reworking of the beading left it with tighter and more precise beadwork than even Ruby has ever done herself. This is what she claims, now; this is not me talking out of my hat. The snipe's wings were literally made up of layers of beaded feathers—its belly a little thicker than its neck, its legs spindly yet sturdy. This bird could fly.

With those lessons and Ruby's enthusiasm, I was ready for my most serious piece of beading. The idea first bloomed in my head in October, just before the first frost, but I couldn't begin on it until I was ready. I hadn't a clue as to when that state of readiness would come, nor how I would recognize it when it did happen, but I would not stop for anything. It began forming itself in the copy machine I used to make my Polaroid reproductions of the hospital photos. Something was right, the second it happened.

WHEN THE COPIES CAME WARM AND TOASTY FROM THE HUMMING MACHINE'S mouth that day, the purples of my bruises had been enhanced by the copier. They were almost pretty. There was something unusual about them. The clerk, he asked me if there were something wrong with my copies, if I would like them done over. No, I told him, but then asked him how much enlargements were. I could hardly afford it, but sacrificed my Sunday-night bingo money and had the enlargements done anyway.

In the new copies, where each photo was singled out, the colors retained the peculiar vividness the machine somehow encouraged, and the patterns were now definitely there. I used Bert's old X-acto knife to release them from their white, filmy borders, eventually pinning them randomly to the broad piece of corkboard Bert had mounted in the trailer's kitchen, where she had always posted competitions.

The enlargements stayed up, and eventually the patterns in the photocopies emerged, becoming clearer and more defined even as those actual patterns faded from my body and mind like an overcast summer tan. In October, under the light of the kitchen fluorescent ring at my new spot on the corner of Snakeline and Torn Rock, the patterns fell into place, almost as if I had tried on glasses for the first time, ending years of a hazy world. Through my rearrangements, shuffling my paper body like a wild contortionist, the skin seemed to no longer be my back, or my arms or legs, or my torso, but instead merely the background for a bed of rich, purple roses.

Bert's traditional-regalia fabric box was filled with bolts of different colored calico; satin ribbon—some already sewn across swatches of the calico; partially completed ribbon clothing; folded sheets of velvet, saved as the background material for beaded yokes, gauntlets, and crowns; and old dress patterns folded in an envelope buried at the box's bottom. From that point, I came home straight from work every day, hitching a ride or walking when I was out of luck. The seven miles were far, particularly after the snow began falling, but the roses relentlessly bloomed against the winter background, keeping my attention at least partially on the road, watching for my father's Lincoln. Every afternoon, my sewing improved, the same way my limited pre-lesson beading had, as I sewed and ripped out the thread over and over again, until the expensive velvet would not be in danger of my botching it.

Designing a patchwork on one of the dress patterns, I divided it up into equal-sized parts to accommodate the velvet swatches. It was unorthodox, but so was the reason for the dress in the first place. When the bodice was finished, a perfectly shaped dress stood before me on the form; but the great number of seams lent it an oddly clinical look, almost as if I had been divided up as a diagram at the butcher training school—by the best cuts of meat.

The white grease pencil from Bert's box—my box—furrowed the velvet as I transferred the patterns from the enlargements at approximately the places where my body was now leaning toward forgiveness. To forgive was one thing, but you can be sure I won't be forgetting—ever.

None of the other cans of Bert's UNFINISHED BUSINESS beadwork had contained a three-dimensional floral piece instantly recognized as Haudenosaunee work. They must have all been sold, or given away, or stolen. There were no patterns to dissect and follow. Though the gauntlet's pattern had been one of roses, they'd been profile roses, designed as if the roses were lying down against the black velvet background. None had been head-on, full-face roses, and that was what I needed; and none had included the thorns so necessary to roses. And that was how I ended up spending the first half of my winter among Ruby Pem's terminal chairs.

By the time Red's jacket was finished, the floral patterns were mine, and my fingertips were callused and nimble. I was ready and armed to sow my father's garden.

Red's jacket was completed in the second week of December, and the minute the last bead had been secured, that black velvet dress came out of its box, and I pierced the line with a seed bead, planting the first of many deep purple beads of varying shades, from "Eggplant" to "Wampum Shell." When my father had blown out my windows, and it had been him, he'd torn down the enlargements from my corkboard and had taken them with him. First he cultivated them, then made them bloom, and finally he picked my roses. It didn't matter. They were already grease-penciled on the velvet, but even that didn't matter. The roses clearly took shape in their proper places along the bodice of the light-absorbing black material. They were a hardy sort, blooming again in the middle of winter. My father's rose garden was of the perennial variety. It would keep coming back.

➤←

AS MY RIDE PULLS IN THE DRIVEWAY, I SLIP INTO MY DRESS OF BRUISED ROSES— the final beads, some "Ivory Bone," in place only an hour ago. In late December, my necessary thorns finally came. Red's leather jacket had been decorated with two dozen small, cylindrical chrome spikes screwed into the jacket's epaulets, twelve for each shoulder. They were screw-on spikes and pretty easy to remove, and the scarred leather was now covered with beaded eagles, one facing each way, to watch for any trouble Red might encounter.

The spikes, they sat in a bowl on my counter for a while, winking in my overhead fluorescent ring. One day not long after, working on the dress, I wandered into the kitchen for a cup of coffee, and the spikes' resemblance to thorns grew obvious. I quickly mounted them strategically throughout the dress, being careful not to secure them anywhere near where I sat. Over these, it was pretty easy to sew small sheaths of calico fabric, and then later, the "Ivory Bone" beads in concentric patterns on top; and now the thorns, while beaded, stand tall on my dress. Though the wind cuts harshly across my recently cleared yard, my deep black dress absorbs the January snow's void as I cross to Minnie's car without a coat.

"Thanks. I really appreciate this. How'd your kids do? They get a lot of goods?" I brush snow from my dress.

"Yeah. They did all right. Better than some, I suspect," Minnie says, pulling onto the road, keeping her eyes out the windshield to the horizon, or locked on the idiot numbers of her odometer, clicking her life forward one-tenth of a mile at a time. We reach the corner of Snakeline and Dog Street in silence. Several houses away from the Old Gym, Minnie pulls her car into a driveway and turns around, finally idling on the roadside. "There you go. I'm not going to the Feast this year, so I thought I'd turn around here. Avoid the jam. Not too far away, is it?"

"You're not even gonna ask, are you?" Her eyes remain fixed on the horizon. "Even in the privacy of your own car. Doesn't some part of you want to know?"

"I got four kids, Fiction. They're gonna have to live out their lives here, too, you know. C'mon, I gave you a ride." Minnie, she steps on the brake and drops the car into drive.

"Thanks. You know, your four kids are gonna have to live out their lives here, too." I repeat, sliding from the seat and into the road. A number of people pull into the parking lot as I reach it, and either wait for me to pass, or rush their asses in ahead of me if they think they can make it.

The expanse of the main gym is filled with tables and chairs, coats resting on chair backs, reserving seats for people already in line. Those on one side are trendy, flashy, will probably be out of style by the time next winter rolls around, and on the other lie dour, heavy woolen overcoats, faded through years of heavy storms. Last night's party had none of this division, the older people who decided to show joining in everything. It is only here, under the Nation's watch, that they don't dare to associate with anyone from Mason's side.

"Trish!" Two-Step, he waves from a table toward the back of the room, where he helps Ruby remove her winter coat. "What's up with the dress?" he asks when I reach speaking range. Ruby, she glances up and then instructs her grandson to get her a plate, telling him specific dishes to avoid.

"Is this what I have taught you?" she asks when the boy is out of hearing range. I nod. "It looks good—tight beads, no crooked places. Thorns. Original. The beadwork should have some of the beader's soul in it. But, you know, the velvet is supposed to only be for special things."

"This is special. One of a kind."

"All right, then. No one can decide that but you. You gonna sit with us?" I join her with my back to the wall.

My father brings Ruby an enormous slice of strawberry-rhubarb pie. "Hello, Auntie," he says. "I have brought this special for my Clan Mother; my wife made it with your sweet tooth in mind." Ridiculously formal, attempting to mimic respect. He repeats several bits of mundane Feast gossip, all the while keeping his back toward me, as if I don't exist. Throughout the meal, anyone who walks past our table takes my father's cue, looking elsewhere—at their shoelaces, the flyspecked dusty skylights, some piece of food spilled on their shirts—anywhere but at me.

Even at the Feast's most dense and hectic period in the middle of the afternoon, when people stand freezing on line in the doorways, waiting to find an empty seat elsewhere, our table remains empty, aside from us, until the evening nears and the last group of people are eating. Big Red and Mason, they step in and join our stark table as the outside sky darkens.

><

LATER, AFTER THE TABLES HAVE BEEN BROKEN DOWN AND CLEARED, AND REPLACED with metal folding chairs, my father, he paces in front of the crowd and holds out his arms, trying to get the group's attention. A young man in the front row stands and sends a piercing whistle around his callused fingers, jagged teeth, and chapped lips, and out into the huge building. My father, he begins the Debate, as the group settles in, explaining his reasoning as to why the Old Men's team should hold the title of "Winning Team of the Hunt." He offers some comical statements, and everyone generally laughs in the right places. Toward the end of his First-Round Speech, he grimaces several times, clearly not wanting to introduce Mason Rollins as the captain of the Young Men's team, though to not do so would be bad form. As he makes a few last remarks, I rise and walk to the front of the room, stopping several feet to his left.

"Heh, Heh. It seems that the Young Men's team has chosen a new captain. One of their more powerful, I'd guess," he says, glancing at me at first and then just staring, his jokes drying up in his wrinkled little chicken neck.

Watching the recognition in his eyes, I step closer. "Real comical, Dad. You know," I continue, stepping into the center, crowding him out, "this was a fine Feast. Wouldn't you agree?" My question is greeted with a quiet rumbling through the crowd. It won't be so easy for them to avert their eyes, now.

"The floor does not recognize this person," my father shouts over the growing din. "Will the captain of the Young Men's team come forward so we can continue the Debate!"

"It seems to me," I begin again, looking through the crowd for Mason's approach from any direction, "that the reason we have this Feast is in part to remind us of the sort of community we are. The sort that comes together for the betterment of all of us. Sharing and giving. So you can imagine my surprise when I woke up this morning to find myself with no electric or phone.

"And then, when I called to see about a repair, I couldn't believe my ears. They told me the Nation voted to cut off all my utilities! Two months ago!"

"The Nation," my father starts, stepping in front of me, "voted that all non-Tuscarora residents, as of January first, be denied utilities, unless they are renting from a Tuscarora. It was a matter of Nation integrity. We could have all kinds of strangers just moving in here, otherwise."

"Yeah, they're lining up at the gates. Step off, Dad. I'm not done here. So, I had to come down here and see if it was true. I figured this was some sneaky act of my father's, here. But it seems to me, by the odd looks I've been getting today, or non-looks, that it wasn't just him, after all. Dionne, did you vote for this? Johnnyboy, you're a Chief. Does this sound good to you? Floyd?"

I get what I came down here to receive. It's pretty clear, by the way I've grown selectively invisible, that it wasn't just him, after all. Dionne Chambers, a young woman I served sloe gin fizzes all last night, she checks out the blue painted lines on the gym floor as if she's going to be painting them herself, real soon. Johnnyboy Martin makes little movements with his closed lips, like he's chewing a mile a minute on something, but no words come out. Floyd Page, he just looks confused, so maybe not everyone here is involved. But then I see Eddie. He won't even raise his head to meet my glance. I had at first thought that for some unknown reason, he hadn't made it here this year; but there he sits, big as life, with those Protestant cousins he's been living with since the eviction. I see it in almost all their faces.

"Then it's true. Seems like, even though you're quiet now, a lot of you have strong opinions in private meetings. Strong opinions that could have easily frozen me to death for your tribal purity. And all this time, I thought it was just your leader here. Well, since you've shared one of your shitty little secrets with me today, I'm gonna share one of mine with you. You see all these roses?" I thought this through all morning, while finishing the last of my dress thorns. I will say everything I have intended.

"These roses should be a warning to you. You see, I was forced to wear them because one of your precious Tuscarora men wasn't satisfied with a Tuscarora woman. I am the proof of the stupidity and greed in your little secret vote. I know that I'm Onondaga, even though my father is Tuscarora. And a Chief, at that!"

"I am not your father!" Bud shouts. "I am not her father," he repeats to the gathered people.

"Then why did you beat me and kick me when I called you that, while you were trying to throw me out of my own house, and off of land that was given to me by someone who trusted you to do the right thing?"

"She's making this up. This girl is crazy. I have no idea what she's talking about," he says, addressing the audience again, his eyebrows raised and his arms open, pleading.

"All of you know the first part is true, that this man was knocking my mother up with me, even while his own wife was pregnant. You all know where I inherited my storytelling skills from. You've known it for years, the same as me. And as for the second part, my father has two different times come into my home and destroyed it, smashing every lamp, shooting out my windows, and stealing photographs taken at the hospital after he beat me. But I have other copies of the pictures; I'm not that stupid. Every rose on my dress has bloomed in a place where he punched or kicked me. He wanted me to wear them on the inside, in secret, like he wants me to wear my identity, like the way you run your meetings. But I can't do that. Maybe you'd all like to see those photographs some time, maybe in an *open* Council meeting.

"You take a good look at these bruised roses, and you think about them long and hard the next time you decide you're better than the non-Tuscaroras living out here. That's a pretty risky decision, if you think he's leading you for the next seven generations. He's not fit for it. He can't even acknowledge his part in the next generation." My father walks over to his wife, who crumples on her folding chair and weeps with my truth.

"What if the Senecas thought this way, two hundred years ago? Did you all forget that someone gave you land to start off with here? What if they said, 'Okay, you can stay there, as long as you pay us rent forever, and by the way, you have no rights. We'll decide what you can and can't have'?" All the Senecas look down, not wanting troubles of their own. "And my family. We've been here from the first. My ancestors came with your ancestors through New York on your way here. You all talk about your long memories, but somehow you just forgot this? Forgot all the possibilities of people out here? Can you guarantee who your kids are going to marry? Or their kids? You think love recognizes such boundaries? You think my father's going to stop with me?"

They might be able to close their eyes today, but they're going to see these blossoms every time he encourages them to think they're better than the rest of us living out here. In that quiet place where they can't sleep, but know they have to get up for work in a couple of hours—when people tell themselves the secrets they hide in daylight—they'll know they can't guarantee their kids will marry other Tuscaroras. Or their kids' kids—or maybe nephews, or nieces, or some family member. They'll know love doesn't necessarily ask you if you're on the tribal roll or not.

And even if they choose to still be blind, theirs aren't the only eyes in this room. A lot of the men here, on both the Young Men's team and the Old Men's team, are Mohawk, Seneca, Oneida, even Chippewa who helped fill the bellies of everyone else with game; and the women in their lives, who've been cooking for this Feast nonstop this whole last week, they're going to see that any one of their kids could be wearing these roses in the future. The room is virtually still, and I leave, shattering this static moment the way my windows have been blown out, into a million irreparable shards, ready to cut deep into flesh.

In the parking lot, feet crunch the frozen snow behind me, and I half expect to be jumped, but it's only Big Red and Two-Step. "Hey, Babe," Red says, throwing his leather jacket around my shoulders, "Wow. That took a lot of . . . wow."

He brings the truck around as Two-Step helps Ruby on the steps. She invites us in to her place for a while, to get warm. Red throws two chairs in the fire and we stay for a little while, until we're sure the blaze will last her the night.

"You know, he was good when I picked him," she says, staring into the fire. "And I think he truly believes in what he's doing, as you do," she says to me. "I know that's no excuse, and I don't agree with what he's doing, but I hope you know I can't call for a dehorning unless everyone believes he's unfit for the role of Chief. And I think you know there are enough people out here who still agree with him that my decision would not really reflect their wishes.

"I hope you understand, hon." She reaches out and touches my arm, covering a rose, and I hold her fragile hand in mine. "What you did took strength. You will make out all right." I nod and, standing to leave, kiss her cheek. "I would give you a coat to wear, but I suspect you are not ready to bury your roses yet." Two-Step decides to stay the night with his grandmother, and he waves grimly in the rearview mirror as we drive out into the icy night.

A few minutes later, my porch light is visible from several houses away. I left it on last night. Red kills the headlights and pulls slowly into my driveway. He reaches behind the seat and grabs a shotgun. "Check that," he says, braking. We get out and walk around. No new prints aside from our own impress the snow around my trailer, so we enter.

Searching the trailer thoroughly and deciding we are alone, we sit together on the couch. "You suppose I really made a difference?"

"Coulda been. I still can't believe you did that. Why didn't you tell me before? I'm gonna beat the shit out of him, the first chance I get."

"No. It can't be that way. I mean, look, I argued the truth, and here— my lights are back on. I can maybe even retire this dress." I stand in front of him and lift the dress slowly from my body. Only my exposed skin lies beneath, and along every inch the deep velvet reveals, Red embraces me gently and kisses the smooth, blank places where the bruises were, as if somehow trying to heal them. Though my mother was as dark as can be, I am kind of on the fair side, and this is even more apparent in the washed-out complexion I get every winter, when the sun leaves us for months at a time around the Great Lakes. In the picture window, my skin almost glows with the dim light. Red's reflection joins mine, and this time does not walk right through it, but connects instead.

As Red nestles himself between my breasts, the telephone rings. We jump. While I am relieved to hear it working again, I have had enough for one day. "Just let the machine get it." I pull him closer, enjoying the warmth of his breath on my exposed flesh, melting down onto him. The machine engages, filling my ears.

"This isn't anywhere near over," a hoarse, indistinguishable voice whispers into my machine. Unable to stop, I stand straight up, clutching the dress in my hand, of course knowing whose voice has just been recorded. The roses bloom all over my body again, bursting forth from the inside on this first night of the year.

>‹

CHAPTER 10 Commodities

Mason Rollins

A small glass of Scotch, neat, sits on the bar. I occasionally lift it to my lips and feel its cold burn for a second or two before setting it back onto the napkin. Fiction leans against the bar, further down, talking to Floyd Page, one of the roofers I used to work with. Periodically, they both look in my direction, Fiction nodding and smiling, speaking in a nearly volumeless rumbling. The early-February afternoon sun spotlights the dusty stickiness of empty booths and stools.

"Not many tips, working this time of day, huh?" I ask across the empty floor. Fiction looks up, glances at her empty tip jar, and shrugs her shoulders, excusing herself and wandering over.

"Yeah, I know. But this way, I can keep working on my beading at Ruby's convenience. Get you something more?" The Scotch is really more of an endurance than anything else—the licorice, acid taste filming over my new-capped, perfect teeth—but it's the price of business lunches. The gin in martinis pounds my head, and this is a little better. Seems to be the drink of choice at charitable-organization awards dinners, political fundraisers, and the like, and not one person at any of them has ordered a beer, not even a Heineken.

"So, why you think your beading is so goddamned important that you give up all the tips of nighttime tending? Shit, you could probably buy all the beadwork you'd ever want with the tips you'd make on the weekends."

"Not the kind I make. Mine is magic. Didn't you see what I can do with it? I got my electric back on and my phone working, in less than twenty-four hours. My father ain't going to cross me again. You can be sure of that. The people know now. They know what kind of man he is, and . . . What are you laughing at?" She throws her bar rag at me, the dense, coarse cloth landing on the shoulder of my new black-pearl Armani cashmere. Years of drunkenness emanate from the rag—stale beer, nicotine, and saliva, soaked up from endless nights of pass-outs, husbands being abandoned by their annoyed wives until the next morning. This dense fog of my past life soaks in.

"What the fuck are you're doing? You got enough there to pay my dry-cleaning bills?" I throw the rag back at her, grab my glass, and slam it on the floor behind the bar, shattering it against the ancient hardwood. "You like using that cleaning rag, clean up *that!*" You work hard all your life to make something of yourself, and some stupid bitch still tries to drag you down.

She doesn't move as the liquid seeps into the void of the floor's cracks.

"Fuck are you lookin' at, Floyd? Least I didn't pay for my drink with an unemployment check!" Floyd shakes his head, drains his glass, and wanders toward the men's room.

"Get out. You're barred for a month, and if you don't think I can make that stick, watch me, motherfucker," Fiction says, sweeping the broken glass with a whisk broom. "You don't own everything, yet, and you definitely don't own me."

"I'll be back in here in under a week. You just watch me. This place couldn't run without the money me and my workers drop in here in a month."

"And you're proud of this?" she asks.

A blast of frigid air sears my lungs when I hit the outside, leaving my favorite bar stool rolling on its legs. She can't possibly know, but she certainly has a knack of bringing me back down, just like Bert.

My old Thunderbird has gone the way of the carrier pigeon, and my new ride has way more style. That other car could have been anyone's, but they all recognize this one, though there are costs. The sluggish purple '67 Mustang needs to be coaxed into action, my loafer gently pressing the gas further and further into ambition. The old radio is still lodged in the dash, so the space here sits heavy with static-filled talk shows, significant elements of the conversation lost in the wind. They'll be interviewing me on one of those shows, sometime. Very soon. But for now, that too-familiar odor has already seeped into the soft, dark fibers of my jacket, and in the rearview mirror, nearly at the visible spectrum, the veins in my eyes are pulling away from the whites, throbbing, growing deep red—my escape attempt hasn't worked after all.

The tenders at Indian bars, knowing the fierce drunks are their best customers, let them sleep the night off for the few hours after closing while they mop the floor, take inventory, and essentially get ready for the next business day. If the sleepers haven't stirred by six o'clock, they're usually nudged awake and shooed out the door into the coming sun.

For years, that early sunlight seared my eyes with pain a vampire must feel. That bar-rag smell often rose in my waking nostrils, my cheek stuck to some heavily urethaned table, ribs sore from being jabbed awake with a mop handle. I have seen myself in men's-room mirrors that are streaked with dried snot, have felt lovers' initials impressed on my cheeks where my face had lain heavily on their carved bar-table confessions. Every one of those mornings, the alcohol crept through even my freshly showered skin, for the rest of the day encased in the scent of hangover.

I still come to The Den, though my roofing belt's been hung up to dry for over a year. The draw here, as it always has been, is Fiction, for two entirely different reasons. She was a long-range goal for years before money came my way, and I asked her out nearly every Friday, assuming she'd be impressed with my healthy paycheck and the fact that I was willing to blow the entire thing on her if she'd just consent to come home with me—figuring the potential in my paychecks would blind her to the fact that I don't really know how to talk to people, don't know the things people talk about. But closing time or early the next morning always saw me in as shitty a mood as I'd been in since she'd left after her shift in the late afternoon, my pay still a hard and stiff bundle in my front pocket. Plenty of nights played out here filled with concentration, efforts to make her spontaneously reappear behind the bar after she'd cleared her tip jar and removed her bear claws, all dwindled to hope for just a few more minutes of opportunity.

I WAITED FOR HER EVERY NIGHT, TRYING TO PERSUADE HER TO SEE MY WAY WHILE she sipped her after-work drink. One Friday night, as usual, she sipped from a large goblet—seemed like the only such glass in the whole damned place.

"What are you drinking? I'll buy us another round." I pulled the thick wad from my pocket and peeled a twenty from the interior layers.

"Uh-uh," Fiction grunted, covering her goblet with those long, slender fingers of hers.

"Why not, *this* time?" Each time she denied me, I forced some sort of rational excuse from her, and she readily complied. Her stories were good, the seam between truth and lie folded under, invisible.

She licked a drop from the glass's rim and waved her fingers to Angie, one of the bartenders who took over after her. Angie strolled over and winked at me as Fiction asked her to reach under the bar and get her another of the usual. "I never pay for this, and discourage everyone else from drinking it. Sometimes, I even lie and say we're out—imagine that. Thanks, Ang," she said, relieving the other young woman. "Here, look at this." She thrust the bottle out toward me, her index finger pointing to a line on the label, revealing that the hard-cider drink was made in upstate New York.

"So?" I said, looking up. Fiction placed the dark bottle back toward the other side of the bar. "A lot of stuff comes from around here—mostly wines—but this ain't a big surprise. You know, this is farm country."

"*So,* I did some research. The apples that were fermented for this shit were grown right here . . . well, not here, but right at home. At my father's orchards. He never, as far as I know, ever gave my mother any child support. So I don't let anyone else drink what we have, and I've been slowly drinking us out of stock, one free drink a day. He's not making any money off of this place. Think of it. All that money, tax-free. And that's on top of what he makes at the plant. He's gotta make—"

"What do you mean, tax-free?"

⇥⇤

THOUGH HEADING HOME ALONE AS USUAL, I TOOK SOMETHING FROM FICTION Tunny that night. She'd actually been telling the truth that time. For nearly a year, a plan brewed in my head with the new tax information that had seasoned it, spiced things up with an advantage embedded within the United States Constitution. As part of the price the United States government paid Indian nations in return for being removed to reservations, the tribes were declared as belonging to sovereign nations within the continental United States, and as a result of this declaration, and the combination of the United

States Constitution, Article 6, Section II and Amendment XIV, Section II, taxes could not be collected on Indian lands.

The government officials probably had a good laugh, signing that agreement, never imagining we would be smart enough to use these laws to our own advantage some day—having been given a perfectly legal right to evade taxes. The Haudenosaunee government also negotiated other treaties with New York State, even refusing to develop a government system which worked with the Bureau of Indian Affairs. Washington, bewildered, finally gave up on trying to entice the Haudenosaunee into full submission, and forced the state to resume its own negotiations. Or at least that's the way I hear it. A lot of this is fuzzy and vague, only implied. Some of these other negotiations included—again for the loss of land—road maintenance, an elementary school, and the health clinic. Thriving under the United States Constitution, though, New York State had to also abide by the tax negotiations which had been set by the federal government. Clearly, no one had foreseen the vision I developed, arriving at a commodity most folks would want, cheaper than any other place could deliver. The answer, oddly, waited in tradition all along. I never smoked myself; one of the few things my parents did teach me was to respect the Creator's gift of tobacco, and casual smoking seemed, I don't know, somehow disrespectful.

One night at Bert's smoky kitchen table, though, I sat discussing the future with the old woman and Big Red. Red spent many hours at Bert's table after his wife died, losing himself in the dim existence of coffee and cigarettes. You never knew who might be there, at any time of night or day. In the living room, Eddie Chidkin lay on the couch, dozing through some stupid game show, where idiot contestants agonized over the price of rice and instant potatoes—all that shit.

"Hey, stranger," Bert said, pouring me a mug. Red greeted me too, lighting a cigarette from the burning end of a previous one. Bert pulled a smoke from the pack on the table. "What brings you around here? Haven't seen you in almost . . . gosh, almost a year."

"Been busy." The tax proof had been easy to locate, even vaguely documented on my tribal ID card, and signing a firm distribution deal was no trouble at all. Trying to find five thousand dollars was a little more challenging.

"What you need five thousand dollars for? Fiction ain't gonna be any more impressed with that bulge in your pants than she is with the one you been showing her every payday," Bert said. We laughed, but blood rushed up in the recognition that I was the subject of dance gossip. "Really—what for, hon?" she persisted.

"I don't know if I really want to do this. How do you deal with the whole 'Creator's gift' thing? You're smokers." I'd been to Longhouse, on other reservations, and had seen tobacco offered, thanking the Creator for the world's gifts at countless dance competitions, and they had both been to at least as many as I had—Bert probably several times over.

"What's to deal with?" she asked, taking a long drag and letting the smoke plume out from her nostrils. "The Creator offers gifts. If you don't use the gifts, what good are they? It's like if I gave you a shirt, and you had some really nice place to go in it, but you don't wear it 'cause it was a gift. You see? So, anyway, cigarettes ain't so expensive that you need five grand to start smoking. Here, you want one? Take one." She held the pack out.

"Creator's gifts. You know, I been hearing that one for a long time," Red said, chain-lighting another cigarette. "Chiefs said this place was one of the Creator's gifts, too, that this is *Indian* land—sovereignty and all that shit. That's why they don't want town water in here. We all know what a load of shit that is. The state proved that forty years ago, when they took a fifth of this 'Indian land' without blinking an eye. Sovereignty is just a word most people out here can't spell, and that's about it.

"And you know if it had been Bud's wife, or one of Johnnyboy's kids who died from contaminated water—sure as shit, they'd be letting the town water lines in. But that'll never happen. The state dug Bud's well and leach bed; he didn't. You can be sure they're as pure as can be. I just couldn't afford to do a better job on ours, and *that* was when I was working. You know, we had a kid to raise. I didn't really know any better, then, either. And Bev, why she was Bud's second cousin, and you can bet he didn't show at her funeral. He knew it was the water. I guess safe water must not be one of the Creator's gifts, at least not for all of us."

"So, what's this about? You still haven't told me what you need five thousand dollars for," Bert asked, getting up to make another pot of coffee.

"I'm thinking about opening a shop." I understood the Creator's gifts a little better. For years, I tried to go by strictly tradition; but what good is tradition if it just keeps you poor?

"Cigarettes are the perfect commodity. They have such damned heavy taxes on them. Without all that state tax, and then the federal tax on top of it, the discounts I could give would be phenomenal. I'd be saving at least eighty cents on the pack, retail, and that's just prepaid taxes, not even counting sales tax. Every pack! Smokes have been climbing so steadily on the regular market, and folks just keep buying them—bitching away the whole time, but still buying them, blaming the government for driving up the prices unfairly with those taxes, abusing the poor smoker whose habit just ain't as cool as it used to be . . . Man! Think how happy they'll be even if I give them a few cents off, just a minor fraction of the break I'd be getting. The rest would all be profit! If I give that fraction and let 'em know it's because the smokes are 'tax-free,' every smoker in Niagara County'll be lining up to buy tax-free smokes, thinking they're getting some fabulous deal. I could buy those people with that 'tax-free' label. I'll be running out of smokes left and right, and I'll be needing bigger pockets than these ones to shove my wad into. And, you know, maybe in a couple of years, I could finance town water coming in here."

"Big dreams for a broke man," Bert replied. Those little jabs, remarks from her, always had a way of forcing me to focus on my most immediate concern, as if she had somehow thrown a dart of awareness into me—even back when I was one of her dancers. The top prize would loom high before me in a haze, and all the while I'd be stumbling on the simplest of steps. Her echoing, stabbing remarks dragged me back every time to the steps, forcing me to walk through them, over and over, until they became natural moves. Only then would she relent and let me dream a little, just long enough to keep me going.

The next night, after the sun had set and Fiction had abandoned me, the door to my future opened when Red stepped through it that moment, looked directly at me, and, cocking his head, called me outside. An envelope passed between us in The Den's parking lot. Red said Bert wanted this to be delivered to me only at the bar.

I broke the seal on my future. The envelope contained five thousand dollars and the deed to all of Bert's land from the south wall of her house to the reservation's edge—plenty of room for my initial business, and the suggestion of so much more . . . a venture I could not then have imagined. But as the money started rolling in, the use of the remaining acreage grew more clear in my mind. It was right.

➔←

THE SCOTCH SCENT LINGERS AND FOLLOWS ME THROUGH THE BACK ENTRANCE AND into the T.R.B. office suite, getting more faint. The meeting isn't scheduled to begin for another half hour, but at least a hundred people mill about, drinking pop and coffee from the concession tables I'd had set out before the doors opened. They're not running on Indian Time—good, good. A business can't run too well on that kind of system. Some compromises in tradition have to be made.

"Hey! Hey! Nice to see all of you." The microphone was right where it was supposed to be, near the rear entrance. "Okay, I know we've been a little slow with this; I wanted you all to have the health insurance right away, but sometimes these things go a little slower than we plan. Now, if you haven't gotten and filled out the insurance and employment forms, you'll have time for that later. Right now, grab a seat. I want to talk about our futures for a while and then leave some time for you to bring up concerns of your own." They all wander over to the west wall and grab folding chairs for themselves. Though the job would have been no trouble for my workers, initiative is an important skill. I want to see how quickly this group will respond to me.

"Okay. Great. Now some of you know how this business got started—at least ten of you—but most of you maybe don't. And I think it's time you should. Now, I'm not blaming you or anything, so don't start getting worried. In fact, I'm here to tell you that I know exactly how you feel.

"Now, you see, when I first got the idea for the shop—you remember, that old purple shack—well, I knew that I would need some money to start up with. More than I could possibly get myself. Living on a reservation, banks won't give up even a first mortgage, let alone a second one. So I had to rely on individuals, and—well, you remember me a couple years ago. Would most of you here have lent me any money?" A few flutey laughs trickle from deep within the crowd.

"Of course not. I probably looked like a drunk to most of you, smelling like day-old beer and my hair all standing up like this." My left hand jabs into my stylishly cut hair, sending wild spears of it skyward for a few seconds before raking them back into civilized layers. "I wouldn't've lent me any money, either. But you know what? I wasn't really a drunk. Sure, I probably drank too much, but I kept a steady job. For the most part, I was reliable. Responsible. But I had that label. I was . . . a drunk," I say, flexing two fingers in front of me in mock quotation marks.

"And I'm sure most of you here can understand that label, too. Now I'm not suggesting that you're all a bunch of drunks, or even that anyone has ever said that about you. But many of you carry a different label—one that, around here, is much, much worse in the eyes of some. You're"—I raise my quotation fingers again—"non-Tuscaroras." All laughing has stopped.

The front doors open, and Fiction walks in. A number of people crane their necks to see who came late, and seem relieved to know it's only Fiction.

"Take a seat." She shakes her head and, dismissing the idea with a wave of her hand, leans against the back wall. "You know, I bet you were all a little alarmed when that door opened, weren't you?" This is much better. I had my speech all prepared, had even read it to a couple of people for their response, but the act of reciting it just now had seemed so artificial. Everything will still come through, but now the freedom—to go wherever my mind carries me—is here too.

"That little alarm should be telling you something. What were you afraid of? The Chiefs? Afraid because your name's not on the Tribal Roll Books? Afraid because it is, and you've just been spotted in the undesirable building? Well, I'll tell you. My name is on those books. And it hasn't done a damned thing for me my whole life. I still drive the same shitty roads you do. Until a little while ago, I lived in the same kind of house you do, improving it only when I could scrounge cash to do something. My name being there didn't get me a loan from the Tribal accounts. Don't even think such a provision exists, really. You know where I got that money from? From you. Ten of you in here lent me the start-up money. But even there, you didn't lend it to me. You lent it to Bertha Monterney—the only person on this reservation who could see past my 'drunk' label. The only one.

"And you know what? She just handed me the money—no rules, no conditions. She let me make my own decisions. Gave me an opportunity. And that's what I'm here to do for you." More and more heads nod with my message, seeing the future through my eyes.

"No, I'm not giving you money. But, you want a job? You got it! And you're gonna get the right kind of training. Let's say you don't like working for me. With the training and experience you get here, you can move on. You see, being on the roll means you got to obey the Chiefs, got to depend on them to do what's right for you, not living your own lives. I'm not a Chief. I don't want you depending on me. I wouldn't have the balls to think I knew what was right for you. I'm here to give you the opportunity to take responsibility for your own lives. I want you depending on yourselves!" The crowd hoots and shouts back at my clenched and raised fist, some raising their fists in the solidarity of freedom.

"Now. Smoke Rings will be open for gas and smokes in a few weeks, but we won't be running at full capacity for about another month and a half. We gotta be ready. You won't believe the number of people we're going to be serving, and who'll be serving us." A number of heads in the group are bowed, people filling out the job applications, checking any boxes they think they might even remotely be qualified for. I've already moved Big Red back to filtering through the applications. No one knows the reservation better than he does. It's time to end while they're still excited, but I have to use my closing.

"Okay! Okay! Keep those pens moving. One more thing, though." The group settles down briefly, and most heads look up and listen. "So, you know, as I said before, I've shared this life with you. I have drunk the same contaminated water you have. But all of that's going to end. We deserve clean, safe water to drink. And within two years, we will have it. Nation and non-Nation members, alike. We are all members of the same nation— Onguiaahra Nation—Haudenosaunee Indians living in Niagara. I don't give a shit what Bud and his books say! We're here!" Another shout rises from the group to accompany my exit.

Red and Fiction join me in my office a few minutes later. "Have a seat. Surprised to see you here, Fiction."

"I don't know why. I believe in what you're doing as much as those people do. Probably more than most of them."

"Hey, listen," Red says, "I gotta run some of these applications down-stairs. We can start hiring more cashiers right away. Get them started in training. And let some of these others know their start date. It's not like there's gonna be any training period for running a gas pump. Whyn't you just stay up here with Mason? I'll be done in a little while."

"Yeah, all right. But hurry up. I had kind of a hard day at work, today." She stares at me until Red clanks down the stairs. "Nice story. How much of it is true?"

"Hey, that's not nice. Every single word of it was true. Who do you think I am . . . you? Look, I'm sorry. It's just . . . oh, never mind. I was just really edgy about this speech. I overreacted. What do I owe you for the glass?" My front pocket is still warmed with the wad of neatly folded bills.

Fiction waves her hand and shakes her head, smirking briefly.

"Forgive me?"

"Cut it out, you cornball." She crosses her arms and rolls her eyes. I still have it.

"Hey, come on. Tell me I'm forgiven."

"Why do you keep trying to flirt with me? I am practically living with your right-hand man, who is, this very second, signing up your work force. Not to mention the fact that I've consistently said I'm not interested in you since you first asked me out. And jeez, I wasn't even legal, then."

"Well, I keep hoping you're going to come to your senses and say yes. And as far as my 'right-hand man' goes . . . yeah, me and Red go back a long way, but the fact of the matter is, if he wasn't working for me, he'd be on the old unemployment line. And you know it. I think if you complained to him, he might just be inclined to quit."

I do need Red, at least for a while. Sometimes, it's so easy to fall into the millionaire gig and forget all of the people I came up with. I would've never even learned to dance if the group's older members hadn't taken the time to show me their own moves. For years, after Bert had criticized my moves, Red secretly danced slowly with me, occasionally guiding me from behind, in a way that was awkwardly intimate for a bad-ass like me. We danced in Bert's dark, middle-of-the-night living room, Red probably exhausted after his twelve-hour Carborundum shifts, until I got the move right; but he never complained. Some of the others, while certainly never going to those lengths, helped out over the years, too. I respected those lessons and never lifted any-one's moves exactly, taking them and developing my own, based on those others. My vision is at its sharpest, now—I can do it again.

"What you could offer me, it ain't that valuable, Mason. I'm gonna meet Red downstairs."

"By the way," I say to her fine back. "Your stupid beadwork dress didn't get your lights and phone back. I did."

"Bullshit," she says, as I reel her back in.

"No, it's true. I just got my lawyer to call both utilities, threaten to sue. Tough break, but you know as well as I do that beads haven't worked that kind of magic on Indians since the selling of Manhattan. I told my lawyer that was your only home, and he said that would be plenty to get them back on. Human-rights issues. It's amazing what you can find out when you got a lawyer on retainer."

"Simple as that? Be nice if we could all afford to keep one on the payroll." Her voice sounds light and faint, almost an echo, like she's lost any momentum she might have built up a few minutes ago. "I still believe in my dress. It had to count."

"Not really, but if you're interested, the lawyer is surprisingly cheap. Although with me, I think he's looking down the road. He wants to be my lawyer when I hit the top, so he's treating me pretty nice these days. He might not give you the same deal. Everyone's for sale, you know. All you gotta do is figure out what that price is; it's just like that game show—you know the one. These folks out there," I motion to my new, large group of employees, "they were cheap. The Chiefs' been fuckin' with them for so long that their price was simple kindness and economic freedom—things they should be able to expect from life."

"That's all they are to you? Commodities? Like government cheese?" She snaps the line free, this time, but I try again anyway.

"When you put it like that, it sounds so shitty. It's not like that at all. Don't you think Bert saw us as commodities? Sure, she loved us, just like I love these people. You didn't see her babying us. I want them out of their miserable situations. I don't want to see one more person die from water contamination, and you don't, either. She looked out for our futures, but she looked out for her own first, to make sure she could help us."

"You and me didn't learn the same lessons from Bert, it seems," she says. "She believed in you enough to do all those things. Do you know how hard it must have been to convince some of those folks that a drunk like you would pay them back their five hundred dollars? She did that for you. She trusted you. It turns out she was right to trust you, by the looks of things here, but you gotta learn trust, man. Trust me when I say that you and me are never, ever going to get together. What's it gonna take, Red and me getting married?"

"If you'll excuse me, I have to go down and hear some of the concerns of my people now, find out what else is going to be involved in their loyalty." I reach for her, touching her on the pretense of escorting her downstairs. She steps easily out of range, walking out the door for good, and as she reaches the stairwell, I shout one more thing to her.

"Everyone's got a price, Fiction. And sooner or later, I'm gonna find yours."

⇥⇤

CHAPTER 11 Fighting and Flying

Fiction Tunny

KEEP HOPING FOR A LITTLE CLOUD COVER, BUT IT DOESN'T SEEM LIKELY THIS morning. The sky is so blue that if Skywoman were falling today, we'd be able to see her for miles and miles as she tumbled towards us. But would we even notice, or would she just tumble to her death while we argued with one another? Or maybe we'd see her and then just argue about whose responsibility it is to save her. Either way, her chances of surviving her fall today would be not so hot. Certainly not as hot as it is here, the unseasonably warm April sun not exactly delivering the time, as I look up into it, more likely delivering a headache—but it seems a little past ten. My yard sale's in full swing, and I don't want to be late for my future. Okay—really, a couple of minutes ago, Two-Step Harmony's tiny form appeared on the distant horizon, making its way up here from the trailer he and his father share, and that boy, he never rises before ten unless it's absolutely necessary.

"Lose something?" Mason Rollins washes into my eyes as they adjust to the light here at ground level. He's pulled up alongside the ditch bordering my yard in that '67 Mustang convertible he's been driving since the new year began. He's added white pinstriping that makes it look like a wampum belt on mag wheels. Too much.

"Yeah, I had this silver dollar that I was going to invest down at the smoke shop a little later, but, wouldn't you know it, as I was sitting here tossing that coin, heads or tails, this damn crow swooped down out of nowhere and snatched my silver dollar out of midair and flew away with it. Heads was for a pack of smokes, and tails was for a gallon of gas for my lawnmower—so I don't get lost in my too-tall grass. Practical or impractical, that's always the choice, ain't it? Can you beat that?"

"Crows are like that," Mason replies. "Get in. I'll take you down to the shop and get you some smokes and enough gas to do your lawn. A gallon ain't gonna do shit here. Amazing, huh? Grass growing this high so early in the year?" He leans across the bucket seat and unlocks the passenger-side door, though the window and the ragtop are already down.

"Bad sign, some would say—drought, famine, maybe locusts—hard to tell. Anyway, I was just kidding. I gotta hang out here 'til I sell all my junk, and then I'll be down, later."

"It's gonna be awful hot sitting here all day. You wanna beer?" He reaches into the back seat and pulls a cold and sweaty Heineken from a fresh six-pack apparently resting on the floor.

"Sure."

"It's back there." He pops the cap on a bottle opener mounted on the Mustang's dash. "Whatcha going to do to occupy your day between sales? I can think of a couple things."

"Sorry, got plans already." I pull a pair of copper armbands from a bag sitting on the table in front of me. On one, the copper is barely visible through the tanned hide and solid purple-and-white beadwork pattern. The other isn't anywhere near finished. "Here, check this out. I made it for Two-Step. He was wearing the copper bands around at competitions, so I told him I'd bead him something on it. Isn't it nice?"

"Who?"

"You know, Two-Step Harmony, Red's boy. What are you, an idiot? He's at your shop all the time."

"Oh, yeah, the kid." Rollins, he tries the copper band on, but it only fits around his thick wrist, the loose threads and my needle dangling. The George Washington wampum-belt design draws him in, the same design he has had pinstriped onto this car—the men joining arms across the car's doors, and the Longhouse in the center of the belt dead center across his hood. "You should make me a couple of these."

"Well, these are his. You know, he was one of Bert's best dancers at the end. He had just taken top awards the week before she died. Young Men's Traditional. Anyway, he was wearing these bands around, and I figured that he should be wearing some traditional regalia if he's gonna be doing the circuit. I'm kinda hoping these will encourage him to dance again. You know, after she died, he just . . . he just stopped competing." He passes the band back into my outstretched hand. "Hey, I was thinking maybe we could get a social going at the T.R.B.—excuse me, 'The Tribe,' I mean. Nothing big, just a show of solidarity for your workers, you know; my father's probably making life not so easy for 'em. You wouldn't even have to do the catering. We could make it a potluck. Give them something back."

"You mean givin' 'em a job's not enough?"

"You know what I mean. It would only have to be a one-day event, just for anyone from here who would want to come. Like the New Year's Eve party but, you know, more connected to us. I mean, what's 'The Tribe' for, if not for things like that? Or were you making resolutions you wanted to break at the New Year's gig?" He doesn't want to deal with this right now— probably wondering what he's going to find when he gets to the shop— but he's not flying away that easy.

When the winter cut us some slack a month ago, these two sides started trading late-night commentaries on one another: tire slashings, mailbox explosions, and midnight "doughnuts"—circles gouged into front lawns by cars spinning their tires. And that old favorite, the lighted bag of dog *oo(t)-gweh-rheh* on the front porch, and who knows what all. His side has done as much nonsense as the other side, but it's kind of nerve-wracking not knowing what the morning is going to deliver you, and I can tell you that for sure. His desire to head out to the shop this morning is certainly legitimate, but I've never been one to keep quiet until the moment was right.

"I don't know. What's in it for you?"

"We haven't had one in a long time around here, and even when we do, they've been kind of, you know, disorganized, small—almost like those stories Bert used to tell us about dancing when she was so much younger. And, you know, we could set up booths, and people could sell their stuff— be kind of nice. Maybe even some good publicity. If you wanted, you could charge for tables, I guess, but it's not really what I had in mind. If I had the cash, I'd have a place; it could be real nice. I could have beadwork, soapstone carvings, paintings, silver and turquoise, all of it."

"So that's it," he nods. "You just want to sell your shit? Well, I don't have room in the shop for any of that. I have a hard enough time finding space for all the brands people want me to carry now."

"Well, I wasn't asking you for any space in your precious shop, anyway. I was just saying what I'd do if I had the cash. You do what you want, and I'll do what I want. You don't have to get shitty about it, Mr. Mason 'Rollin' in Dough' Rollins."

"Will you stop! I hate that fuckin' name. I don't see anyone else out here giving these folks jobs. Shit, most of them couldn't hold down jobs outside." He pauses, runs his fingers through his damp hair. "Sorry, it's just that everybody seems to want a part of me now that the money's good. You want that beer?"

"Nah, maybe later. A little too early for me. Well, think about that social idea."

"Nah, maybe later. A little too early for me."

"Funny. I better get back to selling my rags here."

"Yeah, they're lining up," he says, pulling out.

"Hi, Trish." Two-Step's small voice blooms out of the air in Mason's dust. "What'd he want?"

"Just seeing what I had for sale."

"My dad was just taking off for Grand River Rez. I decided to stay behind." Red went up to finalize all the table arrangements at the Band Council Office for their setup at the big powwow held there every summer. Two-Step usually went with his dad, but confesses he's not ready to see the dancing grounds yet, believing he'd never have the passion to glide through them again.

Red, of course, isn't just trashing his boy's feelings, and he told me one night in bed that he hoped the boy would go with him and face the future. He had to do what was right. A good number of folks from here do a little survival beadwork, and Red has consignments at his table every summer on the powwow circuit, but Two-Step, he has to do what's right for himself. These guys have, for years, sold beadwork, leatherwork, Indian stationery, greeting cards, turquoise, and a few small stone carvings—and in that business, location is everything. A vendor's table can't be too far away from the stands, or folks' money will be gone and in someone else's beaded wallet long before they get to your cold table.

Grand River is almost four months away, but I better get my act together. My main gig right now is a porcupine-quill and glass-bead belt buckle of a hawk's head, sure to bring in a firm hundred bucks at any table, even with those Skins bargaining for "Indian price."

It's funny—quills from such a heavy animal make for perfect feathers on beadwork birds. They use them to fight, and my beaded birds use them to fly. Most hawk's-head buckles look just like eagle-head buckles—the only difference in breed being the little white price sticker where the bird is neatly labeled; but with mine, anyone can tell the difference. It's in the lay of the quills, just like feathers—my buckles *could* fly if they wanted to. My hawk buckles are pretty popular. But my quill supply is just about at its end, and that's why I'm frying in this oddly hot April day, listening to the new music station on my duct-taped radio, with my belongings stacked up around me like a padded fortress, fending off unruly and cunning customers.

Now, eagles have become pretty rare around here, but there are plenty of hawks—graceful liquid movement through the sky making men envious. I mean, come on, airplanes? Who would have thought of that craziness if birds hadn't been having so much fun? And before that, the trapeze—the *flying* trapeze—momentary flings with the sky, only the most ballsy performing without a net, defying gravity and fate among the high wires. Swinging into new plans, quite often without a net, there is nothing like that—excitement driving me higher. Sometimes I know why Skywoman left the Skyworld: just to have that feeling of free flight, not even worrying if something would come in time to save her or not.

This weekend is one of those times. The rest of my life and Bert's legacy depend in part on the revenues of my first-ever yard sale. I want to walk away from the bar, but a woman's got to eat and pay her bills. Be nice if I could do it, making a difference somewhere, and this is my first shot. If I can make enough to live on for a few months, beadwork is going to be my profession, and I'll be able to concentrate just on it and stockpile my work. I've already raked in fifty dollars. My flight to freedom began about an hour ago with a promising start, but it isn't like I've given up my day job.

"So, hey Trish, what you got lined up for this weekend, anyhow?" Two-Step peruses the assortment of my life set up on the ground.

"Well, gotta work tomorrow at The Den, but for today, I decided to move outdoors—you know, give my clothes that fresh clean scent of spring without using dryer sheets."

"Yeah, whatever. My dad wants to know if you can stop in later, maybe stay the night at our place with me. Said you could even use his bed, like when you used to baby-sit me."

"Yeah, he said." I hold up my cordless telephone, and Two-Step nods. "The only thing is that I gotta lug this stuff back inside my trailer before nightfall. I was just gonna leave it out with a big piece of storm-window plastic covering it up, but if I'm not here at night, you can be sure my stuff won't be here in the morning."

I'm practically giving it away. I never had a sale before, but now I feel like a true old Indian woman, and here I'm only twenty-three: I got someone else's kid around, I'm trying to sell my rags, and I'm doing beadwork under a hot sun. "You want a pop?"

The cool shade of the bathroom mirror shines out a dim new reflection, some kind of half-assed mother to this boy who could, by years, be my younger brother. At eighteen, I walked out of my mother's house determined to not be one of those Indian women spending endless reservation nights in toy-strewn living rooms with a bunch of kids from different fathers. Plenty of my high-school friends grew wide bellies and dropped out of school before they turned sixteen, knocked up on Moon Road some drunken night by some asshole who moved on to someone else when she was no longer fuckable. I hate that word, but it's one of the two categories young Indian men seem to throw young Indian women in: fuckable and unfuckable. On the few occasions I wound up on Moon Road, you can be sure I stayed sober enough to talk my way out of any situation and still get a ride home—or at least sober enough to make the guy wear something, if I were so inclined.

The water in the bathroom sink takes forever to cool down. Luxurious, the water slides down inside the baggy arms of my T-shirt and cools my body. The wet T-shirt isn't a real problem, but if the water runs too long, the leach bed saturates and seeps into the backyard. The whole area surrounding my trailer would smell like a sewer, and that's no way to run a yard sale—even novices know this.

"Hey, Trish, how much for this?" Two-Step's holding a plaid flannel shirt up to the bathroom window. Ruby, she stands on the other side of the table, carefully sorting through the other clothes, but keeping her ears open for my response.

"Oh, hi, Ruby. Dollar."

"Cheap," Ruby says, jabbing more intently through my piles of junk. "These are nice for moccasin linings. Look." She holds the fabric up to the sun, showing me the shirt isn't threadbare.

"Mm-hmm. But I don't know how to make moccasins. I tried them once, but I didn't have a pattern or anything, and they came out crooked, like not for human feet at all. Maybe I'll try again sometime, but now I just make regular beadwork the way you taught me. See?" She runs her fingers over a couple of nearly completed matching barrettes, tugging at a few seams.

"Nice work. It's not too many that take the time to sew beadwork this tight any more. You still double stitch, even after your lessons. Good. It takes more time, but you can always tell when someone does it. You learned your lessons well, and you haven't gotten lazy. How come you stopped in the middle of both of these, anyway? You're not supposed to stop in the middle of any piece. You lose your original vision that way. Maybe you didn't learn so well."

"I'm out of long quills. Stubs are all I got left. That's why I'm selling all my rags; I gotta go buy some quills. I usually just drop my old clothes off down at the school. You know, they got that area next to the clinic for free clothes to anyone who needs them. And I've seen some of these younger girls around here wearing my old jeans and tops." There's nothing wrong with them. It's just that when I could, I always dressed to the nines in fashion. Some might say that's not the liberated way of doing things, but to hell with them. I look good, and nobody's old gossip-tongue is going to stop that. But that life was before my big plans. And besides, I never lose my original visions. Just ask around.

Two-Step sits on the steps, idly moving some tiny ceramic animal figurines around a table. I've collected them since the seventh grade, but right now they might be the difference between a future as a barmaid and one as a real traditionalist—not like my father's type.

"Now I've been trying to cut back at work, not do the hours I used to. Seeing people drinking up their lives is one thing, but helping 'em do it is something else entirely. I been spending too much time away from the beads, lately, and I've been catching up on all my past-due bills, so I can't afford to accessorize like I used to." It's not like there was any big trauma or anything, but I want to do this beadwork thing right. I've got a plan, but all that won't matter if I can't sell this stuff and get some quills. No bead-work, no bucks, no Grand River, no future.

"You should give this to me," Ruby mumbles, stroking the flannel shirt. Though the old woman no longer makes moccasins either, she still wants the material. Back at her house, there are boxes of tanned hides, beads, and lining material—denim, rabbit fur, and now, as Ruby folds the material into a compact, even smaller square, at least one swatch of flannel—just waiting for someone to pick them up. Crouching in her closet, they would remain potential moccasins, empty dancing husks waiting to be born, waiting for me to come back for more lessons.

"Now I can give you something." Ruby rummages around in her purse, but I'm not hopeful. It's unlikely she has a bag of quills in there. Plunging her clumsy hand deeper into the purse, Ruby finds what she's looking for. She comes out clutching a crumpled map. "Here."

"*Nyah-wheh,*" I reply. Even though the gift seems pointless, I have to be polite. After all, Ruby taught me the basics of beading over the winter, so my own style could finally come through. The map is of Niagara Falls. Maybe someone would want to buy it for a quarter, and if they find their way out here, maybe they need a map.

"Open it up." Ruby takes her own advice and unfolds the map over the card table, covering my wares. "Here, look here. You see this?" A purple circle of bingo dabber ink blots out Whirlpool Park, on the edge of the city, about a twenty-minute drive from the reservation. "There's a dead porcupine there. It's fresh, too. No stink. No airing out. I was just down there yesterday. I go walking by Devil's Hole, make sure my legs don't turn out like my fingers. Anyway, it's there and you can use it. I was gonna stop down at Twila's and give her that map, but it's yours now. Now you be mindful of those barbs; they got to be snipped off right away, even before you wash them."

She pulls out, and in less than five seconds, Red's phone is ringing in my ear, traveling through the heavy reservation air. "Shit! Not home. I don't even know how to get them off, anyway. And what barbs?" The thought of dequilling a porcupine is not all that comforting, and as good as my stories are, I can't even fathom how you might do it. I've only ever bought bags of cleaned and sorted quills.

"Oh, it's easy. Don't worry about the barbs. I can help you." Two-Step stands and looks through the piles. "You got an old blanket?"

"Sold it earlier this morning. Three bucks."

"I think my dad's got one in the truck."

"Well what good is that? I was just trying to call him, but I guess he already left."

"I told you he did. Weren't you listening? Anyway, didn't he tell you? Mason sent him in one of the new company cars; he wants it broken in with some mileage, but I think he's just afraid of it. It was another one of his police-auction finds, and he's using my dad as a guinea pig; put him up for the weekend there too. Won't be back until Monday. Dad thought it was kind of dumb, but as long as Mason was paying . . ."

We're on the road fifteen minutes later, my garage sale covered in plastic, left with a sign and one of my all-too-many empty bead-sorting boxes—the honor system. A few seconds beyond the border, the reservation is obscured in my rearview mirror by the dike's anonymous giant wall. My relatives are responsible for this, and I am not sure forgiveness is in my heart anymore, for even one more violation. The purple spot we head for looms on my horizon like a dark, setting sun, Two-Step explaining along the way the best method for dealing with porcupines; but I'm beginning to think my habits are rubbing off on him, it sounds so ridiculous.

The Devil's Hole parking lot is empty this early in the year, so no one slows us down on the large flat stones making up the stairway down into the gorge. The stairs were built right into the walls of the Niagara River's lower gorge, a convoluted and shifting path eventually bringing its travelers to the river's edge where the rapids shoot through, angry and loud, tearing at the river's rock walls in a hissy fit. The stairway landings were built at the natural tiers in the gorge walls. Ruby said the porcupine lay on the second landing from the bottom, presently hidden by spring growth. How she climbs these stairs, I have no clue. The carcass lies right where she said it would be—beyond the safety barriers. It's not at all the way I've always pictured porcupines, the quills almost hidden in the animal's dense fur. I must have one of those cartoon kind of pictures in my head. If I didn't know better, those nasty little teeth would have been more of a worry than the coat.

Beyond the guardrail, the leaves rot back into ground. My feet press in, and soft leaves give way. The earth beneath it hasn't yet grown solid in itself, hasn't returned fully, and falls away with a soft and sweet moan, like the sound overripe August tomatoes make pulling from the vine in the sun. Sliding down about eight feet, I come to rest, having barely missed a dive over the ravine—smart, but not smart enough. A few quills stick out of my right palm, throbbing and nagging about where I should not reach my hands out to, even in desperation.

The porcupine lies just a few inches beyond the place I had grabbed it at. Pretty much unmoved, it remains just out of my reach.

"I still need that. I woulda had it, too, if that damn ground didn't give out."

"What?" Two-Step yells. The stairs emerge from the woods right near the lower rapids, and that furious rushing sound of the crashing and swirling waves is all we can hear, a thousand angry birds taking flight. I repeat myself, shouting, trying to work the quills out of my hand, now knowing what barbs Ruby was talking about. With each tug, these nearly invisible hooks dig into my flesh, but they've got to come out.

"How much do you weigh?" he responds. I tell him and decide on the Band-Aid method for the quills, bearing down and ripping them out as hard as I can.

A few minutes later, he's on the other side of the guardrail. Lighter than I am, he leaves only impressions on the soft ground, not forcing it to give. Stepping assuredly, tracing the footprints he had made on his way into the mulch, he has the porcupine carcass pulled and blanket-wrapped in a minute. His feet move lightly, smoothly, the kinds of steps that helped him take top dancing prizes around the Northeast. He tests the ground ahead of him with his toes, after he nearly loses his footing three steps in. The risk heightens his confidence, his sense of the relationship his body has with the earth. His concentration builds. I hang onto the guardrail, ready to grab him if he needs, but he ignores me. He's back. He's always done better at new powwows, on grounds he's not familiar with, saying he doesn't like having home-court advantage. It seems like a cheat to him. Unsure of how long his confidence will last, I share in this return in the only way I can: smiling.

He delivers the blanket and stays on the other side of the rail while I swing the blanket over my head, again and again, enjoying the momentum, almost forgetting the burning sensation in my palm. The porcupine circles spastically with my jerky movements at first, but a rhythm emerges after a few revolutions, and finally, I bring the bundle down gently and open the blanket.

The dequilled porcupine rolls gently out of its spiny bed. Aside from the fact that it's not breathing, there seems to be absolutely no reason for it to be dead—no marks anywhere. What animal would be stupid enough to mess with a porcupine, anyway? Maybe it was just meant to be provided for me. Two-Step places its body in the underbrush, where it can grow back into the earth at its own pace, and I sprinkle some tobacco next to it, thanking the Creator.

"So, what do you think I should debut at Grand River this year?" he asks, smiling, trying to sound casual, as we return to the reservation and turn on to Torn Rock. But before I can respond, he's shouting something about my sale. He points straight ahead toward my front yard, where my empty table sits in the afternoon light, torn plastic flapping in the wind.

Damn it! I knew some son of a bitch would take my stuff. And the balls, leaving me my plastic after they tear a big-ass hole in it. Well, I can probably still make some use of it, and at least they didn't steal the table.

"Uh, Trish . . ." Two-Step holds the white translucent bead box I left for sales. It's been sitting in the grass under the table. A folded sheet of paper sits locked between the lid and the box. The sheet catches on a breeze and nearly floats away when I open the lid.

Each of the bead box's ten compartments has a fresh one-hundred-dollar bill neatly folded into it. The paper's plain white surface is only marred by a brief message, printed in nondescript type, from a Xerox machine or a laser printer—no pressure marks.

SOCIAL—MEMORIAL DAY WEEKEND.
I'LL BE BACK FOR THE REST OF MY PURCHASES LATER, I ASSUME THIS
WILL COVER THEM FULLY. YOU CANT BE THAT GOOD.

We put my table away and then fill up on some microwave dinners before attending to the blanket. Two-Step clears the dishes, tossing them in the garbage, and spreading the blanket on the table, says, "Watch this. It's really cool."

The same barbs that dug deeply into my palm here have snagged the blanket's weave, capturing the porcupine's silhouette in quills, spread across the center of the blanket, stretched wide in full flight. But some quills have broken off and lie among the others, all on the left side, the side it had been lying on. And in that moment, I know how the porcupine died. It had fallen—maybe like I had—after being hit by a car. It probably bled to death internally.

It hadn't been provided, after all. The whole thing was an accident. The porcupine came up against the one enemy it couldn't fight—one that wasn't even trying to kill it, just crushing the animal in its rush to some other destination. It didn't know it should have just laid its quills down and waited for the car to pass. Instincts, fight-or-flight—the porcupine made a bad call this time.

You can be sure a bad call won't get to me that way. Seizing the opportunity Ruby gave me paid off. My lessons will resume by July at the latest, toward making the most supple and luxurious moccasins ever constructed. But I have other things to do before then, and the first is to pick up the phone and turn in my bear claws and spandex. Well, maybe I'll keep the spandex. Angie sounds annoyed that I'm not coming in to The Den tomorrow, but more relieved than anything when I say it's for good. She wishes me luck and says she's going to quit herself and maybe go back to school, just as soon as she catches up on her bills. I can't wait until mine are caught up. This is it.

The broken quill pieces roll out easily with a tip of the blanket, and I set them aside with those that were embedded in my palm, still bearing my blood. All up the stone stairway, they scratched at my palm. I was not letting them go.

Just as I set the quills out on the dining-room table for snipping, Mason lets himself in. That's what I get for not locking the door, but no one on the rez ever locks their doors, and that is one new tradition I have no interest in initiating.

"I'm back for my goods," he says loudly. He must not realize Two-Step is here. I hope the kid is smart enough to stay in the spare bedroom.

"Seems to me you already got your goods, paid in full." I step behind the table. "What do you want, a receipt?" He comes closer, casual, in no hurry whatsoever.

"Maybe later; I got something else in mind for right now." Only a few inches of space exist between us now. He's been drinking, and it isn't beer on his breath. It's that sharp Scotch that used to make him so crazy at The Den. He unzips his jeans and pushes against me, and I shift at the last second to get my right leg lined up just as I need it. He presses me against the wall with the weight of his chest and reaches behind me. "It's collection time," he says, stretching his neck back far enough to look me in the eyes.

He leans back into me, pressing harder, taking a deep breath. "I can still smell your pussy—you been thinking about me?" he says, grinning and flicking his tongue at me.

"Trish?" Two-Step calls from the dark hallway and Rollins, startled, turns. It's enough. I swing my knee up and get him in the balls. He crouches, and I shove him into the table. He puts his hand out to catch his fall and lands his palm straight into the quills.

"Son of a bitch!" he yells, trying to pull the quills from his palm; but the barbs just work their way deeper. Eventually, he grits his teeth and yanks the bunch. He stares at me like there's something he thinks I should be doing with his bleeding hand.

"You might want to go to the hospital. I haven't cleaned those quills. You never know what you might get your hands into here." As he nears the door, his face grows more red by the minute. "Oh, and uh, thanks for pulling the barbs." The quills are back in my hand.

"I meant what I said about collection time." He tries to fit a smile around his grimace. "You ain't paid up yet, Fiction," he says, walking out the open door. His car starts a moment later, and the sound eventually disappears down the road.

"What was that all about?" Two-Step asks, coming out of the shadows, carrying one of my sawed-off lacrosse sticks. "You okay?"

"Yeah, fine. You did great. As always, perfect timing." I drop the quills beside those I had pulled from my own hand, and those that had been broken off by the porcupine's fall.

These broken quills could have been deep in some animal's muzzle, but they're not. These quills hold the magic of potential, and even more importantly, they shout a warning of carelessness . . . of slipping. I will not be careless, and even if I slip, I'm used to flying without a net. I pick up my needle and start binding the quills together, strengthening them.

Into the night, a new pair of earrings comes together: broken and blood-stained quills, bound tightly to one another—fierce magic. Fight and flight. I'll strike a balance, only I won't just fly—I'll soar. Near dawn, I hook them into my ears, the spikes gracefully floating below my lobes. The only animals that mess with a porcupine must have amazing powers of underestimation—animals like my father, or like Rollins. The hair on my neck bristles. Rollins has no idea what sort of animal he's messing with. All his money and lawyers and connections and laser printers and business holdings—they're just dead weight he mistakes for freedom. Rollins is not acquainted with the sensation of free flight. He is going to fall.

➻❮

CHAPTER 12 Undercurrents

Bud Tunny

ARKNESS GREETS MY FRESHLY OPENED EYES, BUT THE FIRST BIRDS OF THE DAY have begun their singing on this Monday in early May, and I feel fine— am in fact looking forward to another unseasonably warm day of confrontation. My name will appear in the lead story of this morning's paper, as it has this past week. That is, my full name, mind you: Deer Clan Chief Jacob Tunny. The name "Bud" was delivered unto me when I was three or four, my mother saying my thick Indian lips were beautiful, a small bud, ready to bloom from within—and like most nicknames out here, it stuck. Even now, at sixty-one and a Chief of the Nation, I haven't been able to lose the name.

That reporter from the *Cascade* has never, at any time he's written about the Nation, included the name "Bud" anywhere. It's one of the few places the name gets a rest. In all these years, really, I've grown used to the name—my supporters calling me by a name they've adopted for me, a nice affirmation. It's another thing entirely when the opposition, only a few feet away, shifts and twists Bud into "Budhead," "Budstard," "Budfuck," and other such concoctions.

The reporters never write any of that, though. They have a sympathetic ear for our fight, as we try to preserve a certain way of life within the Nation, and that is no easy feat, lately. Relief filled me when that reporter had not, in his annual Feast coverage, included any of the girl's antics. He had been there—the singularly short, pale man with closely shorn curly blond hair—Paul, Peter, one of those Apostle names I always confuse. When I finally looked at the paper, well past sunset the next day, there was no mention of her, and no article on Rollins's party either. Those two unrelated forces have conspired to turn this Nation upside down.

Rollins's discovery that he could buy and sell cigarettes within the Nation's bounds without any New York State or federal tax was not a huge difficulty. My family has always used the Nation's foggy tax definition for extra income from our orchards, legally not having to declare whatever we sell—period. Tax is taken from my income at the carbon plant, but that's off in Niagara Falls. Whatever the orchards bring in is mine, free and clear. Though it's been good, the other tax issues had barely occurred to me. The state loses over twenty-five hundred in sales tax every two years from my new-model Lincoln Continentals, but the tax inflation on cigarettes must be outrageous. In this last year, Rollins has virtually soared from pathetic Moon Road drunk to wealthy businessman. He likely now wears the title of "millionaire" with no trouble.

A number of Nation members complained to the Chiefs' Council, but their arguments rang untrue—a few smoking when they made the complaints. They wondered why the Nation hadn't been involved with the business from the beginning. Boiled down, their questions often contained a "what's in it for me?" element. The real reasons they should be protesting Rollins's shop eluded them. They hadn't seen the future—but naturally, that was my job. That job, that status, had remained mine all of these years, until the first day of this year—the day that girl, with her beaded dress and long fingers, called my leadership into question.

As she approached the center of the room in that dress, the Nation forgot that I had only enacted their wishes; but that is part of my responsibility, too. I should have been able to see through my own feelings, should have protested, directing them toward some other solution; but secretly, making the calls to the utility companies was a delight. It was a good idea. How would future generations of Tuscaroras survive if just anybody could live in our Nation? How could that future place even be considered a Nation? They shall see clearly soon, and today, I shall be one step closer to parting this fog from their minds and allowing them the insight that they must fight for the purity of their Nation.

My wife doesn't stir at my leaving the bed this morning. She'll have her own hard day ahead of her, and she should be granted the two extra hours of sleep I'm denied. She'll have to stand with me, a show of solidarity, knowing the stories being told about her just below hearing level, even by people on our own side. Constant reminders—in the telling behind their eyes, in the slightest smirks below the surfaces of even the most supportive faces—will tell her she'd been the only one blind enough to not follow the trace of my long fingers down to the hands of that young woman.

Keeping my wife in the early days of this year had been a true challenge. Though she really had nowhere to go, she packed a few small bags the night of the Feast, leaving the jewelry I'd given her over the years clumped neatly on her dresser. The Debate had ended with the girl's accusations, and we'd driven back in silence. Twila has still never spoken a reason for wanting to leave me. The girl remains shrouded in some unspeakable shadow. On the occasions I've tried to introduce an explanation, Twila has silently returned to her still-packed bags, and only the importance of Nation solidarity has kept her at home. She remains a good Chief's wife, knowing Nation responsibilities are sometimes more important than her own happiness.

The cool bathroom tiles shock the pads of my feet as she sleeps, her slight form rising and falling beneath the blankets. How could I have ever strayed from her, those years ago, so dedicated and trusting every time I leaned my head into the living room, hiding my hardness behind the plasterboard, telling her I was off to check the orchards? She never looked, though—only waved and told me to hurry back, that she would miss me. She never questioned the showers every time, either, accepting the claim that my romps through the trees had made me sweaty. My lack of certainty in my actions lasts only seconds, though, and my answer hurries me along my way.

The door shuts silently on its rollers, and I am in the dark for a moment, hoping my morning routine will wash my answer away. This morning, my toothbrush catches a little on the gold clasps holding my bridgework in. If given no other inheritance from my father, clearly I have received his bad teeth. The fluorescents buzz and flicker at my hands, power igniting in the room, lighting my body and exposing its secrets, my other inheritance. Darkness falls from my ribs in the harsh light, lines drawn across my dark chest pointing shadowy, accusing fingers at the faint hairs growing around my nipples—fragile, tattletale spiders. I tried ripping them from my body in my younger years, but they continued to creep out, spinning their web of my lineage. The vanity mirror ends at my chest, so the line of thick, shiny hair running from my belly button down to my privates remains obscure.

The water from my showerhead pulses like blood flowing over me from an unseen heart. The liquid soap easily lathers, scrubbing and rinsing the night from my body, and the necessarily small dollop of shampoo reminds me why I never bother showering in the dark anymore. The thinning strands dance across my slippery scalp under the stream.

Around the time of my fortieth birthday, I was forced to modify the "What is an Indian?" lecture I'd given for many years to area schoolchildren. My father had done this before me, and I took over after his passing. For years, I stuck my fingers in my thick black hair and proclaimed, with a chuckle, that Indians did not go bald, that baldness was God's way of scalping the white man. At least one bald man, usually the school principal or one of the teachers, was in the room every time, and I would smile gently at this fellow.

My lecture from that time on, though, after my hairline began crawling to the back of my head, included a few minutes of "dispelling the rumors" about Indians. "See," I said thereafter, "we go bald, too. That other story, that is just a myth." Some of the same bald men who'd been in the audience for years now smiled back, but not nearly as gently as I had. They had the power of knowledge, of experience.

Far from confirming my Tuscarora heritage, my gleaming, exposed skin confirms, at least for me, a different tradition among the Tuscarora. Our last names clearly came from a Christian influence—this is a given—but I have grown convinced since puberty revealed my history that white blood mixed into my family line somewhere. The source, though, is entirely unclear. I have come from a long line of apparently closed-mouthed Chiefs, running the course of the clans through the generations, each growing to represent the clan of his mother. My father, however, died with a full head of hair, and before that spent every summer almost constantly shirtless, working the orchards, not one hair marring his deep, brick-colored skin. This leaves my mother's line as the more likely source, and if that were true, according to the Great Law, I quite possibly have no Tuscarora status. Though my entire life has been spent immersed in the culture, I might officially be white.

Whoever would have known this information firsthand is now long dead, and if anyone passed it down, the truth has never come out. The indiscretion of my ancestors played itself out in my genetic makeup, as my own indiscretions have in my daughter's. Toweling off, my chest hairs accusingly thickened with dampness in the mirror, I know the reasons I slept among the apples with Deanna Johns: quite simply, because I could. Any number of Tuscarora women offered themselves to me before I settled down, each hoping to be the wife of a Chief. Only Twila waited until marriage to give in to me, and in that way, let me know she was the one.

The sun creeps softly behind the venetian blinds, outlines the silhouette of my wife in nearly motionless slumber, and slashes my chest with light through the steam rushing out the bathroom door. I love her passionately, even still; but back then, the variety had been an extremely difficult luxury to abandon. The responsibilities of my role kept other Tuscarora women safe from pursuit, but non-Tuscarora women were another matter. I hadn't felt any need to guide Deanna Johns anywhere but under me, among my rows of entwined apple trees.

Deanna was the only one after I was married—married life harnessed me beyond her—but that child remains a flag to me of how easy and seductive irresponsibility is. In a way, I can almost appreciate the girl, her existence proving for me that Rollins needs to be stopped from becoming even more powerful than he already is. The boy clearly doesn't know the responsibilities that come with power. Only the life of one non-Tuscarora woman was disrupted under my guidance; Rollins is playing for much bigger stakes—the integrity of the Nation and its political structure. Rollins's new "big proposal" for the Nation grows a deep fear in my belly, but I have to attend our agreed-upon meeting today, regardless, and whatever the boy's idea is, it will be crushed. Rollins is taking too many liberties. His money is going to his head. There cannot be two sets of people to follow into the future. That simply does not work.

My steel-toed work boots leave heavier, thicker prints across the living-room carpet than the pair of dress loafers I had initially pulled from the foyer coat closet. If today is going to be like every other day this past week, the tan boots are better suited to the kind of *oo(t)-gweh-rheh*-kicking that is likely to come later. These boots have not really done any of the kicking themselves, but they are a show of solidarity with those boots that will grow bloody, if necessary. And that's what our life is all about: solidarity, community.

My permanent-press slacks look odd with the boots, so they go back to the bedroom closet, exchanged for a pair of prewashed and prefaded dungarees. The fade is too uniform to look weathered by real work, but it is an attempt. This will be closer to what everyone else on my side will be wearing. Appropriately dressed, I leave the house silently, drive with the headlights off—as my home disappears in my rearview mirror amid the dark orchards, dancing masses blowing in the early-morning breezes. Vague light from the horizon sun slowly burns the night off of my sleeping Nation.

A few members of the congregation wait in their cars at the Protestant Church parking lot, idling, their exhaust fumes mixing with the early-morning mist. Just inside the front door lean a row of picket signs and several large aluminum pails with lids and dippers. As soon as I unlock the door, Johnnyboy Martin—the Chief who took my father's place—steps up and helps distribute them among our supporters. Throughout this last week, their number has leveled out to a sadly disappointing few, all members of the Protestant Church who have really turned out so diligently to support Johnnyboy, their deacon, rather than for any political motivation.

They haven't shown for me—that's clear. A number of former supporters, while they've not defected to Rollins's side, or at least haven't yet shown on his side of the picket lines, have refused to participate in the protest, and have made it clear that they'd not approved of my handling of the "Fiction situation," as the girl's story has come to be known since January. Though enough have appeared this morning—and every morning for the last week—to make the path difficult for Rollins's new gasoline business, I continue to hope for a line so overwhelming that Rollins would know the people don't want his ideas for their future, would know he's been defeated.

The business property bumps right up to the road cinders, and my crew can only stay in those sooty margins. The New York State Troopers reminded me my Nation's sovereignty didn't allow outside interference among its members without written consent from a Nation official—when I asked what could be done about the business and Rollins's refusal to comply with the Chiefs' shutdown command. Though many opposition members were not of the Nation, the trooper said this was a technicality; if they live within the bounds of the Nation and the problem is within its borders, they're our problem.

The trooper, a notary public, held out a pen and a sheet of paper. All I had to do was give the state jurisdiction on Nation land. The period could be flexible and could be rescinded immediately, by me or by any other Chief, at any time. The paper stayed blank, and the trooper kept his pen. The situation cannot have come to this.

If I signed that paper, which I've contemplated more seriously than I'd like to recall, the door would be wide open for an end to our Nation. Once outside forces entered, the rule I'd used in my first real attempt to remove the girl would be totally useless. Rollins and his lawyers have me for the moment; but once the others see that non-Tuscaroras living among us endanger our continued sovereignty, the girl—my daughter—will be gone forever, with all the other undesirables. If I sign that paper, betraying everything it is my responsibility to uphold, all sovereignty issues will be lost.

I invented a worry that my people might be subjected to violence during our peaceful protest, standing in places not governed by the Nation, reminding the desk trooper that they have issued speeding tickets on our roads as part of state maintenance. I hadn't believed a word I said, but my anticipation of the state's response led me to believe they might be of some use, if only visually.

This morning, sending the Nation supporters out with their signs and pails for fresh well water, confidence streams from me in every direction. The troopers will flank my group again, as they have every day since my complaint, and this will surely bring the media again. The television reporters have been listening to reason and have broadcast features since the beginning, exposing Rollins for the corrupt threat to tradition he truly is. This continued coverage should bring more protesters to the line. On Friday, every Nation mailbox received a photocopied plea for increased attendance; but it appears, by this morning's turnout, that this campaign was a waste of time and paper.

Overgrown and nearly obscured, the ancient manual pump rests between the church's back wall and the incline where Big Crick runs, the place I was baptized. The crick is so close to the church's leach bed, being submerged in its flowing waters doesn't hold the appeal it once had. That more formal ritual has been replaced by a splash on the forehead, another tradition falling by the wayside. Several people stand around while a young man pumps gushing water into the pails, stopping only to exchange a full one for an empty.

The water is the heart of my argument for the media, and really for my people, too. Sadly, most of them know the realities of sovereignty and power and the seventh generation about as well as the media, but the water is something concrete for them to grasp, something to fight for. The gasoline tanks, lowered into the ground, unregulated, gave me the push. At the first protest meeting, they were easy to convince that, being used on Nation land, the tanks didn't have to pass a DEC safety test. Of course, I had to explain that "DEC" stood for Department of Environmental Conservation; but once I made them see a small ocean of gasoline creeping from substandard tanks into their drinking-water wells, they were more than happy to line up on Pem Brook to express their indignation.

The water pushes as a flowing rallying cry, and the people fixed on it. One of Johnnyboy's nephews, Paul Valley, thought bringing crisp, cold wellwater to revive our protesters throughout the day would be an encouragement. He made signs about the virtues of this water. For the past week, unseasonably hot, we even dipped into the pails and poured the clear wetness over one another on the protest line, celebrating in the pure soaking and leisurely drying.

We load the covered pails into the back of Johnnyboy's Bronco, and I tell them that if all goes well today, they will not have to picket any longer. Some nod—others merely drive off, leaving me in a wake of fading music and spinning parking-lot gravel dust.

"You know, Jacob," Johnnyboy says, when we're alone, "they are supporting your ideas, but . . . it's gonna take you something awful big to recover your honor from what you did to Fic . . . that Johns girl. You better be able to take this boy down and bring him back among us, or this just might be the last thing you do as Chief. I know you don't want to admit it, particularly here in the churchyard, but that girl is your daughter, and all these people believed her at the Feast. I can't think of any way what you did to her serves the people, and they can't either." Johnnyboy walks circles in the lot, gravel popping under his feet, shifting with his weight.

"You better be able to show you got someone else's interest at heart here, or you're gonna lose the line started a long time ago by your grandfathers. You're not the only Chief out here, you know. We may have let you act that way for a while, 'cause you seemed to know what you were doing; but I'm not so sure anymore. I hope, and I pray to Jesus, that you know what you're doing. That boy's no dummy, and his vision might be as sharp as yours is." Johnnyboy climbs into his Bronco and drives away, leaving me alone in the churchyard to prepare for my meeting.

It's easy for Johnnyboy Martin to be tough now, when most of the real decisions have already been made, but the apathetic group of Chiefs who welcomed me at my installation during the condolence ceremony spoke volumes about why I was needed. My adult life has been consumed taking this nonfunctional Council and reviving its power, forcing it to reassert itself in this Nation. And now that I've made one decision they feel some guilt about, suddenly I better watch the ways I ride over them. *Oo(t)-gweh-rheh!* I am the one true leader of the Tuscarora Nation—it's me that Rollins always comes to with his ludicrous proposals. The briefcase resting in my trunk is the singular proof that I am this Nation's only hope.

In the Power Vista's main lobby, a few minutes later, a friendly young woman in a blue synthetic blazer greets me; and behind her, in an enormous mural, Father Hennepin—the first white man to see Niagara Falls—"discovers" the rushing water and climbing mists, while flanked by his Mohawk guides. Mason Rollins certainly has a sick sense of humor, picking this place: a tremendous power station, the development of which relied upon my father's inability to stop the state from taking a fifth of our Nation's land—as if we could actually be effective against the United States Supreme Court. These young ones, they forget all about that. All they hear are the stories of how much their families lost—how the people protested then, but that it did them no good. Well, this time, protests are going to work. My reflection in the glass wall—a tired face, cheekbone wrinkles and deep eye circles—blends gently with the natural cracks and gouges along the gorge's sides.

"Bud, glad you could make it. I was beginning to wonder." Mason Rollins approaches from behind, nearly silent in his designer suit and shoes, even on the tiled floor. A similarly dressed man stands a few feet away. Rollins holds out his hand.

"I thought we were meeting alone."

"Sorry, I just want these papers all drawn out perfectly," Rollins says. "Bud . . . sorry, Jacob Tunny, I'd like you to meet my attorney, Richard Overstreet. He'll be helping us with the papers."

"What papers?" I ask, carrying my own papers, also composed with the assistance of a lawyer. In mine, Mason Rollins clearly agrees to immediately shut down his gasoline and cigarette business, pay for the gasoline's safe drainage, and finally have the storage tanks extricated (I really like that lawyer word) from the ground, with a promise to never set up any business venture again without first consulting with the Chiefs' Council. All the documents need is Rollins's signature. Really, the papers are unenforceable, even if Rollins does sign them, without my allowing the New York State legal system—and thus the legal system of the United States—to interfere in our tribal politics. The signed papers (assuming Rollins will sign them) will sit in the safe deposit box with all other significant Nation documents, proof enough.

"C'mon. Let's go up here," Rollins says, climbing a Plexiglas staircase to the next level of the Vista, the observation deck. The other suited man, Overstreet, waits patiently for me to follow Rollins on the stairs before taking them himself. The building appears made up exclusively of glass and I-beams. Rollins moves silently to one of the glass corners, looking out on the expanse and then down. This section of the Vista juts out above the gorge, at a right angle from the rest of the structure, and we seem to be balanced precariously over the ravaged landscape.

"Magnificent, ain't it?" Rollins asks, leaning his belly against the guard rail. "This water just keeps running. Man doesn't stop it; dirt doesn't stop it. Shit, even rock can't stop it. Look at that gorge. Rock worn right off, and even then, is the water satisfied? Man, it just keeps going."

"You brought me here to show me the river? I've seen it."

"I don't think you have, Bud, or at least not really well." He seems to continue staring out at the water. "You see, on the surface, water looks pretty easy to handle, right? Just like a shower." Rollins turns and leans closer to me, inhaling deeply through his nostrils. "You showered today, am I right? That wasn't too hard to take, right? Water running gently over your body. The falls kinda looks like that on the surface, steaming up God's mirror, but underneath . . . oh man, underneath, that water just keeps digging and digging. It's relentless—so relentless, it can wear down rock. It wore down this gorge," he says, slapping one of his hands against the Plexi.

"So?" I have, in fact, never been within these transparent walls before, and have no desire to stay any longer than is necessary—only agreeing to come because Rollins assured me we would earnestly discuss the closing of the Smoke Rings era.

"So, nothing . . . I just like it up here." Rollins turns back to face the gorge again. "So here's the deal, Bud. The Nation's biggest worry over my shop is water contamination from the storage tanks, right? That's why you want me to shut Smoke Rings down?"

"That's correct. We know those tanks didn't even undergo any DEC testing. We know—"

"Actually, they did. They're fine. Think about it, Bud. You think I want to lose all that gas—that I've already paid for up front—into the ground? It just doesn't make any sense. Certainly not business sense."

"I don't care. I want those tanks out of there."

"I know, Bud. It's not the Nation. It's you. Well, I want you to listen for a few minutes, and then I'll listen to you. That's the way it's supposed to work in open Council, isn't it?"

"There are no *cree-rhooh-rhit* at open Council."

"Overstreet's just an observer at this point. He won't say anything now, unless I ask him to. So anyway, here's my deal. I'm ready to offer the Nation city water—chlorinated, clean, safe, Niagara Falls water—all lines laid out at my expense. And," Rollins exaggerates, "full partnership in a new version of the shop, one with an expanded line. There are other things out there that, when they're not taxed, might be inviting. Fifty-fifty, me and the Nation, in the Onguiaahra Nation Products and Sales. I'd never use the name 'Smoke Rings' again for a business, so that way, I would be following the Council's order."

"No," I say without hesitation. "How can you imagine any of those offers would bring good things? You tell me we're going to negotiate your shutdown out here, and then instead, you offer me another invasion from the outside forces and expect me to accept? Your brain must be affected by all those gasoline fumes; you are drowning in the Bad Mind. And what the hell is On-gee-ara, anyway?" I know it's a trap, but I have to walk through anyway.

"Ooh, Bud, you don't know your history too well, do you? Guess you'll just have to find out on your own. Anyway, that's a bullshit excuse. It's not as if there ain't already other outside elements in your precious Nation—electric, telephones, bottled propane heat. Last time I looked, we don't have a power station on the reservation, except where your father sold us out."

"All of those relationships were established under my father's guidance. You can't blame me for his mistakes, and I intend to make none of the same. I know this Nation, in ways you obviously do not, or you wouldn't have made such an offer. You see, there can be no relationship where you stand above the rest of the Nation. We are all about having equal voices. What you propose has nothing to do with our way of life. You will still close your business."

"Afraid not, Bud. But let me get this straight," Rollins says, stepping closer, backing me into one of the glass walls. "Even forgetting the fifty-fifty deal, if I can arrange to have city water lines run through the reservation, at my expense, you're refusing me?"

"That is correct. I told you, as long as I am a Chief, not one more outside force will enter our boundaries." I rush down the Plexi stairs. On the floor below, the word "Onguiaahra" stares me in the face, written under the Father Hennepin mural. It was the word the Haudenosaunee had used to describe the waterfalls, a word obviously Hennepin had been unable to pronounce.

MY WIFE WANDERS UP AND DOWN THE DRIVEWAY, NEARLY BLOCKING MY ENTRANCE, instead of being at the protest line. Then I see what she sees. Something's wrong with the trees lined up on the borders of my neat and orderly rows. Thick, hearty leaves that should glisten in the sun are wilting, curling under themselves on drooping new growth. A ring of bark has been stripped all the way around every tree. Even the old growth seems to have a desire for crawling back under the furrowed earth.

Every tree is the same. The problem is not isolated, and the closer I get, joining my wife, the more my nose burns with chemical scent. The vegetation killer has seeped into the ground. The surface is no longer wet with it, but its scent, unmistakable, lingers in the air as it works at destroying my roots. It'll be years before the contaminant is flushed from the system and things are normal again.

In less than an hour, I make a liar of myself, signing the statement at the New York State Troopers barracks, granting them jurisdiction to operate within the Nation's borders, even before reaching the Nation and consulting with them on my decision. This act will put the girl out of my reach for now, but the Nation's interests must come first. One of the treaties with the government provides that support would be available to the Nation if any hostile party threatened its integrity. The floor fills my eyes, so I do not see my reflection in the barracks' glass doors. My papers remain unsigned by Mason Rollins. A seeping insight filters through my brain: that the most formidable and dangerous hostile party can surface from within the Nation's own currents.

It will be years before things are normal again.

PART THREE

Smoke Dance

Okay, now, Smoke Dance, this is a tough one; you have to be like the smoke itself, shifting whichever way the wind blows. And you know that the one of you who follows the wind the best, through its twists and turns and sudden shifts, and who can anticipate a sudden drop in the wind and stop with it—well then, that person is the best Smoke Dancer. Single competitors, here—every man for himself, cutting your own territory, and at the same time pounding those evils back into the earth; and remember, me and my drum here? We're pretty tricky winds, I can tell you. You never know how we're gonna shift, or how long we'll last. Oh yeah, I always forget this—ladies too, these days. We don't want them nagging, now, do we?"

SINGER, GRAND RIVER POWWOW, SIX NATIONS RESERVE

CHAPTER 13 Snap Shots

Big Red Harmony

HERE IS THE BEGINNING. THE GLEAMING SALIVA ARCS UPWARD IN THE HUMID May air, then back earthward, toward the closer line of divided folks. My lens focuses on the globe, the bubbles locked within, and I press the button, hoping to freeze the missile, to suspend it twenty feet or so above their heads. They could contemplate the significance of this act and conveniently sidestep its path, stopping this nonsense.

It is a hawker without incident, though, peacefully landing in the dust a few inches away from any shoe, boot, moccasin, or bare foot, avoiding the eventual start of an altercation that is surely no more than two days away at the longest. The photo won't likely turn out, but it hadn't been an historic lob, anyway. It was pure luck I even got the opportunity to document it—the sort Zapruder had been afforded in Dallas—though something's going to happen, soon. Surely Zapruder hadn't anticipated the explosion of Kennedy's head under the Texas sun.

Wayne Grayson, locked in the powerful lens a few seconds ago, had for years passed candy out to children at the Clan League basketball games, but now made plans of distributing something else to the young people of the Nation. Nostrils flared, face bunched into an awkward expression, he planned his shot carefully. The thick ball left Wayne's mouth, fury driving it, and my camera, auto-advancing, followed the rocket.

My girlfriend and my son stand just this side of the picket line, watching all the traditional protesters, their Tuscarora Protestant Church charter pins gleaming in the late-morning sun. This hostile line blocks Pem Brook, stretching from the front of Bert's house across Mason's stone parking lot, and even over into the wild bushes still bordering the south end of the business, beyond the ruts Mason's old purple shed left behind—right up to the sign announcing the southern border line of the reservation, where Mason is in the slow process of changing the landscape into parking lot. In a way, I was relieved to see the glob had headed in Fiction and Two-Step's direction—they're generally in control, even as targets.

Cameras that can capture this sort of detail have always floated inches away, their price tags proclaiming they were luxuries only obtainable in the "next-year" world. I found a number of discarded cameras over the years of junking, but most had been thrown out for obvious reasons; and of the few I ever took down to Camera Doctor for a free estimate, none ever came back with a good prognosis.

Before Camera Doctor, I tested my finds, taking twelve-exposure rolls with the cameras and dropping them off at the drug store, picking up the developed shots whenever extra money allowed, sometimes months later. Each time, the glossy photos clearly displayed reasons for the particular camera's demise. Some of the shots streaked their subjects with outrageous color—deranged clowns inspired by Jerry Garcia. Another camera cast brilliant white light over a third of every image, a not-too-distant nuclear explosion occurring at exactly the moment the photo had been snapped. A third gave my subjects glowing red eyes—family photos from a summer picnic in Hell.

All these failures were banished to my work shed—still safe from the junk pile—where they would await their final fates among other, previous failures. They gathered dust for years, and I would occasionally examine a few, arrive at no conclusions, and set them gently back among their pile. Finally, during this long winter, years later, those old cameras grew useful. At first, while my truck warmed up, I dismantled the cameras, removing their lenses, setting them on a bolt of beadwork velvet, and tossing their broken and defective shells. Some lenses had shattered, either in the past or in my removal attempt, but that was alright. Most had been surprisingly intact, clearly not the defective element of the camera, and I only needed seven.

I've had winter hobbies, both before the Mercury coat rack and after, whenever they revealed themselves. These gleaming lenses, jewel-like on the velvet, called in that familiar voice, guiding my hand, telling me what to do. Whenever not out plowing reservation driveways for Mason Rollins, I worked on a new carving, presenting it to my boss on the opening day of Smoke Rings—lugging it, late the night before, to the suite of offices and, using the key he now entrusted me with, mounting the new carving on the wall Mason faced when he sat at the desk.

"What the fuck is that?" Mason asked the next morning, first squinting and then frowning. The carving still hangs in the same spot, though, and that's really more important than any initial reaction to the piece. In fact, this morning the carving had recently been dusted, the lenses even polished.

Some casual shots of Two-Step and Fiction fill the end of this thirty-six roll. The Camera Doctor suggested I never trust anything important to the last couple of shots on a roll. Sometimes the edges get cut off—or the images, under the strain of advancement, grow stretched and distorted, or in some other way undesirable.

Nearly fifty rolls of film this week have run past my camera's shutter, documenting the protest over Smoke Rings' opening in some form other than the ridiculous version Bud has somehow gotten the papers and the TV to agree to—the black-and-white version, where Mason is the corruption monster and Bud remains the noble Chief, fighting for his people's ancient way of life. Shots on each roll are dedicated to Bud and his Continental—which, not surprisingly, never seems to appear in any pictures with its owner in the local news.

Mason reassigned me to this job the day before we opened the new shop, handing me the expensive Minolta setup and the address of Camera Doctor, where I spent the rest of the afternoon in a crash course on photography. The zoom was amazing, and manual focus was easy to master. Twisting the barrel that first day, I captured my images precisely: Two-Step on our front porch, his hair spiked from a full night's sleep; my boy casually dancing to himself, some new move that looks like he is thinking of Smoke Dancing, on the soft spring earth outside our trailer; Fiction lying on the new grass, enjoying the sun and dismissing the fact that her long hair is resting in mud.

The only shot not clearly focused was an attempt to use the built-in timer, consisting of me chasing Fiction in the grass. The camera had auto-focused instead on my old, dissolving retired truck at the far end of the driveway behind us, its pitted surface and even Chuck's hand-painted "Curbside Phoenix" standing out in every sharp detail, while the two figures running from the camera were shy ghosts, sprinting for a getaway car, escaping the camera's stare.

Fiction makes elaborate hand gestures to Two-Step—part of a story I can't quite decipher from here—at the end of this roll, and that blurry shot aches with familiarity. At the last exposure, my camera begins to whine in its automatic-rewind mode, the film finally dropping out neatly into my hand, a bullet of images ready to explode. The used roll goes in the OUT basket, and I pick up a fresh one from the small refrigerator Mason purchased just for film.

The high-tech police scanner on Mason's desk traces its radio waves in blinking red lights—left to right, over and over—searching for any information that might be useful. The red light stops occasionally—reports ambulance calls, domestic disputes, schedule changes and the like—then moves on, searching, sometimes documenting nothing more than a coffee break. Mason keeps the shifting red line and its arbitrary stops on at all hours, the machine equipped with a recorder that only engages after the light has paused for at least four seconds. Though we've gotten a lot of garbage, he hopes this will pay off eventually—exactly how, he hasn't said.

That hazy photo stays with me, reminding me of an earlier camera's tricks—one of my junk finds, and the only one I didn't dismantle for Mason's carving. The camera still sits at my workbench, collecting dust on the sill above all my other junk finds. This photo, though, has nagged at me ever since I had it developed two weeks ago, and the urge to go through my old pictures finally won.

Earlier this morning, before Two-Step awoke, I pulled my snapshot box from the bedroom closet's top shelf. Several black-and-whites of me as a kid curled in on themselves in this box, which also harbored a few heavy cardboard-backed color shots of me dancing, and whatever photos people had given Bev and me of our wedding—documents other people had made of my life. We never got around to buying an album, and we had both grown up in families who used the snapshot-box method of saving their memories.

Any photo coming into the house was slid into the corners of mirror frames, displayed for a while until someone grew bored with it. That person would remove the photo and throw it in the snapshot box, sifting casually through the images—some from decades before, others as recent as a month old—until a suitable replacement was found, and that photo would then occupy the mirror space until the boredom of familiarity set in again.

In this morning's soft early light, I shuffled through our box—an elaborate, deep, velvet-lined cube, ornately topped with embossed-aluminum panels depicting scenes of knights and horses—quite fancy for what was, essentially, a cardboard box. Bert had given it to us as our wedding gift—the earlier photos of me, and their negatives, enclosed. We were very impressed, as Bert had held one of the best collections of the Nation's photographic history, period. Though Bud and some others, including university history folks, had begged numerous times, she'd never given away one picture, not even the rights to reproduce them. I suppose Fiction has those pictures now. She's never said.

✷

BERT HAD STARTED THE PRACTICE OF PHOTO DOCUMENTATION WHEN SHE'D BEEN very young and the dancing was done in secret. The only public performances Tuscaroras did in those days, the first half of this century, had been a ridiculous pageant sponsored by the Tuscarora Protestant Church, where Nation members, dressed in Plains war-bonnets and buckskin outfits, recited the poetry of Longfellow and sang hymns like "Amazing Grace" and "Gladly the Cross I'd Bear" for audiences made up of congregation members from various Western New York Protestant churches.

The dancing, on the other hand, had occurred in clearings in the woods, among the wild. The participants snuck their calico-and-velvet dancing outfits in satchels to the sites, preferring not to be seen by those Nation members who didn't recognize any Longhouse tradition, including social dancing. The men would change into their leggings, loin cloths, and ribbon shirts among the trees on one side of the clearing, and the women, on the other, would slip into their ribbon dresses and velvet beaded collars and cuffs.

Bert had grown up in this practice, her mother taking her to every secret social dance she'd heard of. Even these dances had nearly died during the smallpox outbreak when Bert was twelve. At every dance, they'd had to perform a mourning dance, a dance of remembrance—at least one among them having fallen since the last dance. By the third occurrence, Bert's mother had handed her the old Brownie camera she'd traded an ornately beaded collar for earlier in the year; her instructions had been for

Bert to document the dances before they'd be lost forever. Bert had taken shots of those who were not looking too healthy, not knowing if she'd have another opportunity. Those whose pictures she'd taken experienced miraculous recoveries, and soon every dancer begged to have Bert snap a shot, and she had obliged, believing she was somehow saving her community.

She'd continued documenting the dances in the woods, coaxing new people in as others grew too old to dance or had simply passed on. She'd asked only those she thought had the strength to carry this responsibility on their shoulders, and she had never been wrong. She'd brought her dancers, as they had gradually come to be known, out of the woods and into the arenas in the sixties, when the powwows awakened tradition in so many Indians around the country, when feathers and beads abounded, when it became cool to be an Indian—so cool even one of the Monkees suddenly discovered he was part Cherokee and wore a Lakota war-bonnet to the Monterey Pop Festival, where Jimi Hendrix lit the night with tribal fire. Suddenly, Bert had become legitimate—maybe even in demand.

><

DEEPER IN THE BOX, PAST THE GLOSSY CAPTURED YEARS, A SET OF PICTURES collected in a wax-paper envelope at the bottom waited. I spread the shots out on my freshly made bed. I always make the bed as soon as I step from it. Bev had always loved to sleep in. Often, after she'd died, if the bed were unmade and the covers crumpled just right, she would seem to appear suddenly back in our bed, wrapped in its blanket cave, dozing and avoiding the coffee maker for as long as she possibly could.

The junk-camera photos before me had been cause for great laughter between us. They were from the only camera we wasted more than one lone twelve-exposure roll on. The Pentax seemed to be fine, and in fact, the Camera Doctor couldn't confirm a cause for the anomaly, so we were stuck owning a relatively high-quality camera with a wandering eye. The automatic-focus mechanism had its own agenda. Regardless of what we tried to shoot, the camera focused on some irrelevant object in the viewfinder. Even if we tried tricking it, focusing on a meaningless object when the true subject lurked in the foreground or background, pretending insignificance, the camera still decided on an old water bucket, a broken fence, the rural delivery box for a now-dead newspaper, leaving the person in the frame smudged and cloudy.

For one shot, Bev crouched down and posed, perfectly still, in front of a tossed-out TV set whose picture tube had been shot into, weird concentric circles marking the bullets' paths through the glass. As usual, when we got the roll developed, the bullet holes had been captured in their circular perfection; the dial numbers and even the fake woodgrain stood out clearly on the discarded box, but Bev was some character broadcast across the airwaves from a distant station, a gauzy victim of poor reception. All the photos laid out on the bed had that same weird look: Bev about to vanish from their surface on a random wind if I looked away for even a moment.

Over the years, she's even faded to some hazy lover, her body glowing with that same curious iridescence as we make love in my memories. Aside from our wedding pictures—marred by bad light or streaked motion—these are the only shots I have of my wife. We eventually grew tired of the bitchy camera and put it aside, promising ourselves a better camera when we made it big, when we'd have times worth remembering—the future I promised her.

"All the time with you was worth remembering, Babe," I said to the photos this morning, taking them out to my workshop.

Now, in Mason's office, the recently dusted carving that occupied my old workshop all winter long observes me load this prosperity camera. The carving's center holds a large, circular beveled mirror—an idea I stole from the Mercury rack, but one which made perfect sense for the elements surrounding it. Flanking the mirror in three directions curl carved, interlinked figures of the seven clans thriving on Tuscarora—Bear, Wolf, Deer, Turtle, Snipe, Eel, and Beaver—each staring out with inlaid camera-lens eyes at whoever is vain enough to use the mirror. Above the mirror, an eagle soars above the white pine, the Tree of Peace, its roots surrounding the glass.

Mason won't begrudge a few exposures on my handiwork, you know, as long as the camera's loaded and pretty full for today. Blackness fills the Minolta's viewfinder instead of the watching clans, the cap still on; and besides, it's a zoom, way too powerful for this little room. The heavy lens falls solid in my hand with the quick release. This won't take but a moment. I slip the lens into my arm pit for a minute. The image comes clear in the twisting standard barrel, lens compatible with subject. My prideful grin falters; my own face glides into focus in the cross hairs.

"Guess it works." I hoped the mirror might keep Mason grounded any time he groomed himself here before one of his public appearances, reminding him of the people he's responsible for, keeping him mindful that inside the thousand-dollar suit, he's still one of us and not above us. Through the viewfinder, I move out of the mirror's collecting area, focusing again when no part of me, not even my shadow, appears in the shot.

Gunshots fire outside the building. "Move in, move in. We got the okay, it's all clear," the scanner says, its red light frozen, as more exchanges come across. The forgotten zoom falls heavily on the Plexiglas carpet saver. I click the lens back into place, reaching a window. Below me, the entire dusty parking lot has come alive—a swarm of bees, bodies everywhere, rolling, punching, kicking one another. How can they possibly even see who they're swinging at? What could I have missed in the five minutes I was away at the mirror?

This scene is far worse than any Mason anticipated. The Minolta snaps onto the tripod, and I set the consecutive timer for one-minute intervals and, pointing the camera over the lot, take the stairs two at a time.

Bud's Lincoln is parked in its usual position, on the far side of Bert's house, but Bud isn't in any of the brawls in the stone driveway's expanse. Police in full riot gear have moved on the shop grounds, badges and face shields shining in the noon sun as they drag Smoke Rings employees and supporters through the stones, night sticks drawn and, in some cases, being used. Near the door I lock, two troopers attempt to squeeze into one of the four dumpsters banked near the side of the building.

"Hey! This is sovereign land! What the fuck are you doing?" I grab a trooper who, with another, reaches for a twelve-year-old girl named Shirlee Windson, trying to escape into the dumpster filled with empty cigarette cases.

"Back off," the trooper says, releasing Shirlee long enough to shove my hand away. It's all she needs. She bites the other officer's gloved hand until he lets go, and she dives out the dumpster's back door, running for the woods. "That's it. You're coming in. I've got you on obstructing justice." He reveals handcuffs and shoves me up against the dumpster's open door.

"What justice?" I have to ask, frisked and cuffed, wrists locked behind my back.

"We were in the process of arresting the individual in the dumpster, when you—"

"You were arresting a twelve-year-old girl?" I'm yanked forward and heavily escorted through the stone lot, through similar scenes, many of my friends dragging their feet and stiffening their legs among similar cadres. Every Protestant still remains on their line. "Hey! How come you're not arresting any of them?"

"She's twelve," one trooper says to another. "They haven't done anything wrong. They're merely staging a peaceful protest. Any idea what the girl's name might be? Your cooperation would be noted. And . . . age does not matter. She assaulted an officer—"

"That kid? Yeah, she's real dangerous."

"She kicked an officer in the groin, temporarily disabling him," the trooper says and is then silent. I say nothing. She could probably make it to the woods, and if she has, she'll be free; they'll never catch her. She's Longhouse, and none of those Protestants would recognize her, even from a photograph.

Fiction looks up just in time to lock eyes with me, and I yell to her. She frowns, cups her hand to her ear, and gives whoever she's wrestling with a big-ass slap and runs my way as I'm shoved in the back of a police van. "Will you wait a fuckin' minute," I say to the trooper whose hand is pressing against my forehead, trying to force me into the van. "Take care of Two-Step until we can get this all straightened out, all right? And, uh, see that Mason gets that project I been working on," I yell to Fiction, looking up into the T.R.B. window, where the camera winks in the sunlight.

She nods and runs toward my boy, who is wiping spit from his face and shouting as loud as he can at Wayne Grayson, their faces a few inches from one another. The van fills with other bloody employees, and the two officers riding with us, their weapons drawn, close the door. "They'll be all right," Butchie Jacobson says, trying to wink his right eye, pinched shut under a growing welt. "She's a good kid. She don't take after her father."

"What are you doing here?" Butchie, a sixty-seven-year-old man, broke and bored with retirement, just started at the shop yesterday, doing some landscaping around the buildings. This morning the old guy wandered around with a series of flats, planting flowers in barrel gardens around the T.R.B. and smoke-shop entrances, to make the place seem more spring-like.

"Donnie, it's my place, too. I'd be watching the goddamned *Price Is Right* if I didn't have this job, maybe waiting 'til noon to eat and think about what I'm gonna have for supper, maybe not even waiting that long." I nod and smile at the old guy. "You know, I clocked that Johnnyboy right between the fuckin' eyes. Man, he saw stars and birds, I bet, just like in the fuckin' cartoons. And when he went down, Jex! Uppercut to the jaw. Cracked his bottom plate right in half. I could see the split, right between the two front teeth. But I guess I shouldn't ha' done that. I didn't think all this was gonna happen, but jeez, when he let that Bud do that . . ."

"Do what? What happened, anyway?"

"You don't know?" Butchie straightens out on the bench.

"No. I'm in the back of the building, and suddenly I hear these gunshots, and I come running on out and there's these guys trying to nab . . . trying to nab somebody in one of the dumpsters."

"Oh, jeez. Well, I was planting this flat of pansies, and I hear someone calling me from the line. I just figure it's one of them harassing me like they been doing. You know—they harass us, we harass them—that's the way it's been going. But I looks up anyways, and it's my cousin, Johnnyboy Martin. So I walks over, and he flags me over to the weedy end of the line where there ain't nobody, and he tells me that he's just warning me so's I can get out right then, that Bud has signed us over to these guys here, giving them jurisdiction." He motions with his chin to one of the troopers. "And I says, 'and you let him?' and he says, 'it's already been done, it's outa my hands,' and I says, 'get it back into your hands, you're a fuckin' Chief,' and he just stands there, shakin' his head like it's none of his business, so I clocked him."

"Well, what about the shots? I heard some shots fired." I still find it hard to believe that a good number of people are going to jail and another good number are hiding in the woods behind Smoke Rings because one old man punched another. Johnnyboy had to have been lying. The Chiefs would never sign us over.

"Oh, I don't know. One of their side, just trying to get things more stirred up, I guess. Coulda even been one of ours, too, I guess. You don't believe me, do you, Donnie? About what Bud did? I wouldn't shit ya. Ask this guy, here. He'll tell you." The trooper looks up, meets my eyes, and then nods.

>✦<

WE SPEND A FEW HOURS IN JAIL, UNTIL MASON ARRANGES BAIL. FINALLY, I JOIN Fiction—waiting in the line for my personal effects—stepping behind her and kissing her neck.

"Back of the line," the attendant says monotonously, not even looking up. She must come equipped with some built-in motion sensor.

"Oh, my God. I wondered when I was going to see you. I guess I didn't figure they'd put us in separate areas," Fiction says, as we step out of the line and retreat to its end. "Two-Step's in the hospital. I don't know. Maybe he's been released by now."

"What? What do you mean you don't know? I asked you to watch out for him. What's wrong?"

"He's all right. I had him brought to my house," Mason interrupts, joining us. "He won't be doing any dancing for awhile, but he's gonna be just fine. Now, there's plenty of time to continue this later, outside. I've got a couple of vans waiting, so as soon as you guys get your shit, meet me out there." An unusual number of people mill about with notebooks and mini-recorders. Mason nods and steps out the glass doors. Fiction and I hold hands, waiting in silence, but the entire time, she has refused to look at Mason.

On the way to Mason's new house, just off of the reservation, Fiction elaborates on her arrest—that she was taken in for leaving an impression on Wayne Grayson's head just about the size of her cowboy-boot heel while the two of them brawled in the state ditch. Though she explained to the arresting officers that she'd been trying to pull the man from a boy he'd been sitting on and pummeling, they'd seemed not even slightly interested. It didn't matter to them that Wayne Grayson had about two hundred pounds on Two-Step and had just deliberately leapt on him, breaking the boy's leg; all that mattered was that she had kicked an old man in the head.

Throughout her story, Mason continues a quiet, repeating phrase, alternating Bud's name with some swearing, occasionally punching the upholstered steel back of the bench in front of him. He adds a few things to her story, but she doesn't pause. The driver seems unwilling to speed, even a little, to get me faster to my boy. In the rearview mirror, the blank look in the driver's eyes says he's not being paid to care about my kid.

At Mason's house, my boy lies on the couch, watching MTV. Surgical-steel bars, wires, and pins, glowing neon-blue in the television light, pierce my boy's leg.

"Hey, I brought you this." Mason hands me a Minolta with a zoom.

"You got it. Great! What happened to the film?"

"I already had it developed, but that's not the same camera anyway. Well, the camera's the same, but I sent someone out for a new zoom. The old one's lens was busted. Split right down the center. Here, check out the kind of pictures it took." Mason spreads a series of thirty-six photos on his glass-top coffee table. The first is a shot of the carving in Mason's office; in the mirror, miniature people run across the reflected expanse of the T.R.B.'s main floor. The next exposure shows some blurred version of the carving, only the white pine in focus. All of the subsequent snaps involve groups of people running—some up close, some at a distance—but each of them are split nearly down the middle by a sharp white crack, and each side shows a drastically different angle of the scene. In one, Fiction shouts from the right at the blinding split, and across its arc, Wayne Grayson appears to be pounding at it. Two-Step points to the dark form harnessed between the old man's legs, noting he never has been very photogenic. My arrest is captured on one side of another, the other half revealing a state trooper cradling his balls in gloved hands.

"You still got that old zoom?"

Rollins shakes his head.

"Too bad. I think you're gonna have to find yourself a new photographer, though." I set the camera down near the photos. "I gotta take care of this boy for a while."

"Dad, I can take care of myself. And besides, Fiction can help." The boy struggles to reach for his brand-new crutches. "She's over all the time, anyway." Fiction nods, standing in the front door entryway, out of the boy's sight.

"Your boy's right," Mason says. "And besides, I think I got something else here that might change your mind." Mason slides another set of photographs across the table, Polaroids. They were all clearly taken from outside of a building through the windows—the yellow glow of electric lights shining out into the dark foreground in each. Each photo highlights groups of people gathered—some sitting at a weak and uneven card table, others on a wheezy-looking couch, still others just leaning against walls—but all of the people in the Polaroids have shotguns strapped across their shoulders. "It's Bert's house. While Bud kept you guys busy with the cops, he had the utilities turned on, in the name of the Nation. They've taken it over. They've got our house."

I pick up the fractured photos to add to my snapshot box, and sighing, lift the camera from the table.

><

CHAPTER 14 Bloodstone Mortar

Mason Rollins

THE EARTH ERUPTS WITH THE RUMBLING OF SMALL EXPLOSIVES AS THE BOW TIE falls loose from my neck. The troopers stay just across the road, watching, back behind an invisible shield. The border doesn't really exist anymore, but lots of people still try to pretend it does—and that holds a certain satisfaction, because they can't try hard enough to truly convince themselves. I haven't been able to keep them from my property since the day Bud signed the jurisdiction papers a month and a half ago. In the time since, no more arrests have been made, and Bud's group has dwindled some. They've finally realized the implications the jurisdiction statement holds for their own sovereignty. At a moment's notice, their leaders—on a whim—could alter their citizenship.

Much of that May day Bud crossed the line blew over surprisingly fast, and until a few seconds ago, the situation had settled into a nagging annoyance more than anything—a canker sore that kept rubbing up against my newly perfect white teeth, reminding me of its presence, a blister ready to burst. Smoke Rings Smoke Shop and Gasoline Island still thrived just fine, jamming and rocking all hours of the day and night, maybe more so—the news coverage alerting all in broadcast range of the bargains to be found over the reservation border. The protesters still blocked my driveway, trying to slow my business; my own counterprotesters still joked and hassled their opponents a few feet away; and the New York State Troopers still occupied my land, crowding the shop parking lot with their cruisers, intimidating potential new customers with their blank stares.

Most active hostility just vanished in the spring winds. We had arrived, as they say, at a stalemate, each keeping our own ground and hoping the other would eventually give in. The state troopers maybe even taught Bud's group a lesson by never leaving my land once they invaded it, but I've ended the stalemate and their occupation just now, with a shovel of dirt and some low-grade construction explosive.

Regret pinches me a little—losing the front parking lot as the crews tear into it, but it really hasn't been mine for the month and a half of occupation anyway. This doesn't alter my plans, even a little tiny bit. Those chumps can't occupy my property if it's under water.

These damned bow ties are still a mystery, and Gina Hendricks from my cleaning staff has to do them up for me on these occasions. She's always scheduled for the days my formal attire is required. My tailor suggested a cheater tie, a newer and more sophisticated variation on the clip-on ties I wore to church as a kid, but that would not do. My tailor assured me no one would be able to tell the difference, but I waved my hand away. "I would know." Later, I slowly pulled on the tie in my Mustang's rearview mirror, hoping to unlock its secrets, but the fabric somehow unbound itself without my being able to trace its path.

Though my need for wearing a tuxedo has occurred more frequently of late, no occasion has given me the satisfaction this one affords. Dust snags the sleeve of my jacket. Hazard of the trade. Happens at every damned ribbon-cutting ceremony and groundbreaking I've attended over the past few months. No matter what the official's level of grace, some smudge of dust or string of wayward ribbon always finds its way to the host's attire before the end of the ceremonies. I've just been christened by the earth, its blood anointing me.

"Hey." Red drops into one of the leather office chairs, pulling his necktie loose and lifting it over his head, never completely untying it. Fabric burrs pulling away from his sport jacket shine under the fluorescents.

"So, uh, why didn't you want one of these? You know, if this goes over big, we may just be hosting a few more of these things through the next couple of years." The office closet receives my tux, but the deep green cuff links sit plain on my desk, where they go if I'm not wearing them, their red-flecked surfaces shining in the fluorescents. "Well?" I prompt, yanking on a pair of jeans and a Smoke Rings T-shirt, closing the door on the apartment I recently had added up here.

"You know, you'd probably get a lot more mileage out of this groundbreaking if you'd let people know what it is you're building. Shit, even I don't know." He leans forward in the chair and examines his tie, repeatedly sliding its knot tighter and then loosening it.

"No, you don't understand, man. If they know what it is, then they expect it right away, as if you can just press a button and Presto! There it is. And when it doesn't show up . . . when it doesn't show up *right away,* they get bored. Sick of waiting. They just move on to the next spectacle. This way, I keep 'em guessing, right up to the end."

"So you gonna keep me guessing? Mason, you gotta trust somebody, and that somebody's gotta know you trust 'em. You got people here putting their lives on hold for you, living here—carrying guns, no less—to protect your interests from Bud and those crazy fucks holed up in Bert's house. Hey, they gotta know Bud stole that house from us—our home—and that's a pretty big thing to have over your head; but at least they know what they're fighting for, why they're doing those things. I've been here since the beginning, and man, I don't like being kept in the dark." He stands up and leans across the desk.

"And what's up with these outside contractors? I thought part of the reason for this business in the first place was to make jobs for folks from the reservation. I know ten guys, at least, who could operate that machinery out there. I'm one of them. When you look at this thing," he says, walking over to the carved mirror and tapping its carved wooden wolf—my clan—"you gotta look beyond the shiny glass and your own reflection." He grabs his tie and leaves the office.

The clans, something Big Red definitely believes in, stare at me with their camera-lens eyes. I am indeed a Wolf, but more by nature than by clan. My mother's a Wolf, and her mother, and her mother, too. In fact, I have absolutely no idea what clan my father belongs to; since all of our lines spin out of our mother's bones, that's all the information needed. The only time a man's clan comes into play is in his choice for marriage, and there, he's just not allowed to marry anyone of his clan. Supposedly, if they shared clans, they were somehow related on both of their mothers' sides, and their asses would both be chased off the rez pretty quickly if they crossed that taboo line. But so much of that is blurred, these days. I'm sure if you trace back far enough, almost everyone is related to everyone else somewhere down the line. The clan system's useless and archaic, an appendix in our community body—pointless, but potentially dangerous. Strategic alliances have not been unknown out here. Though I'm a Wolf, and Red a Snipe, I feel more of a connection with him than with anyone in my life, shared bloodline or not.

Bud's been blaming me since that April day for killing all his orchards, tainting them for years to come—even showing big pictures to the news people of the damage. But—and I can say this even in my clan mirror—I had absolutely nothing to do with it, personally. I didn't even know it was being done. But I had my suspicions, once I heard about it. A little inventory check confirmed a significant shortage of the Clear-All vegetation-killer barrels I keep to control the weed problems on the shop grounds. As with just about everything, it was much cheaper in quantity, and I figured it doesn't go bad, and I'm going to have a need for a long time, so I invested—apparently opening a door of opportunity for one of my employees to seek revenge, maybe even crossing clan lines to help me out.

I would never purposefully interfere with someone else's profits. That's just not my style. But I can't generally control the actions of others. However, this was done in my interests without my knowledge, and that can't continue. I've got to bring them all back with me. Without my people, I'll fall, and I've got to start with my number-one man, who is also drifting away from me, losing the clarity of my vision in all this interference.

I had no problem trusting him until he and Fiction got involved. What does she see in him, anyway? He's an old guy with a potbelly and skin that's beginning to grow leathery, and he certainly doesn't have anywhere near the financial resources I have, and he never will.

My retail prices don't even remotely reflect the seventy-five-percent difference I save in not having to pay federal and state excise taxes and the standard retail markup on gasoline, diesel, and cigarettes, but they're enticing enough to bring in a flood of customers, pushing my income way beyond anyone else's from the reservation. It's no surprise that a growing number of local gas-station owners from off the rez have started complaining.

Numbers are powerful things, man. The government takes big-ass gouges on gasoline and diesel, but the franchise owners have been taking their deep piece, too, safely blaming price hikes on prepaid taxes and OPEC and any other damned thing they've wanted to. The truths of tax numbers and volume discounts are the truths Joe Sonoco just down the road doesn't want his buying public knowing. But that buying public knows the score. Joe Sunoco can cry and whine all he wants about me being an Indian, exploiting an unfair advantage, but anyone who has ever bought a three-dollar slice of pizza or a dollar-fifty can of Pepsi from a gas-station convenience store knows that's the price of business. They sell at those prices because they know people will pay. I've just reversed their logic.

Smoke Rings Gasoline Island kicked off with ridiculously low prices, nearly forty percent lower than my next-lowest competitor. Not only did this bring customers in, lining up an unbelievable twenty-four hours a day to buy gasoline—I was amazed at the lengths people would go to for a bargain—but it also put the essential doubt in their minds about the profit margins my outside competition developed over the years. No one likes to be exploited, and it came back exponentially. Man, I smoked those bastards quick.

Then there were the truckers. In the next set of billboards, announcing discount diesel, the truckers were the primary targets. Within two weeks of opening day, it seemed that any eighteen-wheeler passing through the Niagara section of the New York State Thruway now made the brief ten-mile detour down Clarksville Pass to wait in line for my lone diesel pump to fill its huge, two-hundred-and-fifty-gallon tanks at Smoke Rings before heading out again.

Profit from the first two weeks went to adding a third and fourth bank of pumps, and this was still not enough to ease the traffic jams at the shop. Finally, the customers came up with their own solutions, and as the ground hardened in the late spring, they created a long, snaking line in the next field, moving with an amazing patience and orderliness. Even when I began gradually creeping the prices up, finally leveling off at a little under fifteen cents a gallon difference, they still came.

Bud's protester occupation of Bert's house helped me decide it was time to start the next phase of my new empire, the first solidification of my initial dream. The very day that house across the field, across the border, from Smoke Rings went on the market, the possibilities of installing pipes from it pushed through my brain. Though I'd already bought a house, paying cash in full because I could, I felt a little funny not giving anything back to my people. Now it's time to begin working on the gift.

In my private office, a series of secret numbers fall from my fingertips into a keypad mounted on the wall, releasing the lock on the safe embedded next to it. There, a rich brown leather portfolio sits. Laughing my ass off when I saw the miniature lock mounted on its zipper, I had snatched it up immediately.

The portfolio is my balance pole down the hallway toward Big Red's office, the separations in the floor tiles a tightrope across a vast chasm of what Fiction has or hasn't told him—and there really aren't any methods of approaching the subject. *So, your girlfriend tell you I tried to slip it in when you were busy making your powwow plans?* just doesn't seem like a question I could actually ask. That one was probably a mistake, but even my money can't send me back in time. And even if she has kept quiet, surely that kid knew what I was trying to do. I can't imagine they've kept quiet, but then again, Red's still working for me, which suggests he's oblivious to those events. I jump from the tightrope, stroll across the chasm, and land in Big Red's office.

"So, why don't you want a tux?" I ask, leaning in the doorway.

"Look, Mason, I'm kind of busy here. If you want these invoices going out on time, I gotta finish them today," he says, glancing up for a moment from his stack of carbons and then returning to it. I toss the portfolio on top of the invoices, and then drop the small brass key on top of it.

"There it is, man. Key to our future. And I do mean ours. I can't keep this going without you. It takes me a while to recognize things, sometimes, but hey, that's why you're here." Red lifts the key, twists it—gleaming under the lights—between his fingers, and snaps it back down on the leather case, not going anywhere near the lock. "Start the paperwork for a raise for yourself, will you? You're worth much more than I'm paying you now."

"That's not what this is about." He pushes the case back across the desk, knocking against my thigh. The key drops to the floor.

"Yeah, I know. But this is something I want to do anyway." I set the key back on the case.

"Do you play stocks, Mason?"

"Well, yeah, of course; only sure bets, though—Blue Chip. Any smart businessman—"

"Okay. Whatever you wanted to give me as a raise, put in the market in whatever you're investing in, but put it in my boy's name in trust, for when he turns eighteen. I would really appreciate that. I've got to think about his future. You know, I wore a tuxedo once. Most goddamn uncomfortable thing I ever had on."

"Well, shit. It was probably off the rack. They never fit right. What was it for, your wedding? Man, the one I would get you would be custom fit, right down to the fly length . . ."

"No, I didn't mean uncomfortable like that. That's just not me. I'm a more plaid-flannel-and-jeans kind of guy. I only plan to wear a tuxedo one more time in my life."

"Your funeral?"

"No, no, not my funeral. Not my wedding, either." Fiction is still not entirely out of my possible reach. Around her, any discretion simply vanishes, evaporates, almost as if she wills me to misbehave. Since that encounter with her a month ago, she pops up in my fantasies at least once a day.

"So, aren't you gonna open it?" The tuxedo conversation falls boring now that Fiction rests securely single again. Red clicks the lock open and removes the series of paintings and illustrations on hardboard, and the sheets of statistical information. He flips casually through the stack, stopping at a watercolor where a bunch of dark-skinned grownups and kids play, some riding in bright inner tubes, jumping up against these crashing waves in a huge swimming pool. A building in the background is clearly supposed to be the front of the T.R.B. The picture below that one is an aerial view where you can see the whole pool—a giant turtle—perched directly in front of the T.R.B., facing the road.

"You're having a swimming pool built? A turtle-shaped swimming pool? That's your big secret?" He flips through several more pages and pulls one to the front. Across the top of this illustration, extending in an arc over the pool, stands an expansive, wrought-iron gateway, the legend ONGUIAAHRA NATION MUNICIPAL POOL emerging from it in blocky, geometric, pseudo-Indian-style lettering. "You aren't serious about this, are you?" He slides his index finger across the painted sign, slowing down at the word ONGUIAAHRA.

"Hell yes, man!"

"How do you figure?"

"You better catch up on your history, man. The Indians of the area, long before Father Hennepin—"

"Yeah, I know all that. Hennepin couldn't pronounce it and came out with "Niagara" instead. And I remember your little speech, but what's that got to do with us?"

"It has everything to do with us. I thought you just said you remember my speech. It's more true now than ever. We're the new Indians of the area. This place stopped existing as Tuscarora Nation the second Bud signed his name to that jurisdiction statement. Bud can keep pretending all he wants, but he gave up sovereignty with that signature. We're not giving up that easy."

><

I WAS ON THE INTERSTATE, RETURNING FROM JUGGLING FINANCES AND DEEDS AT my lawyer's office in Buffalo, when the call came through to my cellular about the brawl. At the shop, several factions of people wandered around, reconstructing and reliving the afternoon. Toward the road, but clearly on my property, several state troopers sat together on a bench I had supplied for my gas-pump attendants. It had been dragged at least a hundred yards from where it was supposed to be.

"Excuse me. What are you doing on my property? This land doesn't fall under your jurisdiction. You're engaging in a federal offense, just by being here in any official capacity." Overstreet's beeper, tapping out codes, informed me he was otherwise occupied. My fifteen-second message was an urgent demand for my attorney to appear at the shop, but I realized even that would be useless—standing before the troopers, staring at the statement they presented me in Bud's unmistakable handwriting, feeling the first tremors of defeat coursing through me, a familial poison.

Regardless of our different visions for the Nation, I simply could not believe Bud would just sign us over, would relinquish our status as a separate people. My entire strategy relied upon a belief that Bud would always look out for his people's best interests, that Bud would, in essence, remain a Chief. That dusty afternoon, much of what I had worked for had been shot down in a signature, and Bud was sure to somehow turn it around and blame me.

Huddled supporters and employees near the back edge of the property, a few yards before the tree line, sat on empty fuel drums, drinking bottled beer from stacked cases warming in the sun. Folks I pulled dirty and reeking from drunken, Moon-Road hazes and gave jobs—sending other employees, on my time, to track them down so they'd arrive at work reliably—had, in one afternoon, fallen off the shaky wagon I coaxed them onto.

Gina Hendricks, my cleaning-crew manager, stumbled from the crowd toward her car, not even noticing me walking toward her. I stood in front of her until she almost ran into me.

"Hey, Mason. Nice of you to show. 'Scuse me, I gotta go make a run. Those cases ain't gonna last us another hour, I'd guess."

"What are you doing? Where's Big Red?"

"Oh, they cuffed him and popped him in the back of the van after I called you. Fiction, Butchie, a whole bunch more. We were all smart enough," she said, jerking her head back to indicate the group crowded around the cases, "to stop fighting before they could arrest us. I just happened to be inside when it all started, or I'd probably be in chains, too. I stepped outside and I saw those pigs crossing the line with their cuffs and clubs out—man, I hit the fuckin' road back inside. That's when I called you." She burped and fished in her pockets, pulling out a wad of crumpled ones and fives, trying to organize them. "Look, I gotta go." The troopers monitored us closely, probably waiting for Gina to get into her car.

"No. Come on, you got work to do here. Forget about those cases."

"What? You want me to sweep the blood off these fuckin' stones? It don't come off that easy." She rubbed her bare feet on a group of stones spotted with bloody patches. "It's over, Mason. You ain't got any customers, and they ain't gonna come as long as those bozos got their asses parked in your driveway. Face it, man; Bud got you. He just does what he wants. Take a look; that there took him less than a half hour after all this started." Gina pointed across the gravel lot, toward Bert's house, no longer empty. Bud's supporters lined the front porch, one talking into a telephone receiver, the base obviously installed in the house. Even through mid-daylight, electric lights shone through the occupied house where I learned everything about community. "Now grab a beer and get over it."

"No. Come here." I walked her over to the troopers. "Excuse me, officers, would you mind removing yourselves from my property?" One of the troopers started to protest, again reaching for his copy of Bud's statement. "Yeah, I know all that, but possession is nine-tenths of the law, ain't it? Get your fat asses off my bench." I reached between the legs of a female trooper who was sitting on the bench's edge. She shoved herself back, bumping into one of the other troopers. They all stood, and as Gina and I moved the bench back to its normal spot, I said: "You might occupy my land with that little piece of paper, but I sure as fuck ain't gonna make you comfortable while you do it."

"You're not making this any easier on yourself, Mr. Rollins," one of them said, stretching his legs.

"Really. And how much more difficult could it get? You ever had your citizenship taken from you? Didn't think so. Now, if you'll excuse me, I got a business to run, here."

My group accepted my offer, on the honor system, of a dollar for every bloody stone they removed from the lot and placed in several five-gallon plastic buckets around the lot. Within an hour, the red-flecked lot returned to its original gray, and my pockets grew a little over two thousand dollars lighter. Altogether, the stones filled two buckets, which I lugged straight through Bud's protest line, driving them apart. They could feel the blood here, maybe smell it, knowing some of its stones vibrated with their own family's DNA, drying and dying. Every member of the protest group did the old head-turn as I got close, evidently forgetting how much they used to want to watch me.

The door, sitting lazy in its frame as always, pushed easily with the weight of my buckets. The house of my past, cluttered with people who'd just as soon I not have a future, seemed full and empty at the same time. It looked nearly the same as when we left it in late September—maybe a little more worn, but other than that the same, aside from the electric lights illuminating the room. That last day in September, we'd sat on the barren living-room floor, no longer dancing—the only piece of furniture an ancient glass table-lamp at the center of the room, lighting our circle. We remained, laughing and telling stories, until the light had gone dead, telling us the electricity had been officially cut. We'd sat in the dark a while longer and then filed slowly out, Fiction unplugging and taking the lamp with her. She'd said she needed it and no one had questioned her.

"Nice lights." Bud looked up at the sound of my voice from his flimsy card table in the center of the living room. Troopers followed me in and flanked me as I approached the old man. Bud held his hands up, pushing them back like some kind of traffic cop, signaling the troopers to remain in the background. "You see this?" I carefully lifted the first bucket and gently spilled the stones onto Bud's table. "This is the blood of people you've been charged with taking care of, people your Nation supposedly supports. This is blood ripped from their skin. Blood you called out with your little paper. Bet you all thought that was cute, today, huh?" The other bucket came next. "This is more." The table legs wobbled as the pile grew. All looked on, staring at the buckling legs, and the table finally collapsed, the damp spring air filling with its dust.

"Seems to me you didn't support them very well." I pulled four stones from the pile on the shambles. "It doesn't take much to start a new Nation. Just a little support."

"You're as much to blame for that blood as I am," Bud said, unflinching. Not bad, I have to give him that. "I didn't tell them to disobey Nation orders. That was you. We were as peaceful a community as we'd been for the last hundred and fifty years until you came along, with your gas and cigarettes. You don't even respect our symbols. You just start corrupting anything you like, to suit your moneymaking."

"Corruption? Hate to tell you, Bud, but there's lots of people out here who don't believe that clean water is a corruption. Something everyone in America should be able to expect. This ain't Ethiopia." Bud's supporters wore puzzled looks. I didn't think he'd mention my offer to them. This move could not have been more sweet if I'd somehow been able to take the old man's voice away.

"This isn't America, either . . ."

"Seems to me that as of this afternoon, when you signed us over to the Staties, we started living in America. Seems to me your time is just about over."

"I think you better go now," one of the Staties offered, gently tugging on my arm from behind.

"You a ventriloquist now, Bud? That was pretty good. Your teeth didn't even move." I allowed myself to be escorted from the house.

❧

"So, that's why you traded in the gold for bloodstone?" Red asks, picking the cuff links off my desk as I explain that the four stones I took with me are going to be the cornerstones for the new pool. I release the contractors at the end of the day, paying them in full, apologizing for the inconvenience.

The next morning, Red and I walk toward the front of the T.R.B. The basic shape was gutted from the earth by the recently released contractors. My new employees sit listening to their new crew boss, the only man from the contracting crew who remained. Some are ex-dancers. Others stood by me on the line, both before and after being arrested, and some even drank from the stack of warming cases that night in early May and had, for a while, been afraid to come back. Red made calls into the night to round up this crew—maybe thirty people—on such short notice. It's been a month and a half since the Staties invaded our land, but as if it had just happened, we've continued to watch those still here—until yesterday—on the Smoke Rings lot.

We blew the lot away to make space for the Onguiaahra Nation Municipal Pool, and the Staties were forced back onto state land—where they now wait, with Bud's protesters, for someone on my side to cross the line again. My people continue watching, only removing themselves briefly this morning at my personal invitation.

The workers assemble the forms for the expanse of cement eventually to be poured, as I crawl into the deep gash in the earth—smelling the sharp odor of freshly turned dirt—and lay some tobacco, a gift to the Creator, on a fire I started at sunrise. Red helps me back up to the surface. At the south bend of the turtle, I drop one of the four stones into the bottom of the custom cement form—at the northern curve, a second. Red, probably carrying some of his own DNA in his fists, drops the other two into the east and west.

The fire dies its own natural death, exhausted, and our mostly new work force begins assembling the rest of the foundation forms, pouring cement into the wounded earth, creating the footers the forms would shortly stand on, sinking the bloodied stones in with those of the mortared mixture. The support of ONGUIAAHRA NATION hardens and strengthens in the morning air, as I sip my morning coffee.

>‹

CHAPTER 15 Washed in the Blood of the Land
Ruby Pem

I F YOU CAN HEAR THIS STORY, THEN YOU ARE STANDING WHERE I STOOD ON THE day I left, between two groups on a blistering day in mid-July, on an imaginary dotted line marking the borders, watching the Onguiaahra Nation pool fill with excited and sweaty bodies, rejoicing, hitting the cool water's surface, nearly sizzling as they submerged, burning off some essential layer, and yet, in some way, asleep. My actions were monitored closely, so I rarely strayed from the position I'd held all month, occasionally taking gifts of food or water from one side or the other, never showing favorites. The gifts were never lavish, mind you—a cup of coffee, a sandwich—but after a while, even those things did not entice me. Greetings came every morning to my invisible border, as they had from the first morning I decided to appear at the lines, the leaders of both sides chatting with me and sitting in the grass at my side.

I first heard from Roger, my grandson, that the pool's liner was being installed one day in June, and that had been my first day. As I arrived and traced my line between the groups, a small riverbed of neutrality, one of those large trucks rumbled along the road as it pulled in. I turned and saw it was actually three trucks—following a fourth, smaller, guide truck with the "Oversize Load" sign mounted above its cab. The guide truck pulled into the place most enter, at the far eastern edge of the property, where they swung around the back, near the woods, to line up with the diesel pumps;

but this one rested as soon as it had cleared the road. The three behind it parted the groups easily, nearly forcing the two sides to brush up against one another and mingle in their attempts to avoid the trucks' path— straight to the edge of the tremendous hole torn from the ground behind them.

Strapped to the beds of the first two trucks sat two nearly identical halves of a giant turquoise-colored turtle, a dead hostage of the road— maybe plastic, but I don't know. On the third truck rested another section, a wide strip including the turtle's head, the center portion of its shell, and its tail. The turtle seemed to have been neatly cut front to back—an anatomy lesson for giant children, its innards neatly scraped out and flushed away, only the useful shell remaining.

A tremendous crane, controlled by one of Mason Rollins's men, lifted and carried the shell halves and lowered them, upside down, into the large but tidy concrete hole scooped from the earth where the recreation-building parking lot used to stand. Those pieces set loosely in place, one side of the line cheered and the other side shouted abuses, while Mason Rollins himself rode down the crane's heavy iron chain with the turtle's center section, seeming to guide it into place, its eyes looking to the east and the west, interlocked with the other pieces in their neat and solid grave.

His workers, carrying buckets of some thick stuff the same color as the turtle, leapt in after him, sealing the gaps with trowels, filling them in easily and swiftly. I wished, and continue now to wish, that I'd had a similar substance for my Nation: that the three deep cracks in the Nation's shell, divisions of traditionals, progressives, and neutrals, could just be sealed over and sanded, as these had been several days later—buffed to a seamless unity that held tight, even after being flooded the next week, supporting the clear, cleansing water within.

"*Chewaent,* Auntie Ruby," Jacob said on my last morning, as people crossed the turtle's mouth, entering through steps built into the underside of its empty skull; and though he smiled, he noticed the newspaper folded neatly across my lap. "The congregation picked these for you, yesterday. Pickin's are scarce this season." He handed me a stainless-steel bowl of miniature, round blackcap berries, the wild sort that grow on thorny bushes, lurking in the shadowy reservation woods. They're a very difficult berry to domesticate for most, seeming to prefer the unforgiving landscapes of forest to gardens, often perishing among the orderly rows, and so are a delicacy, to be eaten slowly, a few at a time, and shared with those around who are cherished. The berries—their fragile outer layers dark, interconnected globes—glowed in the early sun. They'd been carefully picked, none crushed—the metallic bowl tracing none of their rich purple blood down its sides, as happens most often when you're picking them. The core of the berry, its support, is left on the thorny stem in the picking, and only a thin, natural connecting mesh lining the berry's interior keeps the fruit intact after its removal.

I never had any trouble in growing the berries myself, having long ago cultivated a relationship with the formidable bushes. My garden flourished this year as it always has, and I'd been able to make my grandson three pies already. The continuing dry heat this summer had increased their scarcity everywhere else, though. The number of blackcap pies made this year on the reservation, aside from mine, remained at zero, as far as I knew, and I usually know about such things.

"*Chewaent*, Jakee. Have you had your fill of these?" I've been calling him this since before he started elementary school. I never could see my way to calling him "Bud." I had a feeling about him even then, but I guess that's one of the reasons I was picked as Deer Clan Mother; I had that eye. I'd known, of course, that his father had been a Chief, and while of a different clan, his growing up in a house of such responsibility should have its advantages.

"Yes, Auntie," he nodded, flicking his hands to encourage my indulgence. "Plenty. They were wonderful."

"Here, take some." I offered the small bowl to Mason Rollins, who was walking up with a mug of coffee. I reached for the cup and tasted from it—one quarter milk and two drops of honey, just the way I like it. Roger, who fixed my morning coffee if he were visiting, must have told him. Mason Rollins slid four of the berries from the bowl and held them gently in the palm of his hand.

"I'd like to save them for some of my people," he said, rolling the berries in a circular path along his creases.

"Which ones?"

"I don't know yet. Whoever seems like they might need them the most, I guess. You know, we've only had the pool open a couple days and, well, new equipment, you gotta get the glitches out. Just yesterday, we couldn't get the wave machine working."

"What is a wave machine?" I asked. I couldn't even imagine what sort of item might carry the name "wave machine." The only image I could conjure involved several giant mechanical hands, shifting back and forth, either greeting or saying goodbye. Certainly no such contraption was visible anywhere, and I could see no practical purpose for one, hidden or otherwise, so I assumed I was wrong in my guess.

"Well, it's like a giant doorway. You know, it opens and closes, and as it does, the water circulating in the pool gets shoved through it, so that when it comes back out into the pool, it makes these big waves. And it's timed so there are periods when the water's calm and times when it's like the ocean, all wavy."

"Do you think this was the best way you could help out your people, by giving them a wave machine? Who is this really making waves for?" Mason Rollins remained silent, and that was answer enough. "Here, then, you take the whole bowl. It sounds like your people work very hard at trying to do what the earth does quite naturally," I said, handing them over to Mason Rollins and watching Jakee's face, which remained motionless. I didn't want to appear too interested in the wave machine or any other aspect of Mason's business. I would have later asked Roger for a more in-depth explanation as to why someone might desire that particular item. Mason Rollins thanked me and set the berries down. He sat in the barely damp grass, holding his own cup of coffee to his face, absorbing the steam. He wiped dew from his hands across his Levi's. "You should save that water," I said. "You'll be wanting it a little bit later today."

The dry spell we'd been coping with through the spring had officially been labeled a drought by the weatherman in June. While this caused much grief for Niagara County farmers, advised to water their crops only at night as a conservation measure, in the hope the crops' lifeblood would not just evaporate under the relentless sun, their inconvenience held no comparison with our difficulties on the reservation. The water I pumped from my well, when I'd been able to bring some up, had been a deep rust color for the last two or three weeks. I took to letting the darkness settle into the bottom before I had any. I even began saving a couple of pints from every pail, as primer for the next day's round.

I didn't need much, anyway. The thought of food and water had done nothing for me but cause a grumbling from my innards for the past week. I wasn't alone, either. At the clinic, earlier in the week, the pinched faces and clutched stomachs showed others had lost their appetites as well. The doctor told me it was probably one of two things: either everyone was sharing a bug, a pushy strain that lingered, or it was the heat. The doctor said a bunch of others had come in with similar complaints. The nurses pulled some blood from my ancient veins and said they'd get back to me with the results, but in the meantime, drink plenty of fluids and stay out of the sun.

Trusting more in Indian medicine, I ignored both of those pieces of advice and spent most every morning since then drinking tea from sweet flag, one of the ancient plants that still flourished if you knew where to look. And afterward, I headed out to observe the national division—a disgraceful clot, the dissolving of which was partially my responsibility as Clan Mother. Only the barest nourishment had passed my lips the last few days, and the blackcap burned a hot metal hole in my stomach as I nodded and talked with the two men. They swam casually in heat waves in front of me, incredibly wasting their new abilities to speak beneath the water's surface on small talk.

"Not me, I've got plenty here. This water comes from the town. It's all paid for, and it's clean. Chlorinated, purified, and dependable, fresh out of the treatment center. My ma said her well is all but dry. She's been coming here to fill up jugs for her and my dad for easily over a week now. You want some? I can run right over and get you a tall, cool ice water," Mason said, picking up his bowl of berries and standing.

"No, no. She wants some of our pure well water, don't you Auntie? Who needs all those chemicals, causing cancer and who knows what all?" Jakee said, apparently ready to retrieve me a dipperful as well.

"Yeah, Bud, you should know all about chemicals and cancer," Mason interrupted.

"I'm fine, like a camel. I don't need too much, and besides, if I drink a lot of water, I'll just be having to pee every five minutes."

"City sewer, right here," Mason said. "No more outhouse or nasty leach bed floating a green cloud over everything."

I could not believe my Nation had come to such a point that even taking a drink of water or peeing, two of the most natural acts a person could perform, had become political statements. The time came to ask my question; but what would I do with the answer, regardless of what it might be?

"Was the announcements I been hearing on the radio and this article in this morning's paper true, or what?" I knew right away that, while they looked and sounded like any news articles, they had not come from actual, legitimate news people. I'd seen the "lose weight and gain money and grow your hair back" articles in the papers for years, with their tiny "advertisement" legend written in flea-sized type at the bottom of the article, and had always wondered what percentage of people ever saw those letters hiding in the lower margin.

"Go ahead and tell her, Bud," Mason Rollins said, speaking to the Chief for the first time that morning. "Tell her why you're calling an emergency open Council meeting tonight. Tell her the truth." I had, of course, guessed that Mason Rollins had written, or had hired someone to write, the article that took up—including charts I didn't really understand—a full page of the morning's *Niagara Cascade* . . . and the similar one broadcast at least every hour on the radio shows.

The story, while clearly an advertisement for the opening of the pool and a preview of things to come—claiming this "small pool" was just the beginning—also held, within its "exciting history" of the pool's origins, some interesting news for those who'd recently found themselves on the pot more than at the table. The article told that the pool, against the rumors circulating among some reservation residents, was extremely safe, even getting the written approval of the Department of Environmental Conservation.

The article thanked Deer Clan Chief Jacob Tunny for having brought the DEC in to investigate possible leaks from the gasoline tanks to the swimming pool, attempting to trace the source of a recent reservation outbreak of a severe intestinal syndrome, as a number of the afflicted had swum in the pool. This forgot about me, but I went on anyway. The pool and gasoline tanks had proven not to be the source, as the tanks were well within safety standards, and the pool water had come from an established safe-water source: the water lines of the city of Niagara Falls.

While at the location, though, the DEC scientists had contacted the New York State Health Department, requesting they test some drinking-water wells of residents, and there they'd discovered a high level of a bacteria normally thriving in the lower guts of humans, but which at these levels was deadly poison. They'd speculated to the Chiefs' Council, in a statement now nearly a month old, that a possible reason for these levels was that the drought conditions had somehow altered the configuration of the underground water paths. Now, a bunch of badly installed sewage beds were seeping into fresh-water sources. Regardless of the cause, they'd mandated that no one use well water for consumption at the present time, until some satisfactory means of stopping the contamination could be found.

Concerns were also raised about other strange chemicals, found in spot tests around the reservation, that had nothing to do with gasoline. The scientists asked if the Chiefs' Council would have reason to believe chemical contamination might have occurred at some point, but they received no response at the time the article was written. I remember, and I'm sure others do too, when Ezekiel Tunny told us those barrels we saw being buried under Bite Mark Road at his direction were just there for supporting the weak ground, so the road would not cave in.

The article's conclusion mentioned briefly, in an almost offhand way— claiming irony, whatever that is—that Mason Rollins, in the planning stages for the Onguiaahra Nation Municipal Pool, had offered to pay for the continuation of city water throughout the reservation, but that Deer Clan Chief Jacob Tunny had declined for the Tuscarora Nation, without ever having consulted with its members.

"Well, you see, you remember my father and all of the things he'd let into our community . . ." Jakee began—and I knew in an instant that, regardless of the slight name-calling tone the article used, it was, in its most important areas, true. I wonder when Jakee lost his vision, or if this young man in the fancy clothing somehow blinded him into bad judgment; but I don't really think that's it. I've always known he was lacking something. My stomach gurgled viciously with what I suspected was the same ailment that had taken my daughter, Beverly.

➤◄

I FELT ALL THOSE YEARS AGO, WATCHING JAKEE AND THOSE OF HIS GENERATION dipped into the Big Crick below the Protestant Church, that I'd have a difficult time. His small, twelve-year-old boy's body, strangely old-looking in its dark blue suit, had shuddered for a few seconds as he'd submerged in the minister's arms, his image distorted by the gently rippling waves of his minute struggle. I saw his ghost spring from the crick in that shudder, washed right from him—a brief glint of sunlight on the water's surface blinding everyone but me to its exit. The ghost wore moccasins, leggings, and a ribbon shirt. It looked right at me, smiled, and skated off across the crick's surface, disappearing around a bend in the water's path. And when Jakee resurfaced, he knew something had changed, that something was now missing. I could tell.

I'm a Longhouse woman, but one of the last from this reservation. Even years before Jakee was born, I had to travel to other reservations to attend ceremonies that had any meaning for me. In part, I suspect, this was the reasoning behind my inheritance of the Clan Mother role. I took it gracefully, as I should have, but with concern. I'd been aware of the shift to Christianity in many of the families for some time, but had not been forced into any role of preservation for anyone but my own line. I'd been childless at the time—a young Clan Mother, in fact—and this choice would probably be the biggest decision of my Clan Mother career. Since the responsibilities of both the Chief's and the Clan Mother's roles ended at death, I'd only be electing one Chief in my lifetime. With all of the potential Chiefs coming from Christian families, I'd not known even what to look for. That was not a path I thought particularly healthy for the seventh generation to follow.

I'd known, that day, he'd be the one I'd pick when the time came—not because his ghost had left, but because he'd been the only child to have one. I'd watched carefully, but all the other possible candidates had merely shivered in the muddy water and come up smiling, new official members of the Tuscarora Protestant Church, joyfully wiping the blood of the lamb from their eyes and later flipping through their fresh Bibles over bologna and mustard sandwiches in the church hall.

I always suspected that little ghost held its own secret council with Jakee all these years, as he still had managed to keep the Nation together in its time of sleeping throughout his leadership, even through the period when he had to turn some of his father's mistakes around; but now, he's apparently been blinded by some of those acts. His father had not been a total convert—attending the Protestant church but still sneaking off to Longhouse ceremonies as well, taking me with him in his old Indian car, where I served as his rearview mirror, looking back and letting him know when it was safe to pass.

Jakee told me once, in private counsel, that he'd believed this confusion was the root of his father's problem: that he'd lacked a focus and dedication as a servant of God. He felt a man who could not even choose his faith could certainly not be expected to lead people properly. I asked him if he really thought that indecision had been the case with his father, and Jakee had been unable to arrive at any other conclusion.

✧

As he stood before me under this harsh sun, droning away and having no explanation for endangering his entire Nation's health other than his fear of repeating his father's mistakes, his brown eyes said that he'd never fully washed the mud away.

"This man, here, has disobeyed the Nation. Do you know how this pool gets its water? He's illegally hired contractors to pipe water in from that house over there. He's invaded our land with an outside utility. He's compromised our sovereignty with this act. While he claims I violated sovereignty, he's been the one who has truly done it. These troopers here are enforcing my wishes; therefore, I have not invited any violations. They're acting strictly under my orders."

"Can this man shut off the water and turn it on? Doesn't that mean the water acts under his orders?" I asked him simply, hoping desperately that I could somehow will his sight back. His argument held the logic of a singular mind, a mind that could not look after one generation, let alone seven. I might have soon been asked to perform the ritual no Clan Mother ever has a desire to perform—the dehorning of a Chief she has chosen. The act rarely occurs, and the dehorned man, after the permanent removal of his ceremonial headpiece—the pheasant feathers and deer antlers forbidden to ever reside there again—must live out his life in humiliated Council silence. Dehorned Chiefs rarely remain in their communities, and Jacob Tunny needed his community—but needed it whole before he would regain his sight.

"You know he can do those things, Auntie. What kind of question is that? Is it because your grandson works here, and your son-in-law? They're as guilty as he is. I hope you don't have to be removed as Clan Mother," he said, with no hint of threat in his voice, but instead a sad, incurable blindness. I turned my head to the side, unable to look at him.

"No." At the edge of the woods, a small boy about twelve, in ribbon shirt and leggings, emerged from among the trees between the recreation building and the hectic banks of gasoline pumps. He came toward me across the back parking lot, ignoring the dense line of cars full of people that jogged along to the gasoline pumps or the smoke shop.

"Auntie? Auntie?" the adult Jakee called as the child Jakee arrived next to me and held out his hand. I reached out to take it. I'd recognized him immediately, though nearly fifty years had gone by since he'd wandered down Big Crick and disappeared into the wild.

"Bud, she doesn't look good," Mason said, touching my forehead—his fingers, icicles, draping themselves across my brow. I staggered under their weight. "Holy shit, she's burning up. Somebody call an ambulance. I'll get her over to the pool for now," Mason said, his ice body surrounding me and wrapping me in its harshness. "Try to cool her off."

"No! Put her down, God damn it! She will never enter your pool," the adult Jakee shouted from his side of the invisible line, as the child Jakee silently ran alongside Mason, still holding my hand tightly. We entered the icy water gradually, crossing the turtle's giant teeth and into its skull. Steam must have leapt from my body as we gently moved deeper and deeper, into its protective shell. Mason's eyes, above me, said nothing; they were merely two tiny mirrors, reflecting my gleaming face. A tremendous, smooth wall of water rose above Mason and came crashing down upon us, causing him to lose his balance. We surfaced immediately, and I tried to open my eyes, but they burned with chlorine on my first attempt.

"Turn off the fuckin' waves," he shouted, as a second, forceful gush plowed into us, knocking us into the current again. He regained his balance quickly through that one, and as he helped me stand again, I wiped my eyes. People from both sides of the line, including both Jakees—the adult Jakee standing at the edge of the pool—crowded in together around me: one group. Some stood in the pool and others merely around it. A softer wave flowed around us as I looked about. The water did follow his orders. I pulled away from Mason Rollins, slipping under the water as another gentle wave caressed my body.

Below the surface, I opened my eyes, ignoring the pain and looking about. All of their legs looked identical, and their muted voices sang out in one complicated melody, all the dissonance of the past year completely gone. To my right, the child Jakee floated patiently, smiling the same smile he'd worn all those years ago. I closed my eyes and we left the pool together, two brief glints of the July sun on the water's surface, blinding everyone to our departure.

>←

CHAPTER 16 Mourning Rituals

Bud Tunny

As occurred last September, ten months ago, the graveyard storage shed waits for the return of the Nation's digging tools, resting neatly against the obscured side of the shed. This time, however, the users had not been the Mounter brothers, who usually dig the graves. They've been buying gas and cigarettes at Rollins's shop and, on those hottest days, swimming in his pool, and that's enough for me not to have called them. The tools get only as far as the inside doorjamb, as I'll be needing them tomorrow morning, anyway.

The grave was mine alone to work, quietly in the dark. Auntie Ruby never made it any secret that she wanted to monitor her family land for eternity, to make sure it stayed in her family. Toward sunset, at the end of this impossibly long day, a flickering light peeked through the bushes in that area, an apparent brushfire. This turned out to be a small, controlled bonfire. The familiar black truck, the bird flying across its door, sat in the flickering orange light, parked dangerously close to the escarpment's drop-off. In the shadowy, overgrown area at the graveyard's back edge, Don Harmony, several feet into the earth, burrowed with his own shovel. His boy pulled the free clumps a few feet away with a hoe, leaning on it heavily, until Harmony shoveled enough away that the earth began creeping back into its rightful place.

"What are you doing here?" I dropped my tools on the ground. They looked up, startled for a second, and then returned to their work as if they had never stopped. "She was my Clan Mother. This is part of my responsibility."

"You know, Bud, if you'd stuck to your responsibilities, we wouldn't have to be here right now," Harmony said. I expected that and, jumping into the opposite end of the grave, began to dig as well. The preliminary autopsy report already confirmed my auntie had been suffering with the same bacterial infection found in the contaminated wells. Though the coroner couldn't say for sure yet whether that had contributed to her death, I am fairly certain—as, I suspect, is the Nation.

By the time the ambulance arrived yesterday, she'd been long gone. Rollins tried mouth-to-mouth resuscitation on her at the poolside, but she'd not even come close to a recovery, her body heaving with no conviction. After the ambulance left with her neatly tucked into the back, the lines simply dissolved—washed away with my auntie's life—my supporters meandering over to the Monterney woman's house while folks on the other side stared vacantly into the pool, maybe attempting to will her life back.

"She believed in you totally, you know," Harmony said later, as he and his boy sat on the truck's hood, looking out over the deep chasm ending in my auntie's property, which has likely already been legally signed over to the boy. It'll only be a matter of weeks before official notification comes for the Nation record books. "I been taking her jugged spring water for weeks, but I found all the jugs today in her back room. Not a one of them had the seal cracked. You told her the well water was safe, and she must have thought that drinking the spring water was somehow going against you. Just like Bert. And my wife. How many more, Bud?"

"I drink the well water myself," I return. "I'm not having people do anything I don't do myself."

"Don't try to shit me, Bud. I'm old enough to remember when your well was dug, and to remember that the state did it for you." Harmony hopped from his truck's hood and helped his son slide off, and then lifted the boy into the cab.

"If she did everything I told her to, as you say, and you think I lied as a leader, do you still follow everything Mason Rollins tells you is true and right?"

"Bud, it's late, my mother-in-law is gone, and I'm tired from digging her grave. Can't you just give that shit a rest, at least until we get Ruby buried?"

He climbed into his truck and pulled away, leaving me with the open hole and the expanse of the escarpment in the weak blue light of the full moon.

The fire warmed me, made me sweat, almost purified me. The shadows grew deeper until the moon left the sky and the last flame died out. Only then did I deliver the tools to their rightful place and return to my wife.

In the morning, no protesters stand on line at the Monterney house. Inside, those who've been staying at the house drink coffee and listen to the news of their own inactivity on an old portable radio at the kitchen table, a substantial piece of furniture that silently replaced the card table Rollins crushed in May. I pour cups of coffee for my wife and myself, joining the silent mourners. No active protesters from the other side have appeared either. Small groups of folks congregate outside of that building, unmotivated.

Later in the day, the funeral progresses without incident, in the Council House. No funerals have ever been held here before, but the Protestant Church is not willing to allow a Longhouse funeral within its confines, and the nondenominational Mission is simply too small. The Protestant congregation didn't mind so much, but the minister, who comes out to the reservation on Sundays, objected and informed me this action might jeopardize our charter. Rather than create even one more slice of grief, I decided opening the Council House for the service would be easier—to just get this nonsensical pagan ritual over. The only problem with this choice is that the Council House, the third largest building on the reservation, is still too small. Nearly the entire Nation shows, as well as most of the outsiders, all sitting together wherever opportunities appear in the narrow, ancient rows.

The eulogy I deliver, filled with as many things about my auntie as I can remember, falls short of the present, as we hadn't had much contact since her daughter passed on. As a Chief, and particularly her Chief, I had a responsibility to do something about the circumstances of her death, but the options had not been appropriate. The Nation certainly can't afford to finance its own water-treatment plant, and the only other option would have required me and the other Chiefs to relinquish one more piece of our ever-dwindling circle of sovereignty. Her daughter's funeral lacked my presence, but this one is inescapable: it's my responsibility to escort my Clan Mother from this world.

Nobility falters. The last words I'd actually spoken to my Clan Mother, when she'd begun to fade in the hot July sun, were threats to remove her from power; and though it would have been incredibly difficult to justify and execute, it would have happened. The other—Christian—Clan Mothers might have agreed to take her down, and it would have gotten moving, all in the name of my side. The recognition smoked in her eyes, and she would never have forgiven me, taking me down—dehorning me soon if I hadn't discredited her first—and that I could not allow. Over the years, the horns have taken root right into my head. Though the headpiece is only worn on special occasions through life, they always sweep powerfully above my head, a constant presence, easily able to gore anyone who tries to stop me—the rich stench of entrails dangling from the sharp thorns of my antlers. My head tingles with the inevitable loss. They're being ripped from my head, the roots unwilling to release themselves from the deep crevasses of my brain where they've come to reside, finally leaving bloody, aching stumps that will never heal, no matter how many more years I live.

This path toward the loss of my horns all started with the death of that Monterney woman, and my daughter's sudden belief she would take that woman's place. Rollins is not all that bright, and he couldn't have gotten nearly this far without some sort of guidance. His business could never have thrived without her calculating mind behind it. She has no status, and won't stop until the Nation crumbles, starting with my leadership. Most of my decisions as Chief have been executed with the utmost care, but when it comes to the living proof of an early indiscretion, I make all the wrong choices. It's as if she somehow guides me down this path—that charming smile she uses on everyone burning me, reminding me that lately, I've had nothing to smile about.

She did it privately, at first, but then that dress changed everything. My people seemed to still be standing by me, but the roses imprinted themselves on the backs of my followers' eyes in the same way they thrived on mine. The act would have been much easier to deny had everyone seeing the roses not also recognized the signature beading patterns of my Clan Mother—my own Clan Mother.

When that girl walked into the Feast, everyone saw my auntie's beadwork patterns—some, the same roses my leggings display in formal political meetings with Chiefs from other reservations, leggings my auntie had handed me when she'd announced my ascension to the role of Chief. When she left this world in Rollins's pool, our exchange would never be finished, but with the girl's collusion, she'd apparently fallen to the other side anyway. Her tendencies might have even revealed themselves earlier, if we'd had a long conversation sometime over recent years, but the last extended talk we'd had is now lost to faded memory.

The burial goes smoothly, the outside funeral home which had taken care of the casket and wake providing all the necessary transportation. It is after the body is lowered into the ground that things grow more difficult. Rollins, heaving a shovelful of earth into the grave—one of the first in a long line of people wanting to contribute—announces that an honor reception will be held at that building of his, with plenty of food for everyone, as well as photograph albums to go through and a tremendous display of my auntie's beadwork, including some newly finished moccasins which, because of her arthritis, she hadn't made in over ten years. The girl had helped her to complete them recently, her hands becoming the tools of the old woman's vision.

I decline in a civil fashion, staying to finish the burial. Everyone leaves, our supporters knowing they shouldn't have anything to do with that reception. The unsettled dirt falls easily back to its rightful place. "Auntie," I call, shoveling, "do you know all the decisions you made me face? I had no way of knowing if they were right." She told me once that she had chosen me in part because my father had also been a Chief, and I replied that I thought this reason had been a mistake.

"My father's career was one full of mistakes, Auntie. Perhaps he wasn't best choice for a teacher. Avoiding his mistakes, I made some of my own, just as bad. Bad lessons crop up everywhere. Look what those children raised by that Monterney woman turned out like. They learned to work together, but now it's against the Nation. I thought I took that away when I took the house, but they just keep surviving. Just keep staying together. Even that grandson of yours. The grandson of a Clan Mother should know where to stand, but he's been swayed by that other side. They crave the prize money . . . not the dance."

The grave begins its slow process of settling into the escarpment, near the remains of Harmony's bonfire from the night before. Twigs of tobacco stems with charred ends rest on the lip of burned grass and topsoil. Harmony offered the Creator a gift to accept his mother-in-law back into the earth, part of a traditional burial. A small one, though—sad. Throwing the tools into the shed, I tear away from the graveyard, the filled hole and scorched earth in my rearview mirror telling me my duty. I must give my

Clan Mother the biggest funeral tobacco-burning any Clan Mother has ever received. She will understand my sincerity then.

My father's house, now occupied by one of my cousins, is unlocked, my cousins surely at the Monterney woman's house. The root cellar is full. I carry sharp, brittle branches from the drying nails, filling my arms, jamming the Lincoln's trunk full, and then the back seat. A few minutes later, in front of my house, I construct a large circle of rocks, pulling them from the plowing pile that has grown for years. Death surrounds me. The skeletal remains of my trees hang their heads like condemned men, waiting for rot to complete its job, the poison spread deep.

Even over this, though, the girl's trailer floats clearly in my vision, between my father's house and here, mocking me in its lush growth. It won't any longer, though.

A few minutes later, my reflection greets me in her replaced living-room windows. The closer I get, the more I disappear, replaced by the circles of dancers looking back at me from their wall. Everything she used to keep the Monterney woman's dancers together has sat just a few miles away from my house all this time, but it won't for much longer. The gasoline can from the graveyard storage shed, probably filled at Rollins's place, will be useful now.

Nearly a half an hour later, all the artifacts from various places in the trailer sit heaped in the center of the living room. This starts with her things, the old woman's junk scattered in my search. Things creep in—props, costumes, award ribbons, flyers and posters from past competitions. Her control over them is woven into their history—the old woman's, hers, Rollins's, Harmony's, and the boy's. The set of photographs from the wall completes the pile, and then the gasoline pours slowly, seeping into the layers of their history. Finally, the large dry tobacco stalks lie at the top, balanced, really not part of the pile.

The fire clears its throat, and the air around it ignites as the first book of lighted matches hits it. The plan was to light the pile over and over from various angles until the entire heap was well on its way to vanishing, but the room explodes around me. My skin tightens, and my crisped eyebrows sprinkle their dust into my eyes. The dress, hanging in the bedroom closet with the rest of her clothes, blooms in my mind from behind the Lincoln's wheel. Maybe it could just stay where it hung. It was really as much my Clan Mother's creation as it had been hers. So much of my auntie is already lost, and though my relationship with her is no longer retrievable, the dress might be.

The living-room picture window softens and sags in the heat, so the main door is no longer a possibility. The fire door at the back has already loosened and buckled in its frame, and my hand sizzles on the handle, new paths being grooved into my palm, altering the lines of my future. The patterns of my Clan Mother's beading slide across my dirty cheeks, the scent of smoky velvet heavy around me. The trailer sighs, crumbling in on itself in the flames. That line of unacceptable behavior has been crossed, and my people's response to the situation I have just worked so hard to create for them is unclear. Probably, by the end of the day, that vision will arrive.

Where my eyebrows grew, nothing but smooth skin lies in the furrows. The fire has burned them clean away. The skin has a new tightness. The faulty bridgework I never get around to having taken care of falls from my mouth, my perfect front teeth slipping away from my face. The gold glows with the fire's warmth in the stones. Heat sinks into my soles as I reach the porch's top step and listen to the roar.

"I'VE CALLED THE FIRE TRUCKS, JACOB. YOU BETTER LEAVE NOW," JOHNNYBOY Martin says, appearing out of nowhere, though his car is in the driveway. Maybe that line truly hasn't been crossed. Johnnyboy has always been a reliable ally, and here we are again, playing through the discussions, as we have for years in Council. Open Council is really a myth, and it has been for over thirty years. The Chiefs have always met privately first and decided the approaches discussions would take, and then in open Council, we've merely spoken our already arrived-at conclusions, pacing ourselves for our audience, as if in some complicated play.

"Good. I was gonna stop at my house and pick up some food for our reception when I saw the fire."

"Jacob, it's over," he responds, breaking from the script. "I still can't believe what I suspect of you. But I think you should go home and shower, and maybe bury those clothes you got on. And get ready to remove your horns." This upstart, who officially replaced my father, as they were of the same clan, gives me advice, crossing clans. He never was a real Chief. A real Chief would know better.

"Jacob, you claim the stench of gasoline is all over Mason Rollins, but today it's all over you. Ruby Pem *Geh-heh* may be gone now, but that no longer matters. The Chief is supposed to be the voice of the people, and these good people would never speak for the things I believe you've done today. You have apparently inherited more than a Chief's eye from your father. What we should have done to your father when he allowed those chemical companies to dump their barrels here, we'll do to you today. The sins of the father shall not be the sins of the son. We'll dehorn you, with or without a Clan Mother. We've waited too long already, but today, we're taking back the voice of the people. And if you protest, don't for a moment forget that I can approve jurisdiction papers, too. And as much as I think that's one of the worst crimes a Chief can commit, I will commit it for the people, to bring you down." Johnnyboy walks away to the voices of sirens crying down the road.

"You don't know the first thing about being a Chief!" I shout to his back. "This Nation slept under your guidance. All I did was wake them up! You might be willing to lie down and expose your belly for Mason Rollins, but Deer Clan Chief Jacob Tunny isn't about to give up his Nation that easily."

Fire definitely purifies things. The brittle hair across my scorched scalp turns to dust, completely gone. But my horns, too, have been burned smooth away. The dusty ashes of my leadership catch on a stray breeze and flee into the air, and I want to rip open my shirt—want to check my chest. I am sure the hair will be gone from there, too.

><

CHAPTER 17 Rites of Passage

Patricia Tunny

ASON ROLLINS, HE STANDS IN LINE AT THE BUFFET TABLE, LAYERING ROAST beef on a hard roll, waiting to pour gravy over the entire sandwich. Well over half of the reservation has come, nearly filling the room. Only the most staunch protesters refuse to enter the building, but even they've accepted Mason's offer of food without much hassle. My father wasn't there at the time, and that probably has something to do with their willingness to take what Mason offered.

"Your social's only been postponed," Mason says in a low voice, sitting down next to me. "Deal's off. But we will still have the social."

"We never had any deals, Mason. Look, you bought my stuff. If you want to return it, I'll pay you back in installments, but I already spent the money getting ready for Grand River." I leave, stopping at the dessert table and then sitting back down with Chuck Trost. Mason can't really have changed, ridiculously, overnight. Even my stories aren't that unbelievable. He claims his change has come about because no one ever died in his presence before. What a load of shit. I mean, he was out of town on business the day Bert died, and heard the news from Big Red over the long-distance phone lines, and by the time he got home, arrangements were already taken care of and he had nothing to do but attend . . . but still.

He claimed earlier to everyone that yesterday, in the middle of the wave pool, he felt Ruby's life end undramatically, in a mundane second: no music, no sunbeams breaking through the clouds, no angels—just cold, chlorinated water. One minute she was burning up with a fever so high that her brown skin had baked into a rust color, and the next minute, her body dropped closer to the water's temperature. He continued to hold her as she made her way into the next world, a woman he had barely known and yet had been courting anyway to get her approval. She had asked him a few minutes before if he'd really thought the pool was a good thing for the people, and though it might possibly have saved her life with its cooling waters, he suspected she would still have maintained that its usefulness and practicality were questionable at best. She'd made him realize some people can see beyond their own interests and immediate pleasures very well. He claimed to finally be able to see something of the seventh generation on the horizon, claimed he was gaining Haudenosaunee eyes, shedding his white ones.

He told me before the service that he truly understood now, and he really had all along, that I had learned a lot from both of the old women, and that my interest in a social had virtually nothing to do with the possibility of vending my beadwork, but that it might somehow get the people back together. He'll probably still have that ache for me he's had for years, but he believes he might have a better chance at keeping it in check, now. He wonders what he missed out on in his lessons from Bert. Maybe they had just changed over the years, as he always understood her lessons involved keeping the prize in mind.

"Nice spread, as usual," Red comments, he and Roger sitting down next to Chuck and me. "I'm sure she would have enjoyed this place, if she'd ever felt the freedom to come in. I tried to get her to come here with me a number of times. I even offered her a tour late at night, when no one else would be around, but she always said no."

"I wonder how she'd feel about this reception being held here," I return, and Roger nods. Funny, I just can't get used to calling Two-Step that, but ever since that day in May, he's been correcting anyone who calls him by his dancing name. He had just decided to come back—and then the protests and the fight . . . and here he is, calling himself Roger. His lost name weighs heavily on me, flown away at least in part because of my attitudes. I've always been the sort to take opportunities and chances whenever they arrive, but now it looks as if the last chance I took—spitting back on Wayne Grayson at the protests—cost Roger his dancing career. At least he feels this, and if he doesn't feel the dance from inside, where else can he get it?

He's come a long way from that first day, but one of his former dancing legs still lies heavy with the surgical-steel halos and pins piercing its skin. If he hadn't been trying to save me, he might still be dancing the circuit. He hadn't felt like it since Bert died, but at least before, if he changed his mind, he could physically still dance. Now, I'm not so sure. I have done the only thing I know how and passed him a small bag from inside my purse. It contains my first completed hawk's-head buckle from the Devil's Hole porcupine, along with his completely beaded armbands. No copper shows through the tightly beaded rings. If my magic is still true, he'll wear them all at Grand River and soar back into his name. Before he can open it or say anything, I excuse myself.

Small groups of people float through the room, all recounting some story or other about Ruby and the influence she'd been on their lives. Some wear prominent items of beadwork of Ruby's design, most only marginally matching the outfits they have on. At the doorway to the main entrance, Mason approaches me again, bubbling over, and I wonder if he is able to totally wipe any conversation he doesn't like clean out of his memory.

"There you are. I've been looking all over for you," he says, grabbing me by the arm and escorting me out into the front hallway. "Nice earrings," he says, admiring the shiny and dangerous looking ornaments hanging from my lobes.

"Made 'em just for you. So, what's up? You've forgotten our conversation from ten minutes ago? My first answer wasn't clear enough?"

"No, I just wanted to congratulate you. Red just told me the two of you are getting hitched at Grand River. He even agreed to let me buy him a tux to wear on your Caribbean honeymoon." A number of people walk past us, and we greet each person, smiling. Eddie Chidkin, he initially looks as if he is going to stop, but Mason stares him out the front door. "So, uh, I take it you haven't told him?" Mason asks awkwardly when the hallway is clear.

"And just what do you suppose I would say? 'Your employer's been trying to fuck me for over five years, but he's gotten really persistent since he got rich'? Look, you and I both know what this job has done for him. He can actually help people like he's always wanted. I can't take that away from him. You should be more like that. Thinking you can just take whatever you want. Man, that's gotta change, and here's your first opportunity to learn. It ain't gonna happen with me, not now, not ever. I been dealing with people who don't know how to use power for a lot longer than you've had it. Don't worry about what Red's gonna think of you. You got plenty to worry about with me around. This is for you." The quillwork lapel pin still retains its barbs. His hand jumps; he's been snagged. Other than his hand, though, he doesn't move. Sidestepping in the dark hallway, I reenter the main room, feeling my earrings swinging. I'll never be Fiction again. And for the first time in years, I feel like Mason Rollins might really leave me alone.

From nowhere, and from everywhere, Johnnyboy appears. At first, I am so overjoyed, seeing Johnnyboy and the others in the T.R.B., that I can't possibly think anything is amiss. For those few seconds, the only thing I wish for is that Ruby'd been here to witness this event, to have known that she needn't sit on the perimeter again.

"Fiction . . . Patricia," he starts, my real name somehow leaping out of his mouth as if he has heard my silent declaration. It was a shock he even knew it. Our hands lock, his warmth vibrating into my palm, and I would like nothing more than to hold that recognizing hand for the rest of my life. "I'm afraid that I have some bad news for you . . ." He begins a chorus flowing into my ears, speaking the phrase in a voice obviously grown accustomed to it, rolling its violent syllables out hundreds of times to Nation families, usually followed by a brief description of the way the family's son or daughter has died, on which road they've wrapped the family car around a tree, or where they've been found frozen to death, having passed out in the ditch, having planned on closing their eyes and resting for just a minute on their journey home. I have heard this phrase so often—on television, in books, and in movies—that it's become nearly meaningless; but that phrase exists without meaning only until someone floods the rest of the sentence with your own life.

The people surge in around me as Johnnyboy tells me that everything I own probably no longer exists. Through this, the distant fire sirens grow louder and louder, filling my head with the truth. Squeezing through the crowd and out into the parking lot, I try to imagine my trailer gone, but can't. The trailer itself is of little consequence. I've lived in a number of places in my life, and none were more than shells until Bert's place. That's where the mistake came, comfort blooming long enough to have actually grown some attachment.

If the beadwork hasn't survived, I can probably recreate that, but all of Bert's photos and negatives were in the back bedroom, under my bed in an old snapshot box, the same place she had always left them. I had plans, after discovering the negatives over the winter, to have some extra prints developed and the negatives filed in a safe-deposit box at some bank, but like so many other things, I never got around to it. The documentation of Bert's entire group of dancers has by now become piles of chemically coated, scorched paper, if anything at all remains of them.

Across the sky from Pem Brook to the Torn Rock, a dark column of smoke disperses across the northern sky, almost like a funnel cloud. Heading down the Rock all the way, straight to my place, I tell myself powerful stories, inventing other places for the fire to be. First, I think, my father's—then passing that, the junkyard, the old Catholic Chapel, and on and on, finally even conjuring Red's place, assuring myself he could move in with me now. Johnnyboy couldn't know, anyway. He was just guessing. Had to be.

And then the firemen have the road blocked. They won't let me pass with the truck, telling me to turn around. Jumping from the cab I tell them, and myself as well, that it's my house on fire.

Red flecks from the dress shout across the road. The dress is bunched and crumpled in my father's hands; he holds it to his face, draped over him like a shield. He is shiny and completely hairless, his skin a deep shiny crimson, as he stands only a few yards from the flaming core. Wandering closer to it, he clutches my dress more and more to his face, so much so that he appears to be devouring it. That son of a bitch. It is the only thing I have left in this world, and I am going to get it back. Collapsing onto the crisped grass, first onto his knees and then backwards, he grins and stares splay-legged at the roaring trailer, the velvet garment covering him.

The firemen are not actually putting the fire out, but merely soaking the borders of my property. With no water lines running through the reservation, the only way firemen can even operate out here is to bring in the water-pump trucks, and if they miscalculate the size of the fire and bring even one too few water trucks, we are shit out of luck. These assholes, they calmly tell me my father has forbidden them from putting the trailer out, so they're now using up the entire water truck's contents trying to contain it—to make sure it doesn't spread. One tells another how much he hates these fucking reservation calls.

They try to stop me from crossing the road and entering my land. My father doesn't see me coming. As I reach him, sweating, my braid takes on that strange curt odor only burning hair carries. We're too close. He's much heavier than I would have ever suspected.

In his unresponsive, staring eyes, my transformer shoots brilliant blue sparks in a pinwheel of burnt electrical wires, and for a second I think he is dead. Slapping his cheeks makes the old man focus on my face—not my actual face, but the reflected, fractured version of it in my melted picture window. The similarities dance in the precision-line cheekbones, the sloped forehead, the thick shapely lips, and the direct stares we control. The sharp electricity sparking in his usually angry eyes softens to a bluish glow as tears well there. He sees it too, and for the first time, he recognizes me. Our reflection bends in the window's last shift, and we are grotesque parodies of father and daughter.

Raising him a few inches, I drag him. The dress begins to smoke in the heat. "Spray us!" I shout, and oddly, this is the one thing they will do. Water rushing over me, I close my eyes, smelling nothing but the water—no fire, no smoke, no morning scent of Red, not even my father's cheap cologne. But something comes back in that moment, a scent I recognize from New Year's Day—the smell of wet velvet. I open my eyes. My father continues to clutch the soft black fabric. He resists my tugging. One of the firemen stands at the road's edge and offers me a hand, but I push him away. This is my business.

"Biggest tobacco-burning for my Clan Mother possible," my father shouts, clutching harder as my grip tightens, the velvet's black blood surging out between my fingers. We pull one another out of the mud using the dress, yanking in opposite directions, making our slow progression across the road. Reaching the other side and falling in exhaustion, he releases the dress and stands again, swaying, apparently wanting to absorb every horrible detail he can.

The beaded dress, now a nearly unrecognizable, muddy shroud—small tassels of white thread dangling where beads had been secured—hangs in my arms. All that remains of the roses are fragments of petals, and where the fabric and bead sheaths had been, there now stand, among the bits of torn calico, the chrome spiked teeth of my roses, gleaming wet and sharp under the high sun—they've been freed. Our bodies are both streaked with the black dye. I wrap the dress about my shoulders, protecting myself with the metallic thorns, and turn away from the spraying water competing with flame for the remains of Bert's home, my home. The blaze dies down a bit, the firemen finally dousing what's left of its life with the dregs of their trucks' contents.

Why start now? And then I see the others. Johnnyboy Martin has apparently ordered them to do it. I have no idea how long the crowd's been here, how soon they followed me from the T.R.B., but it seems to have been long enough for them to know I'm not the one who should be named Fiction. None of them even go near my father, who still won't tear his eyes from the wreck.

Wrapped in my velvet shroud, I leave this scene, the blackness tracing its way down my body and seeping into the ground. Red and Roger, they silently follow me and guide me into the Phoenix. I turn the radio on and spin through the dial, looking for the places where no news lies, but even the static won't shut out the sirens. I do not glance in the rearview mirror as we leave, refusing to look back.

>+<

CHAPTER 18 The First Dance

Two–Step Harmony

"**A**ND THIS WAS WHERE I USED TO SIT, WAITING FOR BERT TO FINISH GETTING into her nightgown before we watched the *Wheel of Fortune* and *Jeopardy*," she says, standing ankle-deep in the sooted rubble that had been, until nearly two months ago, the kitchen of her trailer. "And here"— she scans the yellow weeds and dense brush framed by two bent aluminum struts—"was where all the pictures hung." She swings the camcorder down and looks at its various buttons, eventually touching one. "You ever get to see that one of you Bert took? I had it up a while ago, but forgot to tell you."

"Uh-uh. Trish, why are you doing this? You live with us, now," I ask. "Our place is your home, and you know in another couple of years, when I move into my gram's old house, you two'll have the place all to your-selves." I could probably move in there now to give them privacy, if my dad would help me by paying the bills, but thirteen's probably still too young to be moving out on my own. Besides, in the past month and a half, I've taken enough responsibilities to last a lifetime, and they'll definitely last that long.

><

A FEW DAYS AFTER THE TRAILER BURNED, IN THE FIRST REAL OPEN COUNCIL MEET-ing in more years than anyone would care to remember, the Deer Clan women identified their choice for new Clan Mother—Judy Waterson, a second cousin of mine and the mother of Brian Waterson, the only practicing medicine man on the reservation. Standing and officially accepting her position, she had in turn announced that the dehorning ceremony of Bud Tunny would take place before the year was up. I doubt Bud will be a willing participant and give the horns up to Judy, but the ceremony holds, regardless. His only other choice is outside prosecution, and everyone doubts he'd take too well to prison life.

Judy then further announced that her son Brian would take Bud's place as Deer Clan Chief. I have other plans. I have interests in that direction, but right now I'm too young, and by the time Brian ends his time, I'll be too old. Fortunately, the Peacemaker, in the Great Law of the Haudenosaunee Confederacy, made a provision for guys like me. Johnnyboy Martin, sensing my passions, requested in that same Council meeting that I be considered as a candidate for the role of a Pine Tree Chief. What this means is that, though it's unlikely I'd ever be chosen as a Chief because of the timing of my Clan's need, they recognize my vision could be valuable to the Nation. A Pine Tree Chief is one, they say, who has sprung up from the Nation and can never be cut down. Of course, if at some point my vision becomes bad, I can be silenced. A symbolic wood block would be placed in my mouth, and no one from my Nation would ever be able to hear my voice again. Pretty strong stuff for a thirteen-year-old, but I can't turn down Johnnyboy's faith in me. He says this is a special honor, one I can't pass on to anyone else. My role will die with me, but I'm not planning for that to happen for a very long time.

For my training, I'll serve as a runner, attending all Chiefs' Council meetings silently, observing and learning so I'll be passably experienced when the time comes for me to take the horns. I can't be installed until the time of the next regular Chief's installation, and Johnnyboy says he will not be there. I guess he thinks he's the next Chief to pass on, as the role transfer generally only occurs at the old Chief's death, but he's pretty confident that'll be years from now. I wish him a long life, in no way anxious to force my responsibilities any sooner than they'll come naturally. The reality of all my future decisions has already begun to weigh heavy on my mind, the eyes of the seventh generation always watching from the woods.

I've already attended my first official closed Chiefs' Council meeting, silently watching as my dad negotiated a settlement between Mason Rollins and the Chiefs, trying to make each see the visions the other held, and acknowledging acts of mutual respect. Before it started, Johnnyboy Martin walked me around the empty Council House, telling me of its past and at the same time marveling at what Mason had done with the T.R.B.

The Council House had seen us through the first part of the century. Johnnyboy had stolen the first kiss from his future wife in the dusty balcony at an Agricultural Society meeting as a teenager, and had been handed the horns of leadership there at the front of the main room as an adult.

In recent years, though, the boards in the balconies flanking the main floor have rotted and grown unsafe. Volunteers from the Nation reinforced the work for a time, but after a while, the entire composition of the balconies seemed to be reinforcement. Johnnyboy wasn't even sure any of the original boards were even present anymore. In the thaw of 1975, a series of leaks in the roof had shorted out some of the wiring, and it was decided that the overhead cage lights could no longer safely be used. During maintenance week that spring, Johnnyboy had boarded up the entrances to the darkened and rickety balconies as others had brought in a series of donated floor lamps to light the way. He'd wondered how we'd ever arrive at another seven generations if this traditional courting spot were no longer accessible. He'd known it was only a romantic idea, but he'd refused to enter the area of the closed entrances since then, just the same.

Johnnyboy had watched, as he'd entered the T.R.B. that day, the startled look in everyone's eyes, their dismay that the violence was not over yet. He'd even feared the act he had suggested—giving Bert's house back to Trish in place of her burnt trailer—was not the right one; but the people had agreed, and that was all right. Mason Rollins and his group could have interpreted the giving back of the house as a victory and pushed for more, though it hadn't really been a victory for either side. This last year's been a rough one. Not even Johnnyboy could have predicted what happened with Jacob Tunny or Mason Rollins, way underestimating the wrong turns a person might make wearing the horns of any kind of leader.

He'd stepped in through the heavy steel door, followed by his group, and together, they all entered the main concourse of the T.R.B. Though he tried not to, Johnnyboy had mentally clicked off comparisons to the Council House, and at each turn, aside from longevity, he found his building sadly lacking.

The T.R.B. was built with sturdy metal catwalks, a series of second-floor usable areas, and fluorescent lights embedded in a drop ceiling. The ancient back room at the Council House was put to shame by the advanced kitchen, stainless steel gleaming his astonishment across the room. Everything he'd heard was true, and more.

He'd known this was going to be a trickier situation than any he'd encountered before. Mason Rollins seemed to have a love for outside things, including lawyers, as intense as his hatred for Jacob Tunny. Johnnyboy felt that there was just a little too much outside influence entering the Nation lately. He knew Jacob was as much to blame as Mason was, maybe even more so. Mason hadn't signed anyone over to the Staties, and Johnnyboy believed that, had Mason had the power, he still would not have done what Jacob had. And that belief was what had brought him closer to the center of that building. He'd trusted that Mason, in some tiny and probably self-serving way, still believed the Nation should take care of its own situations.

➤←

"So, YOU MUST UNDERSTAND OUR CONCERNS, YOU MUST BE OPEN ENOUGH TO SEE what I see, and be brave enough to tell me when you see something different, if you are to wear the horns," he finished, holding out the *gustoweh*—leather bands layered in pheasant feathers with two mounted buck's antlers protruding from the sides—as the others entered the building. I held it for a moment, feeling its gravity, before handing it back, not ready to even try them on. Johnnyboy nodded at my choice.

Mason entered the room from the back door, as he'd been told, wearing jeans and a T-shirt, his Armani suit nowhere in sight. My dad made note that Mason brought his new proposals in through official channels, having his Chief, Johnnyboy Martin, introduce his plans to the Council.

Johnnyboy seemed a bit embarrassed about this late attempt to function by the rules of tradition, but he explained they all had to realize how inactive they'd grown over the years, bowing to Bud and his ways, over and over. They couldn't blame Mason for having gone to Jacob first, as really he'd been allowed to grow way too wild, and had choked out the other voices—he had become the Chiefs' Council. My dad, here, voiced support at the admission of fault. Forcing them all to share the guilt of past issues, he began the negotiations, starting by inviting Johnnyboy to recite the Great Law, the Peacemaker's blueprint for the Haudenosaunee Confederacy. We sat and listened through the series of lectures on the role of a Chief and the function of the traditional government before even being allowed to speak—Mason nodding and seeming to listen carefully, afterward remaining quiet until recognized.

Among his proposals was a five-stage joint venture between Smoke Rings and the Nation to bring safe, treated water from the city to the reservation—first at several centrally located main stations, with eventual plans for every person who files to have city water hookups and sewer lines. My teeth already grow stronger with the fluoridated water we'll be drinking, my cavities frozen—a tradition I'm happy to be rid of. We also have to address the chemical worries the DEC raised. No one really wants to dig up Bite Mark Road and confirm what we suspect has happened to the barrels buried beneath it—that they've split; that long, deadly chemical fingers have crawled deep within the reservation—but denial sure hasn't gotten us any place good so far. That report and my gram are still fresh in their minds.

The second proposal involved Chiefs' Council approval of any business moves Mason makes, the tearing down of all Onguiaahra Nation propaganda, and the removal of all signs carrying the corrupted "turtle with gasoline pumps protruding from its back" symbol—and most significantly, a consistent relinquishing of fifty percent of all profits to the Nation. In return, the Nation's financial books, long hidden by Jacob, would always be a matter of public Nation record. The talks broke down here, each side growing blind to the other's vision. We'll have to come back at another time for more negotiations.

I understood at the meeting's end, as they all walked out the front door together, why I'll have to attend every meeting, even though I'll be voiceless for several years to come. Though virtually no one else knows it, I've seen the dangerous potential of Mason Rollins's aggressive nature, and following all of these decisions, I'll be ready when the time comes for my silent period to end with the donning of my horns. Though silent, even to my dad, my memory won't fade. I'll be prepared for our long lives together in the Nation.

✦

"YOU READY? IT'S JUST ABOUT TIME," I ASK, LOOKING AT MY WATCH.

"Yeah, just a minute," Trish says, engaging her camcorder again. "This wasn't my place for long," she says, sweeping the camera's lens from the east to the west, "but it was almost home. Maybe this whole place is. I hope so." She presses the stop button and replaces the lens cap, shutting the camera's eye. "So, you think you can get used to this place? After all, it's in your name . . . I guess it's yours, Roger, my friend."

This is something that's going to change as soon as I get the horns. Anyone out here who's enrolled on any Haudenosaunee roll book should be able to own land—anyone from all six Haudenosaunee Nations. That's the way it should be. We're supposed to live in peace under the white pine, but the seventh generation's eyes are on me right away, and they show me the land disappearing. It's not as simple as it seems, but what is? Certainly not dancing; but the difficulty can't stop me, no matter what I try.

"Watch it," I say finally, not liking the sound of that name in her voice. "It's Two-Step."

"Okay, Two-Step it is. Well, let's get going, Two-Step. Good thing your dad's already there, or we'd probably be late."

"Can I drive?" I ask.

"You know how?" she asks. I take the keys and climb into the driver's seat of Curbside Phoenix. "If you dump this, your dad's gonna kill you," she says from the passenger's seat.

I drop it smoothly into first, and though the blackened hulk grows smaller in the truck's rearview mirror, the reek of a burnt-out existence— clothing, furniture, an occasional knick-knack—marks the life within. We pass my dad's trailer, the wheels already remounted on it. Mason's work crews bulldoze Trish's trailer in a couple of days, and we're moving the trailer to her spot. By Grand River Powwow in a few days, we should all be settled on the land.

My dad won't have to be concerned with land rent anymore, and Trish's land won't suddenly become someone else's who might just happen to move onto the land, a trick that's been played on a number of non-Nation residents in the past. Most of our stuff is already packed or taped down for the quarter-mile trek to Torn Rock. I doubt if we'll move the old truck. The body's almost completely rusted through now. Moving it might produce nothing but sharp orange dust. I'll miss it, though. I've got to say that.

We pull into the long stone driveway a few minutes later, bringing the truck to a stop a little far out in the lot, already filling. Trish hands me a paper bag with my name on it to carry with the rest of my stuff, and I'm about to give her grief, but her arms are filled with identical bags labeled with all the others' names. The plastic banner rattling in the breeze proclaims, snapping loudly, that the Haudenosaunee Open Memorial Esplanade, Tuscarora Nation is celebrating its grand opening with the first-ever Tuscarora Grand River Warm-Up Social. These words don't roll right off your tongue, but Mason insisted on another stupid acronym, so he came up with this, to spell out "home."

"Okay, okay," a booming voice comes over the speakers, loud even out here in the lot. "Grand Entry is in ten minutes or so, as soon as our drummers get their fill of fry bread. All you folks running on Indian Time better hustle your buns." That singer seems to think he's at a powwow instead of a social, but that's okay, since it is a warm-up for Grand River. Trish's gone on ahead, crossing the back door of Bert's house. I run and try to catch up.

The house is still fairly empty, but Trish is planning to turn it into a showplace for crafts and the like before the summer is up, seeming not to realize that's in a couple of weeks. She won't move anything in until she has the proof—on paper—that the place is really hers, free and clear. Upstairs, Eddie Chidkin, in his old room, is making some ruckus, adjusting his breech cloth in the broken mirror he's kept around for years. He is surrounded by the boxes of his stuff. Trish is letting him move back in, and he's taken no time to fill the room.

"Hey, little brother," he says, turning to me. "Check these out." He lifts his foot to a large box. "Fiction made 'em." On Eddie's feet are traditional Haudenosaunee-style moccasins, the type my gram always made—a single piece of buckskin sewn into completion, a seam running straight up the center of the foot from toe to leg. She made them even after they went out of moccasin fashion years ago. The top flaps of these are accented with roses on black velvet. My own package holds an identical pair. Closer examination reveals streaks in the velvet, where the dye's been washed out.

I kick off my sneakers and drop my jeans, slipping into my leggings and breech cloth, and then the moccasins, enjoying the soft flannel lining as I tighten the drawstrings. From my regular powwow garment bag, I pull my ribbon shirt and wrestle it on, squeezing the entirely covered copper bands into place on my biceps. The bands are covered with wampum-belt designs, purple and white images, reminding us who we are. The hawk's-head buckle from my belt slips easily onto a satin sash that goes around my waist.

Mason Rollins steps up as I adjust my ribbon shirt, the velvet and roses surrounding his feet, too. "You know, Roger, I been thinking about moving the pool at some point—with Council approval, of course—but bigger and better. You know where I thought the greatest place for an even bigger one might be?" he says, leaning in the door. "Picture it . . ."

"Mason," I interrupt, "I think if the Creator had wanted to keep the waterfalls at the bottom of Redman's Drop, he would have. Don't you? Some things you can't change. They just gotta be the way they are. This pool is fine where it is. And the name's Two-Step." I walk out into the hallway and head for the stairs.

My gram told me all about Mason's plan, and though I'm not entirely against the idea, he needs to learn his place in the community. Other things need to be accomplished before a bigger pool becomes first priority, and besides, that extravagance is ridiculous.

The back parking lot is just full of cars. Even some license plates from as far away as British Columbia—here at our first social. I'm surprised, since there really isn't any competition here—that's not until Grand River. But it seems we're being welcomed by competitors from around the continent. Mason must have gotten ahold of Grand River's mailing list when he made out the invitations.

I can't wait for Smoke Dance; I am there, for sure. Even deciding to stop competing after Bert's death, I could never stop dancing. It just comes out, like breathing. And now, well, my leg's free of its cast, and things are almost back to the way they were. Bert's gone, but things are bound to change with time anyway, to grow.

I hope the organizers took my advice and included categories for other tribes. The Gathering of Tribes the powwow circuit promotes thrives on the acceptance of all tribes as equals. Tradition is one thing, but tradition at the cost of the people is no tradition at all. Powwows celebrate the richness of our survival, of adaptability—the only way to survive. I learned that on the road, but also at home, too. Time to bring the social into the circle.

It would sure be nice if an eagle showed to bless our first social, but they're a pretty rare sight around here—unreliable guardians. But I'll be watching, silent. My hawk's-head belt buckle keeps my vision as sharp as the bird's.

Eddie must have somehow slipped past me. His familiar drum starts down in the living room, and voices, many voices from nowhere, rip the air with laughter, and the itch gets me, and my feet start to move, as if they've never stopped. The entire group fills the living room again and the floor is alive with shifting waves of streaked velvet and beaded roses.

We all begin the same dance, feeling the rhythms of Bert's group being revived in our arms, legs, bodies—as my dad, Eddie, Mason, and most of the others flow into their own steps from Bert's traditional beginning. In our large Friendship Dance circle, I look along the perimeter. There, Trish lifts my dad's Minolta to her face and focuses on me. I soar into a move all my own, one I am inventing right now, a custom Smoke Dance, shifting with the wind, a young wisp with a slightly off-center knee. The flash goes off and I am frozen for a second, alone in the moment, and then I come back, as Trish slides the camera under her shawl and steps in front of me, joining the dance. She changes our direction and leads our dance out the front door, across the parking lot to H.O.M.E., moving with the smoke and the wind, shifting, ever shifting.

>‹

September 12, 1993
July 11, 1995
Niagara Falls, New York

1. A Dramaturg — A thesis: who controls the text?
whose intention is being supported?
what is the end of the production?

Two views.

Dramaturg
|
The Institution.
vital

believes the D is
an artist / bureaucrat

⟵ Paradox

Dramaturg
|
unimportant who the ins'n. serves
The Artist may be undermined

believes the d is unexpected
↘
artist
↘ so sift out the
real
artist and
support him.

Anecdotes
— Charlie. german nanny
— 12th Night: Tiger
— Midsummer:
— Buskers
— Dream Interpretation
I go. I go. See how I go.
— the rest.

— Kunde = hating us.
the gun.

— Gaskill: Helen Cruz.